THE HEARTBEATS OF Aloha

Praise for The Heartbeats of Aloha

Not enough authors are even willing to tackle these tough subjects and, more importantly, do it right. I'm so glad Brooke does and so well. They are a true love letter to all the spoonies out there.

MARTHA H. -GOODREADS

With plenty of romance on offer, this is an action-packed story that I recommend to anyone who needs to believe that there is always hope, and if they wait long enough, their chance at happiness will come.

ANNE-MARIE REYNOLDS, READERS FAVORITE

Brooke Gilbert brings something new to the romance genre, and we could all benefit from what she shares - the heartbeats of aloha. This book was a hug between the pages!

NORMA, F. -NETGALLEY

In a childhood friends to lovers story, full of representation about life and pain, this author brings back romance in a way people have probably forgotten about.

"The sexual tension was off the charts. I was going crazy for a freaking kiss by the time they finally got there."

So much of what we see nowadays has to have some trope or dynamic to it. and ive felt a bit afraid sometimes that we are losing the people in it. the truth in it. the love in it. and its book like this that remind me of what these books do for and to us all and how special they are when done right. this was done right in all the best possible ways. i adored it.

"Adored the letters and lyrics."

"Absolutely loved the ending [and wanted] to continue being a part of their kind and warm story."

Contents

More Books by the Publisher

THE HEARTBEATS OF Aloha

An OwnVoices Romantic Comedy

BROOKE GILBERT

For anyone who has felt the weight of anxiety, the life altering effects of panic attacks, or has suffered with mental health issues. Being brave doesn't have to mean wearing a mask and being alone with your emotions. Being brave can mean loving yourself and accepting your situation enough to talk about it.

"WHY NOT BE YOURSELF, EVERYONE ELSE IS TAKEN."
-OSCAR WILDE

Content Caution

Hello Friend,

As many of you know, I began my journey
writing as therapy and also to see someone
like myself represented in fiction. It's my
greatest hope you will find comfort and
escape in these pages! But I also hope if
you battle mental health or chronic illness
that you will feel seen. So while I hope to
deliver a romance that makes you swoon, I

also know there will be topics that may hit very close to home. Hopefully, this book will touch you in some way while also helping you feel less alone. But that's why I take this content caution very seriously.

I wanted to see mental health representation between the pages of a whirlwind romance set in a tropical locale. And like one of my favorite quotes says, "if you don't see the book you want on the shelf, write it." It's my hope that these characters will provide a journey of healing and acceptance for you while finding a special place in your heart. However, I would be remiss if I didn't note that these characters are dealing with topics that may trigger some, especially since they are based on my experiences. That's why I strongly believe in disclosing potential trigger warnings! I try to do my best with spoilers, but if you're worried about them, you're always welcome to skip ahead!

Mental health is such a big part of chronic illness and "spoonie" life, and one that has affected me greatly. So there will be anxiety, depression, and panic attacks discussed in depth, and panic attacks will be included in this novel.***SPOILER ALERT***

And depictions of childhood illness and infertility. ***SPOILER OVER*** However, I hope romance and humor will balance out these heavier topics for you. Masculinity, male toxicity, as well as past emotional abuse will be lightly touched upon. Themes of self-worth, acceptance, and unconditional love are present throughout to balance these important topics.

My door is always open to discuss modifications and areas to skip if a topic might trigger to you. Please be kind to yourself first and foremost, and if now isn't a good time to read this novel, then I will certainly understand. Perhaps there will be a better time in the future. If you still have questions or specific triggers in mind, I'm available through Instagram (@brookegilbertauthor), TikTok (tiktok.com/@BrookeGAuthor), and email (brookegilbertauthor@gmail.com).

Also, I have taken a few liberties in the novel relating to places that allow our canine companion. Places like Moku Nui are off limits to dogs, but it was so much fun to include Nova in these scenes that I couldn't resist including her. I appreciate your suspension of reality so she could be included.

Also, a ferry route no longer exists between Maui and Oahu. But this mode of transportation worked best for the plot.

This is a 'sweet' novel with no cursing. I hope you enjoy your time in Maui and Oahu! I can't wait to discuss this novel with you :)

Sending you endless spoons and much love,

Brooke

SIGHTS IN THE ALOHA BUTTERFLY KISS NOVEL

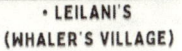

- LEILANI'S (WHALER'S VILLAGE)
- REEF'S APT
- LUNA'S TOWNHOUSE
- AQUARIUM
- MA'ALAEA HARBOUR (TACO STAND)
- HELICOPTER TOUR
- FERRY
- HALEKULANI
- DIAMOND HEAD
- MANOA FALLS

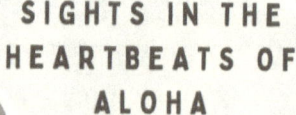

SIGHTS IN THE HEARTBEATS OF ALOHA

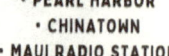

- HALONA BLOWHOLE CAVE AND TIDE POLES
  - MERMAID COVE
  - LANIKAI BEACH
  - MOKULUA ISLANDS
    - MOKU NUI
  - BYODO-IN TEMPLE
  - PEARL HARBOR
  - CHINATOWN
- MAUI RADIO STATION
  - KAANAPALI BEACH
- LOCKE'S BUNGALOW

Travel Map

LUNA & REEF'S MAUI

Find an interactive travel map on Squirl: https://author.squirl.co/books/1450

Luna and Reef's Hawaii

Hawaiian & Music Slang

Learning more about the Hawaiian language and its phrases was a fun part of my research for this novel. Here is a list of terms and definitions used in this novel for reference. ***To make the novel easier to read, most terms will be clarified in the sentence following their usage. Look for the term's definition in 'apostrophes' in the following sentence. That way you won't have to use the index!***

Aloha- hello/goodbye

Châ! - Oh, Ugh, a sign of frustration
Manu Mele- Song Bird
'Anakala-uncle
Ku'uipo- sweetheart
Wahine- woman
Lawa- Enough
Hâmau- Silence
Ohana- family
Tutu- grandmother
Hale- house
"E komo mai!" -Welcome
Mahalo-Thank you (to live in thankfulness)
Nânâ! - See, I told you so!
Laki- lucky
Ailana- moonlight
Hapa- Half. Part Hawaiian and part another race.
Coconut wireless- gossip, to hear something through the grapevine
Lanai- porch/veranda
Auê! -Oh dear/Oh no
Lôlô-idiot
Manu Mele- songbird
Aiâ! - Ouch/ oh no
Mahina Liilii- little moon
Makuahine- mother
Irrahz- annoying/irritating
Honu-turtle
Mili`apa!- slowpoke
Hô! - Wow! How Beautiful!
Hana hou -encore
Pali- cliff
`Oia ana! - I dare you (sarcastically)
Hemolele! - Perfection/flawless

Hûpô- fool/stupid
Brah-Brother (slang for bro)
`Ono! -Delicious!
'Uhane hoa- soulmates
Hapa- half

Spotify Playlist

The Heartbeats of Aloha playlist is available on Spotify. This playlist is unique because the songs written in the book are also included in the playlist!!! I hope you enjoy listening while you read the book. It also includes music mentioned in the novel and/or music I enjoyed listening to as I wrote this book. I hope you will enjoy the playlist.
:)
Songs from the novel are also available to listen to and download on the website's bonus content!!!

Learn how to unlock at the end of the novel or if you're a subscriber, you already have access!

A sample of the playlist:

1. Love on Top- Beyoncé
2. Ocean Eyes-Alicia Keys
3. Best Part-H.E.R.
4. Lika A Star- Corinne Bailey Rae
5. Heartbeats- José González
6. Love Looks Better-Alicia Keys
7. Losing Me-Gabrielle Aplin
8. Feel Me-Selena Gomez
9. Bejeweled-Taylor Swift
10. Praying-Kesha
11. If I Was a Boy- Beyoncé
12. Masterpiece-Jessie J
13. Unwritten-Natasha Bedingfield
14. 10,000 Hours-Dan + Shay
15. City of Stars-Emma Stone & Ryan Gosling
16. One of These Days-Paul Loren, Harlem Gospel Choir
17. Women's World- Little Mix
18. Who You Are-Jessie J
19. Higher Love-Kygo, Whitney Houston
20. Love Song-Sara Bareilles

- Spotify Link: https://open.spotify.com/playlist/4i5Xn-vxyJffI83212OV975?si=2674a4db9ced4c93

  - Youtube videos: coming soon
    - https://www.youtube.com/@brookegilbertauthor
  - Bonus Content (Join The Newsletter Family!): www.brookegilbertauthor.com/bonuscontent.

Prologue

REEF

I n all the many ways I'd imagined her walking back into my life, I was still not prepared for it to actually happen. From my sheltered spot behind the restaurant bar, I watched as a *very* grown-up version of my childhood love chatted with her ukulele fans amidst the glow of tiki torches and shimmering Hawaiian moonlight. When her head slowly turned to gaze my way from across the outdoor patio, I felt as if everything was moving in slow motion. Time had the viscosity of honey. And my feet liquified in place. All it took was just *one* look.

Out of all the restaurants in Maui, she had held her ukulele gathering here. At *my* workplace. I swallowed hard as the glimmering twinkle lights illuminated her figure walking my way. The crisp evening air made the perspiration on the back of my neck feel even cooler. A familiar sinking feeling in the pit of my stomach intensified with each swish of her gorgeous lavender dress as she glided in the moonlight. Her shoulders pushed back with every step she took, chin tilting higher, as if adopting a determined confidence.

And there *I* stood. *Frozen.* A glass fused to my hand, making me look like a tropical version of the rusted Tin Man.

Oh my God, I thought to myself, *she's getting closer.* My pulse thrummed at the tantalizing way her body moved toward me. *Get it together, Reef, get it—*

"Aloha," Luna's sweet, husky voice emanated like velvet from her petite body. For such a tiny frame, she sure had a luscious voice. Great things *did* come in small packages. I couldn't stop staring at her. *Stop it, Reef.*

"Aloha," I managed, pinching my eyes shut, trying desperately to break the spell she had cast over me. Because with her, I never knew if the word meant 'hello' or 'goodbye'. With me, it sure didn't mean 'love'. Finally, I managed to set the glass down from my clenched hand, I immediately started cleaning another one a little too vigorously. It looked like I was going to need *a lot* of dirty dishes to keep myself preoccupied.

Luna smiled at my casual reply and slid gracefully onto a bar stool. She leaned against the counter, her body gravitated naturally toward me, just like it had all those years ago.

Her eyes captured mine, and I swung the dish towel over my shoulder, trying to tame my nervous energy. But it was no use; I had been a goner as soon as her eyes had found mine in the crowd.

"It's good to see you," Luna ventured.

"Yeah, it's been a little while. Can I make you something to drink? We have just about every libation imaginable. I even have fancy umbrellas for the piña coladas. If you get a non-alcoholic one, I can ring it up as a kid's drink and give you a few extra umbrellas." Nervous laughter trickled out of me.

"Reef–" A slightly pleading tone colored her voice. No, we weren't going to talk about it. It had been two decades, and she still had my heart on a silver platter.

Her hand slid across the bar top toward me, and then quickly retreated. An ache pierced me as I saw her hand pull back. Her delicate fingers resting safely on their side of the counter. *Would she try to cross over the imaginary line again?*

Her beautiful brown eyes dared to look up at me. The ones that always made me melt inside. She spoke softly, "How have you been?"

"Good. Yeah, it's been busy here. Can't complain . . ." An awkward tension flared around us. "What about you? I've been reading about you in the news. I always knew you'd make it. Congrats. Dreams really do come true."

"Well, you were the very first one who believed in me. This whole thing has been . . . surreal," her voice trailed off. "Reef do you think?–"

"Luna, come on!" A loud voice called out, interrupting her question. "Time to get started." She bit her lip as she gazed over her shoulder.

"Just a moment," she called back.

"They're growing anxious." A man walked over and raised her ukulele.

Luna nodded and turned back to face me. "Uh, I'm so sorry. I'll come back later." A nervous energy radiated off of her as she slipped down from her stool.

I didn't have any plans to be here later. My co-worker, Nalu, had said she'd close-up the bar this evening. And I certainly didn't have the nerve to wait around for Luna, just hoping. Not anymore.

I allowed myself one more glance over at Luna. People were surrounding her, giving her instructions about her upcoming performance. As soon as I looked in her direction, her eyes magnetized to mine, just as they always had. And for a minute, everything grew quiet as we became frozen in place. And I couldn't help but wonder if her sudden return was more than just a chance reunion.

When someone tugged on her arm, she turned her attention back to the task at hand. She was guided by her handlers toward a makeshift stage. I watched her disappear, just as I had all those years ago. And just like that, the hollow, familiar ache returned. So strong that it dulled all my other senses. But this time, I knew I couldn't let her go without finding out the truth.

Reef

CHAPTER 1 | NOW

" Some say childhood is when we can be our truest selves. Maybe that's why this flame burns so brightly. And feels like nothing can ever extinguish a childhood love.

-CECE LARUE, WHEN YOU WERE MINE

She materialized like a soaking wet reverie with the first bolt of lightning. Everything from her thick eyelashes down to the hem of her long sundress was heavy with rain. Celeste gazed up at him, getting lost in his eyes as she walked toward him. Her face softened when she reached his front porch steps. Her lips tried to say something, but in the pouring rain, she was too far away to be heard. He took a step toward her, leaving the safety of his porch overhang, allowing the coolness of the rain to soak them as the tropical storm raged all around.

He dared to lock eyes with her. And there was a glint in her hazel ones saying, 'it's always been you'. Celeste's lips parted to speak, and she seemed more like a mirage than anything. He'd been waiting to hear an answer from those lips for so long. And he was instantly swept up in the fantasy before him. Too afraid she wasn't real. And just like that, time stood still. When an indistinct murmur from her lips brought him back from his daydreams. "Reef—"

"*Châ!*" I exclaimed in frustration as my name slipped from the character's lips. I swiftly crumpled up the cocktail napkin with my messy words scrawled on it. I was blurring the lines of fiction and *my* fantasy, *yet again*. And that was dangerous. Heat crossed my cheeks as the familiar feeling of failure rose inside me, sending my fantasy world crashing to a halt.

One of these days, the woman of my dreams will realize she was the reason for my novels . . . that she was my muse. And I don't think I'll ever be ready for that day. Especially since the last time we had an actual conversation together was when we were only twelve years old. Right before she broke my heart.

And yet, I couldn't stop picturing her as my main character. In fact, that's how my writing career had begun. I'd always wanted to write, but like so many other people, I had let my dreams go. It wasn't until I came home from an especially hard day at the bar that I picked up my fountain pen. Because I had desperately *needed* to see her again, if only for three hundred pages. And at that moment, it didn't matter if I'd never measure up. Someone at the bar had reminded me of her and the floodgates had opened. And there was *no* stopping them. I wanted to escape with her into *our* world. I needed to belong to a universe where she existed with a 'happily ever after'. Even if I was just the writer and she was my heroine. Because even in my fantasy-land, she still needed to be off limits to me.

It all seemed pretty harmless, especially since my work was only supposed to be a beautiful interlude for me. I never intended for it to be seen on the printed page or on anyone's screen. I easily rationalized that everyone had a muse. But that was before my best friend convinced me to query my work and my writing somehow turned into a bestselling novel. Well, *novels*. So, I lived in the gray now. But, when *I* became the leading man, my world turned vivid colors. Mostly red warning hues.

From my spot behind the faux tiki bar, I lobbed the rejected napkin into the nearest wastebasket, squeezing my eyes shut to erase my errant daydream. I should be able to pull inspiration from someone—*anyone*—else. But when I did, my writing turned flat. And I was already up against a deadline . . . a past due one. Daily reminders from my editor littered my inbox. As if I needed a reminder of the high demand for Cece LaRue's next romance, or that she needed LaRue's revisions—*my* revisions. All for a book I never should have written. Maybe this conflicted feeling was the reason for the heap of dejected napkins in the trash can.

I'd come a little undone when my muse walked back into my life six months ago. Decades of bottled up emotions exploded across the page into a burst of colorful imagery, a.k.a a new manuscript. I guess I had *a lot* of "therapy" work to do. Years ago, my best friend had passed on the sage advice of his grandmother who had wanted to help him with bullies. 'Write down your feelings and then you'll be ready to express them when the time is right.'

In all fairness, I doubt he thought my feelings were going to end up being written down into fifteen best-selling romance novels. All under a pen name . . . About a woman I'd pined for since we were twelve years old. So perhaps when my friend said I'd be able to tell her my true feelings after this process, he intended for me to write directly to her, not publish my emotions as cryptic clues in multiple romance novels.

I stared at the trash can, feeling my emotional repression radiating off the ink from here. I was just about to fish the wadded napkin out of the trash when Nalu interrupted my thoughts.

"I bet it was good," she said encouragingly, while she took inventory of the bar. We were getting ready for the rush of tourists that would soon descend on the restaurant after they had spent a day on the beautiful Maui shores. Until the evening, it was usually pretty dead at the Whalers Village Shopping Center. Occasionally, a thirsty shopper stopped by, but other than that, I normally had plenty of time to contemplate and write. My poor co-worker, Nalu, knew too well about my weird writing habits. With as much time as I spent scribbling, she probably thought I had a manuscript the size of *Moby Dick* lying here around somewhere.

I stared out past the open-aired patio bar to the sandy

shores. A warm glow burnished them, casting everything through a golden hour lens. I'd love to grab my board and go surfing with my best friend, Locke. It would be a great way to get out of my head. Surprisingly enough, bartending helped with that, too. Listening to people's stories was like a healing balm. In a weird way, it made me feel connected to Luna again. Maybe that's why I'd begun bartending.

"Nah," I finally answered Nalu. "The writing was actually pretty awful, but thanks for the confidence boost."

"When are you going to actually publish something, Reef? I've fished out some of your napkins and I think they're pretty incredible—" she stopped herself, as her olive complexion turned a slight shade of pink.

I smiled warmly at her. The encouragement was *really* nice. We'd gotten close while tending the bar together, but I hadn't shared my secret identity with her. There was only one person who knew about my pen name, and that was Locke. I'd never had the courage to put my real name on any of my books. Because these days, it seemed the worst thing to be was a romance author. *Especially* if you were a man. That was even more laughable, not just in the literary world.

Reef

"Cece LaRue!" Locke said emphatically, a slight slur to his words. I discreetly slid the drink away from him on our kitchen island. I knew when it was time to cut people off, even if I was new to this bartending thing.

"What are you talking about?" I leaned heavily on my forearms, feeling the world tilt slightly on its axis.

Locke leaned back on his barstool. "Man, don't you know your porn star name? It's the name of your first pet and the street you grew up on."

I choked on the sip I had just taken. While coughing, I looked down at the contracts below me. The ones *my agent* had sent. How I had gotten one of those was still a mystery to me. But Locke was like a shot of liquid courage.

I exaggeratedly pointed downward in a circuitous manner, as if hitting a bull's eye. "You want me to put my porn star name on this? Even for a romance author, that name sounds like too much."

"Yeah, I do. It's not like we've come up with anything better. And remember, you wanted to be *totally* anonymous. No one is going to think this is you. It's like the most *froufrou* name ever. It certainly doesn't sound Hawaiian."

Maybe it was the drink, but his reasoning was getting stronger. It sounded as good as one of those courtroom drama shows on TV. I could hear the triumphant music swell in the background. I shook my head . . . maybe that was a bad thing.

He leaned toward me, his fingers thumbing through the pile. "Your family would *never* know."

"Give me the pen," I said confidently, making my split-second decision. That was the deal breaker. My father could *never* find out. It would kill him.

Luna

CHAPTER 2

But love isn't so simple,
At least not to a heart like mine.
-Luna Manu Mele, The Man I Could Love

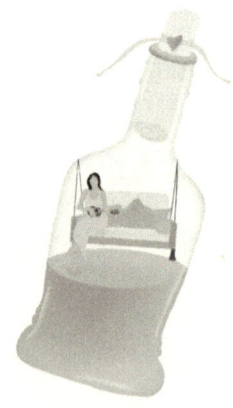

My eyes were glued to the page in front of me as I nestled deeper into my swinging hammock. The front porch was my retreat from the world when my senses needed a reset. And my favorite way to escape was through romance books. Especially tropical themed ones with 'happily-ever-afters'. There was a better chance I'd see someone like myself in between those pages than in other genres on the bookshelves. And recently, I needed those stories more than ever.

The soft island breeze caressed my skin as the printed words enveloped me, pulling me deeper into a beautiful fantasy. Time didn't exist when I was in this private little universe. No stress lived in this microcosm. And no one created a world in which I could so easily escape better than Cece LaRue.

I could place myself in her main character's shoes in a way I never had before. Since I was half Hawaiian, I loved how Cece set all her books on the beautiful islands I called home. And from the very first book I read, I felt a special connection with them, almost as if they were written just for me. But maybe everyone who enjoyed them felt the same way. Maybe that was part of the charm.

But there was something magical about our islands and no one knew their heartbeats better than Cece. I'd give anything to meet her, or even know what she looked like. The nondescript logo she used in place of an author photo drove me crazy with curiosity. It seemed a publicist managed all of Cece's social media accounts. The only thing that seemed to be truly Cece were her books. Well . . . and the P.O. box number I'd magically found.

I'd felt like a stalker when I'd stumbled upon the hidden P.O. box address. I'd been reading about her online—okay, I was doing a little too much research on my favorite author—and stumbled upon it. The webpage had been created so long ago. Probably back when Cece's first book was published, and she thought she'd only receive a handful of letters from fans.

As soon as I'd sent my first letter to her, I'd immediately begun to think about other possibilities. Maybe it was a decoy box manned by a publicist. I still cringe thinking about how I could have poured my heart out to her poor PR team. But I was shocked at the detailed response I received. It felt like proof Cece was real, *and* that her responses were too. They were too heartfelt to be fake. Or maybe her PR team was just that good.

I pulled out one of her letters that I kept as a bookmark. It didn't really matter who had written these letters anymore. They had gotten me through some terrible times when I didn't know where else to turn. And *someone* had taken a lot of time to respond, so I was going to live in the fantasy. The stationery felt more like satin sheets than actual writing paper under my fingertips because it had softened so much overtime. My eyes wandered over the fountain pen ink that gracefully covered the pages. The letters glided seamlessly across the paper. I wanted to drink the words in.

Dear Luna,

Do you feel every atom go still when you have a pen in your hand? Does time stand still? Sometimes that's the only way I know how to make the world right and bring it to a halt. I won't pretend to know what you're

going through or that I'm as strong as you,
but I can relate.

I'm afraid I'm a bit of a recluse.
Writing helped me in so many ways. But while
it's allowed my introverted soul to shine, it's
also given me even more reason to hide away.
It eases the pain and fears, but it's
become a bit of a double-edged sword. Sometimes, what is healing can also be detri-
mental if we seek too much refuge in it. I
now understand the meaning of 'too much of
a good thing.'

I hope you seek your lyrics for solace,
but I also hope you continue to push yourself
to grow with them. To share them. To share
yourself. I have to admit I was curious, so
I looked you up. I think you're pretty incredible. It would be a shame for you to continue
to hide away. The world needs more beauty.
More love. Think about that every time you're
on the stage and take a deep breath for
me. I don't think I've ever believed in anyone
more.

Let the stars guide you,
Cece

. . .

I SHOULD HAVE RESPONDED RIGHT AWAY.

It was one of the most beautiful letters I'd ever received, but it took a while to gain the courage to write her back. I felt I'd already taken enough of her precious time. Or maybe A.I.'s . . absolutely not, *there was no way A.I. had written that—* there was heart and soul dripping off of it. And if I was wrong, then I wanted to stay blissfully ignorant.

And while I knew she wasn't a 'Dear Abby' service, I craved to put pen to paper so I could hear from her again. I felt certain she would understand the pressures I was going through as an artist. And no one gave advice like LaRue.

Romance books don't get enough credit. Some people call them fluff, but the comfort and escape they provided always helped to inspire my creativity. After I finished a book, lyrics poured out of me. Inspiration striking deep in my soul. I sighed, turning another page of the heartfelt prose before me.

He strode over to her with a fire in his eyes. An urgency had reached his lips. As if the words had to be released from his soul. "Malia, you're perfect just the way you are. I thought that from the first moment I saw you. I–"

"Am I interrupting something?" A creak startled me, and I grabbed the worn ropes on the sides of my hammock. In front of me, standing on the deck, was my Uncle Louis. His fedora and suspenders cast a cool shadow over my reading nook. "That was an awfully big sigh." His husky chuckle eased the tension in my muscles.

I let out a little squeal, springing out of my hammock to give him a hug. I always felt like a carefree kid when he was around. Having him back on the island had been one of the biggest blessings. "'*Anakala*, you scared me," I laughed.

"Yeah, I saw that. Seems like you were pretty invested in that book," he teased. "I didn't know the heat affected you so much." He smiled wickedly as he pointed toward my rosy cheeks.

I swatted his hand away as I sat back down. He took a seat on the porch swing, looking way cooler than anyone had a right to be. Louis had this inherent charisma about him—yet he was always so unassuming, which only amplified his effect. Even in his mid-seventies, his charm hadn't wavered. And it carried over to his music career, too. He had such a magnetic stage presence that I'd always admired. I had even tried to imitate his style growing up, but I couldn't duplicate his charm. Swagger was the one thing he couldn't teach me.

A couple of years ago, Louis moved back to Hawaii from the mainland when my attacks had gotten worse. But when he was away, he'd always been there to answer questions about my music career or to talk about a lyric that wasn't working. In short, he'd *always* shown up for me. He'd given me my first ukulele and then taught me how to play it, helping me find music when I needed it the most. Teaching me the most important lessons of life, such as how to channel the healing powers of music to soothe 'my nerves'. Which I would later understand was anxiety. When I felt all alone in the world and darkness felt like it was caving in, Uncle Louis and music were there for me. When I felt like an outcast growing up, they understood me in a way no one else could.

When Louis told our family he was ready to retire and move back home, a weight felt lifted off of me. But deep down, I knew he was really moving back because he was worried about me. He wanted to help me navigate this part of my career. And I couldn't be more grateful to him. For *everything*.

We fell into a harmonious rhythm, just like he'd never left. My front porch held our 'privately reserved' rocking hammock chairs. It was a spot that served as a therapy retreat. And the comfortable surroundings allowed me to open up to Louis about the crushing anxiety I had as an adult. Finally, I felt safe enough to open up about my life: my career, my love life, and especially my panic attacks. I knew Louis wouldn't think I was 'being dramatic' or 'weak' when I shared my truth with him.

I closed my book and showed him the cover, knowing he'd be amused by my reading choice. For a book so deep, the cover was . . . surprising. It gave off a sweeping romance vibe like something you'd find on the shelf of an 80s bookstore. *But what could you tell from a book's cover?* Looking at it, I sure wouldn't have thought the book contained any significant issues between its pages. They certainly weren't mentioned in the blurb. Maybe the point was to disguise some of its heavy content. Maybe they thought that didn't sell.

Louis' smile grew when he saw the cover. "I really should get one of those for Kelani, if you don't think it would make me look *too* bad." He nudged me playfully from his swing.

Even though my 'anakala was in his late seventies, *he still had game.* 'Big-time' game. Maybe it was a musician thing. They never seemed to lose their swag, except for me. I never had any to begin with. I was too shy. Lyrics were how I expressed myself, and the stage was my 'safe' social inter-action. But in answer to Louis' question, I knew better than to believe a book could ever make him look bad. The story of how he'd recently been reunited with his first love was more romantic than any of the books I'd been reading.

Louis looked at me with a creased brow. "I'm glad you're getting some time to relax. But I know you, Luna. You only break out the romance books when things are bad. And you re-read Cece when things are dire."

Louis knew me all too well. Actually, he knew me better than anyone. Romance books were my therapy. And Cece was the best therapist of them all.

I sighed and fished my phone out. The one I had tried to lose in the plush cushions. Hoping a black hole would magically appear and suck the phone away, along with the people sending me text messages.

Slowly, I handed my phone over to Louis, chuckling when I noticed him trying to unlock it using his facial features. People said I looked like him, so it was a nice try. With a goofy grin, he pointed the phone up at me and I couldn't help but smile. That Louis charm would always work on me.

But in a moment's time, I saw a frown appear across his cool and collected features.

"Luna, what are all these notifications about? What exactly am I looking at?"

We didn't keep secrets, but I knew he wouldn't search through my phone. He always waited for me to share things with him. I tucked myself beside him on the porch swing and started scrolling through the label's Instagram feed. Then the text messages from my manager, Steve.

"Honey, why is your ex-boyfriend photographed beside you on these Instagram posts? And why is Steve texting you about boosting your career and doing what is best for the label?" I watched as a protective edge took over his tone.

"It's complicated." I sighed.

"Doesn't look complicated, *ku'uipo*. Looks like they're using you . . . again. Because they think they can. Kindness should never be confused with weakness." He began forcefully pushing up his rolled shirt sleeves as if preparing for battle.

My lips tried to smile reassuringly. "Ever since Azul's big summer hit, he's been the label's number one star, not just in ukulele. So, they want to promote us together. And they'd like us to 'conveniently' get back together for the festival. Apparently, romance sells."

A grimace crossed over Louis' facial features. He'd been pushed around more than his share when he was starting out in his career as a Black jazz musician. He'd told me all about his experiences and how important it was for me to 'stand up' for myself. Louis had broken into the world of jazz music when playing the ukulele wasn't a very popular instrumental choice. Louis had been an enormous influence on my music, teaching me most everything I knew, especially jazz. He'd *never* missed a video call opportunity to teach me new jazz chords. And my musical education came from lying around on our family's shag carpet and listening to the jazz greats on vinyl while he talked about music theory and music history. The real story behind the music.

"No," he said firmly. "I don't want you anywhere near that guy. It's bad enough you have to do the music festival. *No*." Louis' veins began protruding slightly in his forearms. He was the only one I'd confided in about the truth behind my 'glamorous relationship' with the ukulele star.

My eyes shyly looked over at him. I hated feeling like I didn't have any control with my label, especially regarding my music. "It's just one long weekend. I need this contract. I *can't* make it on my own."

"No." His jaw tightened. Water started blurring my vision and the vulnerability I felt was pushing me toward the edge. A heavy tightness taking over my chest. The familiar darkness clouded me. He softened and reached for my hand. "No, Luna. Together, we *will* find another way. One that's safe for you."

Luna

AGE 32

"Babe!"

I'll never forget the moment I heard Azul's ecstatic voice call to me from my living room. I'd been in the kitchen making a snack when his voice called out to me. He'd pretended to be tired of going out in public and 'getting noticed', but I think he just enjoyed seeing me be domesticated. Especially since people hardly ever took notice of us or bothered us on the island, unless Azul brought us to their attention. The people here always tried to be respectful of our privacy.

I lowered the kitchen utensils slowly, reaching for the drinks I had prepared, and breathed out as I strolled into the living room. There, I found Azul hunched over my coffee table, papers in hand. His grinning face immediately looked up at me.

"Babe, this is amazing! You've got a great start here. And I'm . . . Wow . . . I'm *so* flattered."

My stomach bottomed out. I felt like the glass tumblers I was carrying were going to slide right out of my hands as perspiration etched their rounded surfaces.

I set the glasses on the coffee table as quickly as I could, a loud thud resonating from their hard contact, and swept up the rest of the loose papers. Completely oblivious, Azul began reading what was left in his hands. His glee not diminished in the slightest.

Always been told what I needed in life
Always been told how I should be loved right
But love isn't so simple
At least not to a heart like mine

Never been treated right
Not by those type of guys
Never been much of a woman to stand by a
*   man's side*
Just for the status, just for the privilege, just for the
*   right*

Because behind closed doors is different
And there I'd blissfully evaporate into the ether
I stay because I'm loyal, because I'm a 'healer'
because I'm a pleaser, because I'm stuck in a fever

But with you, everything is new
With you, I feel I've come unglued

In a room full of people, no one is equal
I see everyone else has just been the prequel

Because here I realize
You'd never push my dreams aside
Or expect me to compromise

And I'll never be able to hide it
As much as I've been told to fight it,
You are the only man I could love
Forever and always

He looked up at me as he stopped reading. An emotional look clouded his features. One I'd never seen before. "Luna, what's the title? This is such a great start," he repeated.

"It's nothing." I tried to downplay the situation as I reached for the papers *again*. A frustrated sigh escaped me when he pulled the papers away from me. An internal heat filling me like a ball of shame. I'd been at a restaurant with my family when I'd seen my childhood love. He'd been working behind the bar, serving drinks. I doubt he saw me, but all my childhood feelings about him came flooding back. I knew I was playing with fire when I wrote this song. And now I knew what it felt like to get burned. But maybe I'd wanted to feel the flame. To feel *something, anything* again.

"Babe." Azul tipped his head and snapped his fingers impatiently in front of my face.

"The Only Man I Could Love," I told him slowly. *Painfully.*

He murmured the title back to me as if English were new to him. Then he pulled me toward him. Sweetly softening his booming tone. "This could be such an amazing duet. We could finish it together." *Finish?* My mind was screaming as I looked at the pages in his massive hands.

I shook my head, a visceral response overcoming me. This was sacred territory, a piece of me he *wasn't* getting. But I was frozen yet again. Like Ariel, whose voice had been taken away. That's how I felt with him.

He looked at me, determined to change my mind. Or to conveniently interpret my response as a lack of self-confidence. "Don't worry, Babe, it *will* be amazing. We'll make sure of it. I'll change my section to 'the only woman I could love'. It will be such a beautiful ballad for the summer. The label will eat it up." He pulled me onto the sofa beside him, crinkling my papers. As if the thought of him changing the words to my song was supposed to be this huge romantic gesture from him. As if a musician like him admitting his feelings in front of the world was the ultimate gift for a woman *like me.*

And I continued to stay frozen as he kissed me to celebrate, pushing me further into the sofa and his victory. As his body and a crushing anxiety weighed on top of me, I could only wonder . . . *What had I just done?*

Reef

CHAPTER 3

With love, he wanted to trust his gut. But his intuition felt broken. That's why he needed lightning in a bottle to wake him up. And from that very first moment, she was it.

    -Cece LaRue, Pacific Pulse

I crouched below the bar, taking time to restock, when I heard a familiar deep voice. I couldn't stop the smile from spreading across my face. And when I felt a napkin hit me on the back, my suspicions were verified.

"Locke," I said before I even got eye level with the counter. I knew my best friend's signature greeting by now. He was one of the few people who preferred coming to the bar during off hours. And he came even less now that he had found his special someone. I had to admit, I was a little jealous. Okay, maybe a lot. Locke had gone out of his comfort zone to meet his fiancée, so I hoped I could do the same. I wanted the type of relationship he had with Guin. Locke had been waiting on the right *wahine, but* that wasn't my problem. I was just too scared to try . . . *Again*. I preferred my safe "what if" fantasies. Freud would love analyzing me.

"Hey, man, I see you're throwing away perfectly good manuscripts again." He eyed my sad, rejected wads in the waste can.

"Shhhh." I could already feel my neck burning and he'd only been here for two minutes. We'd known each other since we were babies. We literally had our diapers changed together by our grandmothers, who were the best of friends. So, he knew how to paint shades of red on my face better than anyone. And he took great pleasure in this talent of his.

"I don't understand. You're super-talented. I mean, you're a bestseller. Isn't it time to just come clean, *Cece*?" Locke grinned as his voice grew.

"*Lawa*, Locke." I shushed him, knowing my whispers of 'enough' would never work. The *last* thing I needed was for people to overhear him saying my pen name. But my plea only made Locke's laughter boom louder.

"Man, I know women already flock to you, but seriously, you wouldn't be able to keep them away if they knew. We could have a bartending bachelor show. The YouTube royalties would be pretty outstanding."

Locke continued with his newfound confidence. "It would be nice not to have to keep this a secret. Unless you think women wouldn't want to buy romance from a male author, I don't really see a downside to it. Plus, the person you're writing about could finally see—"

"Alright, Locke. *Hāmau*." But I knew my attempt to 'silence him' wouldn't do one iota of good. "Just because you're feeling cocky enough to come back to the bar now that you have Guin doesn't mean you can spill all my secrets." I fired my brotherly shot back.

Before Guin, Locke had a Pavlovian aversion to the bar. I'd kept trying to rip the bandage off and get him to take the plunge into the dating world, but it was like trying to swim against a riptide. Now, he was obviously feeling way too comfortable here. I'd take it though, considering the alternative. Honestly, if we weren't giving each other a hard time, then something was wrong. And Locke had been pretty great about the Cece thing. He could have done some serious damage with that one. That was the nice thing about *Ohana*, 'family' always knew what was too tender to touch.

"Well, I've read *all* of your work, *Cece* . . . Or do you prefer Ms. LaRue? "He teased. "And it still seems very apparent what island girl you're writing about," the volume of his voice only increased, and I scowled at him. It had been such a mistake letting him read my books. Although with Locke, there really was no 'letting'. He'd probably read the books aloud to Guin, too, while she was recovering from transplant surgery.

I looked around, relieved that Nalu had gone to the back, leaving Locke and me alone at the open-air bar. The salty Maui breeze was providing my ever-growing warm skin some cool relief.

"Locke, why did you come to the bar today?" I sighed. I loved this guy like a brother, but something was up. He usually just texted if he wanted to go surfing or to hang out. Locke was a man of few words and activities.

"Can't a buddy just come by—"

"You're ridiculously transparent, Locke. I know you. You never just 'drop by'. You're out surfing or with Guin, so what's going on with you?" I looked around nervously, anticipating Nalu's return.

"Ok, fine. But Reef, you really should just tell her. That's my sage advice." I eyed him because I was pretty sure we'd had this same conversation at the beginning of *his* relationship, when he hadn't been ready to share anything with Guin about his physical disability. I lobbed a raised eyebrow right back at him. Most of our conversations were like a Ping-pong match at a heated family game night.

"Fine," he heaved in surrender. "I'm here because Louis is worried about Luna and he asked if we, well, *you*, might help."

Luna. Her name shot through me like a jolt of electricity. My senses amplified, noticing the starburst of colors from the sunset's glow wrapping us in its warm buttery hues. Images from our childhood flooded my memory, and it felt like I'd entered a golden haze. Everything else around me was suddenly eclipsed by this warm glow. Until Locke burst through it.

"Reef?" He waved a hand in front of me.

"Why me?" My eyes snapped into focus as tidal waves of emotion rushed through me.

"Well, Louis is hoping to find someone who can look out for her. She has this upcoming ukulele festival, and things have gotten out of control. He's really concerned about her. Louis thought maybe I could help, but I don't want to leave Guin. And since my grandmother needs more help right now, Louis wants to stay with her. So, I suggested you might help. Louis wants someone Luna will be comfortable with. So you're perfect. What better person to be her bodyguard? You've certainly been memorizing her body for long enough," he finished cheekily.

I rolled my eyes upward, hoping to find my dignity there. "What part of me says bodyguard Locke?" I spread out my arms so he could survey my lanky frame. My thick, black-rimmed glasses completed the look. "And what makes you think this is a wonderful idea? We haven't even talked to each other since we were kids. Recent pleasantries hardly count. Not for something like this."

"Says the man who is writing romance books about her. Hoping he'll get another shot. I think a *wahine* could get pretty comfortable with that *pretty* quickly."

"You don't know Cece's intentions. That's why they call it *fiction*," I barbed back.

But he just stared at me with his penetrating gaze. "Oh, come on, *everyone* is comfortable with you. That's why you're such a great bartender. Plus, she always holds her ukulele welcome gatherings here. Seems to me she's finding reasons to come here—"

"We have fantastic food and drink—"

He cut me off right away. "No. You've done this for *way* too long. I see the way she looks at you. It's obvious she wants to reconnect. Now, here's the perfect opportunity. The chance you've been waiting for. You've been writing about it for so long, I guess you willed it into existence." He smirked.

I hesitated. As much as I hated to admit it, I wanted to see if he was right. So, I finally asked, "What *exactly* is the opportunity?"

"Uh, I think it's best for Luna to tell you." I raised my eyebrows at him as if saying 'no deal.' He sighed, relenting. "She's been struggling. It's one reason Louis moved back here. Those two have always been close. But her manager is pushing her to do a concert she doesn't want to do, with a pretty personal song. They're determined to turn it into a romantic duet and a publicity stunt with another musician who is under the same management contract. And it sounds like she could really use some help with the situation."

I nodded, as if I knew *anything* about her world. The closest I came to her world was being managed, and enduring the pressure of editing deadlines. Not exactly the same. But I knew what it felt like to lose control over your creative license—not having the final say on your work, and not being able to spark new material. However, that probably paled in comparison to what was happening to Luna. She was a big name in the world of ukulele. Scratch that—she was a ukulele icon. Little girls all over the island wanted to be just like her.

"I still don't see what I'm supposed to do." My eyes looked down at my rolled-up shirtsleeves. They certainly didn't stretch tautly across my forearms like Locke's did. I wasn't a bodyguard. I'd always been the nerdy, awkward guy. And I made up for it with my friendly—albeit quirky—personality. Locke was the one to fill the role of protector. He was the ripped bodybuilder. They had this all wrong.

Locke could see my wheels turning. "Louis is afraid of

how far management will push things. They don't seem to take her well-being into consideration. She's more of a commodity to them. Merchandise. And as you know, romance sells. The song she wrote is pretty hopelessly romantic. Sounds like somebody I know," he said cheekily. But then Locke turned serious. "Perfect for their marketing schemes."

"One More Hour," I uttered without hesitation. Locke eyed me curiously. But of course, it was the song. That one would make a perfect duet. Embarrassingly enough, I knew all her music. Especially the ones she had written when we were kids. Sometimes, I even listened to her discography as I wrote. Because I was a masochist, apparently.

"Reef—" Locke's chocolate eyes showed enough empathy to weaken me.

"Locke, just continue," I said in defeat. I threw a bar towel over my shoulder—one of my nervous ticks—and tidied up.

But he reached for my arm and easily stopped me. Growing up, my gawky stature had been highlighted next to him. Locke, a hulk of a guy, and I, the stereotypical poet. Surfing with Locke helped, but I still felt like the unathletic nerd who'd rather be discussing a literary phrase.

"Reef, why don't you just talk to her?"

"Not what we're discussing, Locke." I pulled away, continuing to tidy up.

He sighed. "Fine." Ironically, the advice tables had turned since he had found Guin. Now, he was the one giving dating advice. The guy who had run from *all* women. "Well, Louis says publicity stunts get out-of-hand fast, and he thinks they will want to market her and this guy as a couple."

The glass in my hand dropped and shattered across the

patio floor as I remembered the photos of her with other men in the press. The glass landed as hard as that news had felt against my heart. I could feel my chest constricting.

Luna had always been a free spirit, but she was so sweet that her polite, people pleasing nature always won out, even above her own well-being. I knew she'd do whatever the label asked. That guy could probably take whatever advantage he liked of the situation. *But I don't look like the type of guy to step in and stop it. No one will believe it for a minute. Luna is such a beautiful woman.* She had her photo splayed across ukulele and musician magazines. And those copies sold fast. Who would buy that she would have such a nerdy, dorky guy as a bodyguard?

"Reef?" Locke called out to me, but I couldn't quite hear him. He sounded so far away. I felt him trying to unclench my fist as he said, "Well, that was quite a response. I'm guessing I can tell Louis you'll do it?"

I heard Nalu's footsteps coming closer to see about the loud commotion from the dropped glass. That snapped me out of it, not wanting her to clean up my mess. I quickly took the broom and dustbin from her, explaining that Locke and I were just fooling around. But she looked at me curiously.

I bent down to collect the little shards, feeling equally broken. This was *Luna*, the only woman I'd ever truly loved. I looked up at Locke as I picked up the fragile pieces.

My voice came out soft yet firm. "What do I need to do?"

AGE 12

The Hawaiian sun was burning brightly in the sky as its rays beat down on me. The heat only intensified the longer I sat watching and waiting on my tiny front porch steps. My anticipation was building like the humidity before an intense thunderstorm. And the more I waited, the stronger the storm brewed.

I'd only received short text messages from Luna this week, and no letters. My heart sunk a little lower each time I went to my mailbox and found it empty, no song lyrics waiting for me. But Saturday was *always* our day. It was as dependable as the sun rising.

But soon the fiery ball in the sky started dropping, and

my legs began to go numb. When I saw Locke walking down my driveway instead of Luna, I couldn't hold back the burning in my eyes. *No.*

"Reef, I–" Locke began, twisting his hands, his muscular build towering over me.

My throat went dry. "She could have told me herself–If she doesn't want to–"

"Reef, it's not what you think. Her family left for the Big Island today. I'm not sure for how long. I overheard my parents talking about it. Apparently, her family isn't telling anyone. Maybe they fell on hard times."

"So, she'll be coming back? When things get better . . . Why didn't she?–" But the look on his face told me exactly why.

I swallowed hard. This was a 'clean break'. Except my heart felt splayed across the dirt driveway. Already collecting debris.

My head kept shaking as Locke reached for me, grabbing my arm as I began running down the road. "Reef! There must be a reason she wanted it this way–"

His voice became muffled as the blood pounded in my ears. My breathing was ragged and labored when I reached her house, the burning in my legs slowing only as I neared her windows. All of my cells screamed not to look inside, but I had to know. And when I did, everything looked as hollow as I felt. She was gone, and it suddenly felt like the best parts of me left with her.

Reef

CHAPTER 4

She slips in and out of my memory
Like a distant reverie,
A word, a sound, a smell
All brings her back to me
She's my everything.

-REEF AKUA,
THE MUSE

Once I agreed to hear Louis' plan, Locke stayed at the bar for the rest of my shift. I guess he thought I was a flight risk. He must have texted Louis that he would secure me, like I was an "asset" that needed to be contained. But Locke knew I'd do anything to help Luna. So, I wasn't going anywhere.

Although, 'plan' seemed to be a very generous use of terminology. Locke had been pretty cryptic in his details. He just said we could meet with Louis after my shift to sort it all out. I should have known these two were up to no good. They were known for their imagination and match-making. Well, at least where Locke was concerned. He had such a good heart, but his hair-brained ideas didn't always execute well.

Since I was too busy wondering about his disastrous matchmaking, my shift became an utter disaster. I couldn't focus on anything except for the beautiful Hawaiian woman of my dreams, and from my romance pages, too. And from what I had seen, time had been *extremely* kind to her. Luna emanated an undeniable elegance and grace. She was like a classic movie star with a tropical twist.

Gone was the young girl who used to race down to the beach for sand castle competitions and who started mud fights in the streams. Before me stood a sophisticated woman. My mind instantly flashed back to humid Hawaiian days from long ago, filled with memories of her. A contagious grin spread across my face at the thought.

Finally, Nalu took mercy on me. "Reef, I'll cover the rest of your shift." She eyed a Bloody Mary that didn't have any "blood" in it. I guess she realized something was off and we wouldn't make any tips this way. Or maybe she thought I was just rushing to get through my shift.

"No, I don't want to leave you alone." I reassured Nalu as I eyed Locke.

"Yeah, because we have *such* a rush," Nalu said sarcastically, looking around. "And because you've been *so* helpful," she smirked, and I blanched. My distractions had led to an array of wrong cocktail mixes tonight. Nalu continued, "It's fine, Reef, go on. I think the patrons would *really* appreciate it, too."

I thanked her and handed over my apron. Nalu glanced my way with a raised brow when Locke led me out of the bar with his hand firmly grasped on my shoulder. Even Houdini would test his limits trying to get out of Locke's hold.

"Locke, I have a car," I said as he pointed towards his Jeep. This would be the *one* time I didn't want him to be a man of few words. But as he led the way, I just shrugged, knowing it was pointless to argue with him.

Taking the path of least resistance, or the one without a Thor-sized-obstacle, I got in his car. My mind whirled at my impromptu decision. Only an idiot would do such a thing in my position. It was like putting an amateur in the ring with John Cena. I winced as I rubbed my chest where my heart rested, still feeling the sting from the last round. Wounds that hadn't healed, and probably never would.

Locke was driving the winding roads at his usual break-neck speed. But the evening air felt soothing as it whipped around us. The celestial charm of the night sky called to me, the moon reminding me of my first love.

It didn't take many hairpin curves for me to realize that this wasn't the way to Louis' house. A screeching kettle sound went off in my brain. It coincided nicely with my head popping out of the sunroof just as Locke took a bump too quickly.

"Locke, seriously, when are you going to drive more like a regular islander? You know, drive on relaxed island time? It's not like I'll jump out of the Jeep to escape if you slow down. There's a reason I don't write thrillers."

Locke began laughing. "Yeah, you aren't naturally inclined to be adventurous. I could go five miles per hour and that still wouldn't happen. You can cross 'stunt man' off your career list."

"Thanks. I guess that's why I'm a writer. I live through things from the comfort of my chair. The only action going on is the wear and tear on the page."

His laughter only grew. "Good to know you're getting action somewhere."

"That's not what I meant. You sure can turn *anything* around."

"Seriously, man, you haven't dated in forever. Come to think of it, you've never really dated, unless I missed something. How do you manage to write bestselling romances?"

"Hilarious, just watch the road, Batman." But he kept glancing over at me for clues, and that, along with his frantic driving, made me nervous. This was certainly a creative way to get people to talk. Gives new meaning to 'interrogation'. I responded, "No, ok. I haven't. Not really. But at least I've wing-manned plenty of people. Same thing."

"No. Um, not at all. And how is that possible? Women throw themselves at your adorable puppy dog face. Every time I'm at the bar, you get at least a couple of numbers a night. Not all telephone numbers, either." Locke looked at me curiously, completely bewildered.

"I'm just not interested. Who wants a one-night stand? Or to be someone's holiday fling? Only tourists come through here. Not all of us are interested in tourists." I looked at Locke pointedly.

"Don't judge until you try it. Mine stayed. And there are some really nice island girls. I see the way Nalu looks at you. Or is she just not the *right* island girl?"

I was getting annoyed by his accuracy. Since when did *his* mixology analysis get so . . . so annoyingly insightful? I countered, "No comment. Are you going to tell me where you're taking me?"

"I remember one summer when you *sort of* had a girlfriend," Locke said in his sing-song tone, completely ignoring me.

"Locke, I was twelve. Doesn't count if you're not even through puberty."

"Yeah, it does, especially if you kissed her. Apparently, that's all it took."

I opened my mouth to reply, but not a sound came out. Because I finally realized where he had taken me. And I was looking at a lavender front door. A cozy porch with twinkling lights, a large porch swing, and matching hammock chairs invited you to stay. An eclectic little townhouse shouted her name. *Luna.* And my body went rigid.

Reef

AGE 7

"He'll never get down from that tree! Whatcha wanna bet me?" a boy down below bellowed.

"It's Reef, so I'm not taking that bet. I'm not losing my Gameboy to you again," another boy called out, as if this was a foregone conclusion.

Locke had gone off in search of an adult to help with the situation and I prayed the adult would be his grandma and *not* my father. I could envision my dad now: hand in pockets, shoulders painfully straight, as he stared up at me and shook his head. I could even hear his words: 'Stop embarrassing me, even your sister could do better. Get yourself out of that tree like a man. Now!' The 'now' would be sharp and laced with warning. Letting me know every last shred of his non-existent patience for me was gone. My little stunt would 'wreck' his weekend and I'd pay for it.

My eyes searched the crowd, praying for a miracle, hoping that Locke would magically appear. After all, he was the one who had dared me to go up here. He was *officially* responsible for getting me down. I didn't care if it was his birthday party.

The boys' cackles became louder, but I had gotten pretty good at tuning them out. My dad's lack of faith in me had been excellent practice. It was like they had smelled my insecurity from day one; the quietness I'd adopted was like a beacon drawing them to me.

Just as I had made peace with the idea that I might be sleeping up here, I saw a tiny figure appear out of the corner of my eye, climbing up the trunk of the tree. I squinted harder, shielding my face from the rays to see who it was. . . a *tiny* girl in a purple floral dress. And she was moving quickly, using everything she had to her advantage to get to me. I caught a flash of her determined expression and knew instantly who it was. *Luna.* The girl from our housewarming party. And she was coming for me. *Me.*

Down below, I saw Locke appear in the crowd with his *tutu.* He and his 'grandmother' were both staring up in awe. Before I knew it, Luna was at the base of my tree branch. Her chocolate eyes, peppered with green, were sparkling with the most magical safety flare I'd ever seen. There wasn't any pity or disappointment in those gorgeous pools. And I wanted to get lost in them.

But all I could do was cling more tightly to the tree branch like a scared little monkey, my eyes wider than a bush baby's. Without breaking eye contact, she delicately extended a small hand to me. Unfurling each of her tiny fingers like a life line being flung out into a raging sea.

"I've got you," she whispered when I didn't move. Her rose-colored lips moved seamlessly. And that's when I knew. She was different from anyone else I'd ever met. I'd known it from the second she'd made that fairy crown with me. But this . . . she was obviously special. Someone very rare to find. And my soul tethered itself to hers.

"Reef?" she said when I didn't blink, consumed by her beauty. Now ready to stay on this branch with her for eternity. It didn't seem so bad anymore. Definitely not scary. Not with her.

"Stay with me." The words slipped out so quickly that they escaped my soul in an exhale. An inaudible whisper. Only my lips made the shape, feeling them out. Not even knowing what those words would mean for me.

"What?" she asked as she tried to inch closer to me and everyone gasped down below. I guess I'd officially made Locke's party memorable.

"Thank you," I said, clearing my throat as I took her hand. A symphony of serotonin overtaking me.

Reef

CHAPTER 5

So long ago, you were the only one
Who could truly see me
The only one who believed

-REEF AKUA, ONE
MORE HOUR

Flight mode had kicked in as Locke struggled to push me out the car door. Locke's laughter ricocheted throughout the car's interior as he took in my slack-jawed expression. He waltzed around to my side of the car like I was his prom date. And I knew there wasn't anything that could motivate me to move out of this safe cocoon in my present frozen condition.

"Come on," he said, like he was coaxing his dog out of the car for a vet visit. "I have some treats in the glove compartment for Penny if I need to use them." His 'dog dad' voice only irked me more, but my butt was glued to the seat like Matthew McConaughey's hand on that nude sculpture in *The Wedding Planner*.

I just looked at him, unamused. "Locke, this isn't funny. How did we go from *one* of us helping Luna in the future, to you waiting for my shift to be over and then driving me *here?* This seems pretty premeditated."

"I know you, LaRue. You'll hide out in front of your computer and find an excuse not to follow through with the plan. As soon as you said yes, I told Louis to make the rest happen."

"The rest?" I asked in disbelief. "You two should not be planning *anything* together. This is how World War Three gets started."

"So dramatic. No wonder LaRue sells out internationally. Come on. You can pine just as well as from the *hale,*" he teased, ushering me into the 'house'.

"That's not funny," I retorted. But he only laughed harder. Locke knew me too well, although I'm sure it was all painfully obvious from my books. I was so glad I'd given him free copies of my novels.

"Oh, and Reef," he began, as I stared at him. "I think

you had the best moves when you were that treasure explorer from book five. *Channel him.*"

"I'm going to kill you," I said hoarsely, as I reached for the door handle.

"Whatever gets you out of the car," he sang.

THE LAVENDER DOOR loomed above us, like an uneasy premonition. The soles of my feet felt clammy as we stood awkwardly in front of it. An unique bro version of *Thelma and Louise* with a tropical twist. I pivoted on my heels, not ready to get dragged down this rabbit hole, but Locke grabbed me right as the door opened.

I turned to see her standing there. Looking even more beautiful than in my daydreams. And I got paid to have *many*.

Luna stood bathed in the light seeping through the half-opened doorway, her yoga pants and long cardigan wrapped around her. Luna's cheeks grew pink as she looked at us. But I loved her like this. She looked like an elegant Olivia Pope without the oversized wine glass. Hopefully, without all the *Scandal*, too.

Hesitantly, my eyes made their way up her body to the top of her head, where loose curls spilled out from her scrunchie. The curls were tied up in what I had learned was called a 'pineapple', secured by a loose scrunchie to contain her long, dark brown hair. She quickly unrolled some of the lavender scarf at the back of her neck to bring the extra fabric over the top of her head to tuck it into the bow at the top of her forehead, succinctly hiding the wavy curls away. But faint wisps of rogue tendrils flew free anyway, caressing her beautiful olive cheeks. I loved seeing her this way. *It was pure Luna.*

She wrapped her cardigan tighter around her as her pupils dilated. *Yeah, she wasn't expecting company.*

"What? . . ." But she didn't get to finish her question. Louis appeared behind her in the doorway, opening it wider.

"Hey," his cool, whiskey tone blanketed all of us. "We were having a chill, music night. It's so good to see you." Louis turned to Luna. "I invited them here, honey, I hope that's ok. I didn't know they would get here so fast." He eyed Locke and this nervous laugh escaped me. I wish I had a different 'tell'. Anything else, really. After my outburst, Locke and Louis cast their eyes over to me. *No, I was not okay.*

Louis continued slowly, "I had something in mind I thought we could all discuss. I don't think I've seen you guys all together since you were little tikes out exploring the world and giving your parents gray hairs. It will be just like old times. You three were always a memorable part of my visit. Why don't I make us some tea if you're up for it?" He glanced at Luna cautiously.

I took in Luna's eyebrows, which had stayed raised. Even her poised expression couldn't hide her true feelings. *Great.* Louis' ambush was even worse than Locke's. I was so excited to witness this exchange right in front of my eyes. She probably wouldn't even want me to be her . . . I have no idea what. But I'm sure Luna would do a better job of being my bodyguard than I would of being hers. When Locke asked me about his little proposition, I assumed Luna had *also* agreed to it. But then again, I wasn't even fully aware of what *I* was agreeing to do. Leave it to Locke. Heat crept over me, preparing for what was to come.

Suddenly, Luna's most welcoming tone interrupted our silence. *"E komo mai!"* Her grace went on autopilot as she 'invited us in'.

Immediately, she began busying herself by tidying up the snacks and a lone drink on the kitchen table. I'm guessing it was Louis'. Maybe *he* needed some liquid courage. I swallowed harder, but all I inhaled was more of Luna's intoxicating scent. The one I'd been trying to recreate in my memory. Somehow, I'd completely underestimated its powers.

"Are your parents here, Luna? I haven't seen them in forever?" Locke asked while she tidied up around the kitchen.

"Oh, no. They're not here now. They also like to stay with my brother. I guess that's the perk of having multiple children. They say it's like having a vacation all the time. Good thing, they're still not over that ancestral art piece you broke."

Locke chuckled. "That's fair."

Times had hit hard here, and like many families on the island, Luna and her parents lived in a multi-generational home. This was the way many people could retire or their children could afford to live here. With the steep prices on the island, this type of living situation was becoming more and more common. It seemed the only people who could afford to own a home here were the tourists who bought and then rented out their vacation properties for an exorbitant fee. Which only caused prices to increase. Many islanders had to leave their homes and go to the mainland where they could afford to live. And while I liked to think part of what made this island so special was the native people, it felt like we were being phased out.

Luna finally stopped moving and extended a nervous hand toward the table. "Please sit. Would you like anything? I have more snacks and drinks."

Locke and I took a seat at the table after Luna's stilted invitation. I began shaking my head as Locke opened his mouth. "Well–" I bumped his leg under the table. "No, we're fine."

"Ok, well, Uncle," she said through clenched teeth, giving Louis the most pointed stare. One I didn't know she possessed. "Would you *help* me in the other room?"

"Oh Luna, it's pretty late. They just said they don't need any snacks or anything–"

"*Now.*" I could see her petite jaw clenching. She led a befuddled Louis out of the room, trailing woefully behind her.

I immediately turned to Locke, who was already reaching for a bowl of nuts. "*She doesn't know?*" I swatted his hand away.

He shook his head at me and blissfully proceeded to the bowl. "Man, all I was supposed to do was get you here. The rest is *all* up to Louis. At least when I set people up, I let them know a few of the details." He popped a macadamia nut into his mouth. I should have known better than to get involved in this. My memory of the surprise double date he set up for his grandmother and Louis popped into my head. I needed to yank my ripcord, now.

"You know more than you're letting on, Locke. I'm pulling the shark card."

He practically choked on his nut. "The *shark* card, Reef? Really? You want to use that now? When I have *no* information?"

"Yeah, I think I do. The nice, warm boat *without* shark-infested waters looked pretty enticing when you got attacked."

He laughed harder. "See, you are a natural protector. Anyone else would have left me to fend for myself with that shark. But you stayed and helped me . . . Ok, fine. As if I'm going to say no to anything you ask me."

I looked at him, waiting. "Locke?" Urgency edged my tone. I could hear Luna and Louis' vigorous discussion in the next room.

"It may be *a little* more 'hands on' than I implied. Let's just say Cece needs to bring her A-game."

My mouth opened, but nothing dared to come out. *What the heck did that mean?*

Reef

AGE 6

I learned early in life that staying tucked away on my front porch steps kept me out of trouble. And I had gotten good at remaining invisible—it was my super-power. My eyes drifted across our front lawn that had been neatly set up for a luau to meet our new neighbors. Stress levels had run high today to make a good first impression. That meant I should stay out of the way.

Thankfully, the move meant Locke was only a few houses down now. Our tutus were best friends, so they'd let us know when this duplex became available. Impatiently, I scanned the crowd for my best friend. Instead, I caught sight of my little sister being my dad's right-hand man. A job I'd never fill. Which was reinforced by the wave of guilt that flowed through me.

I shut my eyes, forcing the feeling back down. Then I opened them back up to look around for *any* distraction possible. A stinging sensation kept tugging at the corners when suddenly I spotted something, or rather, someone.

There was a tiny figure off to the side of our house, bending down beneath our mango tree. Loose curls flowed over her shoulder as she stooped to collect some wildflowers. Purple princess flowers had taken over that corner of our yard, with a few white ginger buds sprinkled in like snow. The dark hair cloaking her face made her even more of an enigma.

"Luna, honey, don't pick their flowers!" I saw her tiny fingers stop their weaving of the floral stems she'd just picked in response to her mother's request.

Luna.

The turn of her head sent my heart racing. I'll never forget the gentle expression on her beautiful face. Soft ringlets and wisps of hair blew around her face in the early afternoon breeze. Everything suddenly got brighter in my mundane world. Like the appearance of a rainbow after a tropical storm.

"Oh, it's fine. Enjoy them, Luna!" my mother called back.

The sweetest smile broke free across her face, and it cracked my heart wide open. I swallowed hard, trying to make sense of the feelings coming over me. My eyes tried to open wider, to take all of her in. But it felt impossible, like I couldn't get enough. I officially had my first crush.

I leaned back on the step, the shadows and my shyness surrounding me. I now hoped Locke would come late as I watched her tiny fingers work, twisting the stems as she hummed to herself. Her voice imprinted on my young ears.

I'd begun relaxing to her soothing melody when I noticed a young boy leave his group of neighborhood kids where they'd been playing. He was making his way over to her. My heart plummeted. He'd seen her beauty and had the courage to do something about it; he'd 'manned up', as my dad would say.

But as words left his mouth, the expression across her face wasn't one of being flattered. An ache sliced through that beautiful smile as her eyes focused harder on the flower chain in her hands. My body moved to the edge of the step, slipping out of the shade. Both my hands grabbed tightly onto the wood.

Leaning forward to get a better vantage point through the wooden railing, I could see the boy's lips pursed at Luna's immovable expression. With a huff, he sliced through her perfect chain, a forceful karate chop ending all her delicate work. Luna didn't move a muscle, eyes steadfast. But mine were glued to him, wanting to send all that hurt back to him.

I couldn't stand the idea of anything taking away her smile. As my hands unclenched, I pushed my feet off the steps, spring boarding forward. I felt a newfound energy in the soles of my feet. Only the sound of my pumping heart keeping my mind company as I made my way toward them.

The boy's harsh tone became audible. "Princesses *don't* look like you. Think you're better than everyone else with your princess crown, over here all by yourself?"

All thoughts left my mind. I pushed the kid slightly, enough to create space between the two of them. Allowing me room to stand between them. The bully's eyes went wide. I was thankful to be tall for my age. And apparently, I looked like the top of the kindergarten food chain.

"Uh, I–" the kid stammered. His friends had taken notice of us. A cacophony of whispers broke out behind us.

I raised an eyebrow. "You what?" At the sound of my voice, the little girl raised her eyes to me. A burst of natural island hues stirred something deep inside me. All of my toughness melted at the sight of them, my fists unclenching.

Thankfully, the boy was too rattled to notice. "I didn't know–"

"Know what?" I looked down at him. The whites of his eyes continued taking on that full moon glow. He took a step back. I continued with emphasis, "That you were messing with a beautiful princess?"

He just nodded his head vigorously. "Yeah."

"Yeah?"

"Yeah, I'm sorry." His cadaverous features paled even further as he muttered his apology. That's what I was looking for. What I hoped she needed. At least he could think about what he'd done and decide to change his way of thinking, or at least keep it to himself. I didn't expect him to change overnight, but everyone had to start *somewhere.*

He continued backing away, doing a frightened moonwalk to escape. I sure wasn't going to keep him here.

I immediately bent down to collect her flower crown. "Sorry, sometimes guys are just stupid and clueless. He was probably picking on you because you're so beauti–" I quickly handed her the broken crown, heat creeping up my neck. *Why had I said that?* But she smiled as my crimson color spread. Well, I'd do anything to see that smile again.

"*Mahalo,*" she said, through her grin. She gathered the broken flower chain, flipping the wilted flowers over in her tiny hands. Something that delicate couldn't thrive in such conditions. Nothing could. Then she said in explanation, "I'm just different."

The downcast tug on her lips squeezed on my heart. "Yeah, me too." For the first time, a hint of pride spread over my chest as I began picking some more flowers.

"What are you doing?" She stared at me.

"Oh, I thought we were making flower chains. You know, I want one too."

The cutest grin greeted me, a dimple flashing at the right corner of her mouth. I didn't even know what to do with the feelings they brought out of me.

"They're princess crowns." She corrected me with a low chuckle. "Here, let me help you," she said, as her hand brushed mine, sending electricity racing up my spine.

Luna

CHAPTER 6

So long ago, we were lost in a dream
Just you and me
So long ago, it seemed you were the only
Place I could run to and be free.

-LUNA MANU MELE, ONE
MORE HOUR

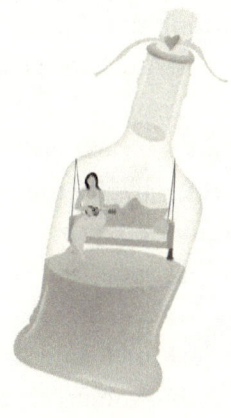

. . .

"Uncle, what do you mean, 'I'll find out what's going on?'" My voice was raising, something it never did, especially with him. My 'anakala, along with the music he'd given me, was my safe place. They kept me from falling into the dark abyss on particularly rough, starless days.

I swallowed harder. I hadn't seen or talked with Reef in almost two decades and now here he was, on my front doorstep. Looking ridiculously sexy with his dark-rimmed glasses and tousled hair that fell perfectly just below his chiseled chin. Bringing back all my dormant feelings as if a ten-foot wave had crashed into me. No wonder all the women at the bar were lining up. He kept getting sexier with age.

His soulful look haunted me every time I saw him. Taking up residence in my fantasies. And once the daydreams grabbed hold, nothing could uproot them. I was still paying for the last time I saw him at my ukulele gathering at Leilani's, the restaurant where he worked. I inhaled deeply as I remembered him leaning over the bar to say hello to me. My mind took note of how his button-up shirt stretched across his chest and forearms. I could feel my heart rate spiking at the memory, solidifying the fact that I'd remember that image for the next eternity.

Frustration bubbled up inside me as I heard my uncle's chuckles. He playfully nodded at my cheeks again. "It looks like you've been reading one of your romance novels, again." Louis eyed my bookshelf, then grabbed one of the offending books he'd just mentioned. He sauntered back into the dining room, giving me no choice but to follow.

"Uhhggg," I groaned, not able to contain myself. I tried

my best to work through the breathing techniques that iron-ically, Louis had taught me. Hoping to regain some dignity.

Why would he do this? Louis knew all about my anxiety. He must think the plan could really help me. His heart of gold sometimes caused trouble, but I figured I should at least hear him out.

I rolled my shoulders back, taking a useless look in the mirror to tidy up. When I returned to the kitchen, three sets of testosterone rich eyes planted themselves on me. I breathed deeper and thought seriously about bolting out the door *Runaway Bride* style. Where was a horse when you needed it? Or a FedEx truck?

Instead, I quietly slipped onto the empty seat beside Louis, right across from Reef. Louis began carefully pouring some tea. "It's peppermint," he whispered to me, as if approaching a wild boar. My eyes slid over to him. *Oh, this was going to be a spectacular plan.*

My uncle would do anything to protect me, so God only knew what he'd contrived this time. He placed the sweet-ener next to my drink, perhaps thinking local honey would soften me up.

His eyes assessed me as he began. "I had this *teensy* idea that I thought could be a lot of fun."

I glanced up at Reef for the first time and saw that his eyes were fixed on me, looking like round saucers as large as a full moon. This was *not* a tiny thing to ask of someone. And he didn't look like he wanted to do it. *At all.* More like he'd been dragged here against his will . . . *Locke!* He was easy to identify as the culprit because he had the biggest smirk on his face.

"Uncle," I said, when I finally found my voice. "I'm sure you have the best of intentions, but this doesn't feel like a small thing. Why don't we forget about it and move on?"

He noted my use of the stern word 'uncle'. He'd always been *my* Louis or *'anakala*. *Never* 'uncle'.

Concern etched Louis' face. "No, Luna. I'm worried about you. Your panic attacks have gotten much worse recently, and I don't want you going to the ukulele festival alone. I think you need a break. But if you don't feel you can take one, then I'm going to figure out a way to help you. And I won't let your label take advantage of you again. We're all friends here tonight and we all *love* you. We can figure something out *together*."

Love. My mouth ran dry at the word. My eyes met Reef's gaze, and a fire coursed through me. The same shade of heat I felt spread up his neck. Great, Louis hadn't even shared his plan of action yet. But I noticed a look of care in Reef's eyes. One that rivaled Louis'. Air felt like it had been knocked right out of me. Enough to make my head spin as I slowly nodded.

"Ok," Louis tried again. "I have a rough plan, so I thought we would get together and see what everyone was comfortable doing."

Comfortable? What strange plan has this man been concocting? My eyes darted to Locke, wondering how much he had "helped".

"Uncle!" My voice went higher, landing in an unfamiliar soprano range.

Louis ran his thumbs beneath his suspenders, stretching them out like 'laffy taffy' . . . Just the way I imagined he was about to bend the rules. "Let me explain, Luna. It might be too impractical, but let's just see." Louis' eyes took on a protective gleam.

I nodded again, since that was the only movement I could manage. My eyes dropped downward, landing on Reef's strong hands, which appeared to have come from hard work at the bar. Flashes of those steady hands holding me tight while I experienced my first feelings of love . . . of romance . . . swirled through my memory. His hands were like an irresistible beacon of light to me. And I felt like I'd been marooned longer than Tom Hanks on *Cast Away*. Not that all of him didn't call out to me. *Not helping, Luna.*

"So, Reef, Locke may have told you, but Luna has a concert coming up on Oahu." I looked up to see why there was a pause. Reef's eyes had gone wider, if that was even possible. He looked like he was going to bolt. I bet Locke had provided Reef with as many details as I had received from Louis.

"Uh," Reef stammered. He adjusted his glasses, the ultimate Reef move. An audible sigh escaped me, one he didn't seem to interpret correctly. *Thank God.* "Oh, I just meant, I wasn't sure. Locke said there was an event and that maybe I could provide some moral support while looking out for Luna. I heard her label might try to pull some sort of publicity stunt. Maybe try selling the idea of a romance between her and another artist to increase sales . . ."

Locke interjected with a laugh. "I told him you were so famous you needed a bodyguard. And you couldn't ask for a better one."

Reef pulled uncomfortably at his shirt collar. "I think you're going to need someone else for that. Locke's the type of guy you want. Maybe I could stay with Guin while he went with Luna." He glanced at Locke, who shook his head. "Well, ok . . . I guess you're stuck with me. I'm not sure how much I can help, but I'd like to try."

I couldn't believe he'd agreed to this much of the plan, but then again, Reef was one of the best guys I'd known. Guess he still was. Louis smiled, his eyes quickly dancing over to me, hesitating for a few moments so I could take in his matchmaking sparkle. He was really something.

"Well, that's the basics." He clasped his hands together. "Except . . . it's a little *more* involved than just being Luna's bodyguard."

Reef's mouth dropped open, and my head whipped toward Louis. "Uncle! You've already asked *way* too much." I spun back to Reef. "Thank you so much, but everything's going to be fine. *Really*. Don't worry about it, *any of it*."

Reef smiled, but it didn't quite reach his eyes, as if he was disguising his hurt. Did he actually *want* to do this? I didn't mean to imply that I thought he *couldn't* do it. Or worse, that I didn't *want* him to. There's *no one* I would prefer to watch my body more. *Stop it Luna, this is not one of those fiction novels. Turn your romance brain off.* But it was too late. Fierce protector lyrics clouded my field of vision, and my fingers twitched reflexively, curling together as if holding an imaginary pen. Reef's eyes landed on the motion, a grin spreading over him. I forgot *how well* he knew me. If I let this happen, it would be like sliding into your favorite worn sweater on the first crisp day of fall. *Perfect. Familiar. Everything you ever wanted.*

He looked at me through his 'professor' style glasses. "Luna, I want to help. I'm *not* going to just forget it. Please, tell me more, Louis." A sudden confidence had overtaken him. I loved when his heart was on display.

Electricity shot right to my core, finally waking me up. He was like lightning. And with him around, it always struck multiple times. Defying all rules and logic. He'd always be my exception. A true good man. Just when I'd stopped believing in them.

Louis' smile had turned into an omniscient grin as he flipped through the pages of my romance novel absentmindedly. While Reef's eyes grew larger with every turn of the page. I guess I'd be pretty concerned, too, if Louis had a romance book. And not just any book. Cece LaRue was a hopeless romantic.

Louis cleared his throat, all eyes landing on him. "So, I might have gotten an idea from one of Luna's romance novels."

It was so silent that the sound of pages being turned was disturbing. Until Locke started coughing. He picked up his water while Reef patted him on the back rather aggressively. "Sorry, but I think we're going to need those drinks." Locke barely choked out.

I stood, happy for the reprieve and ready to grab the bourbon I kept for Louis. He usually enjoyed a drink while we listened to vinyl, dissected the music, and went over my lyrics. And I usually had tea. I hadn't had a drink since my attacks started. Although tonight felt like a good night to break my prohibition.

As I got up, I felt something warm. I looked down to find Reef's hand laying gently on top of mine. "He's *fine*. Don't listen to Locke. He's just joking around. I have a feeling alcohol is only going to make this plan *more* insane. Go on, Louis. Please don't mind Locke's interruptions." Reef's eyes slid over to him in warning.

I had a feeling Reef knew I didn't drink. Usually, I felt like the odd one out. A warmth bloomed in my chest. Time fell away as I felt his familiar care and tenderness. His awareness.

"Ok, if you're sure," Louis replied, but Reef nodded firmly. "Well, I was thinking this could be a bodyguard position with a little extra flare. . ."

Locke snorted. "I'm sorry, please continue."

Louis' eyes narrowed. "Well, I had been curious about

what Luna was reading, so I picked up her book one day while I was waiting for her. I was pleasantly surprised, and—"

No, just no. My insides felt like they were in a vice grip. Like I was that twelve-year-old girl again. The one who had left Reef behind. We were *not* opening that wound back up. I'd already picked at the scab, and it had been a mistake.

"No, Uncle. *No,*" I said firmly.

Louis stared at me, but evidently I wasn't getting his telepathic communication. He continued, "Fake dating appears to be *very* popular. There's no harm in pretending you have a boyfriend, so the label will leave you alone. They can't pretend to sell a romance if you're already in a relationship with someone else. We can post about your 'relationship' on your social media, and when it's time for the festival, they won't be able to do a thing about it. Force their hand just like they have yours in the past. They don't always have your best interest at heart, Luna. Until your contract is up, we have to be smart."

Locke and Reef sat motionless. The kitchen became a silent vacuum. It reminded me of an eerie quiet before a fierce storm. Suddenly, Locke raised his hand like an eager schoolboy. "I'd just like to add that it looks like we've had the right guy for the job all along, Louis. They've already dated. This should be easy. It'll be like riding a bike." His laughter reverberated around the room as Reef's eyes locked onto mine.

Luna

AGE 12

Come on, come on. Just a little closer . . .

I watched as his hand inched its way toward mine. The glow of the screen in the dark room practically blinded me every time I took my eyes off of him and looked toward the TV. From the corner of my eye, I kept looking at his fingers with anticipation. My heart was racing, nerves spiraling, and the roar of the dinosaurs in the background wasn't helping.

Locke, of course, had scooted his pillow up as close as he could to his tutu's big screen, so he could watch *Jurassic Park* in "3D". Or as close to making the dinosaurs leap off the screen as possible. I turned my head to Reef, who laughed lightly from his seat on the sofa next to me. We both took another glance at Locke, whose mouth was now slightly agape. He was completely oblivious to everything except what was happening in front of him.

Our eyes timidly found each other. As they locked into place, my heart caught in my throat. All the starry cosmos in his eyes made my mouth run dry.

With my heart racing, I turned my head back to the screen, biting my lip in frustration. *You could make a move, Luna.* But I couldn't overcome the butterflies soaring inside me. I'd never had them before. Not like this.

I glanced down at his hand with chagrin, the one that had slightly retreated. My stomach fell, disappointment coming over me. But I couldn't look away. I could imagine the nice, warm sensation of his hand on mine. And suddenly, I realized the difference between nervous energy and anxiety.

Nervous energy turned up the frequency of my butterfly wings and the electricity he made me feel. A safe adrenaline rush. One I could lean into. And with that, my hand moved toward his, brushing his ever so slowly, and then rested there. Letting him know what I wanted, and that I was ready.

My heart hammered as his eyes stayed glued to the screen. I smiled as I saw him glance over at me and then down at my hand. His pinky slowly reached out and grabbed hold of mine. And I replied, gently tugging back. An equal force pulling at the corner of his lips.

Ever so carefully, with a newfound confidence, he took my entire hand. Igniting all the nerve endings in my body, even the ones I didn't know existed. And all those pieces felt like they were now completely his.

Luna

CHAPTER 7

Arms intertwined, smiles combined,
Why can't I call you mine?

-LUNA MANU MELE, LAVENDER WAYS

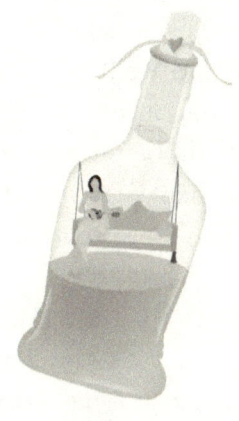

Nervous laughter spliced through the air. Reef covered his mouth, attempting to stop himself, but it didn't help. It was his tell, one I found absolutely adorable. Or at least, I would have if I wasn't so focused on my uncle's creative matchmaking.

"We were *twelve*, Locke," I said defensively.

Locke pointed a finger over to Reef, who was attempting to collect himself, and having no such luck. "*Nānā*! 'I told you' it counted." A crimson wave spread further up Reef's neck.

But Reef pushed ahead, clearing his throat to speak. "Louis, I'm *not* the guy for this. I mean, look at me, *no one* is going to believe it. Luna is a star. She's *stunning*. I'm just a bartender." He shook his head ruefully.

His words hit me right in the tender place that was reserved for him. The one I kept tucked away. *How could he think that?* Reef was the most attractive guy on the island. And the only one I wanted. *Glad you can finally admit that to yourself.*

Louis cleared his throat, grabbing everyone's attention. "We'll make this as easy as possible for everyone. Just go on a few 'dates' together and we'll post some photos. If Reef can be seen with Luna at her ukulele festival and her concerts in Oahu that will be perfect. You don't need to do any more or go *any* further. *Friends* hold hands. So it will be even less than when you were together before." A teasing nature filled his tone.

"We were twelve!" I reiterated. Embarrassment wrapped around me.

"They've totally kissed. Don't worry about it," Locke said, teasing us relentlessly. His childhood grin took over. "Shouldn't be too hard to re-enact it for 'social'. Doubt they need any guidelines either. These two are like magnets."

Reef glared at him. *"Why* are you here again?"

"To be utterly and completely helpful. And *totally* amused." Locke chuckled.

Reef rolled his eyes at his best friend and exhaled deeply. He looked at Louis. "You really think this will work? Will her label leave her alone if I manage to look like her boyfriend? What about anxiety? Is there a way I can help?"

"Reef." His name on my lips felt so intimate. "I'd be so *laki. Anyone* would think I was 'lucky.'" Our eyes met, like familiar strangers getting reacquainted. My heart felt like it was beating too rapidly to withstand, but my eyes refused to go anywhere else.

After all of this, he wants to know how he can help with my anxiety? There was no way I would have believed he was for real if I hadn't grown up with him. His heart seemed to be just as big. And he was *so* gentle with me—*and* my anxiety. I'd never *had* to explain to him more than I wanted. I knew in my bones I wouldn't have to now, either.

Reef held my gaze, and muscle memory took over. The squeezing in my heart was telling me this was dangerous. But I was too content to let those gentle eyes hold me. And I fell back decades into my safe place with him. My happy place.

"Oh yeah, this is going to work just fine. Don't worry about selling it, Louis." Locke bantered, immediately breaking the spell.

I raised my eyebrows at Locke. "Yes, we see how good you are at fake dating."

"Yeah," he jested. "I have a 100% success rate."

I swallowed hard, slowly turning back to Reef to answer his question. "Just you being there will make such a difference. You've always helped with my anxiety. If Louis thinks this will work, I trust him. I can't thank you enough." Reef waved his hand in the air as if this was nothing. Like anyone would do this. But they wouldn't. There weren't many men like Reef. If any. I'd learned that the hard way.

Louis interrupted the moment again, looking quizzically between us, as if putting puzzle pieces together. "I'm hoping Kelani and I can travel to Oahu with you. If she's feeling well enough, we could make it a fun trip for all of us to enjoy together. I'll do whatever I can to help, and I'll try to make it as easy as possible on you, Reef. Really, I can't thank you enough. Luna means everything to me."

Locke chuckled. "Don't worry, Louis. It's going to be plenty easy for him. The best vacation he's ever had." Reef elbowed Locke in the side and he let out a surprising 'oomph'. Reef adjusted his glasses like it hadn't happened, but the massive smirk on Locke's face was proof that it had.

"Ok," Louis said with a grin. "It's settled then. Let's get these two star-crossed lovers reunited."

Luna

AGE 12

"This is becoming a pattern for Luna, and it's not how we want to start the school year," the principal said sternly, shaking his head. "Hiding away in the nurse's office with a stomach ache won't get her out-of-school work. I know this year's workload has gotten harder, but that's no excuse, even if one has . . . *mental health issues*." He spat out the last words as if they left a terrible taste in his mouth, one with which he didn't want to be associated. The bald man looked at me harshly through his thick-rimmed glasses.

The blonde nurse beside him spoke up, her shoulder-length bob bouncing. "Yes, I've tried to explain to her that nerves can cause harmless stomach aches. It's no cause for alarm. Sometimes when we're prone to anxiety, it causes stomach upset. But we have to learn how to cope with the situation. There are lots of exercises to keep her mind busy and school is good for that. If we worry about *every* little thing, we risk becoming a hypochondriacs."

Her sweet tone was mostly gone by the time she uttered that last word. The implication of what she was saying landed with a heavy thud against my chest. And my nausea only grew, as did my stress. I could feel the wet slickness of my palms increasing as I rubbed them against my thighs.

I looked helplessly over at each of my parents as I sat in between them at this mandatory school conference. I'd been feeling so tired and nauseated that I hadn't been able to stay awake in class. And in ways I couldn't explain, I just didn't feel right. I felt sick, and I *thought* the nurse's office was the place to go. But this was *not* a safe place.

The nurse pulled out some more paperwork from the clinic drawer. Literature, which I'm sure was supposed to "educate" us. Probably on being overdramatic. Or lazy. Or possibly mentally unstable. Pretty much everything they had just implied.

The principal pushed up his steel-rimmed glasses as he spread the papers proudly over the nurses' desk, which he had taken over as she sat off to the side. "Now, here is some great, informative literature to help you. And we're going to do our part and not admit her to the school clinic *anymore*. Sometimes, young women just process all their stress internally—"

Suddenly, a loud, feral sound came out of me without warning. My hands gripped the table, mortified that I couldn't find anywhere else to go. And before I knew it, I was heaving all over his pristinely pressed papers. I looked down to see his beautiful white papers stained with a mixture of vomit and blood.

Both of their heads snapped up to look at my parents in unison, the principal's eyes bulging as he slowly looked over at the nurse in horror.

"What *exactly* were you saying?" my mom asked impatiently.

Reef

CHAPTER 8

66 When he kissed her, it was like a part of her became imprinted on his soul. And every time he did so, he gave a little more of himself. Or at least he imagined that's what it would be like if he ever got the nerve to actually do it.

-CECE LARUE, LOVE ON ISLAND TIME

"We *never* kissed, Locke." The words escaped me as soon as we left Luna's house, and I heard the car door of his Jeep close. The words rushed out of me like a dam breaking free.

Disbelief flooded his tone. "What? There's *no* way. You two were inseparable. The summer you dated, you two were practically glued together. I don't—"

"She always seemed really anxious about it, and I couldn't tell if she wanted me to kiss her. I've known she had anxiety since we were little kids. It's just something you innately know . . . at least when you know someone that well. So, I never tried to kiss her. Not even once."

Locke rubbed his jaw like he was trying to hide his shock. "Really?"

"Really. But it doesn't mean that cuddling and holding her weren't some of the best moments of my life. She definitely left her mark on me."

He stared at me. "Yeah, I'd say. So, let me get this straight . . . You're telling me you've *desperately longed* for a woman for almost two decades and you *haven't even* kissed her?"

"Yeah, that's what I'm telling you. And now I apparently get to *fake* the relationship of my dreams."

Locke whistled. "Hey, I'm sorry. I shouldn't have asked you to do this. I just thought it would be good for *both* of you . . . I mean, I knew you've always had feelings for her. But—"

I shook my head, my eyes gazing out the side window of his Jeep. "No . . . I'd do anything for her, Locke, you know that."

Locke looked at me and simply placed a hand on my shoulder. He let out a *long* exhale and then started driving. "Don't worry, you're doing the right thing. You always do. I definitely think this will help her. She hasn't seemed like her old self in a while now. Maybe *you* can help. Plus, fake dating isn't all bad."

"Really? How long did you last?" I asked, as I thought about his fake dating attempt with his fiancée, Guin. He'd done it just to set up a double date for his grandmother and Louis. And now look at him.

"Not even the entire date." He began laughing. "My money says it will be even shorter for you. But isn't that a good thing, Cece? I mean, *you* wrote that book with the fake dating trope. A small part of you *must* have wanted to live it."

I finally released my breath. "Yeah, I think my heart stopped when Louis brought out that book. I'm only going to embarrass myself."

"Well, probably, and I'm *so* here for it." Locke chuckled. "But when you do, it's always endearing. However, I wouldn't be so sure. How did that book end?"

"I don't want to talk about it. It's fiction . . . fantasy. I don't mix the two." A wave of unease came over me, just like it had when I started crossing over that line in my writing. I couldn't let myself believe she might actually want me. I had a line for a reason. It's how I kept my sanity.

"Is this some hard and fast rule you have for yourself, '*Ms. LaRue?*' Because I saw *a lot* of blurring going on in there and it wasn't all one-sided." I gave him a look that momentarily stopped his teasing, and he held up a hand in surrender.

With that, the Jeep revved to life, and we drove the rest of the way in silence, except for the occasional chuckle from Locke. But my mind was too busy contemplating how I was going to survive a 'fake dating' relationship to engage in brotherly banter. I needed to figure out how to keep from revealing all my cards. Which seemed to be a pretty important task since I'd always been an open book with Luna.

When Locke pulled up beside my car at the restaurant parking lot, I asked, "How do you even plan a fake date?"

"Well, it depends on how well you want to fare on it." His laugh rumbled off the metal of the Jeep.

"Seriously, Locke, help me out here."

Concentration covered my best friend's features. A look I usually only saw when he was helping people at his surf shop. "Reef, I think you have two options here. You can plan an activity for two friends, or you can plan an actual date. *Finally*, go for it. I don't understand why you never have. She moved back to Maui some time ago, after all."

"Locke—"

"Also, while we're on the topic of things I don't understand, why are you still bartending? And you're in the same apartment we used to rent together, the one where Cece was born? You could move closer to the beach or get a condo. Shouldn't LaRue have some mega beach house?"

"Authors don't make that much, Locke. We do it out of love. Because our souls need it. Writing is our spirit's expression. Everyone else in the industry is the one making money. Eighty cents per book is a pretty standard publishing deal—if you're lucky. And then you might not have the final say in your work. But you can't compete in this market by yourself, because most likely your work will get buried. It's a Catch-22. And without readers, what is the point?"

"Oh, I didn't realize." His bluntness was always refreshing, especially since he's the only one who knew the real me—*both sides*. With him, I didn't have to pretend an entire part of my life didn't exist. *Maybe this fake relationship wouldn't be so hard after all.*

"No, I do fine, but I'm one of the lucky ones. And I still want anonymity. So, I tend bar and keep the same apartment. Plus, bartending is a way to socialize and helps me brainstorm ideas. Writing can be a pretty lonely existence."

"I don't know how you find enough time to write. I'm sure it's difficult."

I smiled. "I've really cut down on my shifts. They probably think I'm doing something illegal in my spare time. Although some type of posh crimes like black market designer knockoffs or something equally befitting of my dorkiness."

Locke's deep laugh washed over me, a comforting feeling following. "Well, you can always 'help' me at my surf shop if you need to devote all your time to writing. I'll be your beard. We could always use knockoff designer wetsuits. Fendi surfboards—"

I held up my hand to stop him before he really got on a roll. "Thanks. Really. Thanks for always having my back."

"Well, you literally had mine. I'm serious. Luna would be lucky to have a guy like you."

"Yeah, well, I don't know that I'm what she needs. I don't see myself fending off any music label executives. I'm just a romance author," I said forlornly.

"Reef, you fended off a shark. Few people would stay in the water to find their friend and get them safely back to the boat after an attack, like you did for me. You can do this."

Locke looked at me pointedly. "And I've listened to Luna's music, too. Seems like you're not the only hopeless romantic. I'd place a bet that her dream guy writes about love. Maybe she'd even think he was the manliest guy of all. Now get out of here. Go write another bestseller with a fake marriage trope so I can suggest that to Louis next time."

I shook my head at him. "Night, Locke." But as soon as I'd hopped out of his car, I doubled back. "Do you think Luna's read *all* of my books?" I asked, remembering my novel on her kitchen table. The sight of it was like an ice-cold shower. Just an exposed piece of my soul for everyone to see.

"Oh Reef, I saw her face light up. She's definitely read them *all.* Night," he sang out. His eyebrows danced as he drove off, leaving me to think about what I'd just done.

Reef

AGE 9

"**W**here are they?" I could hear my father's voice boom from down the hallway as I sat uncomfortably in my seat. I glanced over at Locke and then at Luna. All of us were posed with ice packs strategically placed in different places. We looked like the Hawaiian *Breakfast Club.* And I knew exactly which one I was. *Not* the tough one pumping his fist up in the air at the end. Not the one who gets the girl.

My eyes widened as I tried to sink deeper into the cold metal chair. Locke glanced over at me. "It's ok, Reef. You look like you won the fight."

But I knew my dad would see through that right away.

And my heart pounded faster with each heavy thud of his methodical steps headed my way. Their noise reached me before his stare did. A shiver ripped through me.

"What the–?" His wide eyes bounced between Locke and me, and then finally to Luna. I squeezed my eyes tightly shut, trying to make it all go away. "What did you do? Are you having *a girl* fight your battles for you now?"

My shoulders fell and my head drooped as his disgusted tone landed on me. He yanked on my shirt. "Sit up straight. I raised you better than this. Tell me what happened because I'm sure the principal will."

"Sir," Locke interrupted, and my dad's face immediately softened. "It's my fault. Really. They were just trying to help me, and it turned into this big fight. We were trying to play kickball during recess and it got heated with this other boy who's been picking on me. I'm sorry."

My father's face stayed frozen with disappointment. "Then why was I the one called first? Nice try, Locke. Brave of you." He turned to me as he waved toward Luna. "She's half your size, Reef. Come on." Luna moved closer to me defensively and I could see her putting more pressure on her ice pack.

Everything Locke said was true, except it had been about me. Locke had been the one to step in, and that's when things got heated. And then Luna tried to help, too. It was a regular playground, free for all.

"Dad–" I tried, but my lip was already quaking. It wasn't enough to be called names, to get my friends in trouble, and to have the girl I loved icing her knee next to me. No, I was about to face more humiliation. And only he knew how to dole it out *so well*.

"Don't tell me you're going to cry. Men don't cry, Reef. How many times do I have to tell you that? We stay strong.

Look at Locke." He pointed to my best friend, who was staring downward, grimacing. I swallowed hard, fighting the tears with everything inside of me.

Locke knew saying something would make it worse, but Luna didn't. "Reef was really brave today, Mr. Akua. He—"

"Let his little girlfriend fight for him," my father finished.

"No, he stood up for himself," Locke intervened, no longer able to bite his tongue. "And if he wants to cry, he deserves it."

"That's it. Get your things, Reef." He pointed forcefully between my friends. "The two of you can call your parents. You're not getting a ride. You can explain the reason to them." With that, he pulled on my arm to drag me down the hallway. I glanced back quickly at my loyal friends. A crack forming in my heart at the pain on their faces and guilty tears appearing in my eyes for being the reason why.

Reef

CHAPTER 9

I'd do anything to keep her
Grasp out into the ether to reach her
But words lie there like vapor
Surrounding me until I put pen to paper
Setting my muse alive again

-REEF AKUA, THE MUSE

Locke's parting words echoed in my mind, and my shoulders sagged in defeat. I instantly felt relief when I finally reached my floor so I could hibernate. But that feeling quickly changed when I spotted Mrs. Aliana standing right beside my front door. I inwardly groaned. *How did she always know?* It was uncanny. *Didn't she have better things to do?* Her last name should mean spotlight instead of 'moonlight' because I knew what was coming next . . . the inquisition.

"Reef," she said brusquely. Her hot pink robe was drawn around her as tightly as her arms. Its hue matched her pink rollers, which were perfectly posed in her hair. They were tucked away under a floral silk scarf, which was tied around her head like something out of a fifties rom-com. Did they need someone to play Doris Day? Because I think I had found her.

Mrs. Aliana's lips pursed, taking on a look of full disappointment in their best nanna fashion. I should be annoyed, but I'd lost my tutu a few years ago and I loved any type of 'nanna' love I could get. Even if hers was more in the reprimand department. Maybe it came from a place of love somewhere deep, *deep* inside.

"Mrs. Aliana," I replied in a cajoling tone, trying to loosen her up. Not that it would work. I continued to wedge my key into the knob. But my fingers only fumbled more under her stare.

"Reef, it's one in the morning. When are you going to get a decent job? Your dog has been whining for you all night. If you had a girlfriend, you *and* your dog wouldn't be *so* lonely." Her lips formed a tight line.

There was the blunt, nosey woman I knew and loved. She pushed up her steel-rimmed glasses to get a better look at me. *Is that what I look like when I do that?* I took in the sight of us out here at one a.m. with nothing better to do. *Both* alone in our apartments. I shuddered. An eerie feeling came over me. I called her *Mrs.* Ailana, but I really wasn't sure if she had ever been married. *Will I be an eighty-something-year-old spinster, too?* I already felt like one.

"Well, we all do the best we can. Would you prefer I bring lots of different women home every night, Mrs. Ailana?"

She scowled at me. "That's not funny, young man. You never bring *anyone* home. I never see you with *any* female companions. One woman is what I would prefer. A nice, sweet girl who watches out for you and your dog."

"Do I need *watching*?" I asked with amusement. I had learned this was the only way to handle her quirky and 'over the line' comments.

"Yes, you never come out of that apartment. And you're always so quiet in there. What are you doing, anyway?" she asked suspiciously. "Probably illegal activities . . . A woman will straighten you out. I'll activate the Gray

Roots phone tree tomorrow. Maybe someone has an unattached grandchild. Just don't be *too* picky."

I sputtered, "How kind . . . But no, Mrs. Ailana. Don't worry, it seems as if I have a girlfriend now." Finally, the key clicked into place. As soon as I opened the door, Nova came bounding out to see me. Her howl was extra commanding. I felt bad for leaving her for so long. She was used to my late bar shifts and weird hours, but I always felt guilty about it. And I hadn't planned on any of tonight's . . . events.

I congratulated Nova on her impressive yodel with ear rubs. Eventually, I dared to glance up, knowing my neighbor wouldn't feel quite the same way about Nova's vocalizations. The disapproval that radiated off of her could melt plastic.

"Well, you should *know* if you have a girlfriend, I would think. If you don't, then you obviously haven't done your job . . . And please do *something* with your dog," she said with impatience as she turned and abruptly went inside her apartment. Her grumpiness leaving a funky aura in her wake.

"Night to you too, Mrs. Ailana." With a shake of my head, I stooped down to pet Nova, who was insistent on licking every part of my face and neck. Nova wasn't satisfied until I'd had a proper face wash. Maybe it was the Vizsla breed, or maybe it was just unique to her, but it had always been her special greeting. And I wouldn't have it any other way.

"Come on girl, let's go out," I said, quickly grabbing her leash by the door. I half expected Mrs. Ailana to be back outside when we returned from our walk, but her door was dark. No welcome mat out there. I silently chuckled as I led Nova inside.

Nova quickly found her spot on the sagging ottoman in

front of my worn leather chair in our special nook. Dedicated to reading, writing, and tons of doggie affection.

I turned on the reading lamp beside me, not having any energy left to write. There was no need to light my "inspirational" writing candles. Yes, I had those. Lighting them was like flipping a switch and instantly becoming LaRue.

More than lack of energy, I just wasn't in any mood to write after the events of this evening. Instead, I focused my attention on Nova's pout. I admired how her dark caramel fur accented her enormous golden eyes so perfectly.

"I know, but can you help me figure out this tangled relationship first?" I asked rhetorically as I petted Nova's head. 'Man points' were flying out the window tonight faster than piña coladas at the local resorts. I was now stooping to doggie dating advice.

With no response, I offered her my thoughts on the matter as I gave her a good ear rub. "I think I should just text her."

Nova's eyes appeared to widen. But maybe she was just soaking up that doggie affection. "Writing is my best medium, so texting seems like my best shot, don't you think? I know I'm supposed to wait for a certain period of time, but I've never understood those rules. Plus, this is all for show, anyway." Nova rolled over on her back, squirming around to show she was already bored and it was definitely time for belly rubs.

I sat up and complied. "Ok, I'm going for it." I sighed as her tongue lolled.

As I reached for my phone, Locke's words raced through my mind, as did his "advice". But it didn't matter, anyway. I realized the phone number I had for Luna was from twenty years ago. Wow, this plan was going so well. *Amazing start, Reef.*

My fingers started typing before I lost my nerve.

> Do you have Luna's phone number? I'm going to text her to get things started.

> How romantic. Wow, I can't believe that charm sells books.

> Locke, do you have it or not?

> Man, there's a waiting rule of like 24-hours at the very least. I know the romance world runs differently, but since you're new to the real world of dating, I thought I'd clue you in.

> How kind. Oh, by the way, how long did it take you to tell Guin she was 'the one'? I forget . . .

> That's a low blow, man. Guin was only in town for a limited amount of time. Ok, fine, here's her number, but don't say I didn't warn you.

> I've known Luna for over twenty years. That's plenty of time.

> And intimately for ten novels. Lol. Good luck.

I would not dignify that with a response.

> Oh, and Reef, let Cece take over. Do not say "get things started."

> Guin agrees.

I was going to kill him. I knew he shared almost everything with Guin, except for the few things I asked him to keep private, such as my pen name. Guin had become like family, so that was fine with me. But now he was really just trying to get under my skin. I closed the chat and opened up a new one. My fingers froze, hovering nervously over the send button.

> Hey, are you still up?

> This is Reef, by the way.

Oh God, this was such a terrible start. I was just about to un-send my messages. Glad tech geniuses had created such a feature for those of us in the 'dating awkward' category when her bubble appeared. I liked to think I was good with people, but Luna must be my loophole. My hands went clammy. I was probably already blowing this. Maybe I should have listened to Locke, as painful as that was to admit.

> Definitely still up. I am really, really sorry about tonight.

> Please, don't apologize. It was great to see you.

Before I could add anything, she wrote back.

> I'm sorry my 'anakala ambushed you. Or us. His heart is in the right place, but he's just very protective of me. We can forget about the whole thing and just keep the memory as something to laugh about.

> Do you want to forget it?

> Do you?

The phone went dark.

I looked at Nova, who was gnawing on her favorite squishy ball. The one she always had in her mouth. But at my expression, she dropped it and made an excited yipping sound, standing up to turn in circles on the ottoman. I'm not sure if she realized I needed the encouragement, but it worked. She always offered her doggie support when I got really excited about a scene I was writing.

> No, that's the last thing I want to do. I could never forget you.

The phone slipped out of my palms at my omission, and I fumbled for it, glad she wasn't here to witness it. Text bubbles floated in and out, taunting me. Well, I'd ventured this far. Guess I should have lit some candles, after all. I was in way over my head. Maybe I should let Cece take over, like Locke had suggested. I hadn't been able to tell Luna how I felt about her for such a *long* time now.

> I'd really like to help you. Or at least try.

> How are you such a good guy?

> In all fairness, there are some selfish reasons motivating me, too. I'd like to spend some time with you again.

The pause of the century continued while I tapped my thumb on the smooth leather.

> You don't need to agree to Louis' plan for that to happen.

Yeah, but I want to help. So, would you like to do something? Maybe hang out like we used to do? I have tomorrow off.

Don't you know there's a twenty-four-hour rule, hotshot?

Reef: Yeah, I'm well aware. Locke warned me all about it.

Haha. Smart move not listening to him. Ok, I could swing by your place in the afternoon. We can play it by ear..

Oh, so you want to pick me up, huh?

You said you wanted it to be like old times. I always walked over to your house when we did something together.

Yes, I remember waiting on my front porch steps until I saw her walking up to my house—it was always the best part of any day. Seeing her still was. I had a feeling it always would be.

Ok, tomorrow it is :)

Tomorrow :)

Reef

AGE 9

The sweltering heat was feeling more oppressive as I sat on my front porch steps, waiting for Locke and, hopefully, Luna. Ever since Luna had extended her hand to me on that tree branch, I'd begun inviting her to join us on our adventures. And soon, we were known as the 'three amigos' around the island.

I was about to go inside when I saw her tiny head bobbing down my gravel driveway. A smile stretched across my cheeks as she eagerly waved back at me.

"Where's Locke?" Luna asked, stopping short.

"Uh, I'm not sure." I swallowed the lump in my throat. It was getting late in the day and there was still no sign of him. I always called Luna's home *after* Locke said he was free. It had never been just the two of us before.

Luna pinched her lips together and sat on the far end of the step beside me. We sat motionless, looking at our hands like they were the most exciting things in the world.

"Uh," I began. "We could do something while we wait for Locke, if you want." I glanced over at her, a quiet grin formed on her lips.

"Yeah?" she asked eagerly. "Do you have board games or a movie or something?"

All inside activities . . . "Uh, how about I show you something cooler?"

Her face lit up. "Really?"

I nodded. "Yeah, follow me." I reached for her hand, guiding her toward the backyard.

I immediately paused, realizing what I'd done. Exactly what I'd kept imagining. "What is it?" Her eyebrows raised.

I glanced down at our intertwined hands and back up at her with questioning eyes. I couldn't believe I'd touched her like this. And she seemed to like it. Shaking my head, I continued on, reveling in our touch. When we reached the corner of my overgrown backyard, I halted.

Her lips twisted with amusement. "My backyard looks pretty similar, Reef." She teased.

I drew my finger upward, pointing to the structure above us, and her lips parted. Electric sparks fired off inside of me without my understanding.

"So, do you want to climb up? I promise it's sturdier than it looks."

"Did you build it?" she asked.

"If I say I helped, are you not going to go up?" A stilted laugh escaped me.

"No, that would make me feel better. If it was here already, I might pass." The sound of her laughter melted into me, warming places no one else had ever touched.

So, I helped her climb up the tree ladder, pointing out any faulty rungs. And just like that, she was standing in my world. The only place that truly felt like it was mine. Her quizzical eyes took in the reading nook and the decorations—my attempt at self-expression. My treehouse "decor" consisted of things that I had found at local flea markets. Many of my market visits with Locke and his tutu added to the memories in this place. As she saw more pieces of my universe, the flecks of green and amber in Luna's eyes grew brighter.

Her fingers slowly trailed over the 'book nerd decor', landing on a notepad I'd picked up in a 50-cent bin. "Do you write?"

"Huh? *Oh, no.*" My brain shut down automatically.

"Really, because this place looks like Mark Twain's hideaway." She remarked as I nervously looked around at the books and maps I'd collected for inspiration. This wasn't a pirate hideout like you'd expect to find on a tropical island. More like a writer's lair for crafting and plotting adventures. "May I?" she softly asked as she reached for the notebook.

My hand landed on top of hers before she could even pick it up. Our eyes locked together with the connection. Both taking a sharp inhale of breath simultaneously.

My fingers uncurled at her gentle expression, and I cleared my throat. "Uh, ok, but it's only nonsense. Just random scribbles."

"I'll be the judge of that," she said triumphantly, plopping down on the beanbag chair where I had written 'said nonsense'.

My palms perspired at the sight of her holding my words. I had to distract myself. So I reached for my little retro radio and started fiddling with it.

"Wait!" she exclaimed as I tried to scroll through the static. And my eyes shot up at her. "That's my favorite station."

A shiver rippled through me as she began humming. The sound I'd longed to hear again. Her soft singing awakened unknown feelings inside of me. Ones I'd been taught to repress.

"Beautiful." The word rushed out of me as my eyes stayed fixed on her.

Luna's cheeks flooded with a rosy hue. "Sorry, I'm not any good, but I love to sing. Can you imagine singing on a radio station like that?" Nervous laughter escaped her in equal measure with excitement.

"I could certainly see *you* doing that. Your voice is amazing."

She bashfully looked up at me through her lashes. "Really? You think so?"

I made my way over to her, adjusting my glasses as I sat on the beanbag beside her. "Yeah, I *know* so." I felt her move. *Toward me.* I swallowed, as my stomach flipped like a fire baton at a luau.

"Well, this is really amazing." She pointed to my notepad. All my words spread out for her to see. I searched her eyes, never wanting to let this feeling go. My body magnetized to hers. She felt like the north to my south.

"Reef!" Locke's voice echoed up to us. "Are you up there?"

Disappointment clouded her eyes as she straightened.

Trying to come back from the moment. But I was still stuck in it.

"Yeah, we're up here," I called out reluctantly, moving away from Luna and creating space between us again.

Luna

CHAPTER 10

Anxiety was my only company
A cycle of belittling
Until you intervened
And took the time to care for me.

-LUNA MANU MELE, ONE
MORE HOUR

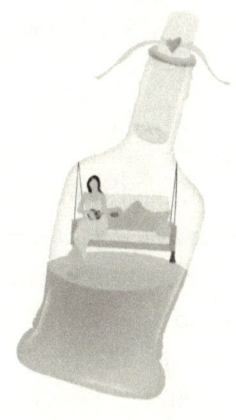

I sat outside Reef's apartment building, taking a deep inhale. *Attempting* to do the breathing exercises for my anxiety. My mind tried to find a soothing spa background track to play, but my brain kept getting distracted. My mind wouldn't quiet down.

I stared down at the brown lunch bag that I always kept in my purse, feeling a dire need to inflate it. There was something about seeing the bag inflate—as if you could see your breath and give it a tangible quality—which relieved me.

And I needed calm right now because dating never seemed to go well for me. I think it was my last experience that made my anxiety skyrocket for any future potential dates. I didn't particularly enjoy being around men. Louis being the exception. My anxiety was skating closer to the edge, tightness grabbing a hold of my body. I had to relieve the anxiety somehow. *Maybe you're not ready for this.*

Just as I was about to press send on a text to cancel our date, I noticed something out of the corner of my eye. I saw Reef standing outside, leaning against the railing of his apartment floor. Like he knew. And the rhythm of my heart slowed. Giving me the courage I needed to leave the safety of my car. Because I knew I'd be going somewhere even safer.

I smoothed out my flowy Hawaiian dress, breathed deeply, and headed up the stairs. While the lavender color of my dress always relaxed me, I was rethinking my wardrobe decisions. *Jeans would have been much more appropriate, Luna.* But that wasn't my style. That wasn't me. And I was determined to be myself on a date finally.

As soon as I stepped onto the landing, Reef's eyes began memorizing me. A headiness laced his expression as he explored my features. As if getting reacquainted with a familiar stranger. I'd long ago stopped enjoying men's stares, but I wanted to live in this one forever.

I felt myself relaxing at the sight before me—sexy glasses, powerful forearms, a collared shirt I wanted to rumple—just when the apartment door next to his abruptly opened. The creak jolted me from the safety of our connection.

An intense, penetrative stare, followed by a disgruntled voice, cut through the tenuous space between us. There stood an eclectic woman in front of her door, wearing a mismatch of bright patterns and colors. She glanced quickly between us as I stood frozen, not knowing what I'd stepped into.

"Reef, is *this* your girlfriend?" She pried. Reef's mouth parted to speak, but she was too fast. "You really undersold her. She's stunning *and* a ukulele star. This will definitely do. She'll be able to keep you well in check. Well, come on in," she said, waving me inside.

Reef's eyes bulged. "What? Oh, no, Mrs. Ailana, we don't have time to come inside, but thank you for your kind invitation." He awkwardly rubbed the back of his neck.

"Now, Reef, I've been waiting for this very day since you moved in. Like heck, you don't have time! Come on *inside*." She demanded. I certainly didn't have the nerve or the heart to disappoint this lady.

I heard a loud sigh from Reef as he followed me into her apartment. He placed his hand tentatively on the small of my back. Ready to pull me out of there at a moment's notice. I raised an eyebrow at him when I saw his neighbor's colorful interior. If I thought her clothes had been brightly colored, they had nothing on her apartment.

The walls came alive with vibrant murals, probably painted by her. It looked like we'd stumbled upon a retro time capsule for a free-spirited art community. Macramé filled the space, hanging from the ceiling and holding little plants. Everything looked handmade, like a little self-sustained oasis. My eyes scanned her coffee table. Amongst the dried-out art supplies was a copy of a ukulele magazine with my photo on the cover.

Reef's eyes continued to widen. Not able to contain himself, he said, "There's no way this is *your* apartment."

Mrs. Ailana's eyes pierced through him. "Well, what did you expect? White-washed walls?"

"Gray maybe," he mumbled.

"I heard that. Did you expect to see concrete counter-tops with no photos or signs of life, too? Like a cult compound?"

"Don't worry, it still looks like a cult," he muttered inco-herently.

I elbowed him in the ribs as she roared with laughter. "Well, I guess I deserved that. I've been giving Reef a hard time for years. It's just that he gives off such sad, loner vibes. Please sit down," she motioned toward the sofa covered in hand knit throws.

I was waiting for something like twenty cats to appear. But there didn't seem to be any felines around. Actually, there weren't any signs of companionship at all. That thought broke my heart. She seemed so vibrant, with so much to give.

Mrs. Ailana continued as we stood, "Actually, he has never brought a woman home, unless you count that dog of his."

I couldn't help but smile, instant relief washing over me. I replied, "Reef is the most fun-loving guy and gets along with everyone, but he can be awfully shy. I can't imagine anyone thinking of him as a loner, though. But I'm sure there's a lot for me to learn . . ." I said in a teasing tone.

"Oh dear, don't tell me I've started trouble." But it seemed she would love nothing more. Teasing Reef appeared to be the best part of her day. She patted the sofa. "Come and tell me how the two of you met, *Luna.*"

"Well," I said, as I tried to find a safe place to sit down on the sofa amongst all the crochets. Reef came over and positioned himself quite close to me. The brush of his arm against mine shot familiar electrical impulses up my spine. Sparks that had remained dormant, waiting for his return. I swallowed past the lump in my throat. Friction was making my mind malfunction like Johnny 5 in *Short Circuit*. *It's an arm brush, Luna. This isn't Austenland. Nothing salacious. Collect yourself.*

"Uh, we met at the bar when he was serving drinks. I couldn't get over his adorable smile and goofy personality—"

"Bzzz!" The abrupt sound from her tiny body jolted me awake. My eyes met Reef's, who appeared just as befuddled. I thought it sounded like a pretty good cover story. Our actual history was too personal to share with anyone. It was only for us.

"Uh. . ." I was just stalling for time when a flash of neon yellow soared into the room. I jumped into Reef's lap with a little yelp. It was followed by an obnoxious, high-pitched sound that echoed around the room. Some yellow thing flew erratically past us.

"Malarkey, I smell malarkey," a squawky call echoed around us.

A bright yellow cockatiel with orange cheeks landed with an ungraceful thud on the lady's shoulder. *So, there were signs of life here.* I turned my head slowly. My eyes wandered up Reef's chest to his broad shoulders, where my hands had tightly adhered. But I couldn't even enjoy the fresh scent of his soft tee or the firm feel of him under my fingertips because of the goofy grin he shone at me.

"No, I want the *genuine* story," Mrs. Ailana demanded, her gaze assessing us closely.

"How did I not know you had a bird?" Reef questioned. My hands were still tightly wrapped around him. At least his arms were still protectively embracing me.

"Oh, who, *Cecile?* Guess I disguised her as easily as *all* the women in *your* life. Such a smart bird, she even named herself. She loves exploring neighbors' balconies," she said innocently. But the raise of her brow told me otherwise.

"I'll tell you the real story." Mrs. Ailana's eyes lit up and shifted from Reef to me.

"Oh, goody. I'll finally get to know more about my mysterious neighbor."

I glanced at Reef's pointed eyes and changed the subject. "Our families ended up living in the same area when we were children. Since Reef, his best friend, and I were all around the same age, we became close friends. We grew up together. Our parents became close, too. So, I've known Reef my whole life. He's always been there for me."

"So he's always had stalker vibes." She jested. The giant bird nodded in agreement and I laughed.

"But—" My eyes glanced over at Reef, who was only a few inches away since I was pretty much in his lap. "The first memory I have of Reef was at a party his parents had for the neighborhood. I was making a flower crown with some wildflowers in his backyard—off in my own world as usual—when one of the neighborhood boys told me it was stupid. That no princess looked like me. That I was *hapa*. I remember him saying that word with such disgust. And I believed him. We didn't have *Moana* growing up, and we certainly didn't see 'mixed' princesses."

I paused, looking over at Reef's face, which had melted at the memory. I swallowed, trying to find the words. "Reef came over and offered to help make a new flower crown with me. He even made one for himself. When I saw him wear that crown just to make me feel better, I just knew . . ." Reef's gaze drifted over my vulnerable expression. ". . . we would be friends for life." I quickly added, not ready to admit I'd fallen for him at that moment. I don't think I could even admit it to myself.

Who doesn't fall for a guy who could wear a princess crown and still be ridiculously cute doing it? A boy who went over to a girl when she was crying instead of running away from her. The type of guy who made her feel like she was beautiful just for being herself. I clung even tighter to him; every fiber of my being was desperately hoping that he was still that type of man.

Reef stammered, "I didn't know if you even remembered . . ." He met me with that caring look of his that always melted my heart. The 'classic' Reef puppy dog look. The one I thought melted *all* the girls' hearts . . . *He isn't yours anymore, Luna.* I loosened my hold. *You made a clean break for a reason.* I'd even *tried* to date other men. *Tried.*

"Ahh, so he's always had an active imagination—" Mrs. Ailana started.

"Ok," Reef pulled us up from the sofa, our limbs still intertwined. *Let go, he's not yours anymore.* An ache tore through me. "I think I hear Nova whining and I'm sure she's dying to meet Luna. So that's all of our time for today." His succinct words brooked no argument. *Oh, he was sexy like this.* I loved when he took charge. *Dangerous thinking, Luna. Reckless.*

Mrs. Ailana's face fell. "Well, good idea. A dog is the

best wingman of all. Don't ruin this Reef, the poor thing needs a companion even more than you."

"Thanks for all the *help*, Mrs. Ailana. Luna is sure to stick around now." Reef matched her sarcasm as he quickly led me to the door.

"Be sure to stop by next time, Luna," she called through the doorway.

Reef

AGE 12

"Luna!" I called, trying to see through the mist. My legs tired as I made my way through the soggy dirt. I pedaled as hard as I could to get here, the pelting rain guiding me.

Luna had left school abruptly. And from what I'd heard through the coconut wireless, aka the middle school gossip, she'd left in tears. I sped up as the image haunted me.

At least I knew exactly where she'd be. Our parents had taken us to the lavender farm on Mount Haleakala when we were younger, and it immediately became Luna's happy place. We'd gotten lost in the serenity it offered that day. It felt like a place where nothing could touch us. And over time, those fields continued to offer us refuge.

As the fog parted, I made out the blurry edges of the lavender. And as I got closer, I saw the outline of a stone bench up ahead . . . and the girl who owned my heart sitting on it. I abandoned my bike and walked toward her. But Luna's head never turned.

I quietly slipped onto the cold concrete beside her. Looking down, I saw tear splatters on her light blue dress, creating an ink stain illusion. In this place of paradise, her heavy breathing felt like the only sound, and her trembling fingers the only movement before us.

The last thing I remembered was hearing Luna's name being called out over the PA system. And I tried never to make assumptions about her. She was the only person I felt I could do that with because she was honest with me. Always giving me the raw truth. So I waited. When her hand wandered over to mine, I interlaced our fingers.

A rustling sound interrupted the quiet as I pulled a plastic notepad out of my back pocket. As I flipped to a page, even the ink looked like it was crying from the rain it had weathered. But I didn't need to see the words. I remembered.

As I read, Luna's eyes crept over to me, red and stained. Marked with a hurt that I couldn't stand to see. But I just kept 'reading' slowly. A warmth covered my shoulder while her head nestled into it. I inhaled the air that was filled with the scents of dewy lavender and crisp earth. It felt like Mother Nature's way of offering new beginnings and second chances.

I paused when I finished reading, looking down at her glassy eyes and soft lips. I tucked her deeper into me. A desperate need to erase any space between us and the aching feeling caused by it.

"Is that for me?" she asked in a hoarse whisper, her eyes landing on the paper.

I gazed at her, noticing that her redness had lessened. "Yeah, you left before checking your locker. We had to pick your lock. I really feel like I should have the code."

She snuggled into me, laughing. "You'd try to steal my lyrics before they were done."

"Exactly. I need some boyfriend privileges." *What did I just say?* My body froze. *You're going to scare her, Reef.*

At my words, her tears fell harder. *What had happened today?*

"Boyfriend, huh?" Her teasing tone returned through the ache.

I swallowed. "I kind of thought that's what I was. Or am I your secret summer fling?" I tried to joke.

Hurt washed over her eyes and she fished something out of her pocket. "You'd never be just a summer fling . . . I was going to leave this for you in the treehouse. But will you pretend I did? Open it Saturday after our date?" Her voice hitched on the last word. My eyes gravitated to her impassive face. *"Please."*

I didn't understand why a vice grip grabbed around my heart. "Ok," I whispered. "Anything for you."

"Thank you," she whispered, tucking herself back into me.

And I slowly murmured the words that peeked through the paper she'd given me 'why did summer have to end?'

"I wish we could stay here forever," she said, snuggling into me. And I had such a powerful urge to make it happen.

"Wherever you are, that's where I want to be," I whispered.

"Huh?" she looked up at me, but I didn't repeat it. I

wish I had. Maybe it would have made a difference. If only I'd known that was the last time I would see her.

My eyes gazed outward at the view in front of us. The lavender fields, with their calming presence, especially as the mist rolled past, protecting us from everything. And from that moment forward, the scent of lavender would always remind me of her.

Reef

CHAPTER 11

> "Trusting someone with a part of you is like getting a tattoo. Exciting, exhilarating, and nerve-racking. And you don't know if you're going to wake up feeling empowered or looking like a fool."
>
> -REEF AKUA, -PACIFIC PULSE

I'd *never* told Mrs. Ailana about my pen name, but somehow she'd figured it out. That sneaky bird of hers must be spying on me. How did I not notice it hanging out around my window? I must have really been in my own writing world. But I needed to focus on getting Luna away from Mrs. Ailana while she was still just toying with me and before she spilled the beans.

Besides, what bird "picks" their own name? And what kind of name was Cecile for a bird, anyway? It was way too close to 'Cece'. And Mrs. Ailana's smirk told me she was quite proud of herself. And the last thing I wanted to do right now was explain my secret writing life to Luna. Especially when I was getting a second chance.

I'd stayed up most of the night trying to 'de-author' my apartment. I hadn't thought it would be difficult to do, but apparently, writing was soaked into my DNA and every crevice of my apartment. My home was literally ink stained, not to mention covered with countless copies of Cece's work in all the different writing stages. I even hid my typewriter, feeling like a dork as it sat next to the fountain pens. I was starting to see why I wrote romances instead of living them. Maybe I'd get lucky and Luna wasn't as observant anymore, but somehow I doubted that possibility.

Slowly, I turned my key in the lock and opened the door, hesitant to let Luna back inside my world. The lock's clicking sound feeling symbolic. As the door opened, Nova came bounding outside to greet Luna. Her long tail wagging exuberantly, tongue primed to give her some sloppy kisses.

"Down Nova, down!" I attempted to use my 'stern dog dad' voice as Nova jumped up on Luna, giving her a wet greeting. The beautiful lavender fabric of Luna's dress started stretching with Nova's enthusiasm. Nova whined as I placed my hand on her back to ground her. My dog might be more obsessed with Luna's dress than I was. All I knew was that it made me swallow involuntarily and my jaw tick.

"Sorry—" I began.

But I didn't get time to finish because Luna was already kneeling down to Nova and accepting all kinds of doggie kisses. Ones I wish I could give her. I was jealous of my dog. *Great.* Little currents ripped through me as Luna's husky laughter filled the air. Especially as she let out sexy, tiny giggles and backed her face away from Nova's increasingly enthusiastic attacks of affection.

"Ok, Nova. Point made. You're ready to go home with her and forget all about me." I teased, pulling her back and giving Luna the chance to come inside. "Sorry about that."

"It's fine, Reef," she promised as she stepped over the threshold. "I've wanted a dog for such a long time. But with all the traveling I do, I haven't been able to adopt one. It wouldn't be fair to a dog. But I've heard they can really help with anxiety, so that would be a wonderful side bonus. Plus, I get *pretty* lonely sometimes."

Lonely. So did that mean there might be room for us in

111

her life? My throat went dry at the thought. *Geez, getting ahead of yourself much, Reef?* I distracted myself by explaining to Luna, "Vizslas are one of the best emotional support dog breeds. You're welcome to borrow her any time. She'd love to get out of the apartment while I'm at work." Nova looked up at Luna with her pitiful amber eyes, as if agreeing.

Emotions flooded Luna's features, and she cleared her throat, glancing over to the bookshelves. A familiar curiosity sparkling in her eyes as she moved toward the shelving. She began brushing her fingertips along the book spines in such an intimate way that I shivered. The slower she lingered, the deeper the currents ran. She'd lost no time delving into my world, and hope ran through me.

"Cece LaRue." Luna's face lit up as she stopped on a book title. "She's one of my favorite authors. I can't believe you have her books, too." Her finger traced the spine, sending electricity down mine. "Wow, you actually have quite the collection. I didn't know you liked romance."

"Yeah, it just depends on the characters. I don't have too many 'man points' left to lose by admitting it," I said, making light of myself.

"What are you talking about?" She straightened up from the shelf. I'd tried to place Cece's books as low as possible.

I shrugged. "I've just always felt like I was a bit of a disappointment in that area. Guess I should have tried harder at sports or something. Or *anything* 'manly.'"

"That old school way of thinking is *so* unappealing, Reef. Usually it comes with strings: male toxicity and belittling women." She blanched at her blunt honesty, as if she'd revealed too much. "You have all the 'man points' you need in my book." Her heated look floated over to me, healing the edges of some of those old wounds.

"So, are you a fan?" she asked hesitantly, returning to the books.

"I guess you could say that."

She worried her bottom lip, trying to hide a grin. "I actually wrote to her . . . And she replied."

I couldn't believe she was admitting this to me. Those letters had been *extremely* personal. This was exactly the gray area I had desperately wanted to avoid. I should have boxed up *all* the Cece books.

"So, what did she say? Did she give you any good advice?" My voice came out hoarse. "I mean, do you think it was actually her writing back to you?"

Luna nibbled on her lip again. "I know it sounds crazy, but I do. They were the most heartfelt letters. She felt like the oldest friend. Like she just understood me." There was this faraway look in her eyes. As if she'd vanished to a different place or time.

"Well, if you want to borrow any—"

"Oh no, I have them *all.*" She left the bookshelves and wandered over to my beat-up leather chair–Cece's chair. Seeing Luna in the spot where I often daydreamed of her made my nerves short out. I gulped, my throat turning to sandpaper. She added with a laugh, "And I've read them *all.*" *Of course, Locke would be right. How frustrating could one man be?*

Her face softened. "I've never read a book where I've felt so seen–as connected to the main characters as I do with Cece's books. She even has a heroine with social anxiety and panic attacks in one of her books. I couldn't believe I was seeing mental health discussed in a romance book. I thought that would be considered 'unsexy'. But it made me feel normal in her world–like I wasn't alone. So many things felt possible. I don't know how to explain it . . . But I didn't feel broken. I had no idea how exhausting that feeling was until it felt 'okay' to be me. Her books gave me the courage to talk about my mental health. And that led me to open up to Louis, and he began helping me with my panic attacks. I had been drowning by myself and I didn't even know it. Not really, not until I got help. I thought I could continue to tread water. But I was so far under, it felt impossible to reach up. So, I wanted to let Cece know what her books did for me."

Yeah; I remember being told that a romance book like that wouldn't sell. But then again, I'd been told *a lot* of things. Luckily, I had a pen name to hide behind. It helped me take risks and stand up for what I wanted to write. Plus, if readers knew a man was writing these books, I didn't know how they would react. I was worried the truth would undo everything I had accomplished. Look at what a difference it had made for Luna. A gentle pulse took over my heart. This moment made the sacrifices worthwhile.

Slowly, I sat down on the sofa, choosing the seat closest to Luna, who was curled up in my oversized chair. Even from here, I could smell the scent of lavender. It was a reminder of home–of our memories.

I swallowed as she arched her brow, wondering where I had gone. It was a terrible author habit of mine. I'd instantly vanished into a field of lavender haze and wistful memories.

Luna made a little noise in the back of her throat to bring me back to the present. "So, Mr. Hotshot, now that you've taken a big gamble and broken the twenty-four-hour rule, what would you like to do with our time today?"

I could tell she was perfectly content basking in the soft

leather chair and stroking Nova's ears, but I had something in mind. "How about going to our favorite place?"

Her face lit up. "You mean we don't have to sell lemonade to earn enough money for our tickets?"

I laughed, "Well, it never worked anyway. Our parents always relented and gave us the rest of the money we needed."

"Yeah, but it's how you got your start at bartending. Crucial formative years." She teased.

"So, I'm taking that response as a yes?"

"Only if you make me a proper drink afterward. I want to see how much you've improved. You still need to earn your ticket." She laughed.

"Oh, it's a deal," I agreed with way too much hope in my soul.

Luna

AGE 12

I pedaled quickly to his house, anticipation flooding me. The short ride felt like an eternity. I hopped off the bike to walk with it down his gravel driveway. But my heart and feet skipped a beat at the sight in front of me.

Reef was sitting on his front porch steps, all dressed up in a button-up shirt and khakis. His hand nervously moved over his pressed slacks. In his other hand, he clutched a single plumeria flower that he'd probably picked from his backyard. Every so often, he adjusted his glasses in a way that made my stomach twist.

Finally, he looked up as I neared, having regained control of my feet. His eyes said it all, taking me in with everything he had. He stood quickly, his hands ironing out his light blue button-up. As if that's what you automatically did when you saw a woman. But I was pretty sure few guys responded that way.

"Hey," he said, pushing his glasses up even higher on his nose. "I–" But that was all that came out. He quickly extended the flower, offering it to me with staccato movements. Giant waves of butterflies propelled me forward. The emotions he always wore on his sleeve calmed me.

I stood in front of him, wearing my vibrant red sundress. The one I'd had to beg my mom to let me buy because she'd said it was too 'grown-up'. I never wore bold colors, but I did for him. Everything was different with him.

I'd always had this constant battle of wanting to be "classically" pretty. Something that felt far out of my reach. I couldn't even get my hair right. My mom had put my hair up beautifully, in a way that worked for my loose, curly texture. But I wanted the straight-haired look of all the other island girls. However, the way Reef was looking at me made me want to change my mind.

"Wow, I–" he began again. Making me feel like I was more than enough–just the way I was.

I tucked a loose strand behind my ear as I looked at the flower he was holding. "Would you?" I leaned my ear toward him and he gently brushed my cheek as he placed the flower. "Thank you. It's perfect," I said as I felt its delicate petals tickle my ear.

But he just stood there, looking at me, his eyes fixated on my lips. The ones I had colored with lip gloss today. I didn't even notice when he stuck out his elbow for me to take. In the silence, I slid my arm through his, and we headed off to collect our bikes.

"Luna," he finally stuttered. "I've never seen anyone

more beautiful . . ." Then he pulled me in closer, wrapping his arm around my waist for our first official date. And every insecurity I'd had melted away.

Luna

CHAPTER 12

*Just give me one more hour
And you'll see, you're the only man for me.*

-LUNA MANU MELE, ONE MORE HOUR

As I drove toward the Maui aquarium, butterflies filled me as I thought about returning with him. It had been so long since I'd felt this way with a man. Since I'd felt butterflies. It was like getting reacquainted with old friends. It seemed my heart had always known the score.

Even if our afternoon was just part of Louis' plan, Reef was the breath of fresh air I needed. He was so different from the musical "stars", or egos, I had dated. And so far, Reef had only been genuinely happy for my successes. I glanced over at him, a goofy grin appearing on his face as we neared the aquarium. And I couldn't help but mimic his with one of my own.

I loved to watch the way men treated workers in the service industry, especially in restaurant settings, on dates. It was a fast way to sum up character. Some men thought they had just "bought" all the power, and that justified treating service workers in any manner they pleased. Now I knew that meant one day they would treat you that way, too.

Reef was different. He treated everyone like a friend. I watched him have a lengthy conversation at the ticket counter with the attendant, even finding out what part of the aquarium her children enjoyed most. By the time the cashier handed us our tickets, a gigantic smile had formed on my cheeks.

"What?" he asked self-consciously. My grin only grew, and he raised an eyebrow. But he extended his hand to me, just the way he had when we were kids. His hand had always been there for me, and I'd taken it for granted. When I slipped my hand in his, I realized just how badly I had wanted to have his hand extended to me again.

We started exploring the nooks and crannies of the aquarium, and it was like catching up with a long lost friend. An ease washed over both of us. Falling back into the warmth of each other felt as easy and carefree as snuggling under a favorite childhood quilt.

We strolled among the sea life, and let the native species entertain us as we filled the space with wonder and laughter. But when we found ourselves in front of the underwater tunnel, I went quiet, feeling an undeniable connection with him again. The flame that had been timidly flickering beneath the surface had now ignited in full force.

"Our favorite place," Reef breathed, as the blue glow of the tunnel bathed him in its rich hue.

"Remember, they had to chase us out of here," I said with a playful smile, as the sharks, stingrays, and tropical fish floated above us. As the sea life soared over our heads, childhood dreams felt possible. Like we still had our whole lives ahead of us again.

Our eyes met, our history playing out between us. As I searched Reefs eyes, his echoed the same longing and ache that I felt. I swallowed hard, trying to contain my feelings, but my words rushed out as quickly as the water running over top of us. "I really loved you, Reef. I don't think I ever told you that."

"Yeah, me too," he murmured as the blue light danced across his face. My heart beat faster.

"I know we were just kids, but it's the truest love I've ever felt. You were the best friend that I've ever had. I just . . . I just really missed you."

He nodded, emotion deep in his eyes. The glowing blue atmosphere of the tunnel was making me feel even more nostalgic. I felt a prickling sensation in my eyes as I inhaled sharply. I chastised myself. *You chose, Luna.*

I glanced at Reef, thankful I could anchor onto his warm smile as he spoke. "Me too. I think we might have been smarter back then and had more things figured out than we knew. Sometimes it seems like the older we get, the more we move away from our truest selves."

Yeah, life gets complicated. I nodded, drifting toward him. Knowing exactly what he meant. He was the person who always put my feelings into words better than I could.

I stared up at him, trying to memorize the subtle changes that years apart had brought. I still saw all my favorite features, and it soothed me. But his adorable, thick-framed glasses hid my favorite feature. Soulful eyes had always been the way to my heart. And his baby gray ones were so patient and kind. They swept me away every time.

"Well, at least we get a second chance now," his soft lips gently mumbled, bringing me back. The lips I'd been fixedly watching. The ones I'd regretted not finding out how they felt. And I wanted nothing more than to find out now.

"Yes, a second chance," I murmured, letting my eyes linger on the boy I'd loved for so long.

Luna

AGE 13

"Luna, honey," my mom's soft call echoed through the thin walls of the apartment we'd rented on the Big Island. I wrapped my blanket tighter around myself, trying to tuck myself away. Even with the extreme heat, I could never get warm. Probably because I always felt like a part of me was missing.

My mom's furrowed brows knitted together even more as she came through my doorway. Her eyes assessed me as I scrunched up into a small ball on the saucer chair by my windowsill. Our view here differed greatly from the one we'd had on Maui. Our priorities had changed.

"Honey, do you need anything?" she asked, sitting on

the edge of my bed across from me. There was a piece of paper in her hand which made me clutch my book tighter. She glanced down in response, as if she'd forgotten, and extended her hand to me. "Another one came."

It took me a while to reach for the paper. I retreated back into myself as soon as I had it, like I could stop the aching in my bones and squelch the nausea. *Maybe if I just curl up tight enough, it will all stop.*

My eyes found their way back out the window as I slipped the letter into my book. My mom sighed. "Luna, why don't you call him?" My jaw clenched at the suggestion, and I repositioned my headscarf. "The letters won't come forever. Give him something in return. Some kind of hope. He must really, *really* care about you to keep writing."

And with her words, everything suddenly looked like it was underwater. I swallowed, pushing down the fear that the letters would stop.

My voice came out as weak as I felt. "I don't want him to see me like this. If he finds out . . . I know he'll find a way to come here."

"Maybe so. Probably. That would be wonderful." My mom looked at the letter that I was rubbing my fingers over indecisively.

"But *not* for him. I want him to remember me how I was. I want our memories to stay just the way they were. For nothing to taint them."

My mom tilted her head, a heart-wrenching smile tugging at her lips. "I think the memories might be more tainted this way, Luna. And sometimes you don't get a second chance, especially if you leave things a certain way."

But a second chance seemed unlikely after the bad health news I had received today. My eyes burned as I held back the tears. Forcefully, I tucked the letter into my book, pushing my feelings down just as hard. I didn't deserve it, but I prayed the letters wouldn't stop. They were the only thing holding me together. *Any* connection to him.

"He doesn't have to know anything yet. Just write him back, Luna."

But he would know. I could never lie to him. That was the one thing I promised myself I'd never do. It was the last thing I felt I had left to give him.

Luna

CHAPTER 13

Lost in a lavender daze
I never wanted to part this way.

-LUNA MANU MELE, LAVENDER WAYS

After our visit to the aquarium, we began wandering around Ma'alaea harbor. Pretty quickly, Reef spotted a nearby fish taco stand, and I immediately saw that boyish mischief light up in his face again. The one I had always loved

His cheeks flushed slightly and he began looking around, probably for a place that would be labeled as more 'upscale dining'. "Are you hungry? I've heard some fantastic things about—"

I cut him off as his eyes continued to scan the area. "Reef, I'd be *very* disappointed if you didn't take me to the taco truck."

A soft, nervous laughter bubbled out of him. "Are you sure because we're not kids now, we can totally—"

"Reef, I'd be extremely unhappy if we didn't get tacos." I pulled my sad face. "I haven't changed *that* much. I still prefer taco trucks. Especially with you. And I definitely expect to split a coconut caramel flan."

"Really?" I nodded at his winsome grin and loved seeing his shoulders relax. From what he'd seen in the media, he probably thought I had pretentious taste. But I wanted nothing more than to leave that world and its tainted memories behind me.

With smiles glued to our faces, we grabbed some fish taco bowls and headed for the pier, muscle memory settling in. Soon our feet were dangling off the dock. *Here.* This was where I wanted to be. It had taken me *so long* to get back here and I never wanted to leave.

Reef stared off into the distance, seeming to fade with his thoughts into the horizon. "Reef," I asked, a little worried.

"Huh, oh, sorry." I bumped his shoulder, playfully

asking if he was okay. "I was just remembering something . . . Sorry about that, my writer's brain sometimes forgets to socialize." He joked.

"What was the memory?" I asked, picking up a taco.

"We don't need to go there," he said a little too quickly.

I put down my taco, staring at it. We had *always* gone there.

He breathed out as I pushed my food around. "I was just thinking back to a time when my dad took me fishing." My eyes looked up at him and hope surged within me. *Was he going to confide in me again?*

Back in the day, Reef's dad had led a team of underwater divers that collected explosive devices left over from World War II. Underwater construction was dangerous work, and it suited him well, especially being the team leader. He was definitely a 'man's man'. Never missing a chance to flex his muscles or make a quick withdrawal from a hug. *Always* ready to be the center of attention in any crowd.

Reef's lips curved halfway as he continued. "Yeah, fishing . . . Locke had started hanging out more at my house when we were in high school. That was right around the time that my dad started to worry that he'd completely failed to make a *real* man out of me. So he started to bombard me with "manly" activities. I remember there was one fishing trip in particular that went horribly wrong." He waved his hand toward the horizon as if that was enough of an explanation.

"Reef, I'm so sorry." He'd always tried to shelter me from that part of his life. Meeting me on his front porch steps. Never inviting me inside or asking me to join in activities with his family.

Reef responded, "It's fine. Locke was like the son my dad never had. But I think the situation made Locke super uncomfortable. He even tried to hype me up to my dad. Nothing worked." He gave a stilted laugh. "My sister fared better on those fishing trips than I did. I think she enjoyed being the 'son' he never had."

"Reef, people like you just the way you are. I hope you know that. We don't have to be one certain way in life. That's why everyone is unique. Everyone has their *own* path." He stared down at his tacos. "The only way I ever enjoyed camping was with *you*. I doubt we did it the "normal" way, but we did it *our way*. And that made it even more special."

He smiled. "Yeah, our way always seemed correct to me. I always felt so normal when I was with you. I never thought about any of that stuff. Things always seemed so much simpler with you . . ." His words left me with an equal dose of happiness and ache. "Anyway, I gave up on fishing a long time ago, but I still enjoy diving and other water activities with Locke. I guess it just took me longer than most people to find my place in the world. Ok, that's enough talk. Remember, I promised you flan. Then, if you want, we can go back home and watch a movie or something."

I smiled at the exquisite evening, while the balmy breeze caressed me. No one had ever been right for me, because no one else had been him. I'd needed *my person*.

After we devoured the creamy dessert, I was ready to go back for that drink he'd promised me. Because I was secretly hoping to see more of his world. To somehow catch up on all the years I'd missed.

As soon as we reached his apartment door, Nova

greeted me with more canine kisses. She appeared so happy to be reunited with me, but perhaps it was the smell of the leftover fish tacos we'd brought back for her. I hoped that would solidify me as a favorite.

Reef looked at my huge grin. "Ok, I see what's going on here. You wanted to come back here to see my dog. That's fine. My pride is only *slightly* hurt."

I loved how he instantly put me at ease. "Guilty. I think I have an instant connection with your dog. I believe Cece calls that the 'insta-love trope.'"

He snorted. "Great, my dog is doing better on this date than I am. *Love it.*"

I burst out laughing as I held Nova's soulful face in my hands. "Just look at her."

"Well, I can't disagree with you on that point." He laughed harder, and I couldn't help noticing that he hadn't said *fake date*.

"So, are you sure you still want that drink?" he asked hesitantly. Reef stepped inside his apartment and began preparing a bowl for Nova with the extra goodies we'd brought back for her. "How about something nonalcoholic? I can still do something pretty creative with that." He raised his eyebrows playfully.

I could tell he was being mindful of my anxiety. But it felt weird that we had missed out on these "adult" parts of one another's lives. Yet, he remained the deepest, most intimate connection I'd ever had.

I teased him, "Don't think you can handle me with a little alcohol?" He shook his head as if he'd mis-stepped. "Think I might be too flirty?" He shook his head harder, now in on the joke. "Think I might make you read a romance book to me?" Now he chuckled as I eyed his many bookshelves.

There were only a few men who I allowed to see this side of me. *All of me.* And while it wasn't a crazy transformation or anything, you could feel the difference when I truly let go. My trustworthy testosterone circle consisted of very few men, including Louis, Locke, who was like a brother to me, and Reef, the boy from childhood whom I'd always loved.

"Well, now I'm just going to spike your drink with everything I have on hand." He jested and then explained, "No, it's nothing like that. It's just that in my experience, alcohol can make anxiety worse. I hate to think that I'm causing you so much anxiety that you're willing to take a gamble on it." A nervous laugh escaped him.

I shook my head adamantly. "No, quite the opposite. You're one of the few people who doesn't make me feel like I need a drink to help with my anxiety." I teased. "But you're right. It can make the anxiety worse after it wears off. That's why I rarely drink." He nodded in understanding. So I continued, "I just feel like I missed all these milestones with you, and I did *really* want to try one of your drinks."

"I feel like I missed out on a lot, too." A cloud of sadness covered his eyes before he could refocus them. "Well, I have some natural herbs my grandmother used as homeopathic remedies. I can mix them in your drink as long as you don't have any allergies."

"Just soy and cilantro, but I doubt you'll be putting either of those in my drink." I joked.

"You'd be surprised." A charming grin crossed over his features as he accepted the challenge. "I can't believe I didn't know about those allergies. Are they new?"

"Oh yeah, but don't worry, I have an EpiPen for them. A lot of our cells regenerate every seven to ten years. I keep hoping I'll somehow outgrow these allergies. But I guess I'm stuck with them."

I could tell what he was thinking. The same thing I had been thinking all day. It was like everything we'd known about each other had been erased. The cells which had once known his touch so well had all disappeared. Reef's touch used to be so vivid in my memory. I could easily recall his warmth beside me to help me drift off to sleep at night, sliding into my safe place. But memory had gradually faded, the feeling blurring at the edges. Until it was like holding the hand of someone completely new. Now, there was an ocean of uncertainty between us. A space that *I'd* created.

I glanced at the assorted bottles and spices he had pulled out, trying instead to live in the moment. "Are these exotic spices? I didn't know we were going to be having fun experimenting with 'herbs' tonight." I bantered.

"Oh no, just some everyday herbs like lavender. Nothing you'd take to a party," he amended, as he slung a towel over his shoulder. "There are some less common herbs my grandma taught me about, but I can hold off on those . . . I've never shared my grandma's lavender syrup recipe with anyone. I think I'm the only one who knows it. But if you like it . . ."

I interrupted his nervous babble. It was a dead giveaway of his discomfort level. Easily a 2.5 on the 'Reef Richter' scale. At least I still knew some of his signals. "Don't worry, you had me at Lavender, Reef. And I think I'd try *anything* with you." I felt my cheeks heating at the implication.

"Well, I don't keep those 'herbs' around." He chuckled. "I've never been much of a party person either, even though I'm a bartender."

He'd probably been the designated driver at parties.

Reef would be the guy to make sure people made it home safe. A warm feeling of security spread through me.

"Well, if you ever feel adventurous, I'm sure you could ask your neighbor for some of her *special herbs*." I jested.

"Yeah, and I'd have to pry them away from her creepy bird. I like you, but not *that* much." He paused, looking me over slowly, as if getting reacquainted. "Ok, maybe I do like you *that* much."

I put my hand out in reassurance. "A nonalcoholic drink is perfect. I don't need a relaxer with you. But I hope you know how to use an EpiPen. No freaking out if my face swells to epic proportions." I only half joked. *It's not like that had ever happened to me or anything.*

"You'd always be beautiful to me," he replied while pulling down some glasses off a kitchen shelf. Reef rolled up his sleeves in one swift, well-honed movement, adjusting his glasses along the way. That sublime combination had my teeth dragging across my lower lip. A quiet sigh escaped me, revealing all my cards.

"Ok, I'm holding you to it." I teased as I eyed the ingredients he was mixing for his special concoction.

"Just so I know," he began as he walked over to me with a drink in hand. "What exactly is it I missed by being 'the good guy?'" He handed me a gorgeous liquid creation. It looked creamy with a lavender liquid on top. Complete with a sprinkle of lavender buds. Too gorgeous to drink. Officially, the most beautiful thing a guy had ever handed me.

Reef pointed to the top of the drink. "The buds are from the lavender farm and the purple liquid on top is lavender syrup. The base is vanilla coconut with a hint of lemon. Hopefully, the lavender vanilla will be calming. I call it 'The Luna.'" He smiled bashfully as he said his creation's name.

I stared down at the drink, feeling too many things all at once. "Did you just come up with that? I'm impressed."

"No, I've been thinking about it for *a very long* time." And his focused gaze implied so much more.

Reef

AGE 12

J ust kiss her, Reef. This is your chance.

Rain was pelting down on the exterior of our cheap tent. The one we'd finally convinced our parents to let us use for camping. Locke's tutu had offered to chaperone us tonight, and we were supposed to set up camp behind her house. But Locke had gotten sick and had to cancel at the last minute. So, we'd decided the wooded area behind our neighborhood would make for a good alternative campground. *Who needed to know the difference?*

"Are you warm enough?" I asked, as a little trickle of rainwater leaked in. We had snuggled up in our sleeping bags early tonight. We were sorely missing Locke's boy scout skills, especially since we had produced more laughter than fire tonight. I'd brought my little retro radio to keep us company, but all we were getting with the storm was static.

"Sort of." A timid look crossed her features.

"Do you? . . do you want?—" But she was already making her way into my sleeping bag. I gulped. It's not like we'd never had sleepovers before, but it was always with all *three* of us. And Locke's tutu was always close by. And usually our sleepovers were a result of falling asleep watching a movie together on her couch.

A crack of lightning sounded overhead, and Luna nestled deeper into me, carving out her spot. The one that would last forever. We were going to get into *so* much trouble for this.

I pulled her into me, feeling a rush of emotions. Sharp electricity ignited all over my body, rivaling the crackling of lightning. "Do you want to go back home? Somewhere safe? We can say we've had the camping experience?"

"No, being with you is where I feel safe," she said quietly, sleep overtaking her. "Until my parents kill me tomorrow."

My heart melted, and I leaned back, taking my eyes off her lips as her head nestled into my neck. I had always wanted to be her safe place. I wanted that more than anything. So I would wait for her to make the first move. And tomorrow, when our parents asked if anything happened, we could say 'absolutely not'. Even though it felt like everything had.

Reef

CHAPTER 14

66 I can't help but see you when I look at the stars. And I wonder, are you looking at them, too?

-REEF AKUA, ECHOES OF THE ISLANDS

We carried our drinks out to my tiny *lanai*. And my mind became barraged with thoughts. I'm sure men had given Luna all sorts of spectacular gifts, but for some reason, she kept looking at her drink like it was the best one. And that's when the real nerves began to fill me, because hope was a *very* dangerous thing.

"Ah," she sighed at the first sip, and it sent ripples through me.

I'd had *a lot* of practice making 'The Luna' drink. Whenever I was stuck on a scene or needed out of my head, I invented cocktails. And I'd made plenty that were inspired by her.

I pulled out a chair for Luna at the patio table, but she walked over to the edge of the porch instead. She sat gracefully on the floor, slipping her legs under the old iron railing that surely wouldn't pass code today. I laughed. Even in the darkness of night, I could see the young girl I knew so well, the stars illuminating her. And I couldn't wait to join her.

I glanced over at Luna while I slipped my legs under the railing beside her. "I know it's not much of a view, but there's not really a bad one here, is there?"

She turned her head toward me. The dark blue hues of the night sky were competing with those from the aquarium earlier today. All we could see in the distance were dark outlines—an imprint of our world. The one we'd been fortunate enough to grow up in. The *only* home we knew.

"The view is magnificent, Reef. And the drink makes it *even* better. You definitely know what you're doing. I think you should have your own mixed beverage line. This drink has such a calming effect. Maybe I need one every night." She laughed, but I would gladly make one for her on *any day. Every day.*

Then she added, "If you're brave enough, maybe you'll let me make one for *you*."

"I'll take my chances, especially *if* there's going to be a next time. You're very creative, so I'm sure it will be good." I'd do anything for a next time. "There's a lot you can do with lavender. My grandmother practiced natural healing, just like Locke's grandmother, so she tried to teach me a few things along the way."

Luna responded, "No wonder I love lavender so much."

I smiled. "Well, there are so many ways to use lavender. There's hot lavender tea which is great for sleep. Or you can take lavender capsules. You can diffuse lavender oil, use it in shower steamers, or in your bath. And of course, you can eat lavender." I nodded at her drink. "Personally, I love lighting lavender candles. I may even have some from the local lavender fields here." She blushed at the mention of *our* place.

"I'm going to have to make better use of lavender. I've been underestimating it." She teased. Then her eyes grew more serious. "Thanks for always caring so much."

I nodded and something swept over me from the heart-felt way in which she said it. *Remember, she's here for Louis' plan. Not for an actual date.* "Uh, should we get one more photo for Louis?" I asked, pulling out my phone.

"Ok, but I don't know why we're sending him photos. I'm not giving him *or* Locke access to my social media. They'd have us married with triplets by now."

I laughed in agreement. "Well, if it's on social media, you know it must be true, right?" She smiled brightly, one of those moments of unspoken understanding blooming between us again. *God, this felt so good.*

I moved closer to her and *tried* taking a 'selfie' of us. Thankfully, she took the phone so she could take over. My arm reflexively reached around her and then halted. I wasn't sure if I was ready for this contact again, no matter how much I wanted it. But as she gently peered up at me, my heart let go of its fear. Just the mere sight of those warm eyes unraveled me, my arm wrapped around her as she leaned into me. Her familiar scent rushed me with memories. The softness of her was nostalgic in all the right ways.

"Reef?" she questioned again, attempting to hand me back my phone after snapping the photo. But I was a little too preoccupied seeing as the air was once again filled with her.

Jolted back to reality, I said, "Oh, thanks . . . Do you want me to send these to Louis?"

"No, the one from the aquarium is proof enough that his plan will work. He can get on social media for the rest." She teased. "Or at least for the ones we decide to share. I want to keep some photos just for us."

My heart raced, thinking about this day with Luna: her in the glow of our underwater aquarium spot. The place I'd almost kissed her too many times to count. I'd wanted everyone to know my feelings for her, even the sea life. Ironic, since I didn't particularly like the idea of posting this photo to social media. Not if it was just for show. The thought had the effect of dumping ice water over me.

I pulled my arm back. "So . . . If our cells regenerate every seven years and these have "never touched", does that mean we should make some ground rules for Louis' arrangement?"

I had to know. No more guessing. I didn't want to be a fool *again*. As much as I wanted to be blissfully carefree and just 'see where this went', my heart told me I had to be smarter this time. *Practical. No more dreaming.*

"Oh." She turned her head toward me with a full blush.

"I guess we should . . . Louis and Locke didn't seem to think we needed much contact to sell this. Apparently, our chemistry still works." Luna laughed nervously. "Maybe our awkwardness looks like sexual tension. So whatever you're comfortable with," she added quickly.

I shook my head. "No, Luna. I want to know what *you're* comfortable with. It's your label and your body." I swear I could see her swallow, almost painfully.

I waited, my errant thoughts running wild. My arm was already itching to resume its position around her again. Wanting nothing more than to keep in contact with her. My eyes traveled upward and got lost in her lips. *Reef, stop. That's not letting her decide. Act naturally.* I tried to straighten, now at full attention. *Now you just look absurd, like you don't want to touch her.* I slouched. *What the heck? Are you doing an ape mating dance?*

Her eyebrows cocked upward. "Well . . . We could take pictures as good friends, *close* together."

"Cheeks touching?"

"Yes," she breathed. "And we could hold hands, if you're—"

"I'm more than ok with that." I heard her exhale at my quick admission.

"And we'll just leave it there unless . . ."

"Unless?" My voice sounded too hopeful. "Unless . . ." I tried to lower my tone.

"Unless they're not buying it. I don't want you to have to do anything you don't want to do."

Dear God, I hope they don't buy anything. I hope they need a ton of proof. I was thanking my lucky stars for being such a nerd and the high probability of that happening.

"I could kiss your cheek . . . if that would help." A little sound escaped her. "*Only* if it helped," I backtracked.

"Well, they may need a little something more." An ache slammed into me with her words.

"They may," I said, letting one of my fingers brush the back of her hand. Her fingers immediately intertwined between mine. An intense need took over me. There was no fighting it. Not tonight. Probably not for the entire trip to Oahu, either. It was like asking someone to stop breathing.

Luna gazed at me steadily and squeezed my fingers. "Reef, I know there are much better ways you could spend your time. So *thank you. Really. Mahalo.*"

"There's definitely not a better way to spend my time." Even from here, I could see her complexion turn rosy as she looked down at her drink. "Plus, if I pass the fake boyfriend test, I think a trip to Oahu sounds pretty incredible. Especially with you."

Luna brushed some hair behind her shoulder and reflexively moved a little closer. The space between us dwindled even more. "Oh, you'll *definitely* pass. But I don't think the trip is exactly what you're imagining it to be. Hopefully, it will be fun for you. It's already greatly improved for me now that you're going."

She nonchalantly rotated the drink around in her hands. I tried to reassure her. "I imagine we can make the trip fun. But you have to enjoy yourself now, so I don't get fired from my 'fake boyfriend' position. That would just be too sad." I nudged her shoulder playfully and she smiled.

"So," I continued. "How are you feeling about everything? I know we haven't hung out in a while. If at *any point* you decide you'd be better off by yourself in Oahu—"

I could easily write a chapter about the disbelief written on her face. "Reef, after *everything* you're doing for me, you want to know if today was ok for *me?* I should be the one checking in with you."

"Well, I'm fantastic. Thanks for asking. 'The Luna' is having quite the effect on me." I winked at her, to which she elegantly chuckled. Something only Luna could do. "Well, I didn't get you a very potent drink, so I just wanted to check and make sure it was working."

"That really has you worried, doesn't it?" she asked.

"I just don't like the thought of causing you anxiety. I've always enjoyed being the person in your life who helped you feel safe. I miss that. *More* than you know."

Her head slowly moved closer to me, relaxing into my shoulder with a familiarity like we'd never been apart, finding the impression she had permanently left on me. A tightness enveloped my chest as her head found its special spot—the one reserved just for her. In the past, she'd always seemed so content when we were together, and it was too hard to believe she might still feel that way.

Her voice called out softly. "I still feel that way. I think I always will. It's like coming home when I see you. I can't tell you how nervous I was before I got here, but those nerves went away when I saw you. I promise the drink was only a luxury because I felt like I *could* have one with you. It hasn't been like that for me in a *very long time*."

My hand found some bravery and wrapped itself around her waist so I could tuck her into me. I never thought I'd hold her like this again. *Ever.* And the tightness around my heart only increased. *I'd never stop loving her, would I?*

Luna set her drink aside and then began leaning back. "Wait," I said. "Let me get a quilt or something. There's no way this lanai is clean. Unless we've just had a *really* powerful storm."

"I'm fine, Reef. We didn't mind a little dust and dirt back when we were kids."

"Yeah, well, you didn't wear dresses like that when we were kids, either." My eyes wandered over her as she rested on her elbows. The sundress that showed off *every* one of her curves made my heart race again. When I saw her coming up the stairs today, I knew I was done. Locke's laughter had rung out in my mind at my defeat.

"It's a pretty casual sundress." She glanced down at herself. "Plus, I remember that I always enjoyed dressing up for our aquarium dates. That's the most effort I've ever put into planning outfits. *So* glad you noticed." She teased.

As if that was the last word, she laid back all the way. Little 'oomphs' escaping her on the landing. So, I laid down beside her and offered her my chest as a pillow. She took me up on it right away, laying her head there as if it was second nature.

"Thank you. I still have some bone pain that's never completely gone away, and apparently it doesn't like the hard decking. I'm not as spry as I once was." A stilted laugh escaped her.

"None of us are. Guess we're both getting older, after all." I gazed at her head resting on my chest, soaking up this moment. My voice came out hushed. "The tank top with the daisies and the cropped jeans."

"Huh?" she questioned as she turned her head so her eyes could meet mine.

"That was my favorite 'outfit' you wore to the aquarium. Although, I loved them all and I *promise*, I noticed them all. You always made me feel special, Luna. I couldn't believe how lucky I was. And this look is *not* casual. Not on you." She snuggled closer, a response I knew well, but one that had frayed in my memory.

After some time had lapsed, I ventured, "Time for two truths and a lie?"

I was hoping she'd agree; I wanted to learn more about her new life. It was one way we'd told each other about our day or about the hard things in life when we were younger. If something was too difficult to talk about, then we wouldn't make a guess. We would just leave it unsaid.

A mist formed in her eyes as she slowly nodded. "Ok," I said. "I'll go first. I survived a shark attack with my best friend. I've written a best-selling novel. And my neighbor is in a cult."

She started laughing, and the mist passed. Something I loved to see. I could see nostalgia wrapping around her with the warm memories. "Ok, my turn," she said emphatically, not bothering to guess. *Well, at least I had tried to tell her.*

Reef

CHAPTER 15

> A Greek myth says we were ripped in two, sentenced to search for our other half–our soulmate–as a reprimand for our pride. But my punishment must be different because searching was never my problem.

-REEF AKUA, -TIDES OF LOVE

In the upcoming weeks, Luna and I continued to spend more time together, all under the guise of getting reacquainted with one another. Or, as Louis liked to call it, working on 'faking it.' Luna eventually relented and gave Louis access to her social media. That way he could 'jazz up' the content in any way he saw fit. And Louis worked hard so that not only her fans but also her manager, would take notice. He believed if he could lay the foundation properly, they would leave her alone at the ukulele festival.

Louis kept commending us on our efforts, but it didn't feel like we'd done anything. We kept the whole thing as authentic as possible for our sanity. We'd labeled our time together as friends re-connecting to take any pressure off. And we snapped an opportune picture or video to post when the opportunity arose. That was the only fake part—or at least I hoped it was. I loved having an excuse to spend time with her. If anything, Louis had done *me* the favor.

However, this appeared to be the easy part. In private, we could frame the narrative. But I had a feeling that the trip could change everything. And my heart wasn't ready for that.

But change is inevitable. No one can hide from it. And it was made clear that I was no exception when I found a crisp letter addressed to Cece LaRue in my mailbox. I had been pretty insistent with my agent that if someone took the trouble to write and mail me a letter, then I wanted to answer it myself. So, we had the letters routed through a decoy P.O. box before they ended up here. The magical PR fairies at work.

I'd been content with my decision to open the first letter I received from Luna. Because it was a way I could be in her life. I'd been sure there was no other way I'd ever be again.

My fingers shook as I stared down at her penmanship on the envelope as I stood in front of my apartment door. I stared harder at the ink as I weighed the pros and cons. A part of me had always felt wrong about answering her letters, but in the end, I'd made peace with my decision. If she'd needed to talk with someone, then I wanted to be there for her. But now, there was no way to justify it. Because the time I spent with her didn't feel like just two friends reconnecting. My heart yearned for it to be more, and that meant there was *no way* I should open this letter.

The sound of an envelope tearing pierced the air. The official sound of so many lines being crossed, coloring me gray. I felt eyes on me as if someone had witnessed my moment of weakness. And sure enough, I looked up to find Mrs. Ailana standing at her front door, eyeing both me and Nova, who was by my side. Her eyebrow arched wickedly. *Not now.*

"Mrs. Ailana," I said brusquely.

"Reef." She nodded in acknowledgment, a heavy

silence falling between us. "You shouldn't read it, you know? Come in and talk to me about it instead."

My mouth fell. *Does she look at my mail?* I countered, "And get attacked by your bird *again*? No, thanks." She simply shrugged at me. "That's a federal offense, you know? Going through someone else's mail."

"Well, I only read the juicy ones. It takes a lot of effort to restrain myself from reading all of them. But it's not like I have much else to do. This one was certainly worth the trouble. *Very titillating.* And what are they going to do anyway, cart off a ninety-year-old woman?" she jested rhetorically.

My jaw fell open, and I didn't even bother to close it. "You're embellishing your age quite a bit, you know. And I doubt the police are ageist. Plus, they might not need to cart you anywhere. Especially if they have to find your body first."

She laughed at that one, a smile forming. "Fair enough. Why don't you come in? I may know more than you think." I gave her a pointed look. I was one invasion of privacy away from snapping. She relented. "Ok . . . I should have said I might be able to help you more than you realize."

"Alright, but if that bird lands on me—"

"Oh, Reef, don't you know a fan when you see one?" I shook my head at her overt omission of the origin of the bird's name, but the unflappable woman just waved me in.

Once inside, she kicked her feet up on the floral-patterned recliner and the bird flew right to her. Her fuzzy, hot pink slippers were on full display. She looked quite comfortable, but I didn't sit down too eagerly.

There was a torturous silence as she stared pointedly at me and the tightly gripped letter in my hand. The letter I couldn't believe *she'd* read. The one I couldn't believe *I* was thinking about reading. Coming inside her apartment had been such a bad idea.

"We all have our muse, Reef." She stated, interrupting my thoughts.

"Oh God, it's not me, is it?" I asked in horror.

"Don't flatter yourself. I only enjoy toying with you." She teased. "Although I would paint the two of you. And I *never* paint couples. Not anymore." I gave her a blank stare. "I haven't seen my muse in fifty years. And I haven't dated much during that time either." She paused, looking out the sliding glass doors. "And I still paint *him* from memory, very similar to what you do in your writing."

She held up a hand to stop my protest. "He's always been the best creative subject for me. I imagine yours is the same. But in my personal life, I'm left surrounding myself with bright colors, trying to convince myself that I don't know darkness or depression. Trying to convince myself that my art was worth the sacrifice. But I'm just fooling myself. I could have had *both*. Maybe with some minor compromises, but nothing I'd have missed terribly if I just hadn't been so stubborn. If I hadn't been so scared. Or if only I could have believed that someone would want *me*."

I couldn't form any words, especially after the "d" one she'd just used. The one that made people uncomfortable, as if it was a 'dirty word'. Like depression was contagious—a weakness to be caught. I'm guessing she knew the word was safe with me after reading my novels. That I wanted a world where discussing mental health was safe—*comfortable* even, especially because of Luna's experiences. Perhaps that's why I fought so hard for those topics to stay in my novels. Or maybe Mrs. Aliana just said what she wanted and didn't let society dictate her.

My lips twitched upward, taking some time to think

before replying. "I don't know depression, but I know lone-liness. You're one of the few people who know my true identity. So . . . what happened? With the muse, I mean. You don't need to tell me if you don't want to."

"Oh, I know I don't." She feistily remarked. "It's not that interesting, really. Same old story. But *you*, now that's interesting."

"I don't believe that for a minute." But she just laughed. I knew by her response that I wasn't getting the story from her.

"I've changed my mind," she said cheekily. "You're in this deep. Why not read it? You've obviously read and responded to *all* her other letters." I gave her a wide-eyed, disbelieving stare. I got up to leave. Really hoping she was joking. "Wait, stay and read it here. I deserve something for helping. Plus, you might need some moral support." I stared harder at her as I slowly sat back down.

Well, she's already read it. I pulled the letter from its enve-lope and took a deep breath.

"Out loud would be nice." I shook my head, and she raised her hands. "Touchy, touchy."

I ignored that and began reading to myself.

Dear Cece,

I'm sorry to write again. I know how busy you are, but somehow I felt you would understand, or possibly have some insights.

I've met someone. Well, we met again. And you know how you were saying there were some men who would be a light in the dark?

That one existed for me—

Mrs. Ailana whistled. She didn't even know how far I'd made it, but I guess heat had crept across my skin. I should not be reading this. She should not have told me to read this. I eyed her sharply, and she looked up at the sky innocently, stroking her bird.

Well, he's that kind of man. And I don't want to lose his friendship. But mostly, I don't think I could stand to find hope in the darkness and it be nothing more than an illusion. A mirage of lost memories. That would devastate me. Especially when I could have a friend. The one I've always wanted. The one I've always needed.

I should just be direct. I'm not making any sense. You're a busy lady. Enough of the analogies. He has agreed to a fake relationship to help me with a situation regarding one of my ukulele festivals. It's a very lengthy story. One I'm sure you could write very well. But I don't think it's worth the risk. I have too much to lose. I'm having so many second thoughts, and I don't think I can pretend with him.

Yours Truly,

Luna

Another loud whistle sounded as I looked up. Mrs. Ailana's voice broke through my trance. "Cece has to respond to *that*. It would crush her if she didn't receive a reply. But there is no way *you* should give advice about your-self," she concluded.

"Well, that was all kinds of helpful. *Thank you*, Mrs. Ailana."

The older lady rocked further back in her chair, kicking her feet up even higher, as if satisfied with herself. The creepy bird repositioned itself, too. Both were staring at me impatiently, waiting to hear my doomed plan.

"Yeah, I don't see how either," was my noncommittal and slightly aggravated answer. I got up without waiting to hear her response, squeezing the letter between my fingers as if I could get an answer out of it. I needed time to think . . . by myself . . . in a bird free zone.

I walked out of Mrs. Ailana's apartment and found my way over to my balcony, the one that was now brimming with thoughts of *her*. My brows pinched harder together as Nova began nudging me with the ball that was positioned solidly between her teeth. Her way of checking to see if I was okay. My lips puckered in frustration as I petted her head in reply.

I exhaled and pulled out my phone to call Locke. As I stroked Nova's ears, my breathing steadied enough that I could start to make sense of my thoughts.

Locke picked up on the first ring, as if sensing some-thing. "Hey, is everything ok?" I almost never called him at his surf shack. Well, I never called, period. "Ok man, just slow down. Start from the beginning. We'll figure it out," he said as a string of words escaped my lips.

"Let's just call the whole thing off. She's having *a lot* of second thoughts and her music festival is this weekend. And

I can't answer *this* letter, Locke. *Not* this one."

"Whoa, slow down. What letters? Do you mean to tell me you've been writing letters to her . . . ?" Locke questioned. "For how long? How have you never told me about this?"

"No, Locke. She's been occasionally writing letters to Cece and I've been writing back. For years. Can you catch up quicker, please?"

"Well, I guess I can when the shock wears off. And when you provide all the puzzle pieces . . . Whoa man, that's a pretty *big* invasion of privacy. *Why* did you answer those letters? Better yet, *why* did you read them?"

"Locke, that's not helping here. That part is done. I already screwed up there. Can we focus? You know, on me not screwing up *more*? . . . If you read the letters, you would understand. She needed someone, and I wanted to be that someone. I didn't think our lives would *ever* intersect again. I thought we were fated to be distant acquaintances. The best known strangers, if you will. So, I wanted to help her however I could."

A long silence engulfed the phone line. "Wow, that's deep. Well, it would help if I heard one of the letters." He fished cheekily, curiosity taking over.

"You're infuriating, you know that?" I let out a loud exhale and then pulled out the letter and started reading. Because *why not at this point?*

After I finished reading, there was a long silence. "Man, you're in deep." Locke whistled slowly.

"Ok, something more helpful than that, Locke. *Please*," I urged.

"Ok, I just need a minute to process," he began. "I think she's just worried about you and your friendship. She just doesn't want to lose you again. That's pretty clear.

Sounds like a good thing to me."

"How is anything in this letter clear?" I asked, flipping through the pages rapidly.

"Just relax. You can't see the situation clearly because it's about you. You never could." I exhaled, knowing he was right.

I stayed silent, waiting for him to continue. "You need to figure out if *you're* still ok to do this. And if you are, then I think you should do it for Luna. It's just a long weekend getaway. You'll go early so she can rehearse and prepare. And you'll act like you're together. You guys already look like a couple, so it won't be hard. And then just be there for her and look out for her. Don't answer the letter until you get back from the trip if you really think you have to answer it. Or better yet, just *tell her*."

"Yeah and say what? 'Hey, I'm the person you've been writing to and sharing all your deep, intimate feelings with? I've known it was you this whole time and I've been answering the letters, anyway?' Yeah, I don't think so. She'll call off the trip for sure. Who'll go with her then?"

"You could always tell her after the trip. And Cece doesn't have to reply. Giving advice about yourself takes things to a whole other level. Maybe save that as one line you *don't* cross."

"Thanks, Locke. You're hilarious. Really." My tone was dripping with sarcasm.

"I have a better idea. How about you just go over to her place with some grand romantic gesture and tell her how you really feel? Say, 'Hey, I'm Cece, but I've also been in love with you my whole life, so I hope that makes it ok.' Then kiss her like you've always wanted to. Just pick one of the hundred ways you've written it. Put her in such a passionate haze she'll have to forgive you." Locke chuckled slightly.

"You're really *laki* you have Guin, you know, because you give terrible dating advice."

"Yeah, I know," he agreed. "But I didn't think that advice was so bad. But, whatever you do, you better decide fast. And make your peace with it."

"Really, Locke. I think you missed your calling as a therapist."

"I know. Aren't you *so* 'lucky' to have me?" He practically winked through the phone.

Luna

AGE 31

I t happened again tonight. My world and my music no longer felt like my own. I just felt like a prop for the music label.

I'd come off the stage, disoriented, the world getting smaller and closing in around me. Steve's words still ringing in my ears. He told me the music label wanted to give my lyrics for the newly titled, *The Only Woman I Could Love, to Azul* as a solo. All sounds had dimmed when I heard the news and my chest tightened. Tremors began telling my body that all systems were shutting down.

A chair off in a darkened corner came into sight. A familiar voice and touch embraced me, guiding me toward safety and allowing my airways to ease.

As the soft tone of a stagehand tried to reassure me, Azul's confident voice broke through my daze. "It's ok, I've got this, babe." Through my hazy vision, I saw him rush onto the stage and grab my dejected ukulele that had fallen off my chair.

When I got back to my hotel room that night, I'd seen Cece LaRue's book on my nightstand. A thin cardboard coaster from the hotel had marked my current spot in the book. I gripped the novel as if it was a lifeline, comfort taking over as I thought about the main character who experienced panic attacks. Just like me. For the first time tonight, I didn't feel alone.

Serendipitously, my eyes wandered over to the desk that was tucked away in a corner of the room. A pad and pen lay there, as if waiting for me. And the words poured out. Words I had kept inside for *way* too long. And I knew I would find a way to get this letter to her.

Reef

CHAPTER 16

66 How can someone smell like home when you just met them?

-REEF AKUA, PASSION IN PARADISE

"What are you doing, Reef?" Luna laughed nervously, fidgeting in my car with a blindfold on. Which, now that I think about it, seems pretty creepy and not at all romantic like it was supposed to be. *Why do these ideas always sound so much better in romance books?*

Luna's hands were playfully feeling around on the dashboard of my car. She looked like a child who had been blinded by the sun but was still determined to explore the sand. Adorably enough, Luna had been throwing out guesses about where we were going the whole time I was driving us here. Calling out the road names as we turned and being uncannily accurate. I didn't expect her to be so good at this game of being 'kidnapped'. However, she was a true crime junkie and a thriller movie fanatic, so I should have known better.

"Can't you just enjoy being kidnapped?" I teased, knowing that would *never* happen. Luna always planned out *everything.* Her cool and collected demeanor was really just a good, protective shield that lent itself to a very nice stage presence. But I sometimes worried she felt she had to be too 'collected'. And in our time apart, this trait appeared to have amplified in her situation with her music label. And I wanted to make sure she didn't feel the *need* to be 'collected' with me.

"Reef, you don't need to take me out to the middle of nowhere." A nervous chuckle escaped her. "We leave tomorrow, and Louis said everything is good to go. The music label knows I'm bringing someone with me and they're very aware of our 'serious' relationship. Heck, they're probably hoping you'll pop the question soon for some great press coverage."

I insisted, "No, today isn't about them. There's some-thing I just want *us* to do together."

"You wanted to kill me at the base of the mountain?" Humor colored her tone.

"No, your true crime skills are seriously lacking. I could have killed you long ago." I teased. "Just wait . . . you'll see."

I parked, and Luna instinctively reached up to remove the bandana covering her eyes—the one I'd taken from Nova's doggie bin.

I teasingly remarked, "No, that stays on."

She said nothing, but I could feel her eyes rolling play-fully. So I reminded her, "You said you would try *anything* with me."

"Reef! What have you done? Is this the part where I die so I don't have to worry about going on the trip?"

Deep laughter rumbled out of me. "No, if anyone has to worry about that, it would be me."

"Ok, that's not helping," she replied as I walked around to open her car door and help her out. As soon as I opened her door, a loud noise invaded her quiet space and a shocked expression registered on her face.

Luna raised her voice over the whirling sound of a motor. "Reef, what the heck? That sounds like serial killer equipment!"

"It's ok, Luna. I promise." I gently reached for her hips to steady her and then started guiding her toward the sound.

"No, Reef. We're supposed to go *away* from the psycho killer noise." But as we traveled closer to the noise, disbelief clouded her tone. "Reef, is this a helicopter? It can't be—"

She stopped walking and was trying to turn to face me.

I laughed. "Well, I guess I can take your 'blindfold' off now."

"Reef, we always wanted . . . I can't believe you remembered." Overwhelm swept over her features, a glassy sheen covering her eyes.

Yeah, it's the one thing we wanted to do the most when we were kids. My words came out softly, "Now's our chance. *Just* the two of us. No photos." Or at least, not ones we're going to share with everyone else.

When we were younger, we didn't have the money for something like this. And if we were going through with our plans for tomorrow, then there was something we needed to do together first.

Luna exclaimed, "But you're terrified of heights. Like actually *petrified.* How did we not think about that as kids? Has that changed?"

"No, it hasn't," I said as I reached to remove the blindfold from her face. Revealing her eyes, which fell intently on me. "But I can get through it with you. That's the point." Realization swept across her face, understanding why I'd brought her here. I didn't want her to be the only one who was going to be vulnerable this week. And I wanted to see if we could still trust each other. Hopefully, for her to see that she could still trust me.

Without waiting a second more, she extended her hand to me. I'd been waiting *so long* to see that motion again. It was one I knew had to be earned. And at that moment, a montage of Luna reels flashed through my memory. Remembering all the times she'd given her hand so generously to me. And I took her hand so quickly that a smile flashed across her face.

As we neared the helicopter, reality began sinking in. But I was pretty numb to it all, riding a 'Luna high' with her hand in mine. It wasn't until we'd buckled in and the engine started preparing for takeoff that the adrenaline began rushing through my veins at full throttle.

"Reef?" Luna called to me as we sat huddled in the back of the helicopter with headphones on. Noise was pummeling our senses from the open windows. I would have opted for windows closed, but I knew Luna wouldn't want to miss this.

My eyes embarrassingly followed hers as she glanced down at my tight grip on her hand. Concern filled her voice. "You don't look so good right now. Are you sure you want to do this?"

"Yeah, I'm fine, totally fine." I nodded as I tried to loosen my grip on her hand. The pilot's voice came through our headphones with the list of safety precautions as he prepared for takeoff. As the helicopter started lifting off the ground, Luna's excited face was in stark contrast to my own chalky white one. Especially as my very active imagination took flight.

"Luna, you're going to need to distract me." A shaky breath left me.

"Reef, just how were you planning to get to Oahu?" Luna teased me.

"By boat," I said through a clenched jaw. My nerves started ramping up to a whole new level. And then to my horror, my stupid mouth began rapidly occupying the space as if I needed to fill the helicopter with words in order for it to stay in the air.

"I listen to your music all the time." The first confession flew out. "*One More Hour* is my absolute favorite. I can actually feel tears forming in my eyes when I hear it. I should probably stop listening to it."

She laughed. "Reef—"

But as the helicopter continued gaining height, my words took flight with it. As we hovered over a gorgeous mountain range filled with lush greenery and the crisp blue Hawaiian sky above us, all I could do was keep filling our tiny space with my humiliating babbling. Turning the inside of the helicopter into some weird pseudo-confessional booth. As if my words could help keep this thing from crashing.

"I lied when we were younger." Oops, confession number two. *Oh no, Reef. Please stop,* my feral self-preservation voice screamed at me inside my head. "I thought about kissing you *all* the time. *Every* moment we were together."

Her eyebrow arched at that one.

"But I've only ever white lied to you. Things I thought you were better off knowing or *not* knowing." *Okay, Reef, now would be the prime time to tell her some of those important things you've wanted to share with her. Couldn't you manage to do that if you're going to purge your soul?*

The pilot turned his head slightly. "You kids ok back there? It's fine if you want to move toward the window and take a look."

I could tell he was more worried about what we might be doing back here as we huddled closely together. Oddly, that made me loosen up a little, a relaxed laugh popping out of me. But Luna stayed *all* business. She wasn't fond of the pilot's interruption at such an inopportune time. She thanked him as quickly as possible so we could get back to the purging of my soul.

"You were saying . . ." Those luscious browns were staring even harder. "White lies . . ."

"Oh, uh. It's fine. You're going to miss seeing everything. Let's move toward the window and I'll hide behind you like a coward," I remarked dryly.

"Are you sure?–" she asked, not even bothering to look toward the window. She just kept massaging my hand–the one I didn't even know she'd taken. I felt her slowly flip my hand over and pull an imaginary string up from my palm like she did when we were kids. She looked at me with an impish smile and when I returned hers, she started drawing a letter, over and over. Her eyebrow raised, waiting for my guess.

"M?" She nodded. And I continued to guess, my breathing slowing at the focal point she had provided. Suddenly, I was in a nostalgic safe harbor with her. "*Mahalo?*" I asked as she drew the last letter.

She nodded again. Her voice came out just above a whisper. "Yeah. It's easy to live in 'thankfulness' with you. Life becomes fuller. Everything gets brighter and clearer. Like it's blooming in color."

And just like that, my breathing slowed. She'd known *exactly* what to do. With a steady smile, she continued, "This is the most romantic 'date' I've ever been on . . . as an adult. So, thank you . . . Now about those dying admissions." She teased.

"So, all it took was a guy almost passing out and then babbling like an idiot?"

"No," she said with a soft firmness. "I just wanted one to *genuinely* care. No ulterior motives."

I stared at her resolute face. *How could I already be this comfortable with her?* Maybe we hadn't outgrown each other after all. Maybe there was still a chance . . . If only she knew how much she *still* set my world on fire. I only wished I was brave enough to show her.

A playful tone entered my voice. "Why are you so interested? Do *you* have white lies you're hiding?"

Her eyes skirted the clear blue skies as she said, "I've

only ever white lied to you, too . . . No, that's not true. I've never lied. I just might not have said everything, but I never lied."

I felt a wave of guilt crash into me. This was the perfect time to come clean, but it wasn't what she needed to hear right now. Not with our upcoming trip tomorrow.

She pointed between us. "That's why this is so special." I tried to swallow my guilt down. I swear I could taste it.

I inhaled sharply as I moved with her toward the window. Luckily, she thought my phobia was getting the better of me. Which was true. It was just that I was battling two phobias right now. Permanently losing her being at the top of my list.

But the look of amazement brightening her face as she stared out at our world melted all my fears. Such a quiet peace came over her, even at these great heights. I could see the girl from my childhood again in her features, especially when she aimed her sweet smile at me. A familiar warmth started sweeping over me.

"Reef, this is incredible. Are you able to look out the window now and see it all?" She wrapped an arm around me, edging me a little closer to the window, pushing my comfort zone just enough. Maybe we still knew just the right amount, so the other got what they needed safely. I'd always thought of a soulmate as someone who would know what you needed better than you did. Because they could see you even clearer than you saw yourself . . . Your missing piece. But it had gotten too hard to believe in the idea after she'd left. Because if I did, that meant a part of me was missing, and I'd never find it again. A sad confession for a romance author.

I tried to bring myself back to the present moment. That Luna magic was working overtime on me, my body moving in tandem with hers toward the window. I was convinced it would follow her *anywhere*. Apparently that hadn't changed, and it was a tad nerve-wracking because friends *don't* respond to friends in this way.

As if slipping back twenty years, her warmth completely calmed me. My breathing was now at an acceptable chill level. And I felt like I was flying in more ways than one. Hopefully, that meant my sweaty palms would settle down, too.

"Well, what do you think?" Her eyes roamed over mine to make sure I was taking in all the scenery. "Is it as good as you thought it would be?"

"It's perfect," I replied. "Just as incredible as I imagined." But my eyes weren't looking outside.

Luna

CHAPTER 17

*Not so long ago, you did what no one else would
What no one else could*

-LUNA MANU MELE, ONE
MORE HOUR

"Luna, do you have everything, honey?" Louis called out to me. He was patiently waiting for me to finish getting ready so he could take me to the ferry, which in my frazzled state of mind was taking extra time to do. After Reef's experience aboard the helicopter, we had decided that the ferry would be preferable to this morning. Plus, a ninety-minute ferry ride definitely beats going through airport protocol.

"Yes, I've got everything." I grabbed my journal off the nightstand and headed for the door. I found Louis calmly standing there, waiting to help me with my luggage. He had made no movement yet since I'd gone back into my room so many times, muttering about forgetting things. Or in truth, just stalling.

"You ok, Luna?" His brow furrowed as he looked at me with concern. "If you really don't want to go, I can figure something out. If you feel you can't—"

"No, I can't let down the people who have traveled so far to be here for this festival. I know I can do this. And Reef is going to be looking out for me. I won't have to be alone. You've made sure I've been taken care of ever since you've come back. I don't know how I could ever—" The words caught in my throat.

"Luna, hey, I just wish I'd come back sooner." His eyes were steadfast. "I'm really sorry, I didn't . . . I just didn't know. But I'm going to make up for it now." He gave me a reassuring smile as he gently took my bags from me.

As soon as he stepped out onto the porch, he turned on his heel. He looked at me gravely and asked, "You do still love playing music, right? It's still a light in the dark for you?" I nodded at him. "If it ever stops being one, you'll tell me, won't you?" It wasn't really a question. But music had never been the problem. It was the lifestyle that went along with it. All the things I never knew it involved. And Louis knew your passion for music had to burn so brightly that it could last through everything.

I nodded at him, and he responded with a steady head tilt. Finally breaking eye contact, I grabbed a silk scarf and locked up my suitcase. I'd stalled long enough. Following Louis to the porch, I began making my way down the front porch stairs when I noticed a feminine head peeking up over the headrests of Louis' sedan. My eyes wandered to his pretty packed trunk.

"Uncle Louis, what's?—"

Laughter filled his voice. "You didn't think I was going to let you go with some guy I barely even knew, did you? I mean, I only met him a few times when you were kids. That hardly counts. What if he grew up to be a psycho, or he doesn't do a good job taking care of you? I'll have to be there to straighten him out."

My laughter came out as a nervous chuckle.

Louis teased, "Plus, Kelani and I could use some romantic vacation time." I looked through the car window, now able to make out his girlfriend's friendly face as she waved enthusiastically at me. With Kelani's Alzheimer's, I knew Louis wanted to stay near her in case she needed help. So that meant he couldn't count on being my only support for the festival. He hadn't known if Kelani would be well enough to make the trip until it was time to go. Should Louis and Kelani need to leave the Festival early, Reef would be available to stay and help me.

Plus, Louis really loved his surprises. He and his girlfriend were both known to have a propensity for matchmaking, especially Kelani. The locals all called her Tutu since she was like a grandmother to everyone. She was only biologically Locke's grandmother, but her warmth and free flowing advice were hard-wired in her DNA and she shared it with everyone. I could already see an impish expression forming on her face as she looked at me. Louis had probably given Kelani plenty of 'insider' information so she could begin hatching a few romantic scenarios.

"Well, are we going to go pick up your boyfriend?" Louis teased. "I'm docking points from him since he's not here with flowers in hand. It's not a great start to your weekend getaway. What kind of fake boyfriend is that?"

"A good one," I remarked. "The kind that lets you have space and doesn't get into your business. Did you bring an organized point chart, too?" I teased back. My uncle loved any type of color-coordinated organizational tool, which is probably where I got my love of them.

Louis laughed harder. "Well, Excel had the perfect template marked as 'pretend relationships'. But Luna, you deserve a man who shows up with a huge bundle of lilies and tells you how beautiful you are, whether it's fake or not."

His eyebrows drew upward and the word 'fake' landed with no conviction. It sounded like he didn't believe it for a minute.

IT WAS A QUIET, scenic drive over to the ferry. Thankfully, Tutu kept my mind preoccupied with her questions about the hotel and our sightseeing plans. But even with her kindness, my mind kept running wild, wondering if I was making the right decision. At least my anxiety was under better control since the excursion with Reef yesterday . . . and also thanks to the letter I'd received from Cece. Reef had put himself out there for me in a big way on the helicopter ride. And getting unbiased advice from Cece had certainly helped, too.

The combination of the two was enough to help keep me calm until we reached the parking lot. When my capricious nerves began rising like a high tide. And I went under fast. I tried breathing through my anxiety as we made our way to the pier. *Breathe, Luna.* But sometimes control was just too far out of reach, especially if you hadn't addressed the root of the problem . . . Like me.

My eyes impatiently scanned the area for Reef, but Louis' laugh interrupted me. I hesitantly looked up at his raised eyebrow and then slowly followed the tip of his finger over to the ferry waiting area. "Guess I spoke *too* soon," he corrected.

There sat Reef, waiting on a bench with none other than Nova. His crisp white shirt sported rolled-up sleeves, and he wore nice dress pants. I don't know who he thought he was accompanying, but he looked ready for a dance rather than escorting me to a hotel check-in for a ukulele festival. If he put on some large black sunglasses, he could easily pull off 'bodyguard'. At least, the image of the one I had in my dreams.

As I continued gaping at him, my rebellious eyes traveled down to the unfastened buttons of his shirt. The image only fueled my racing pulse. *Look away, Luna.* I turned to Nova, but it didn't help. He'd accessorized the adorable pup with a lavender bandana that matched the flowers he was holding in his hands.

"How could I forget lavender was your favorite?" Louis whispered. "Can't believe I suggested lilies." Louis' smile burst forth, loving that Reef knew me so well.

"Well, showing up with a dog is the best, anyway." I teased.

"Sounds like he got *all* the points today. Excuse me, I was *all* wrong," Louis apologized playfully. I gave him a rueful side eye and went over to Reef.

My heart was pounding with each step I took. I'd fantasized about going to a dance with Reef when we were younger, but we'd never gotten the chance. Even after I moved away, that daydream got me through a lot of hard times. Somehow, this felt close enough to that fantasy, and my heart was taking the opportunity to act like a lovesick teen. I hadn't needed any celebrity crushes growing up. And my heart was reminding me why.

I smiled at Reef and bent down to greet Nova, who instantly began licking my face. Reef began tugging her away. "Nova, stop. Luna is dressed for her meeting today. You're going to lick all of her makeup off." He glanced apologetically at me. "Sorry, I shouldn't have brought her . . . I just thought . . . I wanted to surprise you, but–" He trailed off as he looked up at me. "You look so beautiful. Uh . . . these are for you," he said sheepishly as he handed me the lavender bouquet.

I could feel the heat rise in my cheeks as I took the flowers. I couldn't even remember the last time a man had given me flowers. Well, not like these. Certainly not hand-picked. They were sweet and simple. *Perfect.* I looked at Reef. "Thank you, you didn't need to . . . but it's *really* sweet. *Mahalo.*"

He nodded. "Locke said wildflowers weren't flowers you would usually give your 'pretend' girlfriend. He suggested I should at least go buy some lavender roses."

No, I'd had enough roses with strings attached to last me a lifetime. What I wanted now was lavender, especially the ones handpicked from our special field. We both shook our heads, a silent understanding filling the air between us. I glanced down at my purple dress and we both grinned.

"I love the idea of Nova coming along, but how?–"

"Oh, well, I called the hotel and asked if Nova could stay with us. It didn't take too much convincing. I explained that while she wasn't a certified emotional support dog yet, she was still very important to your health and well-being. Um, I hope that's ok– that I didn't overstep. I thought you'd enjoy her company."

Yet . ..Was he actually thinking about having her certified as an emotional support dog, or was he just trying to find a way for her to get to stay with us? He knew all about emotional support dogs from Locke, since he had one named Penny.

He quickly added, "I promised I would share her. Plus, I think she likes you more than me, anyway. Was it ok that I told the hotel that? I used vague language, so I'm pretty sure they think she's your dog. Maybe I didn't think this through."

The flustered motions of his fingers on his glasses made me want to keep my mouth shut so I could keep watching his movements. *So sexy.* "More than okay. It's probably the sweetest thing anyone has ever done for me." *Yet again.* He seemed to be an expert in that area.

"Reef," Louis came over and extended his hand, gripping Reef's firmly. *Uh oh, his protective side was coming out.* Dating was the only time Louis' chill nature slid over to the other side of the spectrum. There could be only one reason for that. He must think Reef was *actually* interested. "You're showing me up today, son. Didn't know we could bring cute, furry companions along on the trip." He teased.

"Sir," Reef said, as he straightened to shake his hand. Oh no, this really was like being picked up for prom. *Please don't let them be like this for the entire trip.* Reef deserved time to relax and enjoy himself. Reef asked Louis, "Are you coming along with us?"

"Yes, I wanted to be there for Luna, too," Louis explained as he continued shaking Reef's hand firmly. Neither was letting go first. This was so awkward.

"Well, I'm glad you could come. I know how much Luna loves you, sir. I'm sure you'll do a much better job protecting her than I could."

"Don't sell yourself short, son. You're the one who'll be doing the heavy lifting this weekend. Seems like all her favorite men are here," Louis replied.

Ok, that was enough. I finally reached for their arms, breaking their hands apart. "Reef, you can call him Louis. *Right, Uncle?*" I asked sternly. "This is supposed to be a relaxing getaway. Well, for everyone *but* me." Louis nodded along reluctantly, as he eyed my fingers intertwined with Reef's. A mischievous smile formed on his face. I didn't even realize I had continued holding on to Reef when I pulled their hands apart.

Reef grinned at me and said to Louis, "Thanks, sir. I appreciate it." To which Louis smiled even bigger. It was no use. I obviously couldn't win with these two. Louis gave me a sideways nod of his head as if to say, 'see, I told you so,' when Reef started helping me with my bags. I gave Louis a 'behave yourself' nod in return. But Louis just let out a loud laugh, which caused Reef to glance back at us.

"Just happy we're all reunited," Louis said, covering his tracks. "You know, Reef, now that I think about it, the times I visited the island when Luna was young, I remember you two being pretty inseparable." His voice increased as we headed toward the ferry. *What little birdie had tipped him off about that? Louis hadn't remembered that so well before.*

"I guess we were," Reef agreed.

"Well good. You can fill me in on all the things I missed on the ferry ride over." And Reef actually relaxed at his words. Maybe he took that as acceptance or approval.

So we found our seats on the top deck, enjoying the view and the sea breeze. Reef gradually relaxed while I petted Nova, who was sprawled across my lap and partly onto the chair beside me. Being seated between Reef and Nova made me feel calmer than I'd been in a very long time, which seemed strange since I was going to one of the biggest events of my career. One I hadn't even wanted to attend. It was hard to believe how quickly things changed. But I felt completely content being with the two of them. And I was going to live in this moment for however long it lasted.

Reef

CHAPTER 18

> " The ghost of her always caught up with me. From simple everyday objects to dinner dates. Everything always came back to her.

-REEF AKUA, WHISPERS OF WAIKIKI

I was usually the 'laid back' one in a group, but I appeared more nervous than anyone today. Going on a 'fake' romantic getaway with the woman of your dreams will do that to a man. Especially while pretending to be her boyfriend and trying to look out for her like some quasi bodyguard. Throw her *very* protective uncle into the mix, who was probably very aware of my feelings for his niece, and I didn't stand a chance.

Louis appeared to have a pretty good idea about how strong my feelings were for Luna. *Had he hinted about them to her? I* swallowed hard. It was probably only a matter of time until he did. So far, Luna didn't seem to realize my true feelings, or she was being politely ignorant. I pinched my eyes together, trying to focus on why I was here. At least Luna was enjoying herself so far, although that was probably Nova's doing. Good thing I'd brought some back up. I was going to need it.

However, when we pulled up to the luxurious hotel, I couldn't distract my brain any longer. The massive resort towered over us with its creamy texture as we reached its elegant overhang, where its friendly staff greeted us with leis. As we stepped into the gorgeous five-star lobby, I already felt out of place. A real Alice in Wonderland moment. I'd never been a tourist in a place this elegant. Having a pen name meant I didn't travel to PR events. But I could be persuaded if the places looked like this . . . Somehow, I didn't think my situation would be quite the same.

I glanced around the open-air lobby, which contained an expanse of white marble, columns, and glistening fountains. Sunlight glinted off the water, and the fresh air was fragrant with plumeria. As we walked through the hotel to the reception area, I could see plenty of upscale shops scattered throughout the open-air walkways. I was so busy absorbing the atmosphere that I didn't even realize we had arrived at the check-in desk.

A friendly staff member began greeting Luna profusely, offering her top-notch service. "We are so happy you have chosen Halekulani for your trip. May I put your flowers in water?" I smiled as Luna reluctantly handed over her floral bouquet. "Ms. Manu Mele, we have upgraded your room," the male receptionist continued excitedly. It took me a minute to remember that she used a different last name for the stage. "We've upgraded you and your guest to the honeymoon suite. We hope you'll enjoy the wonderful view of the ocean and Diamond Head Mountain."

"The honeymoon suite?" I sputtered, my cheeks heating.

Luna's eyes twinkled at me with obvious amusement. From the next receptionist desk, I saw Louis' gaze fall on me as well. *Great, I'm already blowing my cover.* I'm sure the type of man Luna usually dated took charge and made all the arrangements. An upgrade to the honeymoon suite surely wouldn't shock him.

I tried to cover my blunder, but I only made things worse. "I mean, that's perfect. It will be great practice." Luna burst out laughing at my word choice. I turned to her, my neck heated. "*Auê*, I didn't mean it like that. Why is everything I say coming out wrong today? You always were good at finding the alternative meaning . . ."

"Oh, I don't think you need any help. You *never* have." She laughed harder, and I knocked some brochures off the desk. That was the problem: she could set my world ablaze just as easily as she could make me feel safe and comfortable. I fumbled to arrange the flyers back on the counter. I was just trying to shut myself up when I felt a hand on my shoulder. Louis, no doubt, coming to help. *So embarrassing.*

Louis explained to the staff member, "They're just a little nervous about Luna's upcoming performance. Plus, it's their first time away together. You understand," was Louis' cool attempt to smooth over my misstep. The man nodded, but still wore a slightly confused expression. Yeah, who would say anything about being upgraded to the honeymoon suite with *Luna?* A normal guy would take the gift and run with it.

The receptionist handed us a key, not explaining *any more* benefits of the room. For *my benefit,* I'm sure. But somehow, I just made an opening. "Will it be ok for our dog to stay in the suite with us?" I asked, double checking, even though I had called.

"Yes sir, any dog with Luna Manu Mele is *always* welcome." I felt like he probably thought that applied to me as well, but I just nodded my thanks.

Thankfully, with a less than ideal check-in over, we headed to our rooms. Tutu and Louis broke off after the elevator to go down a different hallway. This was going to be fun. Now, I really felt like I was being chaperoned. But perhaps I needed it by the way my body was responding to Luna. My rapid heart rate agreed.

When we reached the clearly marked private room at the end of the hall, I said like a *lōlō,* "Uh, I think this is it . . . Do I need to carry you over the threshold?" I teased, but the pause along with the starry look in her eyes made me want to do it.

I smiled, a determination mixed with desire coming over me. "Well, we only get one shot at it." I set the bags down and made my way over to her.

"Reef, no," she said in mock sternness, shaking her

head. "Reef!" she yelped as I picked her up in one sweeping motion. Laughter followed, just like when we were kids, and the sound filled my soul. I held the door open with my foot and dropped Nova's leash so she could bound inside to check out her new surroundings.

"Reef–" But Luna was laughing too hard to get any more words out. I carried her slowly through the tropical entryway so we could soak everything in. Allowing the suite's soft beiges and oceanic blues to fill our vision. I quickly bypassed the living room area with my sights set on the open doors to the lanai, which was waiting just for us. Loungers with plush white cushions and a corner cafe table invited us to relax on the balcony. It was all perfectly framed by the tops of palm trees. Past the opening of the shuttered wooden doors, we could see the expanse of the sparkling deep blue ocean and the lush greens of Diamond Head behind them. A breathtaking view, just as promised. And, of course, Nova was already spinning in circles on one of the loungers, too overwhelmed and excited to sit down. *My* sentiments exactly.

I gently set Luna down so she could admire the view, but she wasn't looking in that direction. With her eyes fixed on me, she mused, "I was just getting used to being carried."

"Oh, I'm sorry." I reached for her again, but she swiftly backed away as she giggled. I remarked on the view's beauty, "It's breathtaking," but what truly held my attention was the exquisite woman standing beside me. I insisted, "No, really thanks, this is pretty incredible. I'm going to go get the bags before someone steals your uke and sells it on eBay. I forgot how famous you are, *Ms. Manu Mele*."

She rolled her eyes playfully. "I know the term 'songbird' isn't very original. But I was young, and it seemed like an appropriate stage name for a jazz ukulele artist."

"Songbird fits you perfectly." I smiled at her as she tucked some hair behind her ear and then moved to help me with the bags. I attempted to stop her. "No, stay and enjoy the view," but she followed me into the room, anyway.

I hoped she knew I wasn't teasing about her stage name. I just couldn't get over how famous she was in our community and how much she had done to make the ukulele popular, but I should have. I'd always believed big things awaited her.

As stunning as this room was, it was a little awkward being in a honeymoon suite with your childhood sweet-heart. And Luna's face echoed that sentiment. Especially as I set my bags by the sofa in the living room area. I didn't want her to think I _expected_ to sleep in the bed. Honestly, I had a hard-wired memory of holding her, one that I _couldn't_ forget. That meant I needed the couch.

"Reef, you're _not_ sleeping on the couch. Don't even think about it." Luna started.

"I'm sure it pulls out. Don't worry about it. I'll be fine," I attempted.

"In a honeymoon suite? I'm sure it doesn't. Pretty sure they discourage that." A nervous laugh followed.

"Well, either way, Nova and I will be fine."

"Even _more reason_ for you to sleep on the bed." She grinned, looking over at Nova, who already had a pitiful face.

I guess I'd try to be chivalrous again later. So instead I asked, "How about going to the pool? It looked really relax-ing. Do you have some time to unwind before stage prep?"

She looked at her watch. "Yes, we're not doing rehearsal and sound check until later this evening."

I smiled, and we quickly changed into our swimsuits. Thankful to leave our overly romantic oasis—the place I was having serious second thoughts about being able to keep my cool in. But *nowhere* in this hotel appeared to ease up on the romance factor.

So we made our way through the breezeway to the lush outdoor oasis, parting ways to find towels and chairs for the afternoon. As I walked around the cerulean blue pool, I admired the detailed, sprawling orchid mosaic on its floor. The ripples of the pool casting the mosaic in different lights and hues. I quickly grabbed some towels and shaded my eyes, looking for Luna who had gone to secure some pool chairs.

My eyes wandered along the loungers until they reached a pair of beautifully tanned legs. I'd found her alright, looking like a freaking Hollywood star from the golden era as she basked in the sunshine. Luna's petite legs stretched out languidly to capture the warmth of the sun as she sat waiting for *me.* Her retro one piece suit had these adorable mustard and white stripes, and laced up the front. My eyes traced her curves, causing me to inhale sharply. The way the suit showed off her curvy features made my eyebrows raise involuntarily. People were *certainly going* to think we were on our honeymoon. Guess Locke was right after all. *No problems* selling it here.

As if realizing there were eyes upon her, Luna's head slowly turned toward me, finding me among the crowd of loungers and sunshine. Her eyes timidly drifted upward to catch mine. Feeling caught like an awkward teen, I straightened my shoulders to make my way over to her. Trying to hide the fact that I'd just been glued in place, completely captivated by her.

"Sorry, I got lost finding the towels." Not a total lie, since I just got lost trying to make my way to her. She looked skeptically at me as I set my book down on a towel and handed another one over to her. I began rummaging around in the bag we'd packed. "Do you want some help applying this?" I asked, pulling out some sunscreen.

"Oh, sure. Thanks." Luna nodded and turned her back to me, sliding off her straps. That movement instantly made me regret my offer. All I could do was continue rubbing the lotion between my hands, warming it up way too much, while I stared at the curves of her back. I swallowed hard.

"Reef?" she questioned, turning her head toward me after an inordinate amount of time had passed.

"Uh, yeah . . . just warming up the lotion." I managed.

"I'm pretty sure there's none left now." Luna laughed. *Probably so.* I got some more lotion out and finally made contact with her back, trying to keep myself in check. A heat pulsed up my arms and right to my core. Making all logic leave my brain.

After I'd done a *very thorough* job of rubbing in her sunscreen, I went back to my lounger and picked up my book for some distraction. As if that was going to help. I'd brought a Cece book, hoping that Luna would open up to me some more about the letters she had written—especially one in particular. If she would share their content, that would be one less secret for me to keep. I didn't relish having insider knowledge. And I had *way* too much of it.

Luna took the bait immediately. "You brought a LaRue book?"

"Oh, uh–" I looked at the cover absentmindedly, as if I hadn't read over it a zillion times in the editorial process.

"Oh, yeah. I haven't read this one since it came out. Figured it would help with my fake boyfriend role." After all, it was the one Louis had put on the table that night.

She shook her head again. "You don't need any help. I'm pretty sure *every* woman at this pool wishes you would put some sunscreen on them." A coy little smile played on her lips. *So, it had been that obvious. Why did I massage the lotion so enthusiastically?* "I'm just waiting for mine to expire," she teased. And I reached over to shove her arm playfully. More muscle memory flooding back.

She looked at the book, then at me. "You were such a talented writer. Do you still write?" *If she only knew what she was asking.*

"Yeah, I guess. Nothing ground breaking." I sighed and went back to my book. *Great, just keep racking up the white lies, Reef.* My plan had quickly backfired.

Concern covered Luna's features. "What does that mean, Reef? What happened? You're *so* talented." Luna sat up in her chair and leaned over to me. I hated when she did that—had such faith in me. Because it made me believe in myself, too. And that was foolish. Back in the day, I'd garnered so much confidence that I'd told my family I was going to be a writer. My stomach dropped a little just remembering it.

"Writing isn't exactly the manliest thing, Luna. And most people don't make any money from it."

She sat up even straighter, knowing exactly where that had come from. The pained expression I couldn't cover told her all she needed to know. I was hoping she wouldn't still read me so accurately.

"Reef, that's not true. You're definitely talented enough to make it. And I've always thought male writers were *extremely sexy.*"

A flirty smile tugged at her lips as I felt a blush creep up my neck. I rubbed the back of it self-consciously. "Yeah? . . ."

Luna nodded with emphasis. "We grew up learning to respect our elders and I'm very thankful for that, but being respectful doesn't mean they have to be *right* about everything. There's a difference. There's more than one path and each person has to find out which one is right for them. Although acceptance makes it a lot easier." The words landed forcefully. A smile crept across my face. She *still* could be unfiltered with me.

I stared off into the abyss of the deep blue pool. The water rippled over the surface, distorting the outline of the mosaic. "I used to carry a little notepad, and I actually began writing a novel around the same time you moved. I remember the notepad had 'author' inscribed on it. Just something to help me envision my dream and put that thought out in the world so I could believe it was actually possible . . . As soon as my dad saw the notepad he said, 'So what, are you an author now?' I still hear those words in my head so crystal clear. As if my being an author was the most improbable thing in the world for me. It's hard letting down the people you always looked up to, knowing you aren't what they wanted and that you probably never will be. It's even harder when you stop looking up to the people whose approval meant everything to you."

"Reef, I didn't—" Luna began, but I could see hard lines forming on her face. I knew what she was thinking. When she left, I lost the support of her believing in me—in my writing—and things were never the same. Locke tried to fill that gap as soon as I opened up to him about it. But even with his support, I'd never been able to find that same belief in myself. There was a reason I had a pen name on my novels. It was enough of a struggle to see my books out in the world, never feeling like I had truly earned a spot on the shelf.

"Maybe one day," I breathed, and I meant it about so many things. I shook the thoughts away. "Is this one any good?" I asked, pointing to the book on my chair. I was trying to lighten the mood, but Luna just stared pensively at me.

I waited and when some of the fog lifted, she said, "They're all amazing. I really love that you read romance. *How* are you still single?" Her face went pink instantly and I couldn't help but grin. I loved this side of her. The one she used to save for me.

I answered softly, "Too many reasons. But there's one *big reason* in particular." I held her gaze as the words floated between us.

Reef

CHAPTER 19

> If you knew it was the last time you would see someone, what would you do differently?
>
> -REEF AKUA, WHEN YOU WERE MINE

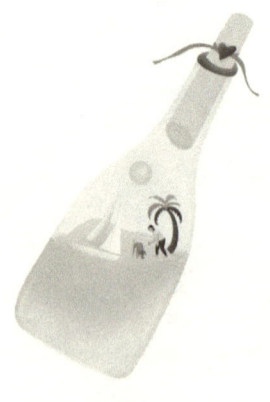

After too much time had probably passed of staring into her eyes, I cleared my throat softly. "Do you ever wonder what romance authors are really like?" It was my feeble attempt to move on from my last confession. *Plus, what did I have to lose?* I couldn't let all these secrets keep piling up. I was tired of pretending not to know about all the intimate details she'd shared with Cece—with *me.* My face flushed, revealing my cards.

But surprisingly, Luna's face went rosier. A rare sight to see. I was usually the one changing colors with my emotions. She worried her bottom lip. "Well, I might have a little insight. I've written to one before. Actually, I wrote to one quite a bit."

"Cece?" I asked too eagerly.

"Yes." She looked down, interlacing her long fingers. "And she wrote back, *every* time. That's one reason she is definitely one of my favorite authors. Who takes the time to *actually* write back? And they were—" She looked at me. "Well, they weren't particularly easy subjects to reply to."

"What do you mean?" *Please open up. Please.* I could feel my heart picking up speed, desperately hoping.

"Well—" Luna leaned over toward me. An enormous weight felt like it was already lifting off my shoulders just when a shadow crept over us. *What the—? Did the staff place an umbrella over Luna?* I wouldn't put it past them—they excelled in hospitality here.

Slowly, I turned from Luna to look up, my eyes scanning the looming figure in front of us. Towering over our loungers was a missing guy from Baywatch. He looked like something off the cover of one of my romance novels; which is not, by the way, what I would have selected to put on them. But I gave up the final say when I signed with my publisher, hoping to get my books out in the world as much as possible. Seldom did my opinions carry over to the finished product.

The brooding hulk had a towel slung over his shoulder that looked *way* too small for his body. What also looked too tiny, and tight, were his toddler sized swim trunks. But this 'Fabio' type proudly posed in his fitted attire, as if he was merely product placement. *Great, some guy has already spotted Luna. Well, at least I'd had a good hour with her since we arrived here.*

"Luna, baby," the man greeted her in a cool, captivating voice, as if he was on the Italian Riviera. My mouth slackened as he continued to speak. "It's great to see you. I was hoping I wouldn't have to wait until sound check." *What? Sound check? No. No, no, no. Please tell me this guy isn't one of the musicians.* I glanced over his muscles again in anguish. *No.* But unfortunately, he wasn't a figment of my imagination or a model come to life off of one of my covers. Either scenario would have been better right about now.

His voice smoothly continued, "You haven't returned any of my calls."

"I believe that's what space is for," Luna replied softly. *No, she couldn't have. Luna couldn't have dated this guy.* I felt my heart squeeze. Of course, this was her type. She could have any guy she wanted. I'd tried to keep reminding myself of that fact, but apparently the universe thought I needed to see said 'type' in the flesh. A perfect, chiseled celebrity. *Aiâ!* I ran my fingers along my brow.

"You really meant that?" Disbelief covered the man's perfectly tanned features. Complete with a jawline that would make even George Clooney envious.

Luna sat silently. "Azul, this is Reef, *my boyfriend.*" She enthusiastically ran her hand over my arm with a glow on her face. She was *proud? Of me?* I was too floored to even move. An enraged expression slowly came over 'Fabio' as he digested Luna's words.

Finally, I unfroze myself. "Hey, I'm Reef," I said as I casually held out my hand like I would with anyone at the bar. But the man of stone completely dismissed it. And my hand slowly dropped.

"That was fast," Azul replied without even glancing in my direction. His chest puffed out like a rooster, trying to make itself the largest one in the chicken coop. As if he needed to do that.

"I'd say over six months is *plenty* long," Luna responded. *Fantastic, they did date.* And *not* that long ago, either.

'Fabio,' responded, "Not when you have a hit song together and are *supposed* to be making more. Steve has *a lot* to talk to you about at sound check today. He has *big* ideas for us." I saw Luna's chest cave inward at his words as the flush began draining from her face. *No, this really isn't good.*

I wasn't a jealous guy. Well, maybe I didn't truly know if I was or not. I'd only really been that way with *one* woman. And I preferred the descriptor 'protective'. Whatever the feeling was called, it was coming out in me now. And *strong.* It didn't matter what the story was or what my chances were. Right now, he was bothering her, and that was something I wouldn't stand for.

"Well, I can't wait to hear those ideas," I said, interrupting the conversation. I *hated* inserting myself like 'that boyfriend', but it felt necessary for this situation. So I continued, "Luna is incredibly talented. I'm sure they have some great promotions lined up so people can easily find her music. I know her music always makes me feel better." Azul harrumphed at that. Not the response he was looking for, I suppose. At least Luna's shoulders relaxed slightly.

I gently pulled Luna over to me and she smiled, moving

to sit in the space I had created in front of me. Letting my instincts take over, I wrapped my arms tightly around her, soaking up her warmth. I wasn't the type of guy to do this. Actually, I hated guys who rubbed their relationship in another man's face. But with this guy, I had no problem flexing the muscles of my *very fake* relationship.

After a little more PDA–which I savored probably a bit too much, especially as Muscle Man's jaw dropped–I pointed to some loungers. *Very* far away. "I think those are free. But it was great to meet you." *Not. So not.*

Luna squeezed her arms around mine. A rush of endorphins flooded over me with her touch. "Thanks for stopping by," she said in a firm voice. That was the Luna I knew and loved. *Good for her.* As soon as he walked away, leaving us with a too vivid view of his buns of steel, Luna turned to me. Her chocolate eyes were already downcast from the short-lived victory.

"Well, that was fun," I teased. "I didn't know you shared a hit duet with someone. I thought I'd listened to all your singles, but I guess I'm slacking."

"I don't. I have a song that I wrote which he took as his own while we were dating. Once I agreed to work on it together, it became a 'duet' and then I slowly got pushed out. If you look at the endless list of credits for the song, I'm in there somewhere. He says it's because I was his 'muse.'" As soon as it left her lips, the word sliced right through me.

"What?!" My jaw clenched. I couldn't stomach someone taking her work—taking advantage of her.

Luna's voice lowered as her face filled with heat. "He's been trying to get me to work on another 'duet' ever since we broke up. Azul is hoping I can help him get another big hit. Now he's even got our manager involved. He makes the process sound *so* nostalgic . . . but we obviously remember it very differently."

"Luna, *no*. That's someone taking advantage of you and being a total–" My words faltered as I looked at her dejected face. Continuing down this path would only make her feel worse. "Luna, you *deserve* to be respected and valued. I'm glad you're standing up for yourself. You're extremely talented and he knows it. Don't let *anyone* dim your light."

She paused at my last word, giving me a thoughtful tilt of her head before reaching for her things. "Thanks, I guess I should get ready for the sound check."

But my instincts had now found their sea legs, and I pulled her in tighter, loving the way her eyes widened. "Come on, *Mahina Liilii*. Let's have some fun and *forget* about him. You deserve it." Her 'little moon' nickname tumbled out of my lips as if it had never left. Its utterance felt foreign, yet *so right* all at the same time.

Before she could respond, I collected my courage and picked her up. The feel of her long-lost nickname on my tongue was driving my adrenaline. And just as soon as I did so, Luna's legs began kicking the air in my hold.

"Reef!" she yelped.

"Better throw the hat off. You're going in," I said in warning as I carried her toward the pool. At least there wasn't anyone in the deep end, because I was pretty sure what I was about to do was frowned upon at such a posh place. It wasn't the 'cannonball and act like a couple of foolish kids in it' type. Which was exactly what I was going for.

Her laughter grew louder the closer I got to the edge, and I knew I'd made the right call. "Reef," she yelled playfully again, and I grinned so widely my cheeks hurt. It felt like those kids had been reunited again. And the last thing I saw before we splashed into the pool was Fabio rolling his eyes.

We surfaced and Luna smoothed her hair out of her face and slowly wrapped her arms back around me. My muscles clenched with surprise, automatically glancing over to see if Azul was still in his chair, but it was vacant.

I turned my eyes back toward Luna, looking for guidance. My eyes lingered over her beautiful light brown eyes, specks of green and amber dancing in them. The variety of colors was even more beautiful in the sunlight. And I couldn't believe those beautiful eyes were looking at me again.

"So, what's his story?" I nodded toward the ego's abandoned chair. I wanted to ask what *their* story was, but I didn't feel like that was my place.

Her eyes quickly looked away. "I don't like to talk about him." I nodded briefly, accepting that there were parts of our life that we didn't talk about now. *Things have changed, Reef. Time has moved on.* But then she looked up at me, a vulnerable glint in her big eyes. "I feel like you're judging me."

"Luna, I'd never judge you."

"There's just not a lot of men who understand or can relate—"

"To being *so* attractive." I teasingly smirked at her.

She shoved me playfully, but her demeanor shifted as she drifted closer to me in the cool water. "No, to being a musician. I just thought it would be better if someone understood about the industry and the pressures that went along with it. . . . But nothing really fazes guys like him. They thrive on the attention and pressure."

She looked away with a flicker of remorse that I hated

to see. "Unfortunately, I just appear to attract a certain type of man. And well, it hasn't worked out too well for me." She removed her arms from around me, crossing them over herself . . . hiding. And just like that, I saw her retreat. An ache ripped through me when she pulled away. A familiar feeling from long ago that demanded I give her some space. She quietly added, "Well, I guess it was a benefit that none of them reminded me of *you.*" A sadness pooled in her eyes along with what looked like regret.

What is she saying? She can't possibly mean . . . I searched her face, needing to understand those last words so they couldn't be misinterpreted. My broken heart couldn't stand to have false hope again.

Luna gazed up at me briefly. "I mean it as a compliment. An *extremely* good one."

"Oh, so that wasn't your way of politely telling me I need to go hit the gym more often?" I tried to joke, but it came out flat. I was feeling pretty low on confidence right now.

"No, *please* don't." The sunlight bouncing off of the water reflected in her eyes, making them sparkle with more life as she floated back over to me. "You're perfect just as you are, Reef."

I looked at her, pretty speechless. Perfect was the last word I'd use to describe myself. But Luna filled in the silence for me. "I always feel my best when I'm with you. The best version of myself. Plus, the water feels pretty incredible right now, too." She joked, and I laughed lightly. "I forgot how amazing water feels, especially on my sore body. Zero gravity is *so* nice. When I'm with you, I take time to appreciate the simple things in life. I've really missed that. And I've finally learned, it's all the little things in life that make it so beautiful. Not taking time to truly enjoy them makes life feel like such a waste. Being with you is restoring my senses."

My eyes scanned hers, looking for any doubt. Any untruth. But I couldn't find any. "Yeah, me too," I said, swallowing hard, holding her tighter as this undeniable urge to protect her came over me. Every so often, I glanced over at Azul's absent chair. Why did I feel there was a lot more to their story that she hadn't shared?

But her words inundated my mind, blocking out all the other ugly noises of our lives. That's what it was like being together. Everything bad dulled to the periphery, leaving happiness in its wake. *I have all my senses back with you . . . you're perfect just as you are . . . none of them reminded me of you.* A warmth only Luna could provide spread over me. Just as suddenly, a welcoming sense of home returned to me. One my body had yearned for so desperately for such a long time.

Luna

AGE 31

C andles on the fine linen tablecloth bathed Azul's face in warmth. Red rose petals lay scattered between us like fallen memories. My untouched red wine glass sat dejectedly off to the side. An ocean of silence settled between us. Finally, I broke my stupor to focus on his overzealous features staring back at me.

My eyes drifted out to the dark sea from our spot on the restaurant patio, trying to gather my thoughts and quiet my anxiety. I'd actually thought he might pop the question tonight and my nerves had only just begun to settle. Well, at least that's what I had thought until the last twenty minutes of our conversation.

My vision landed on the pristine chocolate lava cake. The one I hadn't been able to touch, which was a feat for a chocolate connoisseur like myself. The perfect piece of chocolate lay desolate, like me.

"Well, what do you think? You haven't said anything?" Azul asked with excitement. As if he'd just opened the best present, and I didn't want to play with it.

"Uh, um. Sounds nice."

"*Nice*, babe? I just spent the last twenty minutes talking about our future and your response is *nice?*" He dropped his spoon on the dessert plate with a loud clatter. My muscles clenched at the sound and I leaned back in my chair.

"Uh, well, I think that sounds like a wonderful plan for you . . . "

"For me?" he spit out. I knew this was going about as well as it could. I should have gotten out of this relationship by now. But since we had the same music label, I felt pretty stuck. Especially since Azul had made our relationship public *everywhere* he could.

I pinched my eyes together tightly. "There's just– There's just some things I haven't told you," I whispered so quietly I'm not sure he could even hear me.

His features instantly transformed. "Oh, do you not want that kind of future? Do you not want . . . kids?" he asked more gently, pleased that *he* wasn't the problem with the future he'd painted so vividly for me.

Any other woman would probably have been grinning contagiously in this gorgeous five-star restaurant, but not me. At that exact moment, a ghost from the past filled Azul's place and stared back at me. Haunted memories swept over my soul. I inhaled quickly, the sharp intake forcing my eyes to close even harder.

"No, it's not exactly about *want*, Azul," I remarked with

my eyes still half shut. And even as my eyelids fluttered open, I could see his expression change immediately, a soft smile taking over as he reached for my hand. The one that had stayed frozen on the table, but I now wished it had retreated.

"Oh, Luna. I didn't know. You've never told me." Dark creases formed amongst his face, along with pity. Maybe even for himself. *Oh God, get me out of here.* I felt like I was going to be sick. I tried to look back out to the calming sea, and to the moon that always felt like home. But it was no use. I had gone too far. Down the dark rabbit hole.

"I don't really like to talk about it," I diverged, trying to take back my hand and hoping to end the conversation. It had already been a long thirty minutes, which had felt more like a bloody century.

He tightened his hold on me. "Babe, we're celebrities. We can afford the best doctors. They can *fix* you. There are therapies and solutions. I had a family member with this *same* problem. They can give you treatments and stuff. Don't worry about it, ok? You're with me now. I'm going to make sure you get everything you need or want."

Fix me. The words haunted me. I'd needed "fixing" my whole life. Tears, I tried in vain to stop, ran down my cheeks. There was no fixing me. And Azul would certainly never be the one to do it. And to top it all off, the apparition now stared back at me even harder, penetrating the parts of me I'd kept locked away for *so long*. Like that part of me that dared to hope and believe and dream. That part of me that knew I was good enough to be loved just the way I was. That tiny little, foolish part . . . And I couldn't help but wonder what that ghost might say if he was here. I thought it might break me to find out. *Or maybe it could heal you* . . . That little voice was back, and it was dangerous . . . the little voice of hope.

No, Luna, you made your decision long ago. But as that ghost bored into my soul, offering a kind of illogical warmth, all I wanted to do was see him. My mind raced, wanting nothing more than a pen to release all my pent-up emotions. If only I could have one more hour with him. I could tell him. I could finally see . . . *You could schedule your ukulele meet-and-greet at his restaurant, Luna.* No, that thought was dangerous.

But the thought continued to taunt me well after Azul dropped me off at my door in a cloud of heavy silence. All the way until I pulled out a pen and started writing to Cece. She'd become a safety raft of sorts, a last resort. And it felt time to pull the cord again. But after all this, there was only one thing I knew with certainty: it was time to let Azul go find his future. Because it certainly wasn't with me.

Luna

CHAPTER 20

Always been told what I needed in life
Always been told how I should be loved right.

-LUNA MANU MELE, THE ONLY MAN I COULD LOVE

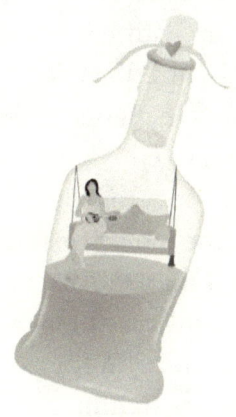

Laying poolside on a fuzzy hotel towel, the sun's warm rays soothed my aching bones and dried my pool-misted skin. This was such a wonderful bubble that I knew it couldn't exist much longer. The real world had already intruded with Azul, and it was only a matter of time until it happened again.

There was too much in my 'new' life that could burst our rosy bubble—that I was ashamed for Reef to see. I used to feel I could bring things inside our cocoon, and somehow, he would make them safe. Make any part of me feel secure. But time and space had made me believe it couldn't work that way anymore. Or maybe I just was too afraid to let him see the new parts of me.

I needed to remember why I had left our bubble—for *his* own good. I glanced over at Reef, who was "reading" his book. The one that was upside down. *Did he bring it because I was a fan and he wanted to know what I liked?* Surely not. But he kept doing things that made me think he was too good to be true.

How had Louis known Reef would be *such a* good match when he came up with his fake dating scheme? *Louis.* That was the wake-up call I'd needed to help me remember why I was *actually* here. He'd gone through a lot to help me get to this place in my life.

Reluctantly, I sat up from my lounger and began collecting my things. On more stressful and tiring days, my pain got a little worse. Like arthritis flaring when it rained. I hoped Reef wouldn't think anything of my sluggish speed. I hadn't meant to say anything in the pool, but I kept slipping back into that safe place with him.

Reef sat up slightly in response, looking over at me as I spoke. "Uh, I do actually need to get ready for a sound check and rehearsal today. But I'll text you when it's over.

Louis asked if we could go to dinner together. There's supposed to be a fantastic restaurant here with incredible views and flame throwers . . . you know, the perfect setting for us to be tourists." But at the mention of sound check, Reef started gathering his things. I reached my hand out to him. "No, you stay. Enjoy the pool and the resort. It's gorgeous here."

But of course, he wasn't listening to me. He'd already begun putting on his shirt, which saddened me *way* more than it should. Because I could still feel his arms wrapped around me from the pool, giving me the warmth only he could provide.

Heat rose to my cheeks as I remembered his words '*one big reason*', as the answer to why he was single. Those words kept racing through my mind. And I especially remembered the way he'd looked at me when he'd said them.

"I'll come with you. I'd love to see the sound check. If that's ok with you," Reef added quickly.

I smiled at his offer, seeing the kind-hearted boy I used to know so well. Maybe he really did still exist inside this man. But Reef was just too good to be true after my experiences with other men.

With anyone else, I would have said no. I didn't want any more eyes on this part of my world. But I realized I didn't want any part of my world to be off limits to him. Not if he wanted to see it. I'd already made that mistake before and I didn't want to make it again.

Before I realized it, the words were out of my mouth, "Yes, I'd love that." The smile he gave in response warmed my wet skin even more. I fumbled, "But it's not glamorous like you'd expect. No judging my many mistakes."

"Like you would make any. They'd all be happy accidents," he remarked cornily, in a way that was reminiscent of our past. "I'm just excited to see this part of your world. I've wondered about it for a very long time." His face heated with his last words.

"Really?"

"Yeah, I mean, it's not every day that your best friend from childhood grows up to become a talented celebrity."

"Oh, is that why you've wondered about it? Well, all you had to do was ask for my autograph."

"Gee, thanks. But I think I have plenty from our child-hood letters. I bet those lyrics are worth a small fortune now."

"Don't you dare—" I began. Conveniently, I had forgotten the way I signed my name on those letters. Maybe out of self-preservation. Getting a letter from him in my mailbox or locker had been the highlight of my day. I'd always felt so grown-up. Wanting to feel like an adult, I'd signed my full name when I reciprocated. Reef had said it was good practice for my career, anyway.

Reef continued, with a teasing grin plastered on his face. "And I also remember I have some burned CDs with your gorgeous voice on them. Original lyrics, too,"

"Reef!" I exclaimed. But his deep laugh made all the joking worth it. Especially his good-natured smile. "If I remember correctly, you actually helped me with a lot of those lyrics. You were pretty good at it. I guess that writer's brain of yours translates into lyrics, too. I may need to tap into your mind again. I've been pretty stuck recently. Actually, I haven't been able to write anything for quite some time now."

"Really?" He seemed surprised. "Well, just say the word. I would be honored. *One More Hour* is my favorite song . . . If I had to choose. But you probably guessed that from the helicopter ride."

Now my face flushed. "That's funny. It's the last thing I wrote. It came to me in a dream." I would not be telling him the lyrics came to me after I'd seen him at the luau. I'd been playing with fire when I'd planned my welcome gathering there. I knew *exactly* what I'd been doing. But I'd had to see him again.

"Dreaming lyrics, huh? Now, that's something I'd love to experience. You always were special." He smiled.

Yeah, the dream kept happening until I finished the song. Like a dogged art piece that my soul had to finish. My manager was especially ecstatic since it had come during a dry writing spell. After Azul stole my lyrics, his stunt hadn't only ended our relationship, but stopped my writing, too. I guess the breakthrough was à propos, since all my love songs somehow came back to Reef.

Louis had told me we all had muses in life. I just wasn't sure how I felt about mine. It was too bittersweet. But maybe that's what made good art. Because as great as it felt to go there, the repercussions always left a sting. Even if I tried to pull inspiration from anywhere else—and believe me, I'd tried—I always knew who the lyrics came back to. Him. Always him.

"That's just about the coolest thing I've ever heard," Reef intoned, enveloping me back in our bubble. "Is it your anxiety?" he asked with concern, noting my vulnerable expression. My facades didn't work with him.

"Something like that." My eyes drifted off to the cerulean blue, not wanting him to read any more into it. "Maybe I just need your help again."

"Anytime, seriously. Writing with you is one of my best memories. And I'd love to see what your writing process is like now. We can hang out on the hotel balcony and see what happens." His warm gaze tried to bring my attention back to the present. Instead, he just changed the subject. "So, are we going to do this? Or are you already regretting inviting me to a sound check?" Laughter filled his tone.

"No, I've never regretted anything with you." *Except not giving him a chance to decide what he wanted.* Maybe I *finally* should.

Luna

AGE 13

L ong, dark brown curls lay limply in my hand. *Not where they should be.* I stared harder as if I could will them back onto my scalp and return to my past life. The one I knew I had taken for granted. My life had segmented instantly into a timeline of before and after. And it was unsettling.

As the locks became damp and heavy from my tears, the inescapable urge to have Reef beside me swelled. Thoughts of all the ways he might make this moment more bearable consumed me. I selfishly wanted nothing more.

I dumped the locks into the bathroom trash can, reaching for one of my nighttime headscarves that had now become a permanent fixture on my head. The one person I wanted here the most was also the one I wanted to shield from this unbearable situation.

I startled as a knock sounded on the bathroom door. "Luna, are you alright? Can I help? You've been in there a while."

My head hung lower at my makuahine's words. Getting sick had become a dreaded constant. Nausea was becoming my faithful companion, as well as the dizziness that had accompanied a few falls. As a result, my mom was much more vigilant about checking on me. But I still preferred to leave the door closed. To mourn losses like this in privacy.

When I didn't answer, she opened the door and looked from the waste can to me. Noting the limp headscarf in my hand she said, "Here honey, let me tie that for you." She always tied scarves better than me, anyway. And relief spread over me at the suggestion. "Just sit down and rest, sweetheart," she soothed while closing the toilet lid gently.

As she worked, I relaxed into her gentle touch, and the voices in my mind quieted. The ones recalling my prognosis and unnerving treatment plan I'd heard earlier today. All the unfamiliar words and things I didn't understand, or couldn't comprehend, were causing chaos in my mind. A swimmy feeling and a thick fog distorting every sound.

Just when I was about to relent and fall into the anarchy, a humming from my mom began. One of her favorite folk songs, *Wade in the Water*, greeted me. Uncle Louis had been trying to teach me the melody on the ukulele he'd mailed to me from California. The practice went better some days than others depending on my body pain. And then there were the days I couldn't overcome the nausea that left me curled in a ball. On those days, I left my laptop open as Louis played to me. He'd sing the chord names as he played an easier song I might enjoy learning. He always picked traditional folk songs that could be jazzed up and told me how we could put our own personal touches on them.

I felt cool liquid travelers wandering down my face as I listened to my mom's beautiful voice. "Luna . . ." Her hands hesitated as she gazed down at me. "Baby, you know we're all here for you, but I think you really need to talk with your friends, too. I'm sure Reef and Locke are really worried about you. I know we thought you'd be able to go back to school by now . . ." her smooth tone trailed off. "Luna, just think about it. Ok, honey?"

But I had thought about it . . . *every day*. And after the news I'd received today, I couldn't answer any of Reef's letters. I needed to be strong and do what was best for him. And what was best for him wasn't being with me.

Reef

CHAPTER 21

" Give a man a gift and he'll be happy for a day. Give a man a dog and his life will be forever changed.

-REEF AKUA, -STRINGS OF SERENDIPITY

Upon returning to our room, I led Nova out to the balcony. That way Luna could shower and get ready in peace. But as I tugged on Nova's favorite tennis ball wedged between her teeth, it seemed that Luna's preparation was taking an extra long time. More along the lines of stalling.

"Hey, Luna!" I called, looking at Nova's cheerful face and her tight grip on the ball. "Do you think they'd mind if I brought Nova to the sound check? I think she'd enjoy going with us. I can always drop her off with Louis if not. He called and said Tutu needed some rest from traveling. I told him not to worry, to just stay with her. And that I hoped she would feel well enough to join us for dinner."

Magically, the bathroom door opened as soon as the word "Nova" met it. I was hoping the word might have that effect. Happiness spread over me as I thought about the special bond they already shared. Simultaneously, this lump formed in my throat as I glanced between two such important pieces of my life. When I turned my head back toward the room, I found Luna. She was wavering in the doorway, her bare feet arching as she rocked back and forth. The fabric of her sunflower yellow dress swishing all around her. Her scent hit me hard. Notes of lavender and vanilla wafted over to me. Like childhood scenes filling my memory.

Luna's eyes looked downward as a small murmur escaped. "Uh, let me just get some shoes."

"Ok. Yeah—" I fumbled, feeling like my awkward, twelve-year-old self again. Exactly like when she'd walk down my driveway. A nervous energy building in my stomach at the same rate at which she took steps toward me. The pounding of my heart matched them. *It's just a sound check, Reef.*

But my heartbeats only quickened at the image before me. Pieced together like a view master. Luna's hair cascading over her shoulder as she leaned over to grab her shoes. The thin straps of her dress being exposed. The ones made to hold up the gossamer fabric covering her lower back. Her bashful eyes looking back up at me. *Breathe, Reef.*

However, the view master only got more vivid. She hesitated instead of putting on her strappy sandals and continued staring at me with this glint in her eye while she walked over to me. It was a carefree look, an echo from childhood. One that asked if I was ready to go. My heart began racing even more at the flicker of trust. *Was she getting comfortable with me again?* My stomach pulsed.

"Ready?" I managed through my tight throat.

Luna nodded and gently reached for my arm. I'd dreamed about this moment around a billion times, but in my fantasies, I was suave. My nervous energy took over as I stumbled slightly forward. But Luna only held onto my arm tighter, looking up at me with an adorable smile. And at that moment, all I could think about was how that irresistible smile would taste.

I leaned into her and whispered, "Thanks. Maybe now I'm ready."

A chuckle left her, and while nodding she breathed, "Yeah, maybe we both are."

WE TOOK a taxi to the amphitheater in Waikiki, which was amply shaped like a shell. It was fit for Ariel and was the perfect festival venue. During the drive, my leg kept tapping without my permission. And to my chagrin, Luna kept glancing at it. This was an area of her life I'd never seen before. And it felt like a test. One I wasn't prepared to take. The proverbial nightmare of showing up to class in your underwear.

By the time we arrived at the event location, I looked like I was flying a la Red Bull wings. I usually went with the flow, avoiding all confrontation, but right now, I was too stuck in my head. And unfortunately, even the impressive venue couldn't ease my nerves.

I tried to take in the scenery. A gorgeous white, vaulted clamshell dome surrounded by swaying palm trees lay before us. The beautiful open-air arena reminded me of the Sydney Opera House in its style. A grand feature set against the botanical mountain hues in the distance.

At least Nova seemed to approve. Her tail began beating wildly in the air, while her nose tried to sniff out everything in sight. I glanced over at Luna skeptically. Somehow, I didn't think management was going to be thrilled with my plan to bring Nova along—especially if this was the same management Louis was so concerned about.

I could feel my muscles clench as we walked toward the hive of activity. Crew members were buzzing around the dome in double time. Despite the currently hectic pace, this setting was perfect for Luna. The atmosphere at sunset would be relaxing and magical under the Hawaiian stars. I just hoped I could help her enjoy it, too.

I reached for Luna's hand, feeling another one of those protective urges. Her head turned toward me with a surprised smile. I hoped she realized that this was real. I did everything with her because I wanted to, not because some label needed it. And I hoped she knew the difference, even if that meant I would discover her true feelings, and possibly face the same bitter rejection. But I'd missed this feeling. I wanted *her* back in my life.

"Luna, baby, you made it." Azul's voice rang out, practically echoing off the shell. Was it just me or was this guy really *irrahz*? *Who calls their peer baby?* It was super belittling and really 'annoying'. Or at least, it was when he did it. My grip tightened on Luna's hand, and her eyes drifted over to me.

"Sorry," I breathed, and she chuckled slightly. "I just–" I didn't really know how to finish that sentence. How did you say to someone, 'I want this to be one of my romance books where I scoop you up and carry you away from the super toxic guy like an overprotective macho man?' Yeah, you didn't say stuff like that. Real life wasn't a Harlequin Romance. *Get it together, Reef.*

Instead, we continued walking toward the stage. Like normal humans. More apprehension flooding my brain. I was *way* out of my element.

"Azul," Luna said aloofly. I wish she would tell him to knock it off with the trivial 'baby' nicknames–tell him to stick it where the sun doesn't shine–but she was way too nice for that. However, the look on her face said she wished she could, and a grin swept over me.

"When did you get a dog?" Azul asked curtly. "There's no way dogs are allowed at sound check." He crossed his arms decisively.

Well, I definitely had a comeback for that. But I'd keep it to myself. Was he always like this? Or had he just turned this way after their breakup? I hoped for Luna's sake it was the latter.

Now it was Luna's turn to have her hand tighten on mine. Unfortunately, that grip was nothing compared to one she used when another man's voice rang out.

A prosaic voice sliced through all our dead air. "Luna, you made it. I'm so glad. We've got everything set up for you . . . Who–Who is this?" The tall man with long curly hair kept stuttering as his eyes fell on me. His clothes were immaculate, but his dark brown hair was unkempt, as if he'd been anxiously running his fingers through it. I think the hair was supposed to be an 'artistic' look, but it didn't quite fit with his uptight business attire. He appeared to have missed 'beach charm' and was now aiming for 'boho creeper' with the number of buttons he had undone.

He reached for Luna's arm, and she flinched backward. "Luna," he leaned toward her and whispered, "You know you're not supposed to bring people with you to sound check. *Especially* not dogs." He looked at Nova as he said it. Although his disgusted tone and look now transfered to me.

"Steve, this is Reef and Nova. I'm *sure* Louis has spoken with you about them. I was told it was cleared for them to accompany me." There was an edge in her polite voice. *So her anxiety doesn't just come from the pressures of making musical content and stage performance.*

"Oh, sure. Louis mentioned *something* when we talked. Luna, you know *you* can always talk to me. Things would be less confusing if we talked directly . . . " he said soothingly, as if she was a child, looking at her with a raised brow.

"Louis has taken over all my scheduling for the time being, thank you. Where may I warm-up?" Luna asked with apathy.

Except for a barely perceptible jaw tic, he obeyed, directing her toward a calmer area, away from the crew's work on the stage. Never acknowledging Nova or me–the fly in everyone's ointment, apparently.

I watched him strut away and turned to Luna. "Are you ok?"

But Luna was lost in the colors of her jazz ukulele, as if hoping she could escape into its beautiful world of melodies. After a while, she began tuning the strings with fierce concentration.

"I'm fine. Sorry, this must be really boring for you. Hopefully, my set won't take long. They just have to make sure the sound is right for the space and that the positioning of the lighting is good, etc. Hopefully, that will all go quickly."

I bent down so I could be eye level with her, speaking softly, "Luna, hey." Her eyes wandered hesitantly up to me. I could sense there was a lot wrong here. Way more than I could hope to fix. "I'll love listening to your music. Nova and I are *both* excited to be here. That's *not* what I'm worried about. What can we do to help?"

She swallowed, then shook her head a little, as if it was a refined technique. "Be here. *Just* be here," she repeated with a smile.

A noise caused both our heads to turn. A friendly female voice came over the PC system, which was a welcome change. "Luna, can you come to the stage, please? It's time for your sound check."

Luna teased, "Ok, make sure you get a good seat. I hear it's super crowded out there." But I could see the trepidation waltzing in her eyes.

"We were promised the best seats in the house. After all, we know people. Nova has connections." I teased and watched the tension in her body melt a little. "Hey," I tugged on her hand. "We're right here, ok?"

She nodded and flashed that well-practiced smile of hers. The one that tore at me every time she felt compelled to weld it. I wanted to replace it with my lips and try my best to put one of her real ones in its place. *Whoa, Reef. Get control of yourself.*

I released her hand slowly, going against all my instincts. Instead, I wished her luck and quietly found a place out of the way to watch as she began warming up.

To the side of the stage, a petite woman wearing all black came to join me. A headset rested atop her short platinum hair streaked with lavender.

"Oh, who is this adorable guy?" she cooed. I stood there for a moment. She wasn't talking about me, right? Or did this crowd just keep getting weirder? Thankfully, in my silence, she bent down and reached her hand out to Nova. I exhaled. "May I?" She looked up at me.

"Oh, yeah, sure. She's super friendly. Lives for tummy rubs and ear scratches."

The woman grinned as she petted Nova. Actually, I think it was the first smile I'd seen around here today. It appeared pretty stressful behind the scenes. *I guess we really have no idea how much preparation goes into the relaxing performances we experience.* Blood, sweat, and tears were about right.

"You must be Reef," the woman said as she straightened. "I'm Venice."

"As in—"

"As in, you won't find one normal named person working on this crew. By way of explanation, my parents met at a Venice concert. The band formed at Venice Beach. But I prefer to think I'm named after the Italian city." I laughed as she continued, "I've heard a lot about you. All great things. And I can see why."

"Really, you seem to be the only one." I joked as more crew came through. I felt her hand land on me lightly as she pulled me over out of the way, closer to the stage's exit.

"Here." She positioned me. "You can see her perfectly from this spot. And she can look over and find you. Best seat in the house." As if on cue, Luna glanced over at me. My jaw flexed as she looked my way. "That bad, huh?" she teased.

"What?" My attention broke from Luna.

"You've got it *that bad*, huh? I knew she did, but you, well, I never know with the men Luna dates." I looked at Venice skeptically. She scoffed, "Come on, Azul is a tool. His ego is the only thing big enough to fit into a relationship."

"Are you allowed to?–"

"I'm team Luna. I'm allowed to say whatever I want. Don't worry, she was miserable with him if you're worried about his 'star power'. Really, what that means is he can tell you all the reasons his smoothie is made wrong. And all the reasons he should be the next big sensation–I can recite all of them for you. Retouching his makeup tests the limits of my willpower. And he can't name one of our names." She looked around at the crew.

I chuckled harder and Luna glanced over at me. I felt this enormous grin tugging on my cheeks. She smiled back, but her head cocked to the side. She pointed at Venice in warning, but Venice simply turned on her headset, which blasted through the PA system. "Ms. Luna, please get your beautiful, talented butt back to work." Luna shook her head, but just chuckled.

I relaxed, seeing that at least *someone* here had her back. "So, the two of you are close?"

"Oh, I'd like to think we are. We've become close friends along the way. I work for the label, so that means I usually work on whatever set she's on." I nodded. "And it's cute you were jealous of these "stars", but I'm glad to see you're relaxing. Don't worry, I've never seen a look from

Luna like the one she just gave you. And I've never seen her so relaxed. I sometimes think the nicest people attract the worst people, you know? . . . The givers attract the takers. I'm glad to see that's not the case this time." She looked at me sternly, as if saying it better not be.

"I'd like to think I'm *not* one of those guys. I've known Luna my whole life. She was my first crush, my childhood sweetheart—"

"*You're One More Hour?*" Her mouth fell ajar. So much so, it was as if I could see a lightbulb going off inside her head.

"What?" I half whispered.

Quickly, she concealed her expression. "Nothing. I rarely know what I'm talking about. I mean, look at me." She pointed to her colored hair and metallic, lavender makeup. Her silver bangles clinking along the way. "Creative here. *I'm totally delusional,*" she sang. "I'm just gonna go check Luna's mic again," Venice blurted as she left my side.

Reef

CHAPTER 22

I can still see her so clearly
a vestige of the past floating through
clouds of lavender hills
Soaking through every ounce of my memory

-REEF AKUA, THE MUSE

After a long discussion about the 'mic check,' Venice finally returned.

"It's all good," she informed me. "You know how tricky these things can be."

"Right . . ." I trailed off. "Actually, I was hoping I'd learn more about this part of her world. For example, you were saying about her song—"

Venice cleared her throat, interrupting me, and pointed toward the stage. "Look, she's about to start. Luna might have the most incredible voice, but her stage presence . . ." She sighed wistfully. "It's so intimate. It feels like you're at a coffee shop where it's just you and her—no matter how many people are around. I wish I had that gift. Luna says she gets it from her uncle. I was hoping to meet him."

Yeah, I thought to myself, *just imagine what it's like when she really is singing just for you, with no one else around.* That can just about end a guy. Or make him write a whole bestselling series for her . . .

I shook my head, clearing the fog. "Yes, but the thing about Luna is she doesn't know how good she is. Never has. I've always wanted to help her believe in herself more." I looked at her for probably too long. Surely revealing way too many of my feelings to this stranger. "Her uncle is unique, but this is definitely *all* Luna. They both have their own special stage presence. He couldn't make it tonight, but I'm sure you'll get to meet him soon."

Venice looked at me, letting the silence linger. When suddenly her voice came back with fervor. "Reef, *listen* to the lyrics."

"What? . . . I promise, I have. I love Luna's music. I have playlists with all of it on them."

"Reef, *just* listen," she said, even more emphatically. And all I could do was turn my attention toward the stage while we waited. A fleeting look in my direction from Luna took me by surprise and I exhaled heavily.

But I continued to follow her routine, watching the series of breathing exercises she knew by heart. And I could tell when she was ready to play. Her eyes barely fluttered open, and it was as if a different person had taken over for her. Then the music poured out. Her soul coming with it.

Luna began her set with one of her oldest songs. One I knew *all* too well—a constant writing companion. It had been easy to recognize Luna's favorite place amongst the lyrics: the lavender farm. The one we must have visited a hundred times. I always wondered if she'd added the romance plotline based on an experience, like I did in my books, or if it was all fiction. Perhaps based on a former boyfriend she'd taken there. But now, Venice's words clawed at the corners of my mind. And I began listening differently, maybe clearly for the first time.

> *Lost in a lavender daze*
> *I never wanted to part this way*
> *Salty, sweet air mixed up with you*
> *All wrapped up in a haze*
> *On that perfect summer day*
> *Arms intertwined, smiles combined*
> *Why can't I call you mine?*

No, there's no way. No . . . Well, if it was us, then it was a very long-ago memory. It was probably her artistic license that resulted in the extra romance. But my rational thought didn't stop the twisted feeling in my gut. Glancing at Venice, I tried to conceal my jaw from dropping as she raised an eyebrow at me.

She wasted no time speaking into a walkie talkie

connected to Luna's earpiece. "You're doing great. Amazing start. Did you decide to go with a coffee shop vibe for the show? Explain your inspiration for each song to the audience?" Luna looked over at us, her eyes slowly scanning over me. A succinct head shake followed. "That's ok, you're doing great. Just move on to the next song, then."

Luna had just begun playing when an exasperated voice sounded from behind us. "Stop coddling her. She's not a baby. She's a performer. This is what she gets *paid* to do. What people would kill to get paid for. So stop giving her choices. She is more than capable of a coffeehouse performance. I don't pay you to give options."

I didn't need to turn around to recognize Luna's manager. I'd heard stories. This guy might just be a bigger tool than Azul. *Were they holding a convention for them here?* I think the "smooth sailing" was over. The look on Venice's face suggested the same thing. But at least he continued to hang back, biting his tongue.

I was even more relieved he did because the chorus of Luna's fifth song hit me like a ton of bricks. I felt like the air had been knocked out of my lungs. I looked at Venice, who fired that knowing eyebrow at me again and nodded with a slight grin. However, I couldn't enjoy her playful manner since the world had gone a little fuzzy. Luna's words were caressing me, her husky tone warmly shrouding me.

> So long ago, you and I
> were lost in a dream
> So long ago, you were the only
> Place I could run to and be free.
> Just give me one more hour with you
> And you'll see

Just give me one more hour with you
Anytime or place will do
And I swear I'll make it back to you
Just give me one more hour
And this time, I'll be the one you need

"**NO, NO, NO!**" Steve cut in, yanking the headset away from Venice. She winced as he bent her headset mic toward himself. "No, *One More Hour* is supposed to be a duet. I thought we discussed this, Luna. Your set can end with the last song and then we can move on to something more marketable." Satisfied, he called out, "Azul, where are you?"

Marketable? My hands turned into fists by my sides. Luna did *fine* on her own. More than fine. She was incredible. I hated that word when it came to art. Nothing cheapened it faster. You had to truly believe in what you were doing with all your heart or else you sold yourself short. Not only cheapening yourself in the process, but possibly destroying yourself along the way. It was hard to live with yourself after you sold out. I would know. I felt like I'd done it one too many times. Never fighting hard enough for my full vision—for what I believed in.

My hands clenched tighter at the scene before me. I'd been witnessing vulnerable and honest beauty as I listened to Luna's voice on that stage. How could someone want to ruin that?

I saw Luna pale. "What? I thought we decided I would do that alone, in *my* set. That I would do *everything* alone. "

But in that short amount of time, Azul had already

graced everyone with his presence. Making himself quite cozy with the mic and taking center stage.

"What, Luna?" Azul teased. "Afraid I'm going to show you up. It's a beautiful song. Why don't you share, baby?"

Steve lowered his voice in what I assumed was supposed to be cajoling. "Luna, don't be difficult. This is what's best for everyone. It will help *both* of your careers," Steve said in an 'end-of-discussion' tone.

At that, Luna didn't put up any more of a fight. I saw the joy and passion slowly drain out of her, the ones which she had just beautifully expressed on the stage. Surrendering, she stood up and slid her chair over, further away from where Azul had placed his.

"Now, Luna," Steve began, waltzing onto the stage. "That doesn't really look like a love ballad. If you're going to do it, then *sell it*," he directed, moving her chair even closer to the 'ego' than it had been before. "*Like this.*"

I could see her body go taut at the proximity to Azul. Out of nowhere, I was overcome by primal instincts, I didn't know I had, toward the stage, only to be stopped by a stagehand. I looked back at Venice for help, but her pale facade told me this was not a battle we were going to win.

"Let's just see how this plays out. We're right here if she needs us. We can't do anything else," Venice said with defeat.

"I can take her home," I said, as if I had any control left.

"Steve always gets his way. At least for now, it's better to just appease him. Let her get through the number, then take her home. We'll work it out later. Doing anything else right now will make it worse."

My eyes continued to stay glued to Luna. I didn't know how to help. *What had Louis thought I could do?* I felt so powerless. And the feeling only reached a crescendo when Azul began to play and Luna clutched her chest, gasping for breath. Suddenly, my protective instincts overrode all logic. My only thought was that I had to get to her. With a fire in my core, I forced my way past the insistent stagehand holding me back.

I could hear the manager's condescending voice as I made my way to her. "Oh God, not this *again*. Luna, you freak everyone out when you do this. It looks like you're having a heart attack. Stop being so dramatic. People would give their right arm to be in your position. You *should* be thankful, not acting like you're dying." The manager's proximity to her only increased Luna's grip, white lines forming on her knuckles. "Please get the diva some water or something. Just make it st—"

But he didn't get to finish because my fist hit his jaw with a force I didn't know I possessed. A force which sent him staggering backward. I guess we all have internal protective bodyguards in us if we're pushed far enough. And my adrenaline sure met his face. At least the shock was keeping him at bay. Even Azul got off his stool and scrambled backward as I neared Luna. I'm sure the idea of anything spoiling his perfect features was enough to make him scurry away. *Good*, because I'm not sure I could land another one of those. My hand was already throbbing from my unexpected reaction.

"Luna, let's get out of here," I tried in a calming tone. But her eyes stayed closed, her fist clenched over her heart.

I wasn't exactly sure about moving anyone in this state. I'd had some experience with posttraumatic stress after Locke's water accident, but this didn't feel the same. Luna's anxiety was different. And the novice Google search I'd done before the trip hadn't prepared me near enough for this. Nothing could prepare you for this situation because everyone was unique.

In my experience with Locke, reminding him he was safe always worked best. And my instincts were telling me to do the same with Luna. Especially to get her away from her triggers. And I was pretty positive I'd identified them. This wasn't purely social anxiety.

"Luna, I'm getting you out of here," I said more forcefully, trying to reach her. My instincts had kicked in, for better or for worse, and I began carrying her.

Thankfully, Venice was right beside me. "There's a place around back where you can take her. It's close to where she was warming up. It will be private."

She directed me toward a tented area with some chairs. As beautiful as Luna's dress was, I opted for the grass. Venice helped by grabbing Nova's leash and holding her back. Nova's whines intensified as I wadded up my jacket to put under Luna's head.

"Luna, hey, you're safe. It's just us," I said as Venice nodded and slipped outside the tent. She was going to make sure we got some privacy.

"Mahina Liilii," I tried again, feeling like that boy stuck on the tree limb. But she softened at the use of her nickname, and her eyelids flickered a little. I reached for her clenched hand and put mine over hers, hoping it was alright. But it felt okay. Better than okay.

"Breathe with me, ok?" I asked her as I started vocalizing my breaths. My voice trembled slightly as I took in the pure panic and dread still written all over her face.

Her breaths remained strained. She was trying so hard to get air. I was worried she was going to hyperventilate. I really hoped Google, or that random Reddit rabbit hole, hadn't lied to me. I'd tried to pick out the techniques that I thought would work best for her. And several people had talked about mantras and visualizing places. *God, I wish I was more prepared for this. It's why I was here, after all.*

"Do you remember our lavender field?" I blurted, pretty confident of her answer after the song I'd just heard. She nodded slightly. Relief washed over me and then I began painting a picture with my words, trying to build an escape for her. After all, words were all I had. The best thing I could give her.

"Remember how the lavender smells so fresh in the crisp morning air? Can you still smell it?" She nodded slowly. "And I can still see the mist rolling in, making our skin dewy. Creating the best kind of chill bumps on us." I could finally see her breathing slow.

So I started repeating what was on my heart, the scariest thing to do. "We're safe. It's ok, because we're together." And the words kept tumbling out, over and over, until she even started saying them with me.

Slowly, her eyelids fluttered open. As if she was coming out of an inescapable, dark pit toward the light. And I'd never seen *anyone* look more beautiful. Any doubts I'd had about being tethered to another person vanished at this moment. My soul was always going to be connected to hers. I couldn't deny it any longer—not even to protect myself. Nor did I want to anymore. I was always meant to be hers.

It was like we were made for each other. Knowing each other's trauma and faults and only loving each other more for it. And so I held her. The frailty of the moment enveloping us.

In the precious space between us Luna whispered, "*Mahalo.*" Suddenly breaking the gossamer air between us, and the transformation as well.

I nodded, feeling befuddled and bewitched. Never

having wanted to kiss her more. Never feeling like I might give into the need as much as right now. Because I had to know if she felt the same way. But an ache was already forming in my chest at the possibility that she didn't want me. *Again.* I was so happy to have her back in my life; the stakes felt too high to take a risk.

Reef

CHAPTER 23

66 One day she'll realize I was always right here waiting.

-REEF AKUA, BEATS OF PARADISE

As I gazed upon Luna's face, I brushed a loose wisp of hair behind her ear, taking my time to enjoy the moment. Thankful for the peaceful smile that had spread over her face. She was coming back to me. Reminding me of how easy everything had been between us.

I leaned down slightly. The exhaustion etched into the creases of her face, came into full focus. "Can I help you to the car?" I asked softly.

"Um . . . I just need a few more minutes. Thank you." Her eyes drifted away, already looking too heavy to stay open. The attack had apparently drained her body's resources. *I had no idea what an attack was like.* I wish I did. I wish I could relate and know how to help her. Ignorance isn't bliss. Not with the people you love.

Instead, I cleared my throat, casting off all questions. "Of course. I'll make sure no one comes in. You're safe here. *I promise.*" I lightly squeezed her unclenched hand. Then I went outside the tent in search of Nova so Venice could get back to work.

Pushing back the flap of the tent, a wide-eyed Nova and Venice greeted me. "Thank you. I really appreciate it. As much as Nova helps Luna, I think that would have been overwhelming."

Venice nodded, her lips parted as if debating her next words. So, I went first. "Does that happen a lot?"

"What, Steve being an overbearing jerk or Luna's panic attacks?" She retorted.

"Both . . . Now that you say it like that," I replied, trying to glean something from her facial expressions.

She heaved. "This is *not* the first attack I've witnessed. And they've steadily gotten worse this year." Venice quickly glanced over her shoulder. "Look, if you weren't the guy from her childhood who she's talked so dearly about, I wouldn't be telling you this. I don't share other women's personal information . . . especially in this industry. Women in this business frequently face inequality and unfair treatment."

I stared steadily into her eyes. "Venice, you can trust me. Meeting Luna is one of my first and best memories of life. That's how long I've known her. And I'd do anything for her."

"I have a feeling it's the same for her as well." She raised an eyebrow at me and I lobbed mine back.

Venice exhaled. "Reef, there are guys in any industry that like to take advantage of women. I guess it's a nice power trip for them. Or maybe they just do it because they can. I don't know, I don't want to waste my time in that head-space. But this industry appears to be pretty ripe with those types. Luna was good for Azul's image and career. Meaning, I don't think it was easy to break up with him. So, I imagine the relationship had to be pretty bad for her to do that since Luna likes to keep things 'pleasant.'"

"Yeah . . . I kind of imagined, unfortunately. He doesn't exactly give off 'woke' masculine energy. But Steve–"

"Well, Steve doesn't like being turned down. *Repeatedly.* Especially when he's in a position where he thinks that *shouldn't* happen. Now, he's just making Luna's life harder for his own pleasure. He wins either way. Like I said, these men like to see *what* they can get away with."

"Yeah, I'm seeing that . . ." I was also seeing red.

"Reef, she needs to break her contract. It might be hard to find another label who will sign a ukulele musician–especially a label that has as much reach and offers as good a deal–but she's got to do something. Once you see how to improve your mental health, you should take the opportunity. Or that's my advice, which I know I have no right giving."

"No, thank you. I need it. We've been out of touch for a while. And I don't–" I couldn't believe I'd known Luna so well–known every detail of her life–and now I was an outsider. How did this happen?

"There's a lot we both don't . . . " Venice trailed off, shaking her head.

My jaw tensed. "When you say turned down? Do you mean romantically?" I drew out the last word.

Venice's eyes went stony as she nodded. "Luna won't say anything, but I don't think he continued asking her *nicely*. He controls her career and contract. Unbalanced power and threats are a swell brand of abuse." Sarcasm laced her tone.

"Right." I gritted my teeth, knowing exactly that type. Because I'd seen all the types sit at the bar. But I never once thought Luna would be the woman sitting across from them. I'd always thought she was with some fantastic guy who would take care of her. Better than I could.

I felt sick to my stomach. I had to get Luna out of here *now*. Those strong primal urges were taking over every part of me. Again.

"Thanks for being such a good friend and watching out for her," I said.

But Venice only smiled weakly. "She's a good friend to me, too. I just wish there was more I could do. I feel pretty powerless." With a downcast gaze, she went off toward the stage.

I let my eyes lay downcast for a moment, too. Then I went back into the tent, this time with Nova in tow. A smile quickly reaching my lips at the sight of Luna sleeping soundly on the grass.

I was just about to find somewhere to wait while she rested and let my adrenaline level off when she stirred. Luna's features immediately lit up when she caught sight of Nova. A large exhale of air left my lungs, which I didn't know I'd been holding.

I gently guided Nova over to her, trying to restrain the massive face bath and neck licking I knew Luna was about to receive. But Luna enthusiastically reached for her and I relented. She seemed to enjoy the doggie affection, giggling as she received endless doggie kisses. Nova's tail rapidly wagged to appraise me of how she felt about the situation: it was the perfect position for surprise doggie kisses.

Luna petted Nova affectionately, whispering to her, "Hey, you. I missed you, too." Then she looked up at me. "Hey, you," Luna repeated.

And when I realized that adorable smile was for me, I think my legs buckled. *Were guys allowed to go weak in the knees?* Probably not, especially according to my father's 'man handbook'. But I think I just did. It felt like little fires were taking off all throughout my bloodstream. With just one look. *How does she keep doing these things to me?* After twenty years, you'd think I'd have some Luna immunities.

"Hey, you," I tried "nonchalantly," as I bent down beside her. "Are you ready to get out of here? You look *way* too beautiful to be lying on the grass. Plus, I have a very fancy dinner and sunset planned at the hotel. Well, your uncle planned it, which is probably a good thing. But I'm going to take credit because I need all the help I can get. I'm adding a walk under the stars and an impromptu dip in the ocean. So, it counts." I teased.

Luna shook her head as she chuckled. "You must feel bad for me—You refrained from making a skinny-dipping joke. And it was *so* easy."

"Well, it's implied," I teased. "Guess Louis should have planned the whole evening, after all."

Luna actually snorted at that. "You're not fooling anyone, Reef. You're the most romantic guy I know. I'm sure it's all you. Fancy dinners aren't your thing. And I love you so much for it. You'd rather eat by candlelight over a meal you prepared on your balcony, and that makes me so happy. Or at a tropical taco truck." She winked.

"Yeah, well, the patio is supposed to be gorgeous. I think you'll really enjoy it. *If* I can persuade you to sit up."

"I'm being persuaded . . ." she mused with an upward twitch of her lips.

"Yeah . . . well, there will be a lot of candlelight . . . ocean waves serenading us in the background . . ." She pretended to think about it. "I'll even get one of those tropical flowers for your hair."

"You'd do that for me?" she asked coyly.

"Luna, I'd do anything for you. I think you know that," I said as lightheartedly as I could manage.

She chuckled slightly and sat up to look at me. Laughter vanished when our eyes became level with each other, meeting in this kismet way. One that felt like it had been waiting for us. We both swallowed hard, our eyes sinking deeper into each other's, while Nova squirmed her way onto Luna's lap.

"Me too, Reef. *Me too.*" Luna's sweet words continued to echo softly in the air. Not a note of laughter to them.

Reef

CHAPTER 24

'Just breathe with me,' he repeated as the world seemed to melt away. And he continued to repeat it until there was nothing but her and their breaths, which sounded like calm waves. And he wouldn't have had it any other way.

-REEF AKUA, PASSION IN PARADISE

Once Luna had been "persuaded," I gently helped her to the car. Inside, I told the driver where we were going, and she nestled against my shoulder. Repositioning herself until she was as close as possible, which sent insatiable warmth rippling over my skin.

While we held each other, her skin's pallor transformed into a lovely rosy hue. The one I adored that was so full of life. "Thank you, *again*," she said into my shoulder, burrowing further into me.

"Of course—"

"No, really." But her insistent words became groggy. "You don't understand what this means to me. You're really—" However, her speech had become heavier, and then suddenly nonexistent. And as much as I wanted to hear the rest of that statement, I couldn't bear to wake her. There was finally a look of peace resting on her face.

I had severely underestimated how draining these attacks would be for her. I had little frame of reference. Locke never talked about his experience, not any more than he had to. And I was beginning to realize there was *a lot* to learn. A lot to experience with someone.

When we pulled up to the hotel, I rocked her lightly. "Hey, we're here. You feel good enough to go inside? I can call Louis and ask him to move dinner a little later."

Luna shone a sleepy smile at me and then looked away, her eyes traveling somewhere else. As if she'd gone somewhere else, too. "Sorry, I just feel kind of strange after one of these. It makes me exhausted."

I put my fingers under her chin and brought her gaze back to mine, something I had learned from her. "Hey, no. Don't apologize. There's *nothing* to be sorry or embarrassed about. We were unapologetically ourselves around each other as kids, and I really loved that." She looked down, as if that was too hard to believe, and I bumped her chin up playfully. Her melodic laugh reminded me of home.

"Yes. I did too. But that was *a long* time ago, Reef. I'm still getting my sea legs with you. The last twenty years have hard wired some things into me more than I care to admit." *Shame, embarrassment. . . guilt.* I understood. All too well. And her words hurt.

Maybe I should have been more persistent in my attempts to communicate. But after a while, a guy gets the message. And to continue trying just felt pathetic.

"The last two decades have been rough on me as well, Luna." Her eyes held fiercely onto mine. As if my words had unlocked something. And all I could do was hold on in those raging seas.

But then she sunk me. "It's really nice to have my best friend back." *Friend.*

The corners of my lips tilted upward, and I opened the car door for her.

She hesitated, wavering, as if she hadn't finished. I was going to ask if she was okay, but it suddenly seemed possible that she might be debating pulling a "runner" and disappearing for another decade. My lungs sighed with relief when she stepped out of the car to join me instead.

"It feels like we can conquer the world together again." She added, chuckling. "Don't let today be a judgement for anything, ok?"

"No Luna." I looked directly into her lush hazel eyes. "I think what you did today was brave. I couldn't go back on stage if I knew there was a possibility of another attack. That's strength, Luna. That's true beauty. Don't let anyone tell you otherwise. They're just trying to dim your light if they do. Or seeing fear within themselves."

Sheltered by the hotel's grand portico, her gaze swept

across my face. Nova, unphased, came bounding out of the car to join us.

"No, Reef. What you saw today was weakness. *Everyone* thinks so." Her features wilted.

"Venice doesn't see it that way. I'm sure Louis doesn't, either. And I definitely don't. I wouldn't worry about Mr. Ego's brainwaves. Or his toxic twin. Their waves are too small to register, anyway." I nudged her playfully, and a small smile spread across her lips. "Come on, I have a very fancy five-star dinner planned. I even packed a tux. Louis said to pack like I was James Bond on vacation. I chose the Sean Connery version."

Luna rolled her eyes with laughter. "Only you. You just want to say 'shaken, not stirred.'"

"Of course I do. I also want the cool retro attire from the 60s, thank you." She laughed harder. "The most gorgeous women were with him, as I recall."

She pointed at me firmly. "If you call me Octopussy–"

Laughter rumbled out of me. In my best Connery impersonation, I said, "Well, see here, Octo, I have been quite the excellent sport. I think I deserve some fun."

"You're lucky you changed that nickname." Luna shook her head, walking ahead of me. She called out to me, "Louis has enabled you way too much," as she began making her way toward our room. I stood there dazed and utterly happy. Then I let my feet catch up to her.

When we reached the room, I could tell Luna still wasn't fully herself. But she continued to tell me she was fine. Another brave front.

"Luna, would you like to rest for a minute? We're not in a rush. You can make me wait as long as you like. Nova will appreciate the company." She chuckled. "I can make you some lavender tea or you could take a lavender bath."

She raised a brow at me. I felt the need to explain, "I packed some lavender things for you—since you appeared interested when we talked about them at my apartment. I thought maybe it would help with the stress of this festival."

"You brought lavender with you?" Her eyes swelled as she stood before me in the entryway.

"Yes, an embarrassing amount and variety, too. So can you at least sit down on the balcony and take a little time to rest to make me feel better?" I teased.

She smiled, those large hazels looking up from under her thick lashes. "I can't believe you packed lavender for me."

"Well, that's what a good bodyguard does. He makes up for his lack of muscles with herbal flowers. Making him *such* a bigger threat." Laughter flowed out of her as she gave me a hug. She stayed with her head on my chest for a long time, tightening her hold around my waist. "Luna, this is not sitting. You're disobeying bodyguard orders, so I may have to employ more types of exotic flowers. It could get ugly . . ."

She looked up at me with a grin large enough to bridge the islands. One I hadn't seen since she wore the flower crown when we were kids.

Her teasing tone sang out, "I'm going, I'm going. I wouldn't want that to happen."

Once she made her way, I used the suite coffee maker station to brew some tea. Then I took two cups for us to enjoy out on the balcony. After a couple of sips, I could see her shoulders relax and I felt my body do the same. That Luna shield was dropping. And I hoped she would see it was okay to still feel her emotions and be herself—*all of herself*—with me.

WHILE LUNA FRESHENED UP, I called Louis' room. I wished I'd had better news about the sound check, especially since I knew he would blame himself. But I was the one who was supposed to be watching out for her. I assumed everything was settled, and she'd just run through her set. Little did I know.

Even though Louis tried to reassure me, I'd hung up with a sense of failure. So, I tried to focus my attention on fastening the rest of the buttons. At the same time, Luna came out, and my eyes did a double take. If I thought her swimsuit was problematic, her current look was far worse.

My eyes lingered up the nape of Luna's neck to where her dark hair elegantly twisted into an updo. She was wearing the same yellow dress from earlier in the day, yet it somehow looked completely different. I didn't know you could 'freshen' something up that much. Her whole back was on display now, causing me to wonder what had happened to the floral lace that had run across her back earlier. *Was this a commando situation? Is that what it's called for women? Stop it, Reef. You've already crossed too many fake lines.* Because none of them felt fake to me.

"Reef? Are you ok?" she asked, stopping in front of me. "Do you need help with those buttons?" *What buttons? Oh, mine. Right, I have those.* I'm pretty sure she'd pushed all of them. She'd already helped more than enough.

"Uh, yeah. I mean, no?" She laughed at my befuddled words. "Just trying to figure out how you went in and came out wearing the same thing, but—" I was going to stop while

I was ahead. I was also going to look at her face more. A lot more.

"That's the power of a travel dress."

"Ok, sure." I said in disbelief.

"It's the lack of a bra, isn't it? Bond could totally handle this, you know?" She sighed, crossing her arms. "My lymph nodes swell and hurt sometimes. So, it's not super fun to wear one. But if you're going to be twelve . . ."

"I actually think I would have handled this better when I was twelve." I joked. She shook her head and headed for the bathroom again, but I reached for her arm. "No, I'm only joking. It's fine. I'll get over taking out a gorgeous celebrity in a little while. Probably after dinner is over, but it *will* happen."

"Oh good. So, you'll be normal for our walk on the beach." Luna jested.

"Yeah, I wouldn't count on it. Isn't there something baggy and unattractive you can wear?"

"Yes, twelve-year-old you definitely wouldn't have said that." And with that, Luna simply headed for the door, abandoning me with my pounding pulse. I swallowed and tried to finish my buttons *again*, but I was failing miserably. Especially as I took in the bare curves of her gorgeous back. I didn't know a back could be so incredibly sensuous. *Well, leaving the buttons undone can be a Bond thing. It's going to have to be at this rate.*

"Come on, Casanova." I heard Luna sing out.

"I think you have me confused with his helpless brother who didn't make any of the history books," I called as I hurried up to her. My hand extended to find a spot on her back, but then I thought better of it. Bare skin wouldn't help this primal side of me. We were off duty and I'd gone back into the friend zone. Except 'safe' didn't feel like what

I wanted anymore. Luna's song lyrics amidst Venice's words were *daring* me to be bolder. But only 'daring'. *That* was the problem. I didn't know how to be bold with her anymore.

As we rode the elevator, my eyes gazed upward, trying to help keep my mind on platonic things. Or at least think of malnourished dogs at the pound to help kill my Luna buzz.

"It's not that bad, Reef." Luna's playful tone greeted me.

"You look like my teenage dreams and my grown-up fantasies all rolled into one. So yeah, it is *that* bad." I looked over at her to see how much damage I'd done. Those light almond cheeks had gone pink. So I'd say a lot. It was no use. I couldn't hide my feelings anymore. Not that my attraction to Luna had ever been much of a secret, but now it seemed really out of control.

To my surprise, I felt a warm hand slip into mine. That feeling of comfort I'd so desperately craved came over me. "Yeah, and you look like *all* of mine."

"Right." I guffawed. "I'm sure a lanky bartender really does it when ripped guys are fighting over you."

Slowly, she turned with this determined glint and she started coming closer to me. The look in her eyes made the hairs on my arm stand on end. "There's *no* competition." Her sultry voice floated over to me and my body inched closer to hers in response. *Magnetized.* Just as Locke had said.

The gap between us continued to wane as my pulse thrummed in my ears. The tension building between us felt thick and palpable. Like the only way to breathe was to expel it. I tugged on my collar as if to loosen it.

Ding. Suddenly, the elevator doors began parting and Louis' voice came crashing into our cocoon.

Reef

CHAPTER 25

T hat omnipresent thought reverberated in his head again. 'No one would ever be her.'

-REEF AKUA, ECHOES OF THE ISLANDS

"There they are—" Louis' chipper words fell off, as if diving off a cliff. Instantly, I moved away from Luna.

There were *no* publicity cameras in this elevator. *No* purpose for me to be this close to her. *No* reason whatsoever for me to do what I'd been waiting to finish for over two decades now.

All the while, Louis' eyes drifted back and forth between us, as if wondering what he had interrupted.

"Aloha, 'Anakala," Luna said without missing a beat. She gracefully slid out of the elevator, leaving me in a wake of romantic stupor. "I'm glad we finally have some time to spend together," she said, wrapping both Louis and Tutu into a hug.

But Louis already protested. "Luna, I feel terrible about earlier—"

"Don't. I had Reef. And I've got to learn how to fight my own battles." She directed a stern expression at him as his features turned pained, appearing to disagree. *We can all use help. No one should have to fight alone.*

Tutu spoke up, interrupting their debate. "It's my fault. I wasn't feeling great. I think traveling got the better of me."

My lips turned downward. I'm sure it did. Being in a new place had to be difficult with her memory problems. And I'm sure traveling didn't help. I'd gone through the same experience with my grandmother recently. And I hated to see it slowly taking over Tutu's life as well.

I cleared my throat. "It's definitely not your fault, Tutu. Besides, what are fake, protective bodyguard-boyfriends for, anyway?" I joked. That's as close as I could get to my very unlikely and ambiguous title. I'd do anything to protect and help Luna, but I'm pretty sure this feat was out of my reach. I'd have to be some type of macho genie.

"Yes," Luna chimed in. "He's definitely living up to his title. He even punched somebody today in order to protect me."

"You *punched* someone?" Louis' tone was heavy with disbelief. "I was mostly joking about the bodyguard thing. I didn't know—" He stopped himself. Yeah, none of us knew I had this in me. I was a people pleasing pacifist. "Well, sounds like you certainly rose to the occasion, son. Thanks for taking your job *so* seriously."

"No, do *not* congratulate him," Luna scolded. "He can't go around punching people, especially at my work . . . and particularly *not* my manager." But there was an upward tug at her lips. She'd never encourage violence, but I had a feeling she thought Steve might think twice before mistreating people in the industry again. At least for a little while.

"Well, of all the men that had it coming—" Louis started.

"There's always Azul," I chimed in.

"Oh, how could I forget about him?" Louis scoffed. "Yeah, looks like you didn't throw enough punches today, son. Go full *Rocky* on them next time, please."

"*Uncle*, Reef has probably never thrown a punch before in his life. Don't ruin him—"

Louis looked at my face, where all the blood in my body seemed to have rush to. "Is that true? You threw your first one for her?" I nodded, gathering even more heat. Another unmanly moment for my father's scrapbook. "Well, that's oddly romantic. Certainly nothing to be ashamed about. You were just saving it for someone special. Not that violence is the answer," Louis said with an overt proudness in his eyes. One that tugged on my heartstrings. Probably *way* more than it should. Growing up, I didn't really have male figures to look up to in my life. Thankfully, Louis had a knack for becoming everyone's cool grandpa, the one you always wanted. Or at least I did.

Luna exhaled slowly, and Tutu laughed. "In a way, dear, it's kind of sweet. Sounds like Steve really had it coming, not that I normally condone violence, either."

"If you met him, you would want to," Louis remarked.

"Let's just forget about him and get something to eat," Luna suggested briskly as she pulled lightly on Tutu, directing us toward the restaurant. But my feet felt frozen, and I hung back with Louis.

Louis looked ahead at the ladies, making sure they were out of earshot. He whispered to me, "You're going to want to ice that." And nodded at my hand. Then he lowered his voice even more. "So, how did it happen?"

"Uncle," Luna called, and he mouthed 'later' to me. His lips quirking upward mischievously.

However, a moment later, seriousness settled on his brow. "*Mahalo*, Reef. I mean it. I knew you'd keep her safe. But I promise, I didn't know this would be part of it. Is she still shaken up from her attack?"

"Well, she appears to be feeling better. I found her a spot to rest after we tried breathing through it."

Louis nodded thoughtfully, processing. "You know, most guys would have freaked out and abandoned her." It wasn't a question. Maybe even a relay of the past.

He paused. "She's usually pretty drained after one of her attacks. This is the best I've seen her after one. I mean, she's fantastic at putting on a good front for everyone, but she seems really solid this evening." He held my gaze, searching. "Reef, I don't know what happened in the past, but things are *different* now."

What? What does that—"I don't—"

"Things could be different this time," he raised his eyes pointedly. As if implying more than I was ready to process. *Was it that obvious that I'd never stopped loving her?*

"I don't know what?—" But I didn't get to finish since we'd reached the hostess stand at the hotel's outdoor dining venue. Louis' expression had stayed in a permanent, 'don't act dumb with me, son' position while his retro fedora loomed, accentuating the look. I simply swallowed and nodded because it felt like that's what a young man should do when faced with a pop star's wise and protective—and equally famous—uncle.

After joining the group, the hostess escorted us through a sea of elegantly lit tables to one overlooking the ocean. As we walked, traditional music performed by a local band swelled in the background and mixed with the rhythm of the waves meeting the shoreline. Crackles from a nearby fire pit hummed in my ears as the bright blaze from tiki torches outlining the walkway lit up the night.

And now I felt bad for all the fun I had made at Locke's expense for being so overwhelmed by Hawaii's romantic atmosphere when he'd met his girlfriend. Because it sure wasn't funny anymore. I certainly wasn't immune. No, I was drowning in the romantic vibes.

I gulped as I looked around and reflexively loosened my collar again, which was already undone. Quickly, I pulled out a chair for Luna and watched as Louis' smile bloomed. He'd continued to watch us closely, as if he could sniff out what was 'fake' and what was 'real'. He had quite the determined look crinkling his forehead, making the pit of my stomach twist even tighter.

Louis cleared his throat, pushing up his rolled sleeves in tandem. "So, please remind me how the two of you first met. I believe it was quite a while before you started dating, wasn't it?" He might as well ask if we were dating now. That's what he wanted to know. But I guess he was just getting warmed up.

Tutu put her hand over his, squeezing firmly. "Louis, they *just* sat down. At least let the poor man order before you interrogate him. I was much better behaved with Guin and Locke. And that was a double date. Luna and Reef are supposed to be off the clock, remember? You have no excuse."

Louis chuckled deeply. "Sorry, you're right, Lani. Reef, please order quickly."

Tutu tapped his hand playfully. "Tsk, tsk Louis. Plus, I know their story very well. I'm sure you do, too. I even witnessed it." Louis just shook his head, but perhaps he was playing dumb.

Tutu laughed. "Fine, I'll indulge you. It is rather cute . . . Locke dared Reef to climb up my banyan tree at his birthday party. As we all know, Reef is pretty terrified of heights. Apparently, going up is not the same as coming down. And well, Locke felt terrible about the dare, so he came to get me for help. Unfortunately, the other kids were being pretty mean and already making fun of him. But when I came back out, there was this tiny girl who had almost climbed to the very top of the tree."

I swallowed hard and looked over at Luna. *Was this mist in my eyes? Great. Why was I always so emotional with this woman?*

"Tutu looked at me gently. Do you want to finish, Reef?" I guess everyone had taken notice. It was pretty apparent—and embarrassing. My un-masculinity was on full display, *yet again.*

But staring into Luna's eyes made me forget all about that outside noise. Somehow those eyes always made me forget about all the bad things in the world and see the good . . .

"She was so tiny," I breathed, gazing at Luna, getting lost in her. Everything else disappeared, just like it had that day of the tree incident. "I was shocked that she would climb all the way up that tree to me. And I remember watching her sit so calmly beside me on the tree branch. The one I had adhered myself to like a scared monkey. But suddenly things shifted, and I never wanted to leave. For other reasons, obviously." I let out a stilted laugh and Luna beamed.

"That is a *very* accurate description," Luna replied teasingly.

"And then she talked me down. I think more than anything, I just wanted to show the beautiful girl I could. Plus, she was going down, and I wanted to spend more time with her. If she'd stayed on the branch, I'd have happily stayed there *permanently*." I joked.

"Yeah, I kind of realized that." Luna laughed as well. "I already had such a big crush on you, it was hard to make myself climb down. I rather enjoyed our time up there."

"Really?" I asked, taken aback, and she nodded. "I thought you were just taking pity and rescuing me."

"But—" Tutu interrupted, "I thought you just met."

"No," I said. "Our first meeting involved flower crowns when my family moved into the neighborhood. But the timing was pretty close."

Tutu gasped with a sparkle in her eyes. "Oh, that's right. I should have realized you would have met before, but I don't know about a flower crown."

"Princess crown," Luna teasingly corrected me.

"Yeah, definitely a princess crown," I reaffirmed. "I sure felt like I'd met one. You were so beautiful." I could see moisture gathered at the corners of Luna's eyes at my words.

Louis had stayed pretty silent, his eyes continuing to linger between us like he was trying to decode hieroglyphics. But he spoke up at that remark. "You don't say, Reef . . . So did you already have a crush on Luna, too? Were you two literally 'sitting in a tree' as the song goes? Or did it happen later for you?"

"Oh, uh." My hands fumbled the place setting as his questions took me off guard. Or maybe it was the fact that he'd caught my hungry eyes, which hadn't stopped staring at his niece.

"Uh, no, sir." I began. "No, I was gone the minute I put on that flower crown we made together and she smiled at me." Luna's eyes searched mine. An overwhelmed expression taking over her features.

I thought Louis was going to continue, but all that surrounded us was an overbearing silence and this moment.

"So, when did you realize you still?–" Louis' voice cut through the air and then halted as if frozen in time. Out of the corner of my eye, I saw Tutu squeeze his hand tightly.

"Enough interrogation, Louis. I'm sure they've had a long day and want to relax. You know what sound checks are like. And you're supposed to help them de-stress from their long day." She reminded him.

Louis nodded and looked over at Tutu, his smile only grew as his eyes landed upon her. As if he was seeing her for the first time. Like he hadn't taken the time to admire her properly this evening in her gorgeous, soft yellow plumeria print dress. And it seemed like he couldn't absorb enough of her. As stares intertwined, their love felt so palpable—even after all these years.

I'd heard their story from Locke, but I still had so many questions. And now it felt only fair. I probably shouldn't have opened the floodgates for questions, especially since Tutu had been kind enough to get me out of the investigation spotlight, but I was too curious. They appeared to have answers you didn't want to miss your chance to hear.

"So, were you two childhood sweethearts as well? What is your secret for staying so in love?" I asked.

"Yes, Reef," Tutu lauded me. "Put Louis in the interrogation chair. He deserves it."

But Louis just continued to look at her softly and chuckled. "Ok, Reef, that's only fair. I haven't taken it particularly easy on you with the questions tonight. Luna is very special to me. But I have to say you've risen to the occasion *repeatedly.*" He turned his gaze to look at Luna with some cryptic meaning. One which made her chest rise in response.

"Well, that was some good deflection." I teased as the server brought us menus and we ordered some drinks. But I could feel us all pretending to look over our menus while we waited for Louis to answer.

"We're all waiting." Tutu teased further, squeezing Louis' hand and leaning against his shoulder. In the silence, Louis had continued to edge his chair closer to hers while she snuggled even further into him. They were beyond adorable. They made each moment count, savoring every one of them. Like each one could be the last. Maybe that was the secret.

"Well, I met Lani when I was eighteen, so not quite childhood sweethearts, but I do feel like I've known her my whole life. It did from the start." He got lost in her eyes again. And I knew the feeling all too well. The moment I met Luna, it was like I'd always known her. Like I was always meant to. I couldn't imagine it happening any other way.

Louis' voice brought me back. "But we were actually apart for most of our life. I'm sure Locke has told you the

story. How we *only just* reconnected . . . thanks to his help."
He looked at me, emphasizing that last part.

"Yes, sir. Locke told me a little about your story. It's really sweet. I've always been a hopeless romantic, I guess. Not exactly something you hear about a guy being—"

Louis spoke up and, as he did, I felt someone lean against me. I didn't realize during Louis' interrogation that Luna had drifted toward me. Her body heat enveloping me as her arm intertwined with mine. All complete with her head resting delicately on my shoulder. Her movements echoed Tutu's, and it unfurled this warmth inside of me. Especially when Luna's eyes tenderly drifted up to meet me. There was a fondness in them—maybe even proudness-that overwhelmed me.

Louis' velveteen voice cut through my thoughts. "Being a hopeless romantic isn't a bad thing, especially for a man, Reef. Creative and sensitive men don't have to finish last. I sure didn't." He gazed over at Tutu. "But in answer to your question of how one stays in love for so long, I'd say it all depends on the person you're with. Taking a chance on reconnecting with Lani was the best thing I ever did. Heck, taking a chance the first time was also the greatest thing I ever did, because it meant I got a *second chance* later."

My eyes opened, thinking about what Louis had just said. I had to agree. . . I wouldn't trade my first experience with love for anything. No matter how it ended.

Louis studied me, lost deep in thought. "The timing wasn't right at first, but if I had held onto that and had not tried again, I would have missed out on the best thing that ever happened to me. And I'm thankful *every day*. I think being grateful for the person you're with deepens your love in unbreakable ways. Maybe that's the key—being thankful for your person and *who* they are. For what makes them special and how they make you feel special in return."

I saw moisture glisten in Tutu's eyes. "Louis–" She tilted her head up and kissed him softly. The love I was witnessing made this bravery bubble to the surface. Because, as Louis was implying, the worst option was not trying at all. His words, 'things are different this time', were finally making more sense. Or becoming more believable.

Tutu slowly pulled back to look at Louis, remarking, "I think that's the best advice I've ever heard. I'm so grateful for you too. *Every day.*" The couple across from us was completely carried away by each other. So much so that I wondered if dinner was going to be forgotten altogether. But I didn't care, I just wanted Luna close. And I got my wish as she continued to snuggle closer into me, the heat inside me only continuing to grow. Until it felt like an uncontrollable forest fire, one I didn't know how to put out. Nor did I want to.

Reef

CHAPTER 26

That omnipresent thought reverberated in his head again. 'No one would ever be her.'

" **-REEF AKUA, ECHOES OF THE ISLANDS**

Gradually, Tutu and Louis came back to "re-join" us at the table. And we fell into the congenial rhythm of sharing stories from our childhood. I forgot how many embarrassing stories Tutu and Luna knew. But to be fair, I knew my fair share of Luna stories, too. And the rest of dinner was filled with more laughter than I'd had in a long time. It seemed maybe the same was true for Luna, as her 'proper' posture continued to melt, especially as she closed the distance between us throughout the night. Something I'd missed deeply.

All was calm until the dessert came. Apparently, Louis thought we needed a little push in the right direction. Or a huge one. Showing so much affection wasn't just playing with fire between us. We'd also tempted Louis too much.

Louis' eyebrow arched as he watched Luna and I share the rest of our molten lava cake. Obviously, we'd been *way* too playful with each other. And I had a feeling that his matchmaking, or inquisition, was about to become a little more blatant.

I was absentmindedly enjoying spoon fighting with Luna over the chocolate like old times when Louis cleared his throat. As he watched our utensils dance across the plate, he intoned, "Why don't you relax after dinner? Maybe take a late-night swim? I didn't see anyone using the pool. Looks pretty romantic all lit up at night. A shame for no one to use it."

Our spoons skidded to a halt. He might as well have suggested skinny dipping the way his whiskey tone drew it out. Perhaps he had the way everyone's jaw dropped, and it went over my head.

"Louis," Tutu reprimanded.

"What? I just suggested a late-night dip? Why is everyone looking at me like that? I didn't say skinny dipping? What? Is it because I lived in California so long

you think it's implied, because I think that's discrim-
inatory?"

We all burst out laughing. "Louis," Tutu began. "I think
'romantic dip' implied what you were thinking, but now we
all know for sure. And it wasn't your 'Californication.' It
was that smoky tone of yours and the way you wield it."

"Well, let me rephrase then," he said with flushed cheeks,
moving his fedora slightly to occupy his hands. "Would you
like to take an extremely boring and platonic swim at the hour
of ten p.m. in the vast pool that's lit by fluorescent lighting,
which is not at all romantic in the slightest, set under the
ugliest Hawaiian clusters of plasma spheres?" He inhaled
sharply, having said it all in one *very* long breath. You could tell
he played the sax. That man had some serious lung capacity.

"Did it hurt for you to say that, *Ku'uipo?*" Tutu teased.
Her term of endearment seemed more pointed than usual.

"Yeah, a little. I think that's the most sterile sentence
I've ever spoken." Louis laughed, nervous fingers running
over his suspenders.

"Now, *I* want to take a romantic swim under the beautiful Hawaiian stars." Tutu looked at him with a raised
eyebrow.

Louis swallowed and then composed himself. "You're
just taunting me with things I can't say now." He looked at
her in mock sternness and everyone laughed.

"Well," Luna began, to everyone's relief. "Reef has
already promised to take me for a walk on the beach
tonight." She turned her head to me, a starry look catching
me off guard.

Apparently, I wasn't the only one to see it because Louis
glanced at me with fatherly approval. I couldn't believe that
this infinitely cool man, whom I admired so much, was

giving *me* that look. Something had shifted between us tonight. Now he seemed just as concerned about me as he was about Luna. Maybe my heart was just that transparent and fragile. No, I knew it was when it came to her. It always had been. But it never used to stop me. I used to be brave, at least when it came to love. *When did I stop?*

"I think that sounds absolutely perfect, Luna." Louis grinned widely. "Way better than my idea." Everybody laughed at his words. "And you know, it seems like just the *right* time for it." He looked at me with all the meaning in the world.

AFTER THE LAST bite of chocolate, Tutu and Luna excused themselves to 'powder their noses'–a term I had not heard since *my* tutu last said it to me, and a phrase only the duo could make sound adorable. As we waited for their return, Louis and I were left staring at each other.

Finally, Louis propped his elbows on the table and cleared his throat, shattering the awkward silence. I leaned forward in anticipation, but he just sat back in his chair and crossed one leg over the other. His iconic move.

I breathed out and Louis propped himself back up on the table, closer this time, and cleared his throat again.

"Sir," I said, my nerves finally having frayed by his stilted movements.

"Reef." His smooth tone shifted to a serious one.

"Yes?" *Oh no, what did he want to say? I should have stayed silent.* He'd already 'said' a lot at dinner.

"You know I'm pretty close to Locke, right? He *is* Lani's grandson. And he's like a grandson to me, too."

"Yes sir, I'm aware. Locke is a great guy. The best."

Louis rubbed his chin. "So, I'm not just guessing at things here."

Ok, that was cryptic. "Excuse me, sir?"

Louis cleared his throat. "I know I seem like the epitome of a creative and spontaneous musician. And I am. Jazz requires a lot of improvising, but I'm not doing that here. I've done my research and I'm prepared. I wouldn't improvise with people's feelings. *Never* with their emotions."

"*Sir?*" I raised my eyebrows at him like he was slightly unhinged. But he was making me feel a little insane, so it felt justified.

Louis heaved a sigh. "Son, for 'a creative', you're being *really* slow here." He turned his head toward the bathroom. "Am I going to need to spell it out for you?"

"Apparently, all of it, sir. You lost me at 'Reef.'" After that, I think we entered a weird vortex of the sixth dimension. I can't speak 'musician', apparently.

He exhaled even louder. "Reef, I wouldn't intervene on someone's behalf or toy with their emotions if I wasn't *sure.*"

Light bulbs started going off. *Creative. Emotions.* Just what exactly had Locke told him? Was this all some sort of elaborate plan?

"No," I started shaking my head. "No, he wouldn't–"

Louis reached around for his jacket that was draped over the chair. I hadn't even noticed it. I was used to seeing him wear a button up and suspenders.

Slowly, he pulled something out of the jacket pocket and my mind went to static, like a TV screen fried by lightning. With one swift movement, he laid 'all my cards' out on the table, and my vision blurred. As if my eyes couldn't find the ability to focus on the small paperback book before me. The one that felt so consequential compared to its actual size.

"When did you–? You still wanted me to–? You still want Luna and me–?" There was no way he knew I was Cece LaRue and that his niece was my inspiration, and still wanted to encourage me to pursue her. *Would he?*

But soft lines formed on Louis' face as he waited patiently for me to collect myself. When he spoke, there was an ache in his eyes.

"Reef, I know what it's like to not feel good enough." My eyes drifted up to meet his as Louis' words resonated so clearly with me.

Since he had my full attention now, he continued, "It's why I didn't pursue Lani until I found out she was being treated poorly. It cost us both a lot of time. Even now, I still live with this imposter feeling. Like I'm not good enough and I could never deserve her. I wish I could tell you it all goes away, but with the right people, it gets better. With the *right person,* the doubts don't control you anymore. That person soothes the toxic emotions and stands by your side to fight those dragons every day."

I exhaled heavily and pushed out my chair from the table. This was too much. I should have known Louis couldn't possibly think I could be a real protector or body-guard for Luna. *No one* could think that.

"Reef, wait!–" But I needed to get out of here. *Now.* Louis' voice sliced through the air. "Reef, I read it."

I froze as his words prickled my spine. My eyes pinched together as my stomach turned sour. Humiliation working its way up my throat.

Louis' voice came through gentler now, "It's her, isn't it? The woman in your novels?"

I swallowed down my dignity, which was fleeting. My voice betrayed me in a quiver. "You don't need to ask, do you?"

"Reef—"

"How long have you known?" Shame was quickly bubbling up and replacing logic. "Did you come up with this entire plan after Locke told you about my books? . . . Did you think, let's ask the romance author to 'bodyguard' the woman who broke his heart with no warning and never told him why? The woman who ghosted him yet he pathetically can't get over? He'll definitely say yes." There was a hardness to my voice I didn't recognize as I yanked my novel off the table, taking back that little piece of my soul. Resentment was coloring my vision. Everything was turning into a blurry merry-go-round of marred colors. *I'm such a moron. Hopeless romantics don't exist. For a reason.*

"Reef." Louis stood up, so he was eye level with me. "No, that's not true. Not at all."

But I'd already turned to go. I'd heard enough. I was ready to pack up my things, take Nova, and go home. Finally, I was ready to let go. I'd wanted closure, to know why Luna had left me without a word, and foolishly to see if I still had a chance with her. But this was enough for me. *Enough Reef. Enough.*

I felt something holding me back and realized Louis had reached across the table and grabbed my arm. Our eyes locked in place. "Reef, I didn't know the truth until after we met at Luna's house. Until *after* you agreed to help. When I saw the two of you together, that's when I realized. I remembered how the two of you used to be so inseparable when I

261

would visit. And while Locke was visiting his grandmother, he may have let it slip that you wrote romance novels and were still very attached to my niece. I also knew Luna had a muse her whole life. *One muse.* Like me. The coconut doesn't fall far from the palm tree. I just never knew it was you. Until now."

I scrutinized his eyes, looking for any sign of deception to keep me there. "Reef, Luna has desperately needed music in her life, but she's needed her muse just as much. Maybe even more. That's where she goes to escape her anxiety . . . her happy place. And I never knew for certain who that elusive muse was until tonight. That's when I knew for certain I had done the right thing."

I wrung my hands anxiously. "I want you to know nothing has been fake for me, but I guess you knew that."

His eyes caught mine with a soft smile. "I know." He placed a hand on my shoulder. "I just wanted someone to accompany her as a friend and only play a fake boyfriend as a last resort. I never wanted to toy with anyone's feelings. But I pushed as soon as I saw you together. I figured you both needed a little nudge in the right direction. And maybe I thought fate needed a little help, like it did for Lani and me. Because, Reef, I may not know what all happened, but I know Luna was devastated when she left you. I know she wouldn't have *wanted* to break your heart. But that was one of the darkest times of her life, and I don't think she wanted you to be a part of it. She would have thought she was doing the right thing, no matter how wrong it might have been."

From the corner of my eye, I could see Luna and Tutu heading to our table. While I knew it was time to act natu-rally, all we could do was stay frozen in our awkward tango. An endless staring contest between us.

"What are you going to do?" Louis managed to whisper.

And an aching feeling came over me. "Please don't leave because of me. Luna couldn't stand to lose you again. That much I know."

His words only confused me more. I was the injured party. "*Luna?*"

"Yes?" she said, reaching the table. Happiness saturated every crevice of her tone.

"Oh—um . . ." I stuttered. Louis' eyes were pleading with me. "I, uh, I was just talking about what a pleasant night it was to go for a walk on the beach. That's all."

A gush of air left Louis, and he looked sick with relief. He really loved Luna. I knew the feeling.

"Oh yeah? You mean you haven't backed out?" she teased as she slipped her arm around me. My body went a little rigid, and she took note, immediately pulling away. Retreating into her shell.

"Definitely not," I replied, tucking her back into me, not ready to lose whatever trust I had regained with her today. A calm smile graced her lips. "Louis was just giving me some tips."

As I spoke, I saw him quickly tuck my novel back into his jacket pocket from where he'd swiftly grabbed it out of my hand. As if it had *never* happened.

Luna

CHAPTER 27

Just give me one more hour
I'll do anything to show you
How much you mean to me

-LUNA MANU MELE, ONE
MORE HOUR

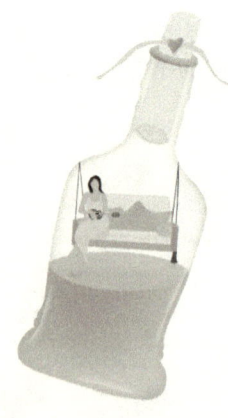

R eef kept his promise as he began escorting me down to the beach. A cool feeling of relief flooded over me with every step we took. *Thank God, dinner hadn't been too much for him.* Even with Uncle Louis.

After our elevator experience, and Louis' inquisition, I thought he'd opt for an activity to lighten the romantic tension that had been building between us. Not something that would surely combust it.

But as we made our way toward the shoreline under the milky way, something inside of me broke forth first: the butterflies that had been hibernating inside of me for decades. They were finally stretching their wings, excited to be back in commission. And their flutters were intensifying as Reef made good on his promise. A man keeping his word set forth this novice feeling of safety inside me, like silky, smooth honey in tea on a rainy day.

My eyes snuck a peek at Reef as we wound our way around the cerulean blue pool. Its sapphire glow cast upon us, reminding me of so many memories. I was feeling a kaleidoscope of emotions, way more than I was supposed to. I'd let myself come undone. But I wasn't the only one, there was this glimmer in his eyes. The one I'd seen at dinner. The one Uncle Louis had spotted, too. *Could it be that after everything, he still had feelings for me? That he'd take a risk on me . . . again?*

Suddenly, my feet wobbled, throwing me off balance. We had reached sand and the start to the beach path. Reef grabbed a hold of me with a crooked upward turn of his lips. *Yup, I hadn't been paying attention at all.*

I slid my shoes off, leaving them to the side. I wanted to feel the cool, soft sand slide between my toes. And I was more than happy to take the hand Reef offered me with the removal of my footwear, even though the expanse before us was pretty flat. But when we reached the water, he didn't let go. The butterflies soared.

"Ok, *Mahina Lūlū*, how about some truth or dare?"

The nickname sent heat down to my toes. I bit my lip, but I couldn't enjoy it because I always chose 'truth'. And that didn't bode well for me right now. Especially since the glint in his eyes was saying there was something he wanted to ask me.

"Ok, dare," I wagered, nerves firing at full speed. Tugging on my lip, in hopes he wouldn't see through me.

"I *dare* you to tell me about your lavender farm song." His eyes searched mine, never breaking contact.

An involuntary breath left me. "That's the same as 'truth', Reef."

"Well, you never did like 'dare,'" he said chivalrously. Of course, a man was finally being chivalrous, and I hated it. I now understood that "hate" speech at the end of *10 Things I Hate About You*.

I stopped, turning to him and the overly romantic glow of the moon. "Why do you want to know?" I asked, focusing on the feel of the cold sand wiggling in between my toes. I held up my dress as a shield from the surf.

"Well, I guess I'm asking because someone told me to really listen to your lyrics today." *Venice.* I thought. *Traitor.* "And of course I have, but . . .this was different." *What else did Venice tell him?*

We obviously needed to have a chat.

I'd been worried when I'd seen Reef and Venice together. So, it was what I thought. She had given him some puzzle pieces. He'd just been waiting until I felt better to ask about them.

"I'm sure you've heard that song before." I waved my hand out to sea, as if washing everything away.

"Yeah, but *not* like today." *Great. Maybe I needed to wave harder.* I tried again. Nothing.

Reef raised his eyebrow at me curiously and then continued softly. "I just assumed you went back there with someone."

There was an ache in his tone, and it wounded me. Right in the place reserved for him. The part I thought couldn't be reached.

"Reef, that's *our* spot." I could *never* take someone back to our place. There were certain spots that would forever be off-limits to other men. Even as big of a pushover as I was. Some things were worth fighting for. And suddenly, I felt that old familiar fire in my belly. *I missed you, old friend.*

"Well, we had a lot of spots and Maui isn't that big." His eyes drifted toward the sea, as if he didn't dare to hope I had saved them.

"Yes, and they've *all* stayed ours." I cast my eyes pointedly at him.

He just looked at me, taken aback. My gut twisted at the longing in his eyes . . . and the surprise.

"Sorry, I shouldn't have asked. Venice just said . . . It doesn't matter," he trailed off.

"No, *it does*," I said adamantly, now having a burning desire for him to realize the truth. If only he had any idea how precious they were to me. I felt a prickling sensation at the corners of my eyes as I held my gaze steadily on him. "The song is about my happy place. It's about you . . . and me. It's the place where I go in my mind when I need an escape from everything. Or just for the world to go quiet. I 'go' to us. I couldn't believe you 'took me' there today." The words barely left my lips.

Reef squeezed my hand tenderly. "I go there, too. *All the time.*"

He looked down at me as we stood together under the full moon, getting to know the grown-up features of one another. Trying to catch up on all the lost time.

His lips parted slowly. "It's a gorgeous song, Luna."

Without warning, a haze rose in my eyes. I don't cry. Not in front of people. It makes them uncomfortable, and me too. While Uncle Louis was helping me work on it, I hadn't made my peace with it. Probably something about not making my peace with myself. But an unavoidable wave ambushed me. Maybe because I felt safe to feel my emotions with him. He was still providing that for me. One of the greatest gifts.

That had never stopped a part of me from worrying about what he'd think of my music, especially if he knew our memories were inspiration.

A rogue tear dropped from my eye and he carefully wiped it away. The softness and hunger in his eyes were unraveling me. As if he could know all of me again. If I would just let him.

The look clawed through all my emergency reserves, and I turned my head to look away. But a gentle finger brought my gaze back to him. And what I found there was the warmest smile. As if he loved our memories being used in this way, having this shared connection. And then his infectious smile spread. He understood. Because in the world I'd created, we both belonged to the same place, and we escaped there together. In some world, we *still* belonged together.

If only he knew *how* connected we were. That all my love songs were about him. That the person I wanted 'one more hour' with was him. And that it always would be.

For the briefest of moments, I leaned into our inconceivable serendipity. Blocking out thoughts about the past or what was 'right' or 'wrong'. I simply allowed serendipity to take over. I was, at least for the moment, done fighting fate. As selfish as that might be.

Reef

CHAPTER 28

" Sometimes I go to our place just to see if I can feel you again. From the breeze to the gentle lapping of the waves on my skin, I find you again.

-REEF AKUA, HARMONY OF HEARTS

A long the serene shoreline, our stroll turned from stolen glances to heated gazes. And neither of us knew what to say.

After we'd let the moonlight sufficiently drive us mad, we quietly headed back to our room. I felt a tinge of awkwardness to be headed toward a honeymoon suite. Especially after our evening had taken such a romantic turn. And I think the fact that I had been pining for her all this time was becoming much clearer.

I slid the key into the door, holding it open for her.

"Thanks," Luna breathed, twisting her fingers self-consciously.

I cleared my throat, staying on the other side of the threshold. "Um, it's pretty late and I really don't think anyone is going to notice if I stay in another room. If you're not comfortable—" I tried to offer again.

"Reef," she looked at me with a crooked smile, "I don't think hospitality is going to move you from the honeymoon suite. At least, not without it causing some gossip. Plus, I really was looking forward to your company."

"Yeah?" I asked hopefully.

"Yeah." Sparks ignited across my skin at her sultry tone. She moved closer to me, her body language inviting me in. "I know it's not a makeshift tent that lets in the rain, but it will have to suffice."

"Well, if that's all you have." I faked a groan, and she laughed. At least our shoulders loosened as we entered the room, some of that tension melting.

As Luna got ready for bed in the bathroom, I called out, "Are you sure I can't take the sofa?" She had continued to be adamant on that point.

"Yes, I'll be done in just a minute, and I don't want to

see you over there. The bed is enormous. Plus, I know you and Nova are a package deal."

"Oh, is that the selling point?" I called as I laid the comforter down on the floor beside the bed. I just couldn't shake the feeling that I was overstepping. Plus, Nova would love bouncing between both of us.

"Yes, a big one—" Luna's voice dropped off, and I turned to see her standing behind me in a long satin slip. A beautiful cream one that dipped down to her ankles. Did she know this was the honeymoon suite when she packed? Because it sure looked like it. That outfit would make any man say 'I do'. I forced myself to swallow. But it wasn't working. I think she'd broken me.

"Reef, what are you doing?" she asked incredulously. Her beautiful body swayed toward me.

"I think I need to sleep on the floor, Luna. I would feel better—" But my words were cut off by the sandpaper in my throat.

She wrapped her arms around herself in response, as if she was cold, and nodded brusquely. Luna quickly went over to the bedside lamp and cut it off. But I had caught the mixture of hurt and disappointment on her features. With moonlight streaming in, we could hear the ocean waves crashing nearby. The only sound we were left with in the room. I had only wanted to do the right thing, but suddenly I felt bad about it.

As Luna slipped into her bed, I called Nova over, but she headed straight for Luna instead. Exactly where I would love to be. So why couldn't I find the courage? With too many thoughts rambling through my brain, one stood out the loudest: I let so much hold me back in life.

"Goodnight," I breathed into the dark.

I'd like to say I was simply being chivalrous, but that's not all this was. I was also building a Luna shield around my heart.

So I retreated. I had just let my eyelids fall heavy and my thoughts wander when I felt a movement at the end of my pallet. And my heart froze at the sight before me.

In the ethereal moonlight, the glow outlined the curves I'd been studying a little too well since we'd reunited. Her creamy satin fabric set aglow in the night air.

Luna's soft voice tumbled toward me, shaking me from my stupor. "I don't think it's fair you get to have a pillow fort by yourself."

She'd bent down and was waiting at the end of my makeshift bed, patiently seeking an invitation. Looking like a dream.

I raised up on my elbow slightly, looking for my voice to respond. "Well, you were always so good at making them."

A woman like Luna, looking so incredibly beautiful, did not deserve to sit by herself on the floor. Without another thought, I extended my hand to her and pulled her toward me. And I loved her response as she giggled along the way. As I scooped her up in my arms, it didn't take me long to find a spot for her. Just like old times. A warmth burst through the center of my chest, happiness coursing through me. And it was like I could feel it radiating off of her, too.

"Are you comfortable?" I murmured, making sure she was still okay. I never wanted to be incorrect about my assumptions with her.

"I'm so comfortable with you. It feels like coming home," Luna said softly.

I swallowed hard at her words, which hit my most vulnerable parts. All the areas still left bare for her.

"Reef," she whispered. "Why can't all guys be like you? I mean, I think I expected them to be. You really ruined me." There was a teasing nature in her tone, but also a dire graveness.

I didn't even know what to say in response. Realizing as much, she clarified, "I mean, I knew there wouldn't ever be anyone like you, but I thought other men would have a good heart like you. But it's really special. Extremely rare. I forgot just how incredible you are. No one treats my anxiety like it matters. They think I want attention or I'm being dramatic. Not you. You've never once belittled me or made me feel small."

I pulled her in closer, tightening my hold. She'd never once made me feel small either, or that my dreams were. It was an awful feeling to be ashamed of your masculinity or think your work wasn't worthy. That it wasn't notable enough. But not Luna. She was the girl who had loved me because I wore a princess crown with her and exchanged song lyrics for poems instead of shorthand text messages with emojis.

Luna continued before I could gather my words to speak. "I used music to run from it all, even from myself. It was my safe place. But even that hasn't been working lately. The lyrics have dried up and I'm even having trouble playing. Louis keeps trying to help me. When he moved back home, he thought he could help me channel my emotions into music again. And his presence has helped so much, especially with navigating the music world, but—"

I let the silence settle over us as I held her tightly, savoring how she felt in my arms. The bittersweetness of the moment and the warmth of her colliding.

I broke the silence, venturing, "I don't know what I would do if writing stopped working for me. I'm so sorry,

Luna. But why didn't you ever reach out to me? When you returned to Maui, we could have re-connected, even just as friends. We didn't have to be random acquaintances who ran into each other and waved from a distance. Or said 'aloha' when they were out with their families. Maybe I could have helped. I've learned a lot through my experiences with Locke. Surely you heard about his accident. You could have reached out to him. He would have wanted to help, too."

Now I felt like I'd overstepped. That this new thing between us was too fragile. And I didn't know what the rules were yet, and I shouldn't be guessing.

"Yes, I heard about Locke and that you were with him when the accident happened. Actually, I reached out to him. We talked on the phone some. I tried to see if there was any way I could help, but he was resistant." What? They'd been in touch?

"Oh, yeah, he got pretty closed-off after the accident. He only let his grandmother and me 'help' him. You know how hardheaded he can be."

She laughed lightly. I couldn't believe Locke hadn't told me Luna had contacted him. Locke kept all things 'Luna' quiet from me. Maybe he thought it was easier that way.

"I just . . ." She bit her lip, stalling for time. "I just felt really awkward about how I left things."

I recognized her 'tell'. The way her eyes skirted to the side said this wasn't the whole truth. And after Louis' cryptic hints at dinner, I was sure there was more. Luna was very good at 'politely' avoiding the entire truth. A nice lie of omission. But then again, I guess that's exactly what I was doing with her.

Omitting my status as a best-selling author was actually a pretty gigantic lie of omission, and I felt horrible about it. She was the one person who had always known everything about me. Even more than Locke. *Why couldn't I just tell her?* She just confessed her song was about me. She'd created the perfect opportunity. Maybe we'd even get a big laugh out of the situation. But I couldn't handle any more rejection from her. Not her. So I just froze . . . again.

"It's okay, Luna. Don't worry about it. I'm sure you had your reasons. I would have been happy to reconnect and help in any way I could. We always had a way of helping each other and being there for one another. I would like to think we still could."

After everything, I couldn't believe I was saying this. I meant it, but deep down, I knew I would always want to know what those reasons were. The scarred young man in me needed closure. The one who had been devastated when he didn't get a response to any of his letters. The boy who closed his heart down for so long. He needed to know.

"No, it's not ok, Reef. I'm really sorry. I don't think I ever properly apologized. But can you just trust me? That it was for the best? That I was doing you a favor?"

Hurt laced every syllable of her tone. And it eviscerated me. *A favor?* Removing herself from my life could never be a favor. *Ever.* But that mist was forming in her eyes again. My kryptonite. And as horrible as it sounds, it made me realize she was getting comfortable with me again. But it also made me realize how much she believed in her declaration. And I was going to have to believe it, whether I liked it or not.

"Ok . . . But that could never be—"

"Reef, just trust me," she said more firmly than I'd ever heard before. This meant something to her. *I* meant something to her.

"Ok," I said more empathically, trying to put my heart into it.

She went silent. As if there wasn't any more to say. Words used to flow so freely between us. About the silliest and most important things. I suddenly missed them. And just like that, I squashed the silence. A question I've been dying to ask, suddenly escaping me like a bubble bursting forth. Finally able to breathe as it kissed the surface.

"Did you get my letters?" I murmured softly into the void between us. There was a sharp intake of air, and even in the darkness, I could see her tears lit by just enough moonlight. So that was a yes. I hadn't meant to ask and now I didn't know how to take it back.

"Sorry," I said into the now painful silence. "Let's go to sleep. I'm sure tomorrow is going to be a big day for you."

"Yes." I don't know how she managed to infuse such an ache into the word. I guess neither of us was going to be sleeping anytime soon. "They meant so much to me. Thank you. I should have responded, but I didn't think that was best for you—" Her words faltered.

I couldn't be more confused. Here, I thought I was the one who would be hurt whenever this old wound tore open. Because I knew it was only a matter of time before it did. *But why was she so hurt? Did her parents tell her she couldn't see me anymore?* Everything pointed toward this clean break being something she didn't want. I couldn't believe what Louis had told me was true. My heart ached at this sapling of hope. Such a dangerous thing. If I was finally being honest with myself, everything she'd done since we'd reconnected was telling me she wanted me. That she'd never stopped. Maybe. Just maybe.

"Well, maybe I should have written you 365 letters, one for each day of the year." I parroted the famous line from

The Notebook. I tried to do a southern accent but failed miserably. At least the attempt was cute because Luna broke out in quiet laughter, breaking the tension.

So, I continued, "Well, *The Notebook* was the gold standard in our middle school days. I figured writing a few letters would be a good move to steal."

Luna laughed harder now, but when quiet fell, her voice came out sober. "It wasn't the letters. They were wonderful. *You* have always been wonderful. And your letters helped me through some really rough times. More than you'll ever know. You have the biggest heart, Reef. Please never lose it. You don't understand the impact a big heart can make."

Well, what was it then?

Her voice broke a little as she noticed my still clueless expression. "I didn't want you to experience that part of my life. I didn't want you to see me like that. Reef, I thought I was doing the right thing for you. I was too young to know, to understand, you would have . . . and I guess I'm still doing it. And I honestly don't know whom I'm trying to protect anymore."

Both of our hearts, it seemed. But it didn't work like that. So I just held her close, prepared to wait until she was ready to open up to me. Realizing I'd do anything for that chance.

And then her voice broke again, and it was like lightning striking me. A moment you knew was going to forever change things. "Reef, I got really sick. And I just . . . My prognosis wasn't good. And I didn't feel like myself anymore. I didn't even look like myself. I just wanted you to remember me the way I was. And there was no way to hide it. My illness affected every aspect of my life. I didn't want you to go through that pain with me. I didn't want you to have to be a part of it."

She finished with quiet determination. One that made me love her even more but also made my heartstrings ache. And I knew that was as much as she was going to share with me tonight. The pain in her tone told me just how hard it had been for her to tell me even that much. So I held her in reply. My silent 'thank you' to the trust she'd just placed in me. With a hope she'd do it again.

Reef

CHAPTER 29

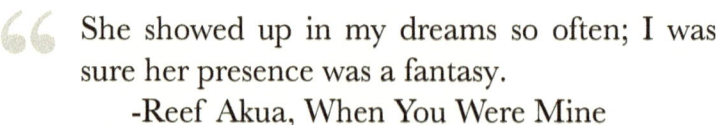

❝ She showed up in my dreams so often; I was
sure her presence was a fantasy.
-Reef Akua, When You Were Mine

Luna's words hung thick like ether as I invited her into me, and she snuggled closer. A silent understanding formed between us as we left the rest of our conversation for the night. Allowing the peaceful silence to shroud us.

I should have slept soundly, but Luna's warmth felt bittersweet as her words raced through my mind. I tried to unscramble the clues like a crossword in the Sunday paper. I should have been relieved that I hadn't done something 'wrong'—that it wasn't me—but the young boy inside me felt no victory.

At least my mind took a break when I awoke to the sunlight streaming in upon her features. There was something so delicate about Luna, yet so strong. She was the best paradox. *How I had missed her petite frame and the way she tucked herself away inside my tall one.* Like nesting eggs, sized just right. Because after everything, she still felt like home to me, too. She still fit. I knew in my heart she always would. And just like that, the ache returned.

I held her tighter and breathed her in. Her essence instantly took me back to all my favorite memories, conveniently blocking the sour ones. The scent you can't describe, yet it's your favorite one in the world; the one that makes everything better when you smell it; that was Luna. I couldn't get enough. And just like that, her soothing presence was easing me back to sleep.

Suddenly I felt a tap on my foot, and I could see her sleepy eyes trying to focus on my feet, which were sticking out from under the blanket of our makeshift bed. I couldn't imagine how much this room cost and yet here we were on the floor. But it was truly perfect for us.

"When did you get that?" she asked groggily as her foot tried to nudge mine again.

"*Aiâ*! Your feet are like ice, Lun," I said as Luna's cold foot rubbed mine.

"Sorry." She giggled as she rubbed her foot playfully against mine.

"Come here." I reached for her feet, tucking them in between mine to warm them, shivering along the way. They were like little Luna popsicles, but I loved them. A warm relief spread over me at the familiarity.

"Thank you for taking such good care of me." She smiled, sending heat throughout my body. Her words only added to the effect.

"I try. I just wish I could do more." *Especially as much as she would let me.* She looked away slightly, as if realizing the same thing.

Luna's chin straightened as she looked at me head on. "Well, are you going to tell me about your tattoo?" She teased coyly, successfully changing the subject.

"Are you going to tell me about the changes to your body?" I replied cheekily, hoping she'd drop it. She did not. I doubt she'd gotten any crazy piercings or tats, though, so I was out of luck, anyway.

Luna replied, "I think you've noticed the changes to my body. But I don't have any tattoos, if that's what you're asking."

I snorted. I couldn't believe she was calling me on how much I'd checked her out. A smile I couldn't control took over my features. I loved when she was bold like this with me. Even if it was at my expense.

"Luna, I'm supposed to be your fake boyfriend who's obsessed with you. It's part of the job," I teased.

"Uh, huh," she replied.

"An *extremely* nice part of the job," I admitted.

She grinned wickedly. "I've enjoyed getting to see you as

an adult too, and *all* of your changes. Now, I want to know about the tattoo," she said brazenly as she bumped my foot again.

I sighed heavily. This was going to be embarrassing. "Can we not? There are things that are better left unsaid from our time apart. I'm sure you have some of those things, too."

She eyed me. "You get *one* secret, Reef. Choose wisely," she teased.

But I could tell she still felt bad about not telling me what I wanted to know last night. So, she was letting me have a lie of omission as well. If only she knew what she was doing. Well, this certainly would *not* be my 'one'. I had much bigger fish to fry.

"Ok . . . Well, can you please not get weirded out over it? I was drunk."

"What?" Her eyebrows shot up in surprise. "You don't seem like you drink. But you took me up on that 'one' pretty quickly. You must have something you want to save your pass for . . ." She eyed me suspiciously.

I chose to gloss over that for now. "There was a time when I drank. Too much. I was trying to numb some things." I couldn't meet her eyes. "Anyway, it's a surf-board, a ukulele, and *honu*–the unity, faith, and good luck turtle."

"Ok, well, that's cool. What's wrong with that? Sounds like a pretty tame tattoo." She moved to get a better look, but I didn't want to let her out of my arms. "Reef," she giggled. The melodic sound made me let go, and unfortu-nately she moved to inspect my ankle. Her eyes immediately turned up to mine when she saw the designs up close. "So, the surfboard is for Locke?" I nodded. Of course, she'd be able to figure it out. The native designs I'd had the artist put on each one were a pretty clear indicator. "And the ukulele is—" She stopped.

"Yeah, it's for you," I said, beating her to the punch. "It's the three of us. Like how it used to be when we were growing up. Like I said, I was really drunk and pretty young." *And idiotic.* You don't get a tattoo of someone who *doesn't* want you. But it served as a reminder of the happiest time in my life and the Ohana I'd had. It had been us against the world. A perfect little 'family'. And it served as a reminder of home and gave me guidance. It was my first step forward every day.

"But were you? Really drunk?" I looked at her, confused. "Seems like a pretty deep tattoo for a drunk person." Her eyebrow twisted upward wickedly. *Sometimes it would be nice if she wasn't so in tune with me.*

It was a variation of the tattoo I'd drawn and wanted to get before she'd left. The one I'd drawn so many times as a kid I could draw it with my eyes closed. So, of course, that's the request that had come out in the chair. But I wasn't going to share that. I needed to have a wall, too. Or at least some semblance of a shield.

"Ok, enough ogling the tat," I reached for Luna and pulled her back. "I know it's *super* sexy, but—" I said sarcastically.

A little sigh escaped her. "It actually really is." And there was something about the sound that made me feel like I had to change topics. For my sanity.

"How'd we end up on the floor again? There's a huge and very expensive bed that Nova is enjoying for us." I peered up at it. Yup, there was Nova sacked out at the edge, enjoying her honeymoon suite.

"Well, *someone* decided to be difficult and sleep on the floor," she teased. "But I'm really enjoying this."

"Yes, it's pretty perfect for us," I said, allowing myself to get dangerously lost in her eyes for the briefest of moments. Ones that felt like they'd been passed down through the depths of the sea and a long mermaid lineage.

"Yes, although maybe I can convince you to upgrade to the huge bed tonight. I'll even stay on my side if it makes you feel better."

"No, you won't," I joked as I rubbed her feet, which were finally warming up.

She grinned at that. "Yes, please don't make me."

I swallowed even harder, knowing I wouldn't survive another night like this. Not easily. Not without all my feelings becoming impossible to manage.

I cleared my throat, needing to distract myself as much as her. "Are you still up for some sightseeing today? Will you have time?"

"Yes, the welcome gathering for the festival isn't until much later and I would love to take my mind off of it."

I nodded. Sound check had been hard enough. I could only imagine what the next step would be like. This was the only part of the trip I felt mildly qualified to handle—distracting her.

"Great, I'm just going to give Nova some breakfast and take her out. Then we can get some before heading out?" She nodded with that dimpled smile. The one that made it hard for me to untangle myself from her.

AS SOON AS I was outside with Nova, I dialed Locke. Thankfully, he picked up on the first ring.

"Hey, are you married yet?" he teased right away. Apparently, he was just dying for an update.

"Locke, that's not funny."

"No, it's not. I'm supposed to be your best man. If you're eloping, you *better* invite me." I rolled my eyes. I was even more perturbed that he couldn't see my gesture.

"So, how's the honeymoon going? Heard you decided to just skip the wedding entirely." His deep laughter rumbled through the phone line.

"Locke," I said sternly. He must have already talked to Louis. I'm sure neither could resist debriefing after last night. "How do you know that?"

"Well, I was worried about how you were fairing, so I gave Louis a call. Plus, I wanted to check on Tutu to see how she was doing." *Uh, huh. Sure.* He was such a gossip.

"Right . . . I'm glad you're having so much fun with this."

"Oh, it's the best." He laughed. "Only *you* could get a *real* honeymoon suite with your *fake* girlfriend. Hey, by the way. Have you told her yet?"

"What? No. Well, I sort of tried, but it didn't go so well. Apparently, Louis knows. He brought a copy of *Tropical Love Lines* to dinner last night."

Locke was quiet. For once. "Locke?!"

"Huh? Um, well, Louis was asking all these questions, and I just figured it would be better if he knew. He was *supposed* to keep it to himself, though."

I smacked my forehead, almost dropping Nova's leash. "Uh, huh. Great. The more the merrier, right?" My sarcasm leaked out. "Well, anyway, that's not why I called."

"Oh, you have something else bigger than a new wife and honeymoon? Perhaps twins on the way?"

I rolled my eyes, frustrated that yet again he couldn't see

it. "*Yes.* I don't know if I'm asking for help or advice. I haven't decided yet."

He chuckled. "Better figure it out fast. This is going to be good. You must be all out of options. Let's hear it."

I exhaled forcefully. "Luna's friend hinted that her song was about me and, from there, we started talking . . . It doesn't matter, I'll just cut to my quandary. Neither Luna nor Louis will tell me why she ghosted me. Luna keeps saying to trust her, that it was for my own good. I told her I would have wanted to help her in any way that I could, especially with her anxiety. I told her you would have, too. That we would have understood, especially with what you went through with the accident. She said she talked to you. So, I guess what I'm asking is . . . Do you know something you're not telling me?"

"Wait, wait, wait. Back up," Locke said emphatically. "You mean *she's* writing songs about you and *you're* writing novels about her?"

"It was *a* song. Luna told me about it last night. It's about the lavender farm we visited together. But her friend said to really listen to the lyrics of the last one she wrote so there may be another—"

"Yeah, there's definitely more than one, Reef. I've heard the lyrics too. God, you two were always so in sync. This is crazy. I actually was a little jealous growing up. I never thought I'd find a connection with someone like that."

"Locke, can we get back to my question? I don't have a lot of time. I'm out walking Nova."

"Oh, right, I forgot about your fake wife waiting in your gigantic honeymoon suite. How quickly things change."

"Locke!"

"Reef, this is *perfect*. Exactly what you wanted. She obviously feels the same way about you. That was the perfect time to tell her about your novels. There's no way she can't take it as a compliment when she's doing the same thing. I don't see how she could be upset. Seems she would think it's romantic and sweet. *That* was your window. You *didn't* tell her?"

"No, Locke, I didn't. It's *not* quite the same. And I choked. Plus, she didn't get rejected . . . repeatedly." My throat clenched on those last words.

"Yet, you still write love stories about her," he said definitively. His tone brooked no arguments. "You still have to be holding onto hope. Or believe there's a good reason she didn't answer you."

"Uggghhh, you are so infuriating to talk with, you know that?"

"Yeah, kind of like talking with you right now." Locke sighed, growing serious again. "Does it matter, Reef? You were kids. Things happen. You've both changed and grown up. The feelings she has for you right now are what matter. If she says trust her, then trust her. Go with hope and good reason. Take the victory. Goodness, you've wanted it for long enough."

"So, you don't know—"

"Reef, man! Come on." He sighed, relenting. "We talked a little about panic and anxiety attacks on the phone a few times. As you know, I didn't want to do anything in person, especially when I was recovering and doing physical therapy. I have a few guesses about what happened from the things she said, but no, I don't know for sure. You know, I always wondered, too. And no, I'm not telling you my guesses. I will keep those conversations private. Although, I will tell you she asked about you and how you were doing, many times. And there was an ache in her voice when she said your name. It appears she's been through a lot. So, I think you need to decide if you can have a fresh start with her or not. If not, then don't put her through anything more. Be honest with her. *From the start.* Making up for falsehoods later is like trying to dig out of quicksand: only for fools and magicians. You're hopefully neither."

I don't know how this turned so quickly. I wanted to talk with him about how to avoid getting my heart broken and somehow we ended up worrying about hers. That was the theme of late. But I knew he was right—she deserved all of that and more. I just didn't know if I could risk my heart again.

Luna

CHAPTER 30

Anytime or place will do
And I'll make it back to you
Just give me one more hour
And I promise this time, I'll be the one you need

-LUNA MANU MELE, ONE
MORE HOUR

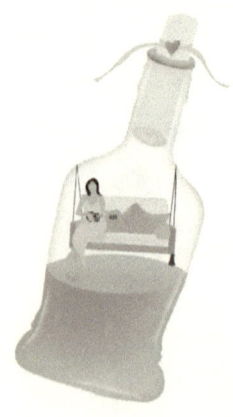

I waited out on the lanai, absentmindedly tapping my foot as I tried to take in the view. As gorgeous as the scenery was, I couldn't focus. I stared off into the rich salty abyss, not really seeing it. My head hung low, feeling too heavy now. A vulnerable feeling settled over me, thinking about the fact that Reef knew I had written a song about him. And the feeling only kept growing and twisting in the pit of my stomach at the thought that I *still* had more songs to tell him about . . . Especially since I only started writing again after seeing *him* that night.

Azul had thought *One More Hour* was about him. But it couldn't be further from the truth, which I felt guilty about. The people pleaser in me couldn't help it. But I'm pretty sure if he gave us one more hour alone, one of us might not make it out alive.

The song's intimate nature only heightened my vulnerability. It implied just how much I'd wanted Reef and for just how long. *I'm not ready for him to know. For the consequences.* But the letters he wrote to me were so brave. They evened the playing fields . . . *a lot*.

My thought bubble burst as a click sounded in the door's key slot. And within no time, Nova came bounding over and hopped up beside me on my lounger. Good thing I'd left some space for her. She proudly took up every inch.

"So, how do you feel about being a Hawaiian tourist today?" Reef asked as he leaned against the wall by the sliding glass door most seductively. He was still in his boxers and t-shirt. *Only Reef.* Had he walked Nova looking this way? *Auê*, he looked so hot. Where was a pen when you needed one? The song lyrics were practically writing themselves.

"Lun?"

"Huh? Oh, yeah." He laughed at me. I could feel the unladylike open gape of my mouth, and I closed it quickly.

"You ok?" Reef asked.

"Yeah, it's just going to take me some time to get used to this grown-up version of you. That's all."

He chuckled harder. "You mean gangly me, just taller, lankier, *and* nerdier? So, *this* doing it for you? I got all dressed up last night, Bond inspired and everything—"

"The button down and pants? I didn't see a Bond tux." I teased.

"That was island style Bond. And that's dressed up for me." I scanned over him some more, *so* glad he liked to dress down. He turned sheepish. "Lun, seriously. Now, you're just making me feel self-conscious." But laughter still filled his tone.

"Sorry, it was dark last night. I'm getting a redo. Since when have I made you self-conscious?"

"Since I became your fake boyfriend . . . and we entered this honeymoon suite." Our eyes met, toying with each other. Playing a game of chicken and begging the other to surrender first. My heart rose into my throat like a balloon floating toward the sun. I could feel the tension mounting. It was going to pop at any second. No way could it survive that pressure.

Our eyes stayed locked. And at that moment, we both knew what we wanted . . . For this to be real and to make good use of this room for *very real* things. *He could start with that kiss he never finished.* But then again, a part of me felt like he'd sworn me off in that way. Like he had to protect himself. Even if he was feeling something. Maybe that was smart. No, it absolutely was.

He cleared his throat, blinking quickly. "So, I'll just go call Tutu and Louis." He spun around to go inside as he continued gazing at me and then promptly slammed into the sliding glass door. He rebounded off the glass like a Bugs Bunny. *Oomph. That had to hurt.*

"Reef! Are you?–"

"I'm fine. Told you, just clumsier. Not one ounce of a suave spy in me."

"No, I never said that." My lips curved up to the side.

His chest reddened, a whole Hawaiian sunset spreading out before me. He turned slowly, bracing himself against the glass door. Then slid his way down to the open doorway, making a big production of avoiding running into the glass again. A little more *Pink Panther* than *James Bond*. I chuckled inwardly, wondering if he knew how cute he was when he wasn't even trying.

Reef rambled, "So yeah, we should . . . we better get ready to go. Out of all the places we considered visiting, I think we should go to Diamond Head first. Before the humidity gets any worse. So, should I still ask Tutu and Louis if they want to join us?"

I nodded, wishing I could read his thoughts. He always appeared to read me so easily. I felt at a disadvantage since I never had the nerve to ask him what was on his mind. "That sounds good. They can always hang out around the park area. I hear there are benches at the base and the foliage is really pretty there."

Reef agreed, and I started working on moving the very comfortable Nova. Once I had convinced her to go back inside, we got ready to meet Tutu and Louis, eager to include them in our plans. But I hadn't really packed for anything other than the festival and hanging out by the pool. So, I put on my most casual sundress, with a swimsuit underneath, and tied a cardigan around my waist.

"Uh, Luna," Reef began. "I doubt you want to–" I

looked at him with a raised brow. He continued, "Did you really not bring any shorts or pants? Well, I can come up with something pretty creative just for you." His brow line deepened. I could see him slipping into overprotective mode.

"No, it's just that I packed for the festival. I'm fine to go walking in this." I lobbed an eyebrow right back at him.

"Ok, well . . . Locke told me I was crazy to take Tutu to Diamond Head, anyway. He said there was an easier trail that could be a relaxing walk for all of us. It's at Manoa Falls. He said Tutu would probably enjoy walking some of it. And since you're in a dress, I think that decision would be better. He mentioned the trail was pretty flat. So, no one can—" He stopped himself.

I raised my eyebrow even higher. "Reef, I have a swimsuit on." But that fierce, protective gaze only grew. Heating parts of me I was sad had been dormant for so long. Growing up, I had sometimes felt like I was in the Hawaiian version of *Twilight* with Reef and Locke as my overprotective vampires. Often, I'd just wanted them to believe I could handle myself. But now, the heat that was spreading through me in response to Reef's primal care was making me rethink things.

"You can borrow something," he said, less as an offer and more as a request.

I shook my head. We *were* twelve again. "Your work out shorts won't exactly stay up on me." He brought a pair over to me anyway, and I relented, trying them on with a sigh. But I started laughing when he pulled the drawstrings closed within an inch of their life to get them to stay up. I felt like I was in the Amish country. "How's that workin' for ya?" I asked teasingly as the pants swallowed me. This was going to look *so* sexy with my dress.

"Wait." He held up a finger in an adorably determined way. One that made my already heated insides melt.

"Reef, really, a swimsuit is fine. It was a good attempt. But it's not medieval times. No one is going to come after you for not protecting my honor." *Well, maybe Louis.*

But Reef came back quickly. Even more determined . . . with a pair of boxers. "Ok, trade me."

"Somehow, I don't think my panties are going to fit you." I laughed as his chest reddened even more. Ahhh, maybe I hadn't seen the *whole* Hawaiian sunset yet.

"Fair, I deserved that. I should know better than to set you up like that." He handed me the boxers more emphatically. "These should fit better and still work as shorts."

"*Jurassic Park?*" My cheeks were aching from smiling so hard.

"They filmed the movie here. Do you have something *against* paleontologists?"

I laughed. "No, I'll just go hiking with dinosaur slashes across my butt. That's totally better than swimsuit bottoms. Attracts *so* much less attention."

"Well, I was going to give you a t-shirt that you could tie so you didn't have to wear a nice dress, but now I really don't feel so inclined. I'll put one in the bag, though." He was *such* a softie. And I loved it. You didn't meet many men like him. Actually, I *never* met men like him. *I couldn't believe how much I'd taken for granted when I was younger. How much I'm sure I still did . . .*

"Well, only if it matches."

He shook his head. "You're getting the most obnoxious one I have now. It was going to be a solid color." Our eyes met as our private rhythm was restored. Reef cleared his throat and quickly threw the shirt into a bag for the hike. "Hey, what do you think about taking Nova?"

I looked down at her. She was already pacing in between my legs, rubbing herself against me to make sure I didn't forget about her. I nodded enthusiastically at the suggestion. Nova's presence brought this instant peace. Probably even more powerful because she was a part of Reef.

I petted Nova's head in appreciation and looked up to see a far off look in Reef's eye. He rubbed the back of his neck, his long, shaggy hair swaying as he did. "Uh, yeah, I think I have everything in the bag. Are you ready?"

He extended his hand to me again. And I wondered if it was just a reflex. Or maybe he just wanted the leash. But it felt like a fresh start. I wondered if I could ever truly get one with him. Maybe I had to give it to myself first.

He'd been my reprieve growing up. Where the sun always shone. The one place I didn't have to be a people pleaser and I could do what I wanted. Ask for what I needed. And I was so tired of running from everything, especially from myself. And now, I was all out of reasons. Clean out of dumb excuses. No shields left to wield.

Want was now overriding everything. I'd crossed that line last night, and I didn't want to look back. So, I put my hand in his and took the leap of faith, letting his warm smile greet me. I realized at that moment how unlucky fools were and that I had been one of them for way too long.

Luna

CHAPTER 31

As the sun lowers
And the waves inch higher
A burst of warm colors fly by us
Basking us in a Kaleidoscope of Maui

-LUNA MANU MELE, 365 DAYS AROUND THE SUN

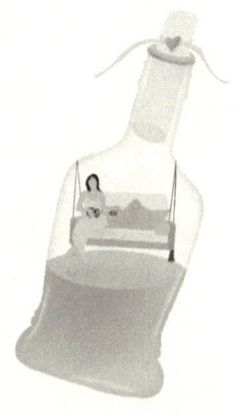

We found Tutu and Louis waiting on a bench in the lobby by one of the oversized tropical planters. Louis' arm was wrapped lightly around her as they drank their to-go coffees. Their picturesque nature made them easy to spot.

As soon as we neared, I could see Louis' mind race, his eyebrow raising at my choice of attire. "Luna, honey. I'm sure Lani would be happy to lend you something."

"Yes, dear, I always over pack. Louis is very kind to lug my enormous suitcase around without a word."

He laughed lightly. "I'm happy to do it. I can use the exercise. And I think there might have been some words yesterday. I'm showing my age." He looked at her and they both giggled. "But uh, Luna, why don't you take Lani up on—"

I cheekily raised the hem of my dress and turned to the side so he could get a good look at my 'dinosaurwear'. I turned my head backwards to take in their expressions.

"Reef already beat you to it, 'Anakala. He was quite concerned about my attire. I guess protective, big brother instincts die hard."

Reef was shaking his head, reddening. "You don't *need* to show them off."

"Oh, no, I was actually going to tie my dress up so I could *really* get the full effect of them on the hike." He only shook his head harder.

Tutu's laugh deepened, and she turned to Louis to explain. "Locke and Reef used to have sleepovers at my house when they were little, and they *loved Jurassic Park*. About broke the VHS. Luna would come over for movie night, too." She looked at us fondly.

Yes, those were some of my earliest memories of realizing I had a crush on someone. I would snuggle up to Reef in the scary parts where the dinos were about to eat someone. And Reef would wrap his arm around me and pull me close. It's when I learned what a 'safe person' felt like with my anxiety. He dulled all the harmful noises and heightened the good. It was magic. *He* was refuge.

I looked over at Reef under eyelids that were heavy with daydreams. So weighted, I barely heard Louis' voice. "Never mind. Please show them off. I didn't realize their significance." A little knowing smirk appeared where his wise age lines usually gathered.

My eyes tiptoed curiously over to my uncle. He never liked any of the guys I had dated. To be fair, I'd not chosen particularly well. Then again, it was difficult when I'd set these arbitrary rules to stay away from anyone who reminded me of Reef. As if that would keep the wound sealed like in a mummified tomb. It didn't. It only left space to create fresh ones.

But the way Louis reacted to Reef made my heart lift. He loved the way Reef took care of me. Louis appreciated the classic old school ways of romance. And I had to admit, with Reef, I did too. Because I knew with Reef, I was safe within them. I would never be held to old school gender constructs. He treated me as an equal. As a partner.

Louis cleared his throat and my eyes shot over to him. "I'm just going to grab the daily paper for us to read in the park." And with a smile at Tutu, he stood to make his way to the sundries' store. He was so old school. And it was so adorable. I knew he'd only buy one paper to share, too. Guaranteed. Finding a man like my uncle who could pull it off without toxic masculinity had seemed like an impossibility. But then I looked beside me.

Reef spoke up as Louis got up to leave. "Well, Locke

suggested Manoa falls. He said it was much more relaxing and we could have an easy, laid-back walk."

Tutu laughed. "So it's old-people-friendly. Sounds like Locke. He probably freaked out at the mention of Diamond Head."

Louis grinned, recognizing the truth there. "I like the sound of old-people-friendly. But I'll still get us a paper for when we decide the visitor center looks better."

He hurried off and Reef quickly added, "I don't think any of us were thrilled about the difficulty level of Diamond Head."

Tutu laughed at his remark. "Only if you're sure. We're happy to explore the park. But remember to take what Locke says with a grain of salt. This is the grandson who won't even let me cook dinner. Not that I'm complaining."

Reef smiled. "Normally, I'd agree, but the Diamond Head hike sounded pretty exhausting. I think this will be better for everyone. Plus, I think they filmed some of *Lost* at the falls."

"Really?I interjected, and Reef gave a tender nod. I knew they'd filmed it in Oahu, but I'd never known where. We had watched anything that was filmed on Hawaii growing up. It was kind of our thing. We'd try to guess the island or location. Apparently, we were going down memory lane today.

Louis came back with a newspaper tucked under his arm. Adjacent to his suspenders and the rolled-up sleeve of his Columbia button-up shirt. Only my 'anakala. And he was giving *me* a hard time about wearing a dress. Guess this is what artists looked like in the wild.

"Ready?" he asked as he offered Tutu his arm and we nodded.

I pulled Reef off to the side, letting them go ahead. "Do you remember when we watched *Lost*?"

He rubbed the back of his neck, a sly grin taking over his face. "Yeah, Locke was so into it, we could have done anything we wanted. Now that I think back on those movie nights, he was *super* unobservant."

"I think he thought I was just a big scaredy cat." I chuckled.

"*Lost* wasn't scary, Luna." Reef's eyes scanned mine. Heat building in them.

"No, but your hand finding mine sure was nice, anyway. The plane crash was pretty intense." I managed dryly.

"I knew there was a reason I did it," he remarked playfully. I bumped my shoulder into him. Nova just looked up at us, like she was trying so hard to understand what we were saying.

A fierce, nostalgic look filled Reef's eyes as he gazed at me. "I was so nervous. I had convinced myself you'd find a subtle and polite way to pull your hand away. I always felt like I should make the first move, but it was nerve-racking."

"I thought it was pretty obvious what I wanted. I had put my hand like an inch away from yours."

"No Luna, the one area where I could never read you very well was regarding your feelings for me. I always felt like I was going to get it wrong." My stomach twisted. Verbalizing what I wanted had always been hard for me. I wish I'd made it clearer. I certainly was going to try now. He deserved that. I did, too.

Suddenly, a wave of guilt came crashing in. It was a mistake to revisit this. Fake was fine. Real was *not*. He should be with someone who could give him *everything* he deserved. Someone who wouldn't hurt him. Who could be *everything* he needs. Someone who was enough.

And just like that, my words ran dry. I didn't tell him what he'd been desperately waiting for and *needed* to hear. If I didn't tell him why I left, then the barrier stayed.

As we reached Tutu and Louis at the hotel entrance, a painful wave emanated from my heart, and I closed my eyes.

"You kids alright?" Louis asked. "It's far too early for you two to be so lost in thought."

"Yeah," we both said in unison as our hands broke apart, which only made the searing pain grow. Louis' brow furrowed in response.

"Ok . . ." his voice trailed off as a cab pulled up and we quickly hopped in.

I opted for the front seat since motion sickness wasn't my friend and I figured Reef could use some space. Nova apparently wanted the same option as she tried to hop in the front seat with me.

I began closing the door. "Wait, don't you get motion sickness, too? I almost forgot. You probably have it worse than me, Reef."

"I'll be fine," he assured me as he ushered Nova into the back.

UNFORTUNATELY, something had gone tense between us. And being separated didn't help any. The picturesque drive, complete with quaint roadside stands and breathtaking mountain vistas, failed to calm my nerves.

I kept sneaking glances at Reef in the rearview mirror,

seeing his complexion grow paler. *Liar.* His eyes finally met mine in the mirror and a standoff began.

But when he went putrid, I abruptly called out to the taxi driver. "Please, pull over."

"Uh, I can't really–this isn't–"

"You're going to need to," I replied urgently. I knew green when I saw it, especially on Reef.

The driver heeded my advice and parked on the edge of a precariously narrow road overlooking the Oahu mountainside. Reef immediately rushed out of the car to the side of the road. Instinctively, I reached for the car handle, but Louis put a hand on my shoulder. I looked back at my uncle's calm face and relented, leaning back in my seat.

With a nod, Louis made his way to Reef's side, placing a hand lightly on his shoulder. In barely audible tones, that I'm sure no one was supposed to hear, Louis said, "Chivalry only goes so far, son. Or at least the right woman will only want it to. Respect your limits. Let her take care of you, too." Reef looked over at him and Louis continued, "There are many types of strength and all different definitions of being a man. Suffering shouldn't be one of them." He patted Reef's back again as more of that green color on his face took care of itself.

"Ok, son, this isn't just a *little* motion sickness." Louis was half teasing. "Do you want to talk about it?"

Reef straightened. And I wondered if they had any idea how much their voices carried on this highway. I looked back at Tutu and she shook her head.

I turned back to them and I could see Reef's chest heave. "It's just that I don't feel very . . . manly. Things like this–I'm never going to be–I've seen the type of men Luna has dated. They're the guys that fathers want their daughters to end up with. The type that fathers want their sons to be."

Louis clutched Reef's shoulder tightly. "Reef, if Luna ended up with that Azul guy, I would roll over in my grave. Don't confuse toxic masculinity with being a man. Sounds like someone might have confused the two. I *hated* the way Azul treated Luna. I wanted to make sure he stayed away from her this weekend. And I hate to admit it, but there's more than one reason you're here. I'm afraid I haven't been doing an outstanding job—"

With that, I started getting out of the car. It wasn't true. However, Tutu lightly reached for me. "*Ku'uipo,* let Louis try." I squeezed my eyes shut and stayed in place. Hoping Louis could help him.

Louis continued to explain. "Unfortunately, I think Luna's manager is worse than Azul. Those types of men think they can get away with treating women any way they want. That's not 'manliness', that's abuse. And should never be confused. Just like kindness should *never* be mistaken for weakness." I opened my car door against Tutu's protest. *This wound would stay sealed.* Enough. Their heads turned and Louis patted Reef on the shoulder again, knowing his work was done, and headed back to the car.

"You ok?" I asked Reef, taking Louis' place. He nodded, looking back out over the ravine. But his eyes still averted from mine as I came to stand beside him. "So, I guess I didn't remember *well* enough about your motion sickness."

"No, it's kind of gotten worse," he said sheepishly.

"Tell me next time, *please.* I want to know. Something like this would never make me see you any differently." He nodded slowly, and I placed my hand on his. "You've always been the type of man I wanted." His eyes looked over at me hesitantly as he stayed silent. And I couldn't swallow the guilt I felt in my throat. I'm sure there's no way he believed me. But I meant it with all my heart.

I squeezed his hand lightly, wishing I could at least give this to him. "Do you feel you can continue the trip if you sit in the front?" He nodded again, and we silently made our way back to the car. But when he held the front door open for me, I said, "Reef, we just went over this."

He tipped his head at the cab driver, who shrugged and nodded. I'm sure he'd prefer no one got sick in his car. Reef hopped in quickly, not giving the cab driver time to change his mind. Then he pushed his seat back and extended his hand to me. I laughed slightly as I positioned myself snuggly on his lap. Rather enjoying this new arrangement as I nestled into his warmth.

And I heard Louis whisper, "That's how a man does it."

Reef

CHAPTER 32

" She always made him feel like a 'man'. No matter what current trends dictated that definition to be. She let him choose his own descriptors of masculinity.

-REEF AKUA, TIDES OF LOVE

It certainly didn't feel like that's how a man did it, but I appreciated Louis' help. Locke often spoke about how much he'd enjoyed having Louis in his life, and I was seeing why. So, I was going to take the victory and enjoy Luna on my lap.

My breath left me, and with it, a sense of perfect unity with another. The perfectionist in me had always felt so bonded to the people pleaser in her. There's something special about finding someone who can empathize with your faults and not love you any less for them. And as she sat on my lap, I realized our connection was still just as special. Maybe even more so because it had survived distance and time. As if reminding us it would always be there waiting.

I gave Luna a little squeeze and she turned toward me. "I like this better, anyway."

"Yeah, me too," I whispered back. "Anything is better with you." Our smiles reunited, making the world feel righted, like only she could put it on its axis correctly.

Once the taxi dropped us off at the falls, we made our way to the trail's entrance, which was decorated with eclectic dinosaur stickers. A surefire indicator that this was indeed the location for the *Jurassic Park* filming. Besides the decals, the prehistoric feel instantly transported us to the movie's world.

As we began winding through the tropical forest, Louis' posture visibly relaxed. I guess he'd been more hesitant than he'd admitted. Tutu's smile widened as she took in the stunning scenery, and so did his own. Plus, the cool morning temperature and the forest's abundant shade made the journey easier.

When we got to the rocky area Locke had warned me about, I thought they'd want to turn around. But Tutu and

Louis just grasped hands and continued on. A testament to the value of a strong partnership. Something I could learn from. My intuition told me my education was just starting.

By the time we reached the large waterfall pool, we were all dewy and out of breath. With eager anticipation, Luna began removing her dress to dive into the refreshing water.

"Whoa," I began. "I know you want to show off your Jurassic gear, but Locke said there was a possibility of leptospirosis here. I had a pretty stern tour guide talk from him this morning. Or from Google. No way did he come up with that bacteria name off the tip of his tongue."

Luna laughed. "Ok, but I thought swimming here was the whole point. I was ready to cool down."

"Yeah, me too," Tutu chimed in. Looking down, I saw Nova panting in the heat; she appeared to concur.

"Well, Locke said there was a beach with a blowhole not too far away. But there's supposed to be a pretty cool Japanese temple and some botanical gardens close by, too."

"Unless we can swim in the koi pond, then I don't vote for that." Luna remarked.

"Ok, the beach it is." I chuckled.

The group trekked back with much less enthusiasm. Our spirits lifted, though, when we arrived at the soft, sandy beach, and spotted the blowhole Locke had described. It was pretty hard to miss the geyser erupting, its white foam shooting high into the sky.

"This is where they shot *From Here to Eternity*," Tutu said as we stood on the small beach looking out onto the raging waves and sparkling sea. A cozy, dark cave nestled within the rock formations nearby caught our eye, and I was eager to investigate. Out from the shoreline, the *Halona* blowhole was spouting water twenty to thirty feet up in the air. It certainly lived up to its 'lookout' name and was making quite the show for us. It was a passionate spot with the intensity of the roaring seas. One, we were all getting swept away by. This was the perfect romantic getaway.

I instinctively looked at Luna, letting emotions I'd only allowed to surface within the safety of a fictional world finally run free. They coursed through me harder than the waves against the jagged rocks. Remnants of long-lost love and hopeless romantic notions came over me. Maybe I had been too young to know my true feelings for her. But I was pretty sure you knew this type of love at *any* age. It's just that when you're young, it's so much harder to know what to do with it. How much it's worth fighting for. That's why I was terrified I wouldn't survive losing it again.

Unexpectedly, a surge of intense emotions slammed into me. *Hard.* I swallowed back the bittersweetness of the salty air and stolen memories, trying to push some of them down. But it was too late. The gates had opened. And there was no slow release.

Luna must have noticed my overcome look, because she playfully threw her dress at me. It hit my impassive face, landing with surprise.

"Come on, I'm ready for one of those sandcastle competitions." Mischief twinkled in her eyes.

I scanned over her boxers, which she had rolled up adorably, inhaling sharply as I took time to fully appreciate them.

"Yeah?" I asked as I picked up her dress. Then started following her as she ran off toward the shore to stake out her claim.

"*Mili`apa!*" she called.

"Are you sure that's the competition you want to pick?

Yours never got past the first level." I teased. Her call of 'slowpoke', egging me on.

She laughed as she shot me a determined look, which sent currents of electricity rippling through me. As we started digging through the sand, I looked up to see that Tutu and Louis had already found a spot to set up their blanket. They definitely looked much more like the iconic romantic movie couple. But I was okay with that. I loved seeing this side of Luna.

Lost in the world of our sandcastles, I was concentrating on my castle's second floor when I felt someone's arm brush against mine. I looked over to see Luna's first level was already crumbling. She truly was horrible at this. An adorable fact which I loved. So I waved her over, and she started picking out shells to decorate mine. Even Nova was pretty happy to chew on a piece of driftwood she'd found beside Luna. I told Nova we'd play catch in a minute, but honestly, I think she was pretty content gnawing on her new treasure.

Luna studied a shell, flipping it over in between her fingers. "Do you ever want one of these for real?"

"A sandcastle?" I teased, as she created some shell windows. She bit her lip *way* too seductively, making my answer slip out seamlessly. "Yeah, I do."

"What do you see in yours?" she asked quietly, continuing with her nautically inspired interior design.

"Nova for starters." She nodded at me, her eyes way too intent on the sand walls. "And a woman who understands me. One who encourages me to pursue my dreams the same as I do for them. Someone who I can create a safe home with, who I trust and respect. Who I can build a life with." She looked at me.

"Is that all?" There was this intense expression on her face that I couldn't decipher.

"Yeah, I mean, I think that's pretty amazing. Don't you?"

She nodded vigorously. "Yes. Reef, but–" She faltered. I tried to encourage her to continue as I patiently waited. Her face suddenly softened. "That's what I want, too."

A heaviness fell between us as a longing burned in both our eyes. After a few moments, words slipped out of me to lighten the mood. "So, are we going to continue down memory lane today?" I raised my eyebrow, and she looked at me suspiciously. "I think there are some tide pools over there and a cave as well." I nodded my head in their direction as her face lit up.

We brushed ourselves off and began exploring the cave together. It was just a small, one-way-to-the-back cave, and it got dark pretty quickly. But it reminded me of when we were kids. Although, I hadn't wanted to kiss her quite this badly then. Or maybe I had. I just didn't feel like I could control the desire any longer, especially with all the privacy the dark cave afforded us here. All I could think about was backing her up against the cool rock face while I let my eyes linger over her in whatever light remained. Then I'd brush my fingertips along her lips to convey my intentions, before finally tasting them while pressing against her and the chilly cave wall.

I blinked to refresh my mind instead. Then, I reached for her hand and led her out of the cave, feeling like it was time for the tide pools in a *very public* area. Somewhere I could compose myself and think clearly. Sensing the abrupt switch, Luna's head tilted slightly, but she still followed.

It took little convincing since tide pools had been one of our favorite things to explore growing up. Thankfully, we hadn't outgrown it. There was pure joy on Luna's face as we searched the pools and we pointed out different tropical species to each other. They were mostly filled with sea urchins and mussels today. But it was the search that mattered.

"Remember our aquariums?" She chuckled.

"How could I forget them?" Luna had this far off look in her eye as she bent down by one of the pools. We only put what we caught in them. That was the rule, and we got to name each other's finds. "Yeah, I think Mr. Helmet Head was your crowning glory." She laughed at the name she'd given my helmet sea urchin.

"Well, I think it was more creative than My Little Pony for the baby seahorse you found me." She laughed some more. "I really liked Mr. Helmet Head." *Yeah, I did too. I loved everything she gave me.*

The waves slapped against the rocks that sheltered the pools, breaking my trance. A little oasis tucked away from the harshness of the world. I looked at Luna, feeling like she was exactly that for me—a little tide pool of comfort and security. I prayed it still worked both ways.

I gazed back out at the rough water. "So, are we going to try swimming here, or is it too dangerous?"

"I think if we stick together, it'll be alright," she said with meaning. So that's what we did. We waded into the water, past everyone else. Feeling brave because we had each other. I held her tightly amidst the waves, hoping we carried that tidal pool feeling of safety wherever we went, as long as we had each other.

Luna

CHAPTER 33

But with you, everything is new
With you, I feel I've come unglued

-LUNA MANU MELE, THE ONLY
MAN I COULD LOVE

It wasn't long before the currents increased in strength. I was hanging on to Reef as if he was a harbor buoy. Greedily enjoying the warmth of his skin and the rush of adrenaline it provided. Any excuse to lessen the distance between us was welcome. I'd gladly take on the raging sea just to cling on to his body.

Before long, we spotted Louis on the shore waving his arms.

"Guess this isn't the best swimming spot, after all," Reef said. "But I'm rather enjoying fighting off the waves with you." A sweet grin overtook him.

I just continued to mold myself to him as if we were in the calmest seas. "Yes, I agree. Nice to have my life raft buddy back," I said as I gazed into his eyes rather fearlessly.

Growing up, we had both agreed that we'd pick each other as our *Castaway* companion. Our personal Wilson. If I had to spend the rest of my life on a deserted island, I'd gladly spend it with him. I wanted to be the one who always bailed the other out. No questions asked.

With one last nod, we made our way to Louis, who suggested we head to a different beach further up the coast, where there were hopefully calmer seas. Watching us, Louis' brow visibly furrowed; he and Kelani were clearly avoiding those waves. So we agreed. I wouldn't mind seeing more of this beautiful island.

When we arrived at the beach Louis had suggested, he and Tutu found a spot on the shore and sat with their feet in the surf, arms intertwined, while we went off to explore some more. They'd been kind enough to keep Nova so she could stay cool in the shade of their umbrella. The driver had talked about a spot that only the locals visited and we were eager to see if we could find it.

We made our way to the end of the beach, where it

turned into craggy, bleached lava rocks. Reef reached for my arm to steady me as we walked over the uneven terrain, finally coming to an opening that exposed the sea. Below, a little mermaid cave peeked out that would be all our own.

I eyed the rickety ladder that had been left in the opening and tied in the hole. I really wasn't sure how it stayed there when the fierce tide rolled in. My eyebrow shot up at Reef.

"Ladies first?" He teased as he looked at the questionable ladder. Then he relented. "I'll go first. I'm taller, so I can probably just pull you down. Plus, if I get stuck, no one will miss me at the ukulele festival."

"I would certainly miss you, but I'm definitely going to take you up on your offer and let chivalry resuscitate." The bright sunshine and a satisfied grin danced along his lips at my reply.

Once he reached the sandy bottom, he looked up at me from the little grotto. He could actually extend his arms and reach the top of the rocky hole.

"It wasn't bad. I'm right here," he reassured me.

Breathing out, I moved forward. And it was at that moment that I realized I trusted him. *A lot.* My usual calculated and careful self didn't do things like this.

Cautiously, I found my footing, and descended slowly into the hole. I didn't even know his hands were on me until I was further down the ladder. I turned slightly, realizing there was only a short jump left, but he was already there to help me. His hands were firmly on my hips. All I had to do was put my hands on his shoulders and let go so he could lower me slowly down.

I exhaled, and I grabbed onto him tightly. *Time to see about that trust, Luna.* A potent friction arose between our bodies as I released the ladder and slid onto him. Its power felt like a deliberate attack on my nerves. Reef stopped lowering me when our faces were level, and my breath hitched. I wasn't used to seeing him this way. All I wanted to do was wrap my legs around him and feel even *more* of him.

Especially those lips. The ones that were beckoning to me, only inches away. *Show him, Luna. Show him he's the only man you could love.*

The thin fabric of my bikini and cover-up did little to shield me. Every touch felt amplified, and my heart felt like it was pounding into him. Then he blinked, lowering me all the way down until my feet touched the ground and reality. My heart plummeting to the rocky floor with me.

However, I didn't remain in that state for long upon observing the breathtaking world around me. Being in this little mermaid cove, away from any prying eyes, felt amazing. Ever since we'd gone in the last cave, I couldn't wait to be alone with Reef again. Somewhere *other* than the honeymoon suite, with its preconceived notions and pressures.

But this little oasis was perfect for us, with its tranquil water reflecting on the low cave ceiling. Hints of natural light spilled in from gaps in the lava rock. Past the stones, a small, shallow beach basked in shade. You'd be completely unaware of this world. So much simmered underneath the stony exterior of this grotto.

I waded through the water and the rocky bottom, taking my time to enjoy the ethereal effects of the cave as I made my way to the beach area. I intended to lie out on the 'shoreline' like a beached mermaid and sift my hands through the sand to search for shells. Enjoying the nothingness and the overwhelming beauty all at the same time. With my mental health, sometimes that's all I could do and exactly what I needed. And I was learning it wasn't selfish to take care of yourself. That finding stability looked different for everyone and was such an important piece of life. One that should be beautiful, not judged.

Reef's eyes tracked me as I situated myself, stomach down in the sand. Allowing myself to feel the sand's textures as it molded into me. There was this hungry look in his eyes that I hadn't seen before. A mature longing. Even deeper than before. And I allowed myself to bask in the gaze of this man, leaning into the feeling it provided. A fire unfurling through my veins. Knowing he truly saw me for all that I was.

Quietly, he came to lie beside me. "All this cave to explore and you're beaching yourself here?" he said playfully, his tone barely above a whisper.

"Oh yes, I intend to look for prehistoric shells." I half laughed. After all, this place looked like an ancient world.

My eyes intently searched through the sand, my hand digging through the grains, when I felt his touch. His hand gently brushed beside my arm, sending ripples of electricity through me. A pulsing in my belly daring me to reciprocate.

But I only managed a glance at him, finding his eyes intently on me, fixated on my lips. The pulsing quickened as a stormy look crossed his face and his fingers moved down my arm to my hand, as if he'd found what he was looking for. Without taking his gaze off my lips, he intertwined our fingers, and I felt all my skin go on alert, especially against my light aqua blue bikini.

A little sigh escaped me, and he raised an eyebrow, his glasses moving with it. "Good thing we have those fake relation rules in place."

"Oh, yeah?" I barely choked out.

"Yeah, I've been thinking about your lips for so long, I

don't think I could ever 'pretend' to kiss them. Tasting you could never be fake."

I swallowed, a heat swallowing my body. His boldness took me by surprise. The cave must really be affecting him, too. *What was down here? Mermaid endorphins?* Maybe this was exactly what we needed. No distractions. To get out of our heads and into a world of our own. *Just the two of us.*

I tried to steady my voice. "Well, maybe we should practice in case it's needed. *For real.* Just so it doesn't take you by surprise. I wouldn't want you to be *totally* unprepared. Louis would give you such a lecture." The sultry tone that I reserved just for him was finding its sea legs, coming back to me so easily. Just like my love for him.

"Yeah, I think I could use some practice. I don't usually get to kiss gorgeous musicians who once stole my heart."

Stole. That's exactly what I did. And ran off without a word, leaving him bare. I swallowed against sandpaper and a fleck of worry crept into the corners of his eyes, tinging our bubble. I shook the thoughts away, trying to return to this oasis.

I brought my hand to his jaw, running my thumb along the stubble. Trying to get used to all his changes that were driving every atom of me mad. I needed him to know how badly I wanted this. Wanted him. That he wasn't alone in this need and desire. I wasn't going to leave him alone again. Not if he wanted *me.* Not if he chose me.

My lips began drifting toward his, already feeling their warmth. Endorphins had my imagination running wild when Louis' voice came crashing through like a rogue cymbal in the middle of a prelude.

His voice broke the spell. "Luna, honey, the tide is coming in! You don't want to be down there for that. Plus, we should get you back to the resort so you can get ready for tonight's event."

His words hung between us like thick smog as I looked at Reef. Our eyes were still hungrily fixed upon each other.

"Coming!" I called back. A shared sadness filled the small space between Reef and me. I didn't want to leave this world. Because this world didn't feel like 'pretend' at all to me.

Luna

CHAPTER 34

Some forces are stronger
Some tides pull harder
Some darkness falls faster
Time was never our friend

-LUNA MANU MELE, 365 DAYS AROUND THE SUN

. . .

I was surprised how well our sightseeing excursion went today, especially after last night's dinner. Now, if only I could be so lucky with the welcome gathering. But I was worried about what Reef might see of my musical business world. The glimpses Venice and Louis had given him were enough. All embarrassingly true. I'd let them use my anxiety and faults against me. And I'd believed all the things they'd said in order to keep that control. Making me feel so helpless and small.

"Luna?" Reef found me on the balcony, gazing off into infinity. He took Nova off her leash from her after-dinner stroll. The fabric of my light blue gossamer dress swished in the light of the waning sunset, making me feel like Cinderella. "*Hô*! You look–Wow, Luna, you look *stunning*." His jaw ticked as his eyes roamed over me intensely. The words 'how beautiful' leaving his mouth hit my chest like a power punch.

"You too," I said way more breathily than I'd meant to. "Way better than Bond. I think Cinderella just got an upgrade tonight."

"Yeah?" he asked, fidgeting with his hair self-consciously, before he halted himself. He'd even styled it away from his face, sweeping it back in this sexy way.

He lowered his hand and started walking toward me. The bodice of my dress suddenly was feeling too tight, like I couldn't breathe. But . . . not in a bad way.

Reef lightly brushed his thumb along my jawline as he gazed into my eyes. Letting his fingers travel to my bottom lip, so he could outline it slowly. Sparks tingled everywhere he touched, cascading down to the soles of my feet.

Suddenly, his hand dropped, and my eyes shifted back and forth in confusion.

"We should go. They'll all be waiting for you," he whispered.

My heart sank; as if in a freefall. I *still* didn't have the nerve to make known what I wanted. And my heavy heart said there must be a reason he stopped. So, I simply nodded.

We awkwardly headed down to the courtyard where the hotel was hosting the luau. With nothing but silence between us, a chaos of tumbleweeds in my mind. Thankfully, conversation flowed easily when we found Louis and Tutu. And other than my brain over-analyzing what had almost happened on our lanai, the night was going smoothly. Even Azul and Steve were staying away from me. And Reef's easygoing nature and personable skills took the pressure off of me. I think the patrons ended up liking him more than they did me. However, the more they laughed, the more side-eye stares we received from Azul. And the closer Reef pulled me into him, the harder he glared. *This is why you don't date people at work.*

I glanced over my shoulder at Louis, who was at a table nearby, his jacket and arm wrapped around Tutu. He gave me an encouraging nod, happy to see everything going well. I tucked myself closer beside Reef as he spoke with the couple in front of us. He truly was home. Everything I had been searching for was right in front of me. *Support. Safety.*

Finally, I could relax enough to enjoy meeting people. And Reef made sure we met only a few people at a time, so it was an easier one-on-one situation. And every so often, he'd bend down and whisper in my ear to check on me. My heart swelled a little more every time he did. So much so that I found it a little hard to continue doing my job of meeting and greeting people. I just wanted to be alone with Reef in some pitch-dark alcove under the blissful stars.

As thoughts of being alone with Reef swirled through my head, I noticed Azul's looks had turned to hard glares. *Oh no. Not now.* He was knocking back drinks harder than a scorned bridesmaid at an open bar. And Steve was scolding him, since he was completely ignoring the guests. Those two should sail off into the sunset together in *Some Like it Hot* style.

I tried averting my eyes from them for the rest of the evening and I was pretty much succeeding. Everything was falling into place—laughter and hors d'oeuvres framed the brilliant Hawaiian sunset—when Steve snuggled up to the microphone. Equipment magically started appearing all around him. *Oh no.*

"Ahem . . . Hmmm." He cleared his throat on a mic screech. The crowd winced. My sentiments exactly. "I thought it would be nice to see if Luna would grace us with a little of her musical musings tonight. How many of you love *One More Hour?*" The crowd started cheering. *Grace us.* I rolled my eyes internally. "How many of you would love to hear it as a duet?" *What? . . . No.*

I took one look at Reef and suddenly found a plan. Not waiting for my synapses to catch up, I reached for his hand, finding all the courage I needed there. I was finished being manipulated. I was done being used and treated as weak. I *was* a fighter. I'd fought before. And I needed to remember that. A flicker inside of me was becoming a flame, ignited by the heat of Reef's hand inside mine.

Surprise lit up Reef's face as he looked at me. "Can you still sing?" I asked.

His brow arched. "Why?" he reluctantly stage-whispered back to me before his eyes followed mine toward the mic. Reef's eyes grew in size. "Luna, you don't want me to– I can't play. *At all.* Zero musical talent here."

"But you can sing." Or at least he could when we were kids. I loved his voice. I still heard it in my dreams. He looked at me, stunned. "Please," I begged.

He gave an apprehensive nod, and I squeezed his arm tightly. Reef graciously set down his drink and followed me, letting me guide him toward the "stage". Within minutes, we had reached the front of the crowd. I guess this was karma for putting Tutu and Louis on the spot by asking them to play together at my luau a few months ago. But this was pushing things *too* far, and Steve knew it.

"Oh, Luna," Steve began innocently, handing me a mic, enjoying every minute of my discomfort. "There you are."

"WHY HERE I AM, STEVE," I said in my best 'talk show host' voice, appeasing him.

An alarmed smile replaced his Cheshire cat one. "Yes, the one and only," he said, recovering. "And she's thrilled to do this duet with Az–"

"Yes," I quickly interjected, "with my boyfriend, Reef. This is a love song, after all. One I wrote about him." I turned to Reef and saw a calmness overtake his eyes. But his mind appeared to have gone somewhere else. "Reef, would you join me, please? There are two stools."

Reef hesitantly leaned toward me. "Luna, are you sure?" he said through ventriloquist lips, self-doubt seeping in.

"Yes, *positive*," I whispered in his ear. He moved closer, pulling me in by the waist passionately. Then he kissed my cheek softly, lingering on my skin as his breath ebbed and flowed at just the right spot. Effectively making it look like we'd been whispering sweet nothings to each other. The crowd swooned. Reef had just tied Steve's hands.

I looked up at Reef, wishing the crowd wanted more. Because I needed more. I was pathetically shaken by just that touch. I didn't know how I was going to play now. Especially as the squeezing sensation in my chest increased. The warmth from his lips was thrumming heat throughout my entire body. Lighting me up in a way no one else had ever managed.

I watched like an immovable statue as Reef took a seat on a stool and I waited for them to bring me a ukulele. *I was frozen.* This was supposed to be the other way around. I was glad he had told me he knew all the lyrics to *One More Hour.* And I hoped that would still be true under the spotlight.

I finally found my stool and leaned over to whisper to him, "We'll alternate verses and sing the chorus together. Just like when we were kids. If you get lost in your verse, I'll sing with you." I slipped the ukulele strap over my head. He nodded, but with a most apprehensive expression. "Ready?" I asked.

He nodded again, looking like he was ready to leave his body and start levitating. Reef was *not* a crowd person. He didn't like the attention. But his eyes stayed anchored to me. From the moment I mentioned writing him a love song, they'd been fixated on me. I was overcome with worry that I'd said too much, his deep, searching gaze and heavy chest making me worry I'd divulged too much.

However, the song started really well, and the tightness

in my chest released. I was more relaxed than I ever had been while performing on stage. Reef had a way of making me feel calm, even in the worst of situations. If the world was ending, I think I'd just pull out a board game and quietly enjoy the end with him. Or perhaps after this, just grab my ukulele.

I sang the first stanza and when Reef's voice came in for the chorus; it was like a shockwave to my system. His eyes continued to capture mine and the desire I saw in them sliced through me as my lyrics took on new meaning. That night six months ago at my welcome luau, when I finally approached him, had left a deep impression on my memory. And those desperate feelings were now igniting my voice.

As the second stanza rapidly approached, I became a little nervous. However, Reef took over seamlessly, as if we'd practiced the song in his tree house a million times. He sounded even better by himself, and waves of nostalgia melted over me like honey. His voice had deepened in ways that sent shivers through me. And I began relaxing into his classic, singer-songwriter tone, being transported to a place where just the two of us belonged.

But something tugged at the edges of my mind, snapping me back to this world. My mind kicked into high gear when I realized the lyrics were changing. *Oh no, he needs help.* But as I studied Reef's face, it was completely serene. He was replying. Writing his *own* stanza. Like we used to do. He was swept up in the moment with me. As the stanza rapidly neared an end, I realized I had a choice. I could play it safe, like I always did, or I could reply, just for him.

> *So long ago, you were the only one*
> *Who could truly see me*

The only one who believed
So long ago, it seemed we had forever waiting
And were always meant to be
Just give me one more hour with you
But I'd gladly spend forever with you, too
Just give me one more hour
And I'd give anything to show you
How I've kept loving you
Just give me one more hour
And you'll see, you've always been the only one
    for me
Please let the stars guide you
Because I've always been here waiting

MY BREATH CAUGHT in the last verse. Something clicked in my mind. *Let the stars guide you.* It was clawing at my memory. I stared at him with tears building in my eyes. It was like he was delivering his heart to me on a silver platter. *What more could I ask for?*

Time had run out. The words left me without a second thought. And it was then that I realized that with him, I would *always* go with my heart. Because I trusted him.

Anxiety was my only company
A cycle of belittling
Until you intervened
And took the time to care for me
Not so long ago, you did what no one else would
What no one else could
Just give me one more hour with you

Anything will do
Just give me one more hour
I'll do anything to show you
How much you mean to me
Just give me one more hour
And you'll see, you've always been the only one
  for me

MY UKE STOPPED ABRUPTLY, my soul emptied before him. I was clinging to my strings in the dead silence while he stared at me with his heart completely exposed. Shockwaves replaced my heartbeats. *What had I just done?* A tear silently slipped down my cheek. Brief flashes went off in the distance, capturing the time of death for my resistance.

Steve abruptly stood in front of the mic and the crowd started calling him away, upset that he was interrupting the moment. *Our moment.*

"Well, that was certainly something." He couldn't keep the displeasure out of his tone. Annoyed, we had pulled off my crazy idea of singing a duet without any practice. "Let's give them a round of applause and see who we have next." The crowd went crazy, shouting *hana hou* and 'encore'. Steve started quieting them immediately.

Reef reached out his hand to escort me back to my seat. But he quickly retracted it, as if he wasn't sure what to do. Like maybe it was a good idea if we didn't touch after what had just transpired. I had to agree. My feelings were so electrified at this moment, it was best to go back quietly before I gave these people a proper show. Perhaps I should go into damage control mode, but there was no going back after what had just happened on that stage.

As soon as I slipped into a seat at the table, Louis eyed me curiously. A tender smile played on his knowing lips. "I didn't know it went like that."

"It does now. It *definitely* does now," I replied with all of my heart.

Reef

CHAPTER 35

> When did we stop seeing people and only start seeing their labels? I certainly wanted to be seen as more than that. Not to love her wholly would be such a mistake.

-REEF AKUA, WHISPERS OF WAIKIKI

. . .

I 'm not sure what all had happened on that stage, but my heart had flooded out. And it seemed I had received hers in return.

None of this was for show. Nothing ever had been. And all I wanted was some time alone with her to make that clear. It was driving me crazy. Forget an hour. Just give me a few minutes.

When I didn't think I could take it any longer, Louis said he would cover for Luna if she needed to get some rest. He'd pass along any other information she needed for tomorrow. Most of the patrons had dispersed, anyway. So, we quickly took Louis up on his kind offer and began walking in a stupor through the open-air corridors.

As we walked, a cool night breeze, salty with the scent of the sea, gently blew through the archways. I wrapped my jacket around Luna, and she blushed in gratitude. Which was followed by an exchange of coy glances ricocheting between us down the rest of the corridor. The insanely romantic backdrop of the properly named 'heaven on earth' hotel only made our glances more heated. Her lavender scent, mixing with the sea air, only intoxicated me even further.

We were just about to cut through the lobby to the elevators when I spotted an off balance 'Fabio' catching up to us. Staggering toward us, he broke through our blissful bubble. *Great. Exactly what this evening needed.* Tonight had been what I needed to muster the courage to lay my heart on the line. I'd gotten the declaration of my dreams and I didn't want to lose my nerve.

Azul's rough voice soared through the air, catching me off guard like a horror clip sliced into a romance film.

"This one is damaged," he shouted as we entered the hotel lobby, taking full aim at us with his inebriated words. He staggered closer with more force now. Pointing at Luna like she had a scarlet letter on her chest.

I pulled her to my side reflexively, but he began raising his voice even louder, as well as his drink. "You hear me?" he asked aggressively, looking directly at me. There was a vitriolic undertone to his words, and I hugged Luna tighter, not knowing what else to do. Feeling this inherent power-lessness.

Whatever protector instincts I possessed, I now wanted them to come out in full force. It didn't take years of mixology to spot *his* type. I'd known Azul and Steve were decidedly toxic. And I wondered how many more like them were skulking about this industry.

Azul continued bitterly while sloshing his drink around. "Yeah, get a refund before it's too late. I just thought you should know because I sure didn't. Unless you're magic or something, you'll find your product is defective. And I highly doubt you're up to the task, Mr. Nobody."

My hands curled into fists at the word *defective*. What a hideous human being someone had to be to call someone 'damaged' for dealing with their mental health. Luna was beautiful and brave to perform with panic attacks, and to *keep* performing. *Not* damaged. *Not* broken. If anything, I only loved her more. I only found her *more* beautiful. They had shaped her into the person she was today.

My hands clenched tighter as his words burned in my brain. I immediately started toward Azul, but Luna grabbed me. "Reef, no. He's drunk. He's *not* worth it."

I glanced back at her quickly, intending to shake my head, but then I saw her face. A hollowed out expression etched on it that I never wanted to see there. As if Azul had just fractured her on the spot, knowing how to pinpoint her vulnerability so succinctly that he shattered her with one blow. I had to get her out of here, as far away from him as possible. Nothing else mattered, *especially* not him.

"Yeah, you better run, glasses," he slurred. "Take your broken prize with you—"

But I wasn't listening anymore. I had Luna pressed against me as tightly as possible. My jacket wrapped around her like a protective shield. "You ok?" I stupidly asked.

"Can we just go back to the room?" she whispered, and I noticed her shaking slightly. I nodded, glad I could at least do something for her. No matter how small.

I swallowed nervously, searching for courage and the right words. Yes, I prayed I found the right words. "Luna, don't listen to that jerk. Panic attacks and anxiety are *not* something to be ashamed of and they are certainly not something that makes a person 'damaged' or weak. If anything, I think, you've been strengthened by them. I know you don't have a choice but to get through them somehow, but you also don't *have* to live your life this way. You could make it so much easier on yourself, but you *choose* to keep helping people through your music, to keep living your dream, to endure more episodes than you have to. You choose to endure them with positivity and grace. And I know *that's* a choice. I'm sure, a *very* hard one. *That's strength.*"

Her misty eyes looked up at me. Green specks overtaking them. A whole wilderness in them just for me. And I wanted to get lost in their beauty again. Wander amongst her secrets. "Reef, that's not my 'damage'. At least not all of it." A glassy sheen threatened to spill over her beautiful eyes as we made our way to the elevator lift.

As soon as the doors opened, she went to a corner and

tucked herself away in it. I quietly took a place beside her and watched the doors close. A numb confusion taking over me.

As soon as the doors closed, I turned to her. "Luna," I breathed. I didn't know what to do, but I was being drawn to her, the tether from earlier pulling at me even harder. I placed my hands on either side of her hips, grabbing the cold railing with everything I had, desperate to be close to her.

Then I leaned into her slightly. "He's just an idiot who's upset he lost the best thing he's ever had. Nothing in the world could make me want to 'return' you. If you were mine, I'd do *anything* to keep you."

Her eyes became even glossier as they drifted up to meet mine. "You don't even know what it is." She looked away. "I didn't think I needed to tell you since this is all . . ."

"This is all what?" I asked her more pointedly. Her lips parted, but she said nothing. I could see the ghost of the word 'fake' on them. I gripped the railing tighter. "I never wanted any of this to be pretend. Not one second of it has been for me. Has it been for you?"

She shook her head methodically, as if knowing what she was unleashing, and my lips curved upward at her response. Especially when her body gravitated toward mine like she couldn't stand to be apart.

I started to remove my glasses, knowing this was the first time my feelings and intentions would be on full display for her. The first time, nothing would be covered up under the guise of Louis' plan.

"Luna, why did you write *One More Hour*? Was what you said on stage true?" I asked with urgency.

But her face said it all. I didn't need the words her lips

mouthed so sensually . . ."Yes . . . It was *you* I wanted. I've *always* wanted you. I still do."

As I went to pull off my glasses, she stopped me, shaking her head emphatically. I felt like a dork, with the goofiest grin on display.

"What? You want me to keep them on? I was trying to look less like a nerd." I laughed nervously as I leaned even closer to her, my hands clutching the railing beside her.

"Yes, they have to stay on. It's required." But she was only halfway teasing, and I loved it. "Do you know how many fantasies I've had about this?"

"No, why don't you tell me?" I began coyly.

"Enough to have a bet with myself about how fast I can fog them up." She smirked.

"Oh, I'm seeing the appeal now. Maybe this nerd thing can have some perks," I mumbled. But all my cockiness left me as I became overwhelmed by her. Especially as she reached up for the collar of my dress shirt and tugged me toward her. The smell of the plumeria flower in her hair and the scent of Luna overcoming any hesitation. I wanted to bottle her scent along with this moment.

Our faces were only inches apart, warmth radiating between us. And I was ready to close any of the distance between us. Need taking over in a way I'd never known, when she breathed out, "Why didn't you ever kiss me?"

"I couldn't tell if you wanted me to." A pain twisted at her cheeks with my words.

There was a hard tug on my shirt collar. A very clear sign of her want. And with that, all space and time vanished. It was just her lips on mine as I leaned into every part of her. Every part I knew intimately and loved . . . *all of her*. Allowing myself to taste her for the *very* first time.

I pulled back suddenly, and her eyes looked simultaneously confused and incredibly disappointed.

"Wait," I interjected, and her face fell. I pushed off of the handrails and moved toward the elevator pad. Quickly, I pulled the emergency button, halting the elevator.

"Reef, you can't do that." Her eyes flashed with mixed amusement and sheer concern.

With a confidence I didn't know I possessed, I strode back over to her. "Oh, but I think I already did." I readjusted my glasses to look at her, the ones that were already fogged up. "Now, where were we?"

She laughed as my hands slid around the back of her thighs to pick her up, gently propping her against the elevator railing. Her legs seamlessly wrapped around me like they were always meant to be there.

"Oh yeah, here." The words tumbled out of me.

Luna only laughed harder and then raked her hands upward through my hair, pulling me in with more force this time. I met her heady passion with a strong desire of my own this time. But I was becoming increasingly aware that I had kind of cornered her. And what started out feeling sexy now felt like it could cause anxiety. And that's the last thing I ever wanted. I spun us around, effectively swapping our positions, hoping to give her more space and control. I was *absolutely fine* with her cornering me.

Luna looked at me and her legs squeezed even tighter around me as her fingers dug deeper. Sending shockwaves through my scalp and back. I guess I'd made the right call. Especially when her lips melted over mine and then started roaming, making use of my neck in ways no one had ever properly done before. I had gotten everything wrong in my novels. No kiss I wrote could ever compare to this. I was going to need to make a few revisions.

"Miss!" the intercom burst forth from the elevator speaker. We looked at each other with wide eyes. "Miss, please disentangle yourself and step away from the gentleman." I started laughing and Luna gave me a look that said it wasn't funny. "We're going to be overriding the elevator panel and resuming normal functions as soon as . . . you . . . huh hmm . . . *Remove* yourself."

But Luna just stayed glued to me, like a scared monkey. Her face was a mixture of shock and embarrassment. "Ma'am," the booming voice rang out, *"Please* don't make me call security."

"Yeah, stop mauling me, Luna. Geez." Now she was laughing, too, as I helped her stand beside me. She appeared as off balance as I felt. Her knees even buckled at the point of contact with the floor. With a sly smile, I pointed to the other corner of the elevator. "You better go over there, just to be safe."

She just shoved me lightly, like when we were kids, and the elevator started moving. The booming voice thanked us for our 'cooperation,' no matter how unenthusiastically we had complied with the request. And then Luna's long, petite fingers found their way in between mine. A peaceful reverberation echoing throughout my body when she did. She was like that first cool breeze coming off the ocean at the end of the hottest day. She was my happy place. Everything that made our island special, she encompassed it all so well. The heartbeats of this place were the people. The heartbeats were her.

My eyes dared to glance over at her, and the intimacy of this moment changed me. I would never look at love the same way. She had just cracked something wide open inside of me. Right at the place that had been scarred so many years ago, and then forever placed herself inside it.

Luna

CHAPTER 36

Why did summer have to end?
Why did the darkness creep in?
What do I have to do to make it back to you?
I'd gladly travel 365 days around the sun
Just to steal one more day with you
So until the summer sun rises,
Just know I'll be missing you
And you'll always be my one

> -LUNA MANU MELE, 365 DAYS
> AROUND THE SUN

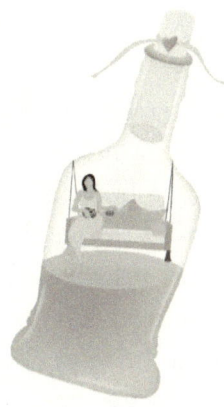

Mauling people in elevators wasn't something I did. I showed 'passion' in one area: music. It was the only space where I allowed myself to lose control. Where I was completely honest with myself. And Louis was the only person allowed to take that journey with me.

Ding. The elevator doors opened, and we exchanged smiles. Reef reached for my hand and my heart picked up speed, knowing exactly what he could do to me now.

We started our journey down the hallway, which felt like a never-ending labyrinth. Especially since a quiet threatened to consume us. Reef opened the door for me, releasing my hand, and we walked into our room in quiet contemplation.

The dimly lit entryway revealed his tousled hair, wrinkled shirt, and crooked glasses—the ones I'd quickly fogged up. I really had let go in the elevator. And as I took in his adorably sexy appearance, it made me want to do it all again. This time letting go of the self-restraint I always had so perfectly in place.

But something icy tugged at me harder and it was winning. Reef's brow furrowed in response. But I began before he could. Because I knew I couldn't put it off any longer, nor did I want to. I wanted him, which meant I had to tell him everything. If I was going to let him have a choice, he needed to know what that choice was. I just hoped he wouldn't do the 'nice guy' thing. I wanted more than anything for him to choose me, but I'm not sure I had it in me to believe it was possible.

"Reef," I breathed out.

His words left in a rush. "Am I making you uncomfortable? What happened in the elevator doesn't change anything. I'll still make my pillow fort—"

He was always so aware of me. I'd chalked it up to Reef and his ability to read people—his ease with them. But now I realized he was always meant to read me. As if I were a language written only for him.

"Reef," I tried again. "About what Azul said—"

He moved to me, his height making it easy to close the space like my body wanted. "Hey, just forget about him."

"No, I *need* to tell you. You deserve to know." The words ached on their way out.

Reef's eyes poured over me, liquefying every piece of my body. His tone turned soft. "Azul doesn't know what he's talking about, and I don't *need* to know anything, Luna." He placed his hands tenderly on my hips. "Nothing is going to change how I feel about you. I'm pretty sure a quarter of a century is proof of that."

"But I *want* to tell you." He looked softly at me as he held me like I was something precious. Then he nodded slightly. The entryway of this gorgeous suite suddenly felt dark and heavy. The weight on my chest was returning, and I forced myself to relax. *To breathe.*

"Reef . . . my family moved to the Big Island when I was young so I could get medical help. They kept it quiet because they were hoping we'd be able to return home quickly and I could go back to school. They didn't want people to treat me differently. Only close family members like Louis knew, and they kept it to themselves. There were more facilities and technology on the Big Island, and I needed them. My family uprooted their whole life for me and left everything behind. They burned through their savings, trying to get me help because our insurance wouldn't cover most of the things I needed. Especially experimental trials and holistic treatments and therapies. And my family never said no to anything. My type of leukemia was rare and aggressive, so it wasn't a fast or simple process."

My eyes drifted away, remembering. The weight became leaden on my chest, and I knew I was riding the edge. I didn't want to fall off the cliff in front of him. But for the first time, with a panic attack, it felt like I might have a safe place to land. Like I might not have to crash alone.

"It's one reason Louis is so protective of me. He didn't get to be here for all of my treatments. It happened during the height of his career when he finally broke through the glass ceiling as a Jazz ukulele musician. But he did every-thing he could to make it up to me. He bought me my first uke and gave me the gift of music—the salve to ease my anxiety. Louis gave me the encouragement to write lyrics to heal my soul. And I don't know what I would be without music. It's the only language my heart knows. Nor would I know what to do without Louis' love and support to follow my dreams. Your support, too. What began as a tiny dream in your treehouse grew into something beyond my wildest imagination.

A pain swallowed his features, one that cracked me open instantaneously. "Luna, I didn't know. I never knew why you left. Is that why you have so much bone pain and your anxiety got so much worse? Is it why you started having attacks?" he asked, trying to process my words. I nodded slowly at his questions. "But you just stopped all communication. I would have wanted to be there with you through everything. Or at least try to be there. *Any* way I could."

There was a deep ache on his face and I knew out of everything, this was the part he was going to have the most trouble with. Because he was selfless and filled with this innate goodness. That's what I saw when I looked at him. And the world hadn't tainted it. He was so different from other men, especially guys like Azul. The weight on my chest eased, the tightness releasing some of its vice grip.

"I know." My voice split. "But I never wanted you to see me that way. I never wanted to share that pain. I never wanted you to go through that with me, especially if the outcome wasn't good. And I didn't want you to have to settle for me."

Anger blazed a trail across his features. An intensity in his eyes that I'd never seen. "Who put that thought in your mind? There's *no way* anyone would have to *settle* for you."

How does he always know? It was true, once some seeds were planted, they couldn't be unsown or at least not easily. They would always be a part of the soil. The landscape forever changed. Once people saw you a certain way, it's hard not to look at yourself differently, too. Everyone's reaction feeds it, no matter how much they try to hide it. I closed my eyes briefly, opening them to this new intense gaze of his.

"Reef, it's not just bone pain. I mean, I'm better now. I've been in remission for a long time and I still take things to help with the lasting effects like Claritin. Oddly, that helps. But illness leaves its damage on you–an everlasting scar. Like a vase that's been chipped repeatedly. It will never look the same no matter how you glue the pieces together, so you just throw the rest of the broken pieces away. Saying that's as good as it gets."

"Luna, *no*. That's *not* true. You're the best person I know. The most beautiful–"

"Reef, they think the radiation and chemotherapy damaged my uterus. I can't have children." The words burst forth like from a dam. And they just hung there as he looked back at me. Holding on to my gaze as if he needed an anchor, too. "You should have seen the poor doctors who had to deliver that news to me. And even worse was how they looked at me from then on out. Like I was going to be broken my whole life. And *I am* defective . . . damaged. I knew it from the look in their eyes. And they were right.

There was now a crushing weight on my chest as my breathing became amplified. The panic attack was coming for me. It always did. A visible warning label of my defects.

But I suddenly felt light, and I realized Reef had gently picked me up. A reprieve washed over me, as did this new floating sensation, when he gently set me atop the side table in the entryway. His eyes were now level with mine while his hands slowly rubbed up and down my arms.

"You're *not* broken, Luna. You hear me? Nothing could ever make you 'damaged'. You're the best person I've ever known." He looked at me, assessing, his eyes roaming over my face as I averted mine. Because my breathing was becoming more erratic. "It's ok, I'm here." He breathed.

Then he just kept repeating the phrase in his soothing tone, telling me I wasn't damaged, hoping I would absorb the words. His gentle voice and caring eyes were bringing me back around. They wrapped me in a net of security. The crushing sensation ebbed with each intentional word he spoke. My ragged breathing and lightning pulse now matched the pace of his rhythmic mantra. My senses were coming back to me and focusing on *him*.

And just like that, he had witnessed a panic attack right in his arms. Not off to the side of the stage like yesterday. And I waited for the fallout to come. I was haunted by a peculiar feeling after each attack; a dark, shrouded rain cloud only I could perceive. My personal reaper, ready to taunt me.

But Reef just smiled at me through the darkness and tucked a piece of hair behind my ear. He was bringing light and hope to a part of my world I never thought possible.

"You're *not* broken. You mean everything to me," he repeated one last time. "You wouldn't have been broken to me then, and you sure aren't now. I would have loved you just as much as I do *now*."

The nervous tick of his hand adjusting his glasses gave him away as his words fell off. Letting me know just how honest and vulnerable his words truly were. He cleared his throat as I tried to settle back into this foreign comfort.

"I knew, Luna," he whispered in an exhale.

"What?" A tiny voice escaped me.

His eyes cast downward for the first time. "Louis, pulled me aside . . . He was only trying to protect you."

"You've known this whole time and—" My throat constricted. He'd still agreed to everything. He still wanted *me*. Just then, every one of his actions became intensified.

All he could do was nod as he took his glasses off, nervously cleaning them on the hem of his shirt. As if he didn't want to see my response. But an intense desire was building inside me like nothing I'd ever felt before, and I took the glasses from him. His eyes snapped up to meet my stunned grin.

I gently placed them back on the bridge of his nose. "So perfect," I breathed out.

And as weird as I felt—and knew I would continue to feel after my attack—a blissful euphoria swept over me. Reef felt just as safe. He hadn't changed in the ways that mattered. He was still the Reef I'd known and loved. Reef could never grow up to be like some men I'd known.

His words wrapped around me, creating a delicious, protective warmth. And within this perfect bubble, my chin tilted upward reflexively to invite him in, and my legs moved so he could close the space between us. I needed him. After twenty years, I was finally going to let myself.

"Say it again, please," I whispered.

His features softened. "I've *always* loved you, *Mahina Liilii*. I'll always be yours." My body responded to each of his words, bringing him even closer, and he smiled as the space disappeared.

Still, he stayed somewhat hesitant at first, as if not believing this moment had finally come. So, I continued opening myself up to him, needing him to know this was exactly what I wanted. He'd left a generous amount of space between us before, especially when he was comforting me. And I wanted it *all* gone.

As I reached my arms around him, my words tumbled out; an ache breaking free. "No one has ever been you. They *never* will be."

His eyes danced over mine with a renewed, happy rhythm. A heart wrenching expression of longing appeared on his features as his endearing expression searched me. The one that absolutely melted *every* part of me. I pulled him in tighter, grasping at his crisp shirt. Letting him know it was okay as I molded deeper into him. By the way his body responded, I knew I definitely wasn't the only one who wanted this.

"Reef, no other man could ever compare. I couldn't even date anyone who was the tiniest bit like you. 'The only man I could love' has always been you." I thought of my lyrics as a realization dawned on him.

A warmth spread over his features. "Even Azul?" He teased me.

"*Especially* Azul," I said emphatically, growing serious. "*No one* was ever you, Reef."

A flood of emotions fled across his eyes as an over-whelming heat bloomed inside me. A feeling no one had elicited since him. Reef slowly ran the pad of his thumb along my bottom lip, outlining it ever so lightly. Picking up exactly where he'd left off earlier. A moan spilled out of me without my permission. One I didn't even know I could make, and he smiled, only deepening my desire. Even with everything my body just went through, I was still desperate for him.

Unlike in the elevator, I could tell that he wanted to take his time, so he could savor this moment. He lingered over my lips, drawing out every touch of his fingertip. Then suddenly he pulled away, as if a switch was flipped.

A soft tone left him. "Uh, you probably should get some sleep. I'm sure tomorrow is going to be exhausting, especially after tonight. How about some more lavender tea or a hot bath?"

My heart sank. I would have felt completely rejected if it was *anyone* else. But I knew Reef. He only wanted to do what was best for me after such an intense attack. He'd just put his desires in check.

And maybe that was the right call, except it only made me want more. I could still feel his warmth and the softness of his breath on my lips, even though he'd taken a step back. But it was quickly dissipating as he gave me space. Ironically, something I usually wanted with men, but not him. *Never him.*

I shook my head, "Reef, I still can't believe you packed all those lavender products for me. The bath sounds amazing. But 'no' to all of it."

His expression shifted like he'd done something wrong. "What—?" But then I saw his face relax as understanding took hold.

"Don't stop," I murmured. To which he rubbed a hand over his jaw. Now it was my turn to be confused. My eyebrow quirked up at him. "What is it?"

"It's just—I've fantasized about this moment so many times that it doesn't feel real."

"Well, let me make it feel *very* real." I pulled him toward me and wrapped my legs around him again. An even louder murmur emptied from me, and it felt like my soul left with it. He'd unraveled every part of me, even pieces I didn't know existed. I was feeling too many things. Over two decades' worth. And it was exhilarating.

"Well, we are in the honeymoon suite," he began cheekily. "Guess we should properly use it. That means no more floor palettes and a proper threshold protocol." His mischievous expression wafted over to me as a boyish look took hold. The look I'd known so well and one which had always kept me such good company.

"Reef. . ." A warning laced the notes that made up his name.

But before I knew it, he was carrying me. "Cuddling sounds good for anxiety. Probably even better than lavender tea." His eyes sparkled as my arms latched around his neck.

"I think you're just good for my anxiety." The words left me with ease. Reef was nurturing to the soul. I kissed his neck softly as he carried me over to the bed. My silent thank you.

He just instinctively knew this was what I needed after an attack. Light humor, no stress, and comfort. And he was going to make sure I got it. *How could someone know you so much better than you did yourself? How could they see you and your potential so well?* It sure felt like a miracle to have them in your life.

Reef laid me down on the bed and tucked me in beside him. I curled up into the nook I'd left so long ago, getting reacquainted and making it mine all anew. I turned my head back to kiss him gently, a new beginning forming between us. So in a way, maybe that's *exactly* what this room was used to seeing.

The care he provided me made intimacy feel safe for the first time. And I reveled in that realization as he tenderly kissed my neck. The soft pulse of his breath provided a new found security beside me. His tighter embrace felt like a comforting blanket during a thunderstorm, overwhelming me with love. A rush of nostalgia blooming with it. Only so much stronger this time. Because tonight, I realized all the alternatives that could have been. All the alternatives that had been before him. And just how long I had denied myself happiness. How long I'd thought I didn't deserve it.

As his breathing grew heavier beside my neck, so did my eyelids. A peaceful contentment finally closing them, allowing me to be enveloped by him and the security he provided. The safety of his beautiful heart embracing me.

CHAPTER 37

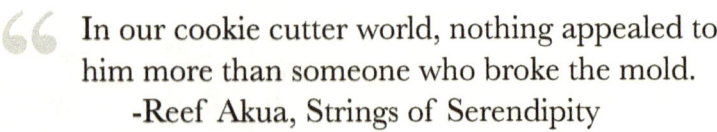

" In our cookie cutter world, nothing appealed to
him more than someone who broke the mold.
-Reef Akua, Strings of Serendipity

My eyes attempted to adjust to the light streaming in through the open curtains. As my one true love lay tenderly on top of me, I realized my mind was going to need much more time to adjust than my eyes.

All this time, I'd had the narrative wrong. I figured a clean break was the simplest way to spare my feelings. And yet, I'd always hoped for a different story. But the puzzle pieces that had slipped into place last night were bittersweet. And the biggest piece gutted me, especially the fact that I hadn't been there for her. I would have found a way, if I'd only known . . .

As I looked at her beautiful features, I recalled how much pain had filled them as she recounted her 'damage' last night. The truth which she'd *already* told to Cece.

I'd been *very* aware of how important her question at our sandcastle construction had been yesterday. And I had also been completely honest. I wanted her. I always had. And I was certain I always would.

But I was still having trouble with the dishonesty–the lies of omission–that I'd let stay between us. I should have come clean about Cece last night. About the letters. About the reason, I knew.

On a technicality, I hadn't lied. But that didn't make me feel better. Louis had pulled me aside one evening. It was just at our dinner the other night. And when I told him I'd known, the same reaction had fallen over him.

However, there was still a lot I didn't know. Things she had told *me* last night. Luna had focused on the present in her letters. I'd never known the *why*. And the inadequate words I had sent back to her were now seared vividly in my mind. Clearly inked across the page, burning in my memory.

I never should have written her back. I had crossed *so* many lines. But it was Luna, and I could feel her pain dripping off the page. And it was a way to have a connection with her again. The only one I thought I'd ever have with her. My only chance to help her. And I took it.

What would she think when I told her? I cringed as the ink became brighter in my memory. Until it was all I could see. The invasion of privacy and all the lines I had crossed over becoming too bright to ignore. *Trampled over, was more like it.*

Dear Luna,

My favorite Martin Luther King quote goes like this "only in the darkness can you see the stars". But perhaps the moon would be more appropriate because I have a feeling that you shine the brightest when it's dark. The best thing about darkness is that you can find the people who are a light. And if they can shine in the dark for you, then, they can always be a source of light. Search for your north star. For a man that will shine bright enough to be worthy of your moonlight.

What good would it be to find a man when the sun is always shining? It's an advantage. You immediately find out people's character in difficult times. And I could sit here and say I'm sorry, but I won't do that because you're a strong, beautiful woman with so much to give. And there's no way someone wouldn't be incredibly lucky to be a part of your life.

I hear stories about IVF, surrogacy, and adoption all the time. You'd be surprised what people share with writers. Stories of how they could never have children, or they shouldn't have children, and now they are happy parents with beautiful children. Science doesn't always know. Sometimes the heart is much stronger. And it appears to me if you want a family, you can have it. Seems to me you can have anything you want. You just have to look for the stars in the dark and use that pure heart. Have faith and believe that there's a reason. That this is how it was meant to be. Be proud of your journey. Who knows, maybe there's a child looking at the moon for some light right now. One who could be yours. And that would be a pretty spectacular reason.

Let the stars guide you,
Cece

My heart had torn wide open after I'd finished that letter. Never had it felt so raw. And then I'd poured it into my next manuscript. The one my agent was currently faxing me about and still requesting my revisions on.

After Luna came into the bar, I felt conflicted. I had wanted Luna to see someone like herself in romance. To feel she was loveable—and so very wanted. More than anything, I wanted her to have a happy ending. Even if it was just in fiction for now. It was important to believe it was possible. Maybe that's what kept me writing.

But when I'd written the story, I'd never expected anything to happen between us. Remorse ambushed me even harder as I held her. I looked down at Luna's arm laying tenderly across my chest. Her hand, resting on my shoulder, gave an adorable twitch. I'd never forget how she stirred in the mornings. The memory of waking up together was one I had safely stored away. A precious moment you try to memorize because you can't imagine being able to live without it.

Luna stirred, feeling my presence. She propped her chin on my chest and I could see her stage mask fall into place.

"Morning," I said. My smile met her shy, polite one. "Waking up to you is just as good as I remember it. But this time I won't have to face my furious parents. They made me call yours and apologize, if you recall."

Luna's husky laughter filled me slowly, like the first cup of coffee in the morning. "How could I forget? It's one of my favorite memories. Falling asleep in your arms was definitely worth all the trouble I got into. Well, at least it wasn't too much trouble, since our parents thought we were just friends."

I snickered. "I don't know if anyone ever thought we were *just* friends, Luna. I've always had it pretty bad for you."

The sound of her sweet laughter filled me. "Yeah, me too. I've revisited that night so many times."

"Well, maybe you can relive this one now, too," I half-joked.

"Oh, I definitely will. Even if there weren't any stars or s'mores. At least you kissed me this time," she said with a cheeky grin.

"Even back then, you wanted me to kiss you? Luna, you should always tell me what you want."

She brought her head closer to me, a contented sigh coming out of her as she nuzzled my neck. "Ok . . ." A newfound confidence claimed her. "I want you to continue what you started last night."

My mouth went dry. "So, you're feeling better?"

"Yes, *much* better," she murmured as she kissed my neck, the heat from her lips waking up my skin. Only Luna could turn me on this fast.

Unfortunately, my nerves immediately tightened, feeling like a wound string that was about to snap. There was a tiny complication I'd forgotten to mention: I'd never actually been with anyone.

I usually got to a certain point, and it just felt off. We both knew it and we called it. It was better that way. Forcing things wouldn't have been fair to anyone. No one had been *her*.

I pinched my eyes shut. This felt worse than admitting I was a romance author. A guy my age not having been with anyone was like an eight-legged unicorn. Luna began moving up my neck, which I'm sure had turned crimson. Continuing to kiss me passionately in *all* the right ways. And here I sat, frozen. *Frozen.* I had pretty much every guy's fantasy—*especially* mine—and I couldn't do anything about it.

"Reef? Are you ok?" she breathed, as my body held onto its tension.

"Yeah, I just think we should take it slow. Like *really* slow. It's all so new," I said, looking up at the ceiling like all of Michelangelo's paintings were up there.

"Ok . . ." she said hesitantly. Rejection smeared all over her face. Her expression looked like I might as well be saying, let's salvage our friendship because this will never work. She quietly rolled over and laid beside me.

"It's just a big change. I don't want to rush anything." *It's not like you've wanted this for twenty years or anything, Reef.*

"Yeah," she mumbled, pulling the covers up. They were practically under her chin. *Great.*

"So . . ." I tried. "Do you want to explore some more today? I had something in mind for just the two of us." My mind was completely in the gutter on that one. All I was thinking about exploring was more of her. I added quickly, "There's a cool little island off the coast I've heard about."

"Oh, uh. Sure." I looked over at her to see if she was even listening. "Yeah, sounds great."

"Luna, I haven't ever been with anyone." The words left my mouth in a heated rush. I felt myself trying to pull them back as they left me. As if I could tug them back out of the air like catching capricious fireflies.

That certainly got her attention. Her eyes snapped over to me, looking lost. "Never?" she breathed.

"Luna, I kind of think that's what that means."

She pinched her lips together as she reached for my hand, absentmindedly tracing abstract shapes on top of it. "I kind of thought you'd have been with *a lot* of women, especially the way they act around you at the bar. I didn't know—"

"Well, that would be *very* inaccurate . . ." *They weren't you,* I thought as I trailed off.

A flood of emotions tore through her face. "Does it make me a terrible person if I say that makes me happy? I've been having a terrible time envisioning you with all these women ever since I moved back." She looked at me protectively and I had to say, I liked it. I hadn't seen her be this way with other guys.

I laughed, thankfully releasing some of my tension. "No, I still feel bad about punching Steve and almost hitting Azul. So, I may have the same difficulty. But I did that for other reasons. *I promise.*"

Luna chuckled. "Yeah, I'm sorry you had to do that, too. I don't exactly attract the best guys. You've always been the exception." She moved closer to me, laying back down on my chest. Thankfully, decreasing the distance between us.

"I think you just attract everyone. That type is just a little more persistent. You're incredibly gorgeous, Luna."

She fell silent as her eyes locked with mine, growing serious. "It never felt right with anyone else for me, either." Vulnerability seeped into her stare. "My anxiety doesn't particularly make intimacy easy. I decided after my last relationship that I would make sure the next time felt right and that it was a safe situation for me *and* my anxiety. I wish I could go back and do things differently, but I . . . I was determined to let you go. I wanted you to find someone who could give you everything you deserved."

Her intense brown eyes roamed over mine as her words tore at me. No one should feel that way about intimacy. It should be the safest space. My hand gripped onto her tighter. I'd do whatever it took to make sure she felt safe with me.

"She's *right* here." I ran a finger along her jaw and then brought her chin toward me. Her lips began lingering on mine, little moans telling me to continue as my hand kneaded slowly into the hair at the nape of her neck.

Eventually, I pulled back, whispering into the small space between us, "I always want you to feel safe with me. That's why I never kissed you. I never wanted to cause you *more* anxiety."

She studied me thoughtfully, a soft smile on her full lips. "No, Reef, *you're* my safe place. I'm sorry that I've not done a better job of showing you that. You've always been so kind to ask me about things, but you shouldn't have to guess. I'll try to be more open about what I'm feeling. I just never wanted to push my anxiety on you."

"You could *never* do that, Luna." I brushed a hair behind her ear. "We're supposed to share everything. To live our dreams together. That's what we always wanted. That means I *want* to know how you're feeling."

She nodded. "That's what I want, too." I heard her throat hitch. "To live life with you." And with that, she snuggled back into me, nuzzling my neck again, letting me know it was all okay. Her words felt perfect and warm against my skin. "But just so you know, I feel completely safe with you. I've never worried about you taking care of me."

I pulled her in tighter, feeling her heartbeat against mine. Allowing her words to wrap me in unrivaled happiness. She probably thought I didn't feel completely comfortable with her, but that wasn't the problem. I was home with her. She was my safe harbor, too. I'd wanted this—wanted *her*—for so long. But I needed to make sure this time was different for her. That she felt nothing but safety and love.

CHAPTER 38

> When you fit with someone, it was easy. You felt it in every fiber of your heart and soul.

-REEF AKUA, SPARKS IN THE TROPICS

I practically floated to the front desk to ask about borrowing a car while Luna finished getting ready for our excursion. What I thought was going to be a difficult task turned out to be an incredibly easy one. Actually, it was too easy.

I knew the hotel had reserved cars for guest use, especially for celebrities such as Luna. But I didn't even need to give them her name. I didn't have to persuade them at all.

"Anything for you, Mr. Akua." I looked inquisitively at the receptionist.

"Thank you . . . Luna will be really grateful to have a car for the afternoon." I hesitated.

"Luna? Oh, that's right, you're with Ms. Manu Mele." A small wink took up her tone, a sparkle lighting up her eyes, and an uneasy feeling settled over me. She dropped her voice, leaning toward me conspiratorially. "Ms. LaRue, I know this is your vacation, but we had some urgent paperwork come through for you. We've kept it secure. Thanks to your friend, this will be of the utmost discretion."

My world spun, feeling like I'd just been cast in Hitchcock's Vertigo. My friend? Had Louis been here?

"Your friend said he'd wait to make sure the paperwork got to the right person. Thank goodness he was here when it came in. I'm so sorry, Mr. Akua, we didn't realize . . . Usually guests tell us their aliases, so any type of miscommunication can be averted."

What did she just say? She couldn't possibly know . . . I felt all the blood drain from my head as my hearing went fuzzy. No, no one could know about this. Especially no one around Luna. I hadn't found a way to tell her about my books yet.

The receptionist kept looking at me like I'd just had a medical episode. "Sir?"

Maybe she was questioning if I was really LaRue. Perhaps I could throw her off. After all, my "friend" could be wrong. No one knew what LaRue looked like. I'm sure they didn't even know what Reef Akua looked like until a few seconds ago. I was just Luna's plus one to them. No one knew me as Cece or Reef here, and I liked it that way.

How did my agent even know I was here? She was like a literary bloodhound. Her superpower was tracking down rogue authors or illusive information. If she could find every plot hole in your manuscript, that also meant she knew you pretty well, too. I'm sure a quick Google image search had led her right to Luna's social media.

When I just stood there speechless, the young woman started ruffling through some papers, handing me a stack. "The caller said it was urgent. I can fax them back when you're finished or send them wherever they need to go."

Really? This couldn't wait a week? My agent must have something big. I adjusted my glasses to see a contract from a publisher for my latest novel. I flipped over the cover page and scanned down to see the manuscript title with my pen name and given name on full display. My manuscript with the infertility representation. Guilt ripped through me like lightning. As I flipped through the pages, I found my sample with notations, bleeding in red ink. Of course, they could fax in color here.

I glanced at the receptionist, who innocently averted her eyes. I flipped back through the contract pages as if they weren't real. Blank lines for Cece and Reef to sign appeared, magnified in my field of vision. I always signed both names because yes, having a pen name was super complicated.

Well, I guess they liked my sample chapters. The revisions had flowed out of me once Luna came back into my life, but I hadn't given them to my agent yet. I couldn't. But I guess they'd seen the potential in the book, anyway. Apparently, my agent had shopped it around, and when a contract was on the table, she didn't lose any time in getting it to me. The industry was too competitive to waste precious time.

My throat ran dry as my stomach went uneasy. I didn't know how I felt about continuing these romance books now that Luna was in my life. Especially not this one. I needed to come clean and see how she felt about it. She was the inspiration, after all. My muse. She deserved to know.

An obnoxiously loud throat clearing startled me; and I slowly turned to see a hunk of muscle leaning against the reception area.

"Reef," Azul said as he tipped his head slightly. He managed the action so dismissively, spending the least amount of energy possible.

No. No, no, no. He surely can't be "the friend" that the receptionist had spoken to me about. A guttural sound escaped me, and I heard a deep laugh come out of him. I nodded back nonchalantly, remembering to breathe.

"Seems like you're in high demand. They've been looking for you and were confused about which guest Reef Akua was. Luckily, I was around. Of course, I was happy to assist them. I wouldn't want them to end up with the wrong person. Especially when discretion is of the utmost importance to my friend."

"Here you go, sir," another receptionist said to Azul, handing him some sort of message.

"Work never ends, does it?" he asked in a way that sent a shiver down my spine. Then he turned and strutted away.

HAUNTED BY A BARRAGE OF QUESTIONS, I

meandered back to the room. Luna and I finished gathering our things and put Nova on a leash for our excursion. Before I knew it, I was driving in a daze toward the east coast to see the Mokulua Islands. All the while, trying to forget about the contract and how much Azul might know. He was way too smirky not to have seen or overheard something.

"Are we going to the beach?" Luna asked. I had been vague about what I had in mind for today, hoping to surprise her. I think she'd forgotten all about my mention of an island at the beginning of the morning.

"You'll see," I said as I came around and opened her car door.

"Reef, you know I'm way too impatient for surprises."

"Well, good thing you don't have to wait too long," I said coyly.

I led her down a path to the paddleboard rental agency that the hotel had recommended. I pointed offshore toward two small volcanic islands on the horizon, explaining their origin to Luna.

"They were created by a volcano falling into the ocean. The bigger of the Mokulua islands on the left is named Moku Nui. That's the one people can visit. Seabird Sanctuary protects the other one. Moku Nui is supposed to be a really cool place to explore. I thought we might enjoy an opportunity to get away from everything today."

She beamed. "I love the idea of it being just the two of

us. This couldn't be more perfect. And I love that Nova can come with us, too." Luna reached down to pet Nova's head in confirmation.

I smiled in agreement. "What else could we need?" And I honestly couldn't think of a single thing.

Luna

CHAPTER 39

Because here I realize
You'd never push my dreams aside
Or expect me to compromise

-LUNA MANU MELE, THE ONLY
MAN I COULD LOVE

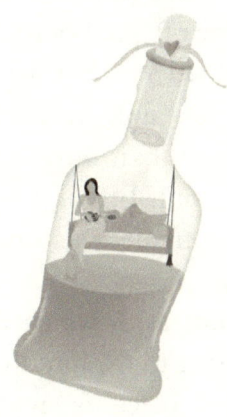

The journey to Moku Nui island from Lanikai beach was utterly idyllic. Especially since the water was much calmer than I expected it to be. We treated our paddleboards as kayaks, enjoying a relaxing paddle while taking in the beautiful aquamarine scenery.

I kept waiting for Reef to topple off his board since Nova was throwing off their center of gravity. Despite everything, she was quite well-behaved and stayed still. I think she must have sensed the consequences. Usually, she couldn't hold back her excitement.

She quite enjoyed being the leader at the head of the board. Our adventure gave me a great sense of what life with those two would be like, as we glided along. And my heart warmed at the thought. I loved living life with them.

The thirty-minute water journey went by in no time. Before I knew it, we found ourselves at a secluded beach on the island. Where we parked our paddle boards in the sand. Away from the beach, Moku Nui resembled a massive rock formation. The area boasted hiking trails, natural pools, and even rock ledges to sit on in the sheltered water.

I wasn't sure what Nova was going to think of the rocky terrain, but Reef let her off the board and she immediately went to explore. Delighted with her new environment, especially since she wasn't left alone in the hotel room. A dog's life was so much shorter than ours and I loved that Reef made every moment count. I think I could fall in love with a man just by how he treated his dog. Perhaps I already had.

My happiness grew as I watched Nova, excitement bubbling inside me, eager to explore the island. Connecting me to an adventurous piece of my soul that I hadn't accessed in such a long time.

Although the island beach was initially crowded, the

world became quieter as we ventured away. A private oasis of black lava rocks and crystal blue water awaited us. The heaviness I carried in my body began floating away, dispersed by the sea breeze and the waves of the sea. Decompressing before tonight's big event was the most helpful thing I could do. My capacity for attending large social gatherings was limited. A gift of social anxiety and being higher on the spectrum. Reef hadn't forgotten about that. He appeared to remember every significant detail concerning me. I had remained important to him. That thought hit me as hard as the heat radiating off the lava rocks.

As Nova led us, I took his hand, and he smiled at me. "Thank you," I said, but he just tipped his head in question to me. He didn't realize how special he was. Reef never had. He was one of those rare people who never took bandwidth. He just gave. And I felt foolish for being worried about the type of man he'd grown into. For being scared to share with him.

As our fingers intertwined, we wandered around the island, searching for a secluded spot to unwind. Smiling, I looked at Reef as we spotted a calm pool nestled among huge rocks. I stashed my coverup in Reef's backpack and went straight to the tanning ledge. Submerged under only a foot of water, it looked perfect for soaking up the sun's rays.

"What? No *pali* jumping?" Reef teased as I positioned myself on the ledge. But his eyes were gazing over my outstretched legs, sending fire to my core. The look he reserved only for me. It made my heart flip like it was being tossed in a raging sea, just like it had the very first day he'd ever looked at me.

I saucily retorted, "I had my eye on the relaxing mermaid spot, thank you very much." He laughed at me, but his eyes were doing *very* different things. They were drinking me in as I slowly leaned back on my elbows in the water. His sweet look turned very heated. "Going to join me? Or are you planning to show me how to jump off that 'cliff?' `Oia ana.`"

"Yeah, that's not exactly height phobia friendly." He chuckled, quickly deciding what his choice would be. My 'dare' wouldn't entice him. He had his eyes set on the spot beside me, and I was thrilled about that.

Reef glanced over at the rocky cliffs encapsulating us. This was perfect, like our own little world. As he looked back, his hungry eyes scanned over me. And with a whisper, the word, *hemolele,* slipped out under his breath.

I blushed at his not so silent admission, gulping as the word 'perfect' lingered on his lips. Sound really carried on the water. But the expression written on his face said it all. I felt a surge of warmth while waiting, only to be interrupted by Nova's arrival before him. She was at the edge of the water, standing timidly at the end of the dry rocks. Trying to decide if she was going to brave it and join me. She glanced back at Reef, who was coming over to wade into the water. As soon as he took his first step, she bounded over to me.

I laughed and wrapped an arm around her. "So, are you going to tell me the story of how you got Nova?" I asked as he began positioning himself on the ledge beside me.

He didn't quite know what to do with himself, and it made him look even more adorable. Reef always had this effortless, easy-going nature, even when he felt awkward.

"Uh, sure." He wavered, trying to find a relaxed position like mine.

"You don't sound so certain." I looked over at him.

He'd finally found the least awkward way to sit on the rocky bottom. "It's just that I've missed out on so much of your life. I want to fill in the gaps."

My lips tried to turn upward, but it was difficult when I knew the reason was my fault. But at least I could make up for it now. And he truly seemed to have forgiven me. He'd never been the type to want someone to feel guilty. For him, my apology would be the end. But it was a little harder for me. I had to live with what I'd done, even if I'd thought I had the best of intentions. I would know better than to take someone's choice away from them next time.

"Ok, well here's the two truths and a lie," he said, and I immediately wondered why he needed them. "She reminded me of you. Locke didn't force me to get a dog. I kind of named her after you . . . I was thinking of a 'super-nova' . . . a reference to the night sky."

I stared at him. So, reverse the one about Locke and they were all true. I couldn't believe it. He looked even more unsure of himself as he sat in the water, running his hand along the glassy surface, playing with the ripples. I had thought this was going to be a really easy topic of conversation.

"Did she really remind you of me?" was all I could think to say as I petted her. *He'd continued to think of me—and not just in his writing?* Enormous rock formations on each side of the cove shielded us from the outside world. A small space was left, giving us a window to see outside our protected world. Just enough to feel completely insulated, yet still witness all the beauty beyond.

Reef continued distracting himself with the palette of oceanic colors beneath his hand. "It's embarrassing, Luna. I was kind of hoping you wouldn't ask about her. I should have changed her name."

"Reef, considering I've been writing music that you inspired, I think you're much better off than me." I rubbed against his shoulder playfully, but he didn't relax.

He glanced over at me. "Well, Locke had rescued Penny and I guess he could tell I was kind of lonely. So, he suggested a dog. Or sort of dragged me to the shelter and forced me out of the car. Nova took care of the rest. I'm pretty sure Locke would have just brought a dog home for me if I hadn't gone inside. He probably thought we could be bachelors obsessed with our dogs together and it would be less weird. It wasn't. Probably made it worse."

He laughed. "Nova became one of my closest friends— as sad as that sounds. So, Locke was right—just *don't* tell him. But I didn't name her for the longest time because she just kept reminding me of you and all the names I thought of . . . Well, you can imagine what the name ideas were like."

"No, I really can't. You probably need to elaborate." He shook his head at me. "So, what did she do that reminded you *so much* of me?" Curiosity overcame my politeness.

"I don't want to tell you."

"What? Reef, now you have to."

He exhaled heavily. "I'll probably offend you. It was just all these little things. Like she loves all my lavender scented stuff. She's terrified of thunderstorms. Nova has to curl up next to me or bury herself behind me when they happen. I have this thunder-vest for her and it came with different scented pads to calm her, but of course lavender is the only one that works. Along with lavender hemp chews."

I burst out laughing. "So, she's a total scaredy cat, and you thought of me?"

His cheeks lit up with redness. "It was more the way you would bury yourself into me during terrible thunderstorms, especially when we went camping. Or when we watched scary movies. And Nova loves your music. I play your music for her when it storms or when people set off fireworks." His eyes slowly looked over at me. "See, embarrassing. Locke has made enough fun of me."

"So, Locke has known this entire—"

"You couldn't pick up on his not-so-subtle hints at the 'meeting' Louis held?"

"Maybe Locke should have officiated that meeting. Things would have gone a lot faster." I teased.

Reef replied, "Well, apparently Louis has known about us for quite some time, too. Locke told him how we 'dated' when we were young. So, we had a lot of help. I'll have to remember to thank them." He beamed.

"Me too." An overwhelming feeling came over me as I sat with the man I loved in this seaside oasis. His look unnerving me now more than ever; love and respect flowing freely in ways I'd never known. I inched over to him as I watched his Adam's apple bob up and down, and I placed my forehead against his, nodding in agreement. And I loved the feral sound that escaped his lips when I touched him. I planned on doing that a lot.

I ran my nose along his until our lips aligned. Looking into his eyes stirred up feelings I'd suppressed for too long. Ones I had buried so deep I was sure no one else could evoke them. Maybe I was worried not even he could bring them out of me anymore.

I gently pushed him backward as my feelings took over. His hand reached to feel for his surroundings, gripping onto some rocks as he began leaning that way. Allowing me to express and delve into my emotions as we found ourselves intertwined in the water, pressed against the rocky pool's edge.

His eyes wandered over to the side, and he broke

contact with me. "Uh, Luna, did you realize Nova is just staring at us?"

I turned my head in the same direction to see Nova just standing there, tail wagging ferociously. I burst out laughing. "Guess she's pretty happy for you. Or she's worried you're getting attacked."

That broke Nova's trance. She came over and started licking both of our faces. "Nova!" Reef attempted to keep her an arm's length away. But it was no use.

"She's *so* happy for you." I managed in between laughter and complete contentment. "Guess she was as worried about you as Mrs. Aliana."

Reef broke out in laughter, too. "So, she didn't ruin the moment?"

"No, Reef. Nothing can ruin a moment with you. Especially not Nova." He swallowed. "I mean, she is named after me."

He swatted the water at me playfully. "You're never going to let that go, are you?"

"Nope, and I also think I dared you to jump off some cliffs . . ."

He hugged me tighter as I rested on top of him. The embrace of water, along with the sunshine, made this moment feel even more tender.

"You really don't forget anything. Ok, I'll man up."

I looked at him, hating that term. His masculinity had never been a concern for me. I loved the way he defined being a man. I wished he would see that. "Reef, does this need saying while I'm practically mauling you *again*?"

He averted his eyes to Nova. "I doubt anyone's going to force you off of me here. I don't see any elevator staff around. Well, except maybe Nova. But certainly not me."

I laughed lightly. "No, Reef, that's not what I'm talking

about. I love the way you define being a man. Your masculinity has always been one of the biggest attractions for me. I don't want you to 'man up.'"

I could tell my words were fueling his desire. His lips parted slightly, but mine got there first. "Say it." I leaned into him and rested my hands on the rocks on either side of him, caging him in. I wouldn't let him run from this any longer. "Tell me why you enjoy being this type of man." I looked straight into his eyes.

"Luna, we're not kids. The tell me thing isn't going to—"

I kissed his neck lightly. "Tell me," I tried more forcefully.

He cleared his throat. "Well, the kissing thing is a new, unfair advantage." I nibbled on his earlobe lightly and he chuckled. "Ok," he said as he looked at me. "I like the type of man I am." I gazed at him sternly. "Because I experience much more when I'm open minded, I don't have to be confined by stereotypes, and I hope I can treat you better because of it."

I nodded. "Because you're considerate, nurturing, supportive, and ridiculously sexy. And you're the only man I could ever want or need. Just like the song says."

He laughed. "Ok. If you say so . . . Azul's song?"

"Yes. Unfortunately. Ironically."

His eyes went hazy as he tried to take in what I had just told him. His voice came out softly, "Alright, I'm ready to jump off a cliff with you. Because we'll be together."

"I like that answer," I replied, kissing him to let him know just how much.

AFTER WE'D JUMPED off the cliff and returned to the mainland, Reef suggested stopping by the Ho'omaluhia Botanical Gardens or the Byodo-in Temple. Since both locations were close by, I voted for the temple.

The kids who loved exploring and goofing around with each other were out in full force again today. My lost zest for life was finally returning after all these years. Something my mental health had robbed me of. It was hard to notice and appreciate the little things in life when a weight was forcing your head down. Amazing how different the world could be when people around you helped you look up. I hadn't realized how many pieces of myself were missing until he restored them.

The vibrant red color of the Japanese temple replica, with its traditional style, stood out against the native Hawaiian landscape. As we approached, a peaceful feeling came over me, growing stronger as we wandered around the grounds. As a trio, we adventured through lovely gardens, featuring native plants and koi ponds. When we got to the massive gong, the not-so-inner child in me came out again.

"I need one of these at home," I teased.

"Yeah, and what would you be ringing for, my lady?" he asked in a British regency accent. Thoughts of Reef at home watching Jane Austen adaptations filled me with fireflies.

I raised my eyes upward, pretending to think about it.

"Hmmm, tea and biscuits." He laughed. "And my romance book." He nodded. "And you, of course."

Reef teased, "Of course. I'll even come with full regency gear." I was flushing all over. Him in those regency adaptations getting much more vivid.

I countered, "We better just ring this thing." I got up to take my turn, but he came with me, wrapping his arms around me from behind. His hands slowly slid down my arms to reach my tightly clenched hands. All other thoughts, but ones of him, left my mind. *Well, now I know what I need for stage anxiety. Can I perform like this?*

He leaned down to whisper slowly in my ear. "What's wrong, Mahina Liilii? Don't want to ring it anymore? Afraid of what I'll look like in regency gear?"

Yeah, very concerned. "Oh, you'll be buying some now," I said as I started our hands in motion and he softly chuckled into my ear. All of me melting into him and the safe world he continued to create around me.

Reef

CHAPTER 40

66 If only she could only see herself as I did, then she'd never doubt herself again.

-REEF AKUA, HAWAIIAN HEATWAVE

That evening, I went with Luna to the Waikiki Shell; however, it wasn't for a rehearsal. The moment we got in the car, I saw a change in her. Proper posture and tense muscles took over as her mind went somewhere else. At least Tutu and Louis were meeting us there. Maybe they could help relieve her tension as well.

Hopeful I might find something to help Luna, the writer in me did some quick research before leaving the hotel. I searched Google for anxiety techniques, and quickly got lost down the Reddit rabbit hole. The results varied widely, since anxiety was unique to every person. But I realized there wasn't a one-size-fits-all solution. However, I knew Luna, and I needed to trust my instincts and rely on what had worked best for *her*.

Upon arrival, a catered meal awaited the crew. We found a shady spot beneath palm trees for our meal, just the two of us. But even that didn't seem to help.

"Are you doing ok?" I asked as she took a bite of her pineapple. Luna nodded slowly, with a faint smile. So that really meant no. "You know, you don't *have* to perform in front of people to be a musician. There are other ways. We can figure something out."

"Tell that to Steve," she said with a sharp inhale.

"Well, I don't think Steve has the answers, at least, maybe not for you." Her eyes gazed up at me. "Luna, you can't compare your path to everyone else's. Just because that works for them doesn't mean it's right for you. And besides, there's something special about being different."

She speared another piece of fruit as her eyes cast downward. I hope my music will resonate with people and provide them comfort, as music has done for me. Whether it's just an escape or the lyrics mean something to them. I don't know how else to do that—"

"You could release your music on livestream. There are other ways to perform and interact that could be healthier for you. And you could get back to your online community where you can chat with people through messages. There are so many other ways to interact. Your music will always affect people. Maybe even more so if you're doing it in a way that works for you. Why don't you just forget about Steve and the label?"

"Breaking my contract isn't so easy. Louis worked on it for me. It would be so hard to come back from what I'd lose."

"So, take the penalty, Lun. I'll help you. I know Louis will, too. There are people that will always support you. Don't let what other people think stop you."

She nodded slowly and reached for my hand. "I've really missed you, Reef. Did I tell you that?"

"Maybe," I said coyly.

"I really love you," she said boldly, and the words filled me with warmth. I expected her to go shy, but she just held my gaze, even as her cheeks heated. Something had changed. "Things always feel so possible with your support. *Mahalo*."

"I really love you, too," I replied. I let the words fill me, lost in her gaze.

VENICE FOUND SEATS FOR TUTU, Louis, and me close to the stage in an area that was reserved for the festival cast and crew. Since our talk, Luna appeared more relaxed. Maybe she was thinking about her options and what I had said. I sure hoped so. I never wanted her to feel trapped.

I'd barely settled in when the festival's opening act began, and I noticed someone sit down next to me. I thought perhaps Luna had snuck away to join us, but the thought vanished when an overpowering cologne hit my nostrils. It had the scent of a perpetually-scratched men's catalogue ad. *Oh no. Not now.*

The muscle man leaned over, bumping me with his protruding biceps. "Hey," he whisper-shouted, because quiet wasn't in his vocal range.

I looked straight ahead, trying to find Luna. Needing an anchor and also to know that she was okay with this man being in such close proximity.

He commenced speaking, neglecting to acknowledge my presence. "So, I heard through the *coconut wireless* there was a mix-up at the hotel." What was he trying to pull? If he said they meant to put Luna in his room, there was going to be another poor excuse for a *Fight Club*. I sure wouldn't win, but I could at least throw a few more amateur punches.

"What are you talking about now?" I sighed.

"Well, usually when a big contract comes in, it's for me." This enormous cocky grin cascaded across his features, but also a hint of jealousy. It was one thing when Luna was dating a 'nobody,' but quite another now that I had a name for myself. My body went rigid. I could feel a clamminess taking over my palms, gradually transcending over my body.

"What did you say?" My head snapped toward him.

He stretched backward, interlacing his fingers behind his head as his elbows outstretched. He looked like a bully who was enjoying watching an upside down kid with his legs flailing out of the top of a trash can. "Yeah, if I was going to have a stage name . . . Well, I don't know that *Coco* is exactly who'd I'd take my inspiration from. It would probably be something more masculine. Like Butch. Yeah, I'd take the Butch Cassidy route. Or Rocky."

Or Fabio meets Freddy Krueger. I rolled my eyes. Coco was not Cece. *Hûpô. So, did this mean Azul wasn't a stage name? Could have fooled me . . .* "What was the name of your first dog?" I asked him, trying to shake off my thoughts.

He waved absentmindedly at Luna up on the stage, who was staring at us with unease. "What?" he asked, as he grinned like a fool at her. He clearly loved getting *any* type of attention from her. I looked at him with annoyance. "Uh, Sweetheart," he mumbled. "My sister named him."

"Yeah, so did my sister. We think she was probably saying 'sea, sea', but it stuck. So, you grew up on what street?"

"Plumeria." I raised an eyebrow. "Wait–" He started laughing. "Are you f–" he looked over at Tutu and Louis and cleared his throat. "Are you serious? Your *porn star* name? *Brah.*" He was dying of laughter and Luna looked more than a little concerned. Oh, no, she looked like she was considering coming over here.

"Ok, *Sweetheart Plumeria.*"

"Hey, *watch it.*" He pointed his meaty finger at me. He cleared his throat again, straightening himself and his pristine linen suit. "I have to go perform now. Oh, by the way–" He leaned over to me, practically hissing, "I guess you didn't need the heads up. You appear to know all about your damaged goods. I told the front desk my friend was insanely talented. That beginning had *such* a nice hook. I'm just wondering if Luna will think so, too."

My fists clenched as his eyebrows arched wickedly. So,

he'd read the pitch and the sample—probably the whole blasted thing while he casually waited for me. He'd probably said he'd make sure I got it. He'd been in the right place at the right time and intervened. I gulped.

So why hadn't he already told her? What was his angle? Was he trying to blackmail me, hoping I'd convince Luna to write another song with him? I would never do that. Not so he could steal it and take all the credit again.

I watched as his eyes tracked her on stage, some type of sorrowful longing in them. *Was there actually more to him?* She did date him, after all. I wanted to believe there was good in every person. Perhaps somewhere deep, *deep* inside of him. Maybe he was enjoying messing around with me, but still wanted to do the right thing by her. Maybe, just maybe, he was showing me he was being the bigger man. Waiting for me to fail on my own so he could swoop in however he wanted. Whether for his career or love. Perhaps he didn't think she was broken at all, because that was the last thing I could imagine anyone seeing when they looked at her. Maybe in his own way, he still loved her.

Azul waved to Louis, who was trying to pretend he didn't see him. Louis was always polite, just like Luna, but apparently that only went so far. "Louis," Azul tried again before walking away. Of course, he didn't even bother to say anything to Tutu.

Louis leaned across Tutu, over to me. "What was that about? If he was here, nothing good could have happened."

"Nothing good, indeed." Regret filled my tone.

"Reef," he warned. "Talk to me. Please."

"A contract came for me today. I don't know how my agent knew where I was staying. Sometimes I think she has a tracker implanted in me. But she's also *very* good at doing research in this industry. She must have seen Luna's social account. Anyway, Azul was hanging around reception when my contract arrived . . . I'm not sure—"

Louis looked at me pointedly. So I continued explaining, "Azul knows. He convinced the receptionists that he was my good friend, and I guess he overheard them talking while he waited, or he persuaded them to let him see the fax. Definitely appears like he's read it, and he's thrilled about his luck."

"Well, he's not that bright. So, don't give him too much credit. Maybe he hasn't figured it all out. You still have time. Just tell her. That's all you need to do." I nodded. "You'll find the right moment, Reef."

Tutu spoke up, "You can't go wrong with the truth. I promise. All that matters is you *want* to share with her. Trust her with yourself, Reef." I looked into Tutu's kind eyes that had always been there for me and nodded. "Don't lose her *again*, Reef. You two have been apart for far too long. And you look at each other just as you did then. With so much love and respect. That's something you fight for."

I nodded again and swallowed. I knew exactly what was on the line to lose because I'd lost it *all* before. In a blink of an eye, my entire world had changed. I'd spent the lasI spent the last twenty years doubting myself and my self-worth. And that was the problem. I was afraid.

AFTER THE CONCERT, we said goodnight to Louis and Tutu in the hotel lobby. The successful evening visibly relieved Luna. And she was excited to make plans for tomorrow afternoon before she had to perform at the festival again.

"So," I said as I wrapped an arm snuggly around her. "How do you want to celebrate?" She looked pretty tired, but I thought we should commemorate her big night somehow. She'd played so beautifully and she'd looked stunning doing it, too. And her singing had felt like a completely new experience for me, since her songs had a whole new meaning now. She'd even looked directly at me while she sang, as if I was her mooring. Completely unraveling me. It was just about the sexiest thing I'd ever experienced.

"I don't know. What do you have in mind?" She laid her head on my shoulder.

"Well, if you're too tired, that's ok. I just thought you deserved to celebrate after tonight. We could walk on the beach again. Or—" My eyes wandered over to her. "What about room service? Chocolate cake? I bet they have a fantastic one here. We could watch a movie or sit on the lanai."

Her eyes lit up at 'chocolate'. It was nice to know I still knew her so well. I loved that so many things about her hadn't changed. Maybe it was a childhood crush thing and the fact that we'd grown up together, or maybe it was just Luna, but I couldn't imagine ever wanting anyone else. I loved knowing her and being comfortable with her. There were enough surprises in life, plenty of things to discover together, and people were always evolving and changing. Why wouldn't you want to do that with someone you knew and loved? Someone you trusted to change in ways that just continued to make them better.

My arm wrapped around her tighter, knowing exactly what I had beside me. Her eyes danced over to me in response. "You know I'm never too tired for chocolate."

I chuckled as I nodded. Picking up our pace to the room, we set up a spot on the lanai where Nova excitedly greeted us. Luna had insisted on pajamas and the incredibly soft hotel robes.

"I feel like that kid in *Home Alone.*" She joked as she took a bite of chocolate cake. "I'll never get used to stuff like this. Come here, you've got to try this. `*Ono*," she sighed as she took another bite and then readied the spoon for me. But the 'delicious' cake wasn't what had me gravitating her way.

I reached for a piece of chocolate that was already smeared on her lips, wiping it away gently. "Yeah, me too. I feel like this is what we would have done as kids."

"Well, maybe. We'd probably have built a pillow fort out here. And I would have beat you at cards." She teased.

"Oh, both can be arranged." She grinned at me questioningly when I left to rummage through my suitcase.

"What are you doing?" she called, leaning in her chair through the doorway to sneak a peek.

I came back with an old, beat-up pack of cards. They featured different cocktails. These had helped me pass my bartending class. We'd played with them so much I'd memorized the ingredients. We used to feel so grown up playing with them and my parents never found out what happened to their lost cards.

"*Nooo*," she began. "I can't believe you brought these."

"Oh, I intend to win at Hollywood Gin, Luna. It's a new decade, and it's my time now."

Her husky laugh sent intoxicating shivers through me. "You keep thinking that." She teased. "We've got chocolate, robes, and cards. Now we just need some booze to complete the classic Hollywood film scene."

"We've got booze on the cards," I said more seriously.

"It really doesn't bother you that I don't drink?"

I could tell this had been a problem for her before. Actually, I'd been able to tell there were a lot of things that had been a problem in other relationships, and I hated it. It made me see red. Azul's words from earlier kept ringing in my ears.

I explained, "No, I've been around enough drunk people to last a lifetime. Plus, women just start throwing themselves at you and I don't need any more help in that area with you." I teased her, and she shoved me playfully. I caught her arm, bringing her toward me. "Plus, I can work on my charm this way."

"Is that so?"

"Yeah," I said as my fingers moved toward her cheek so I could caress her features. Tilting my face toward her, I let my passion crash over her lips. The taste of chocolate mixed with her was driving me absolutely mad. I groaned and pulled her closer.

She graciously accepted and settled onto my lap, a perfect fit as her arms encircled my neck. The bright Hawaiian stars floated around us. A crescent moon angled right above our heads.

Luna's eyes wandered over me as she tucked a strand of hair behind her ear in the soft light. She ran her fingers along the side of my face, moving down my jaw. Leaving goosebumps in her wake as she felt my stubble. I loved seeing her in control as she guided my lips to hers. Leaving me with that rich taste of chocolate and her essence intertwined. A taste of the perfect night. Of what every night could be like.

When her lips parted from mine, I immediately brought her back in, desperate for more. Feeling all the space and time between us from when we had parted. I'd missed her so much, and I needed her to feel just how much she meant to me.

"Do you have any idea what you do to me?" I asked in a raspy voice. One I didn't even know I owned.

Her familiar lavender scent enveloped me along with the moonlight. This had to be the most exquisite spot on earth, combined with the most beautiful woman. I couldn't believe this was real. It was embarrassing to think about how many times I'd dreamed about this. A feeling of warmth washed over me, knowing we'd been thinking about each other. All along, she'd been missing and wanting me, too.

Reef

CHAPTER 41

Just give me one more hour
And you'll see, you've always been the only one
*   for me*
Please let the stars guide you
Because I've always been here waiting

-REEF AKUA, ONE MORE HOUR

W e woke up covered in the sea air and morning dew. The smell of fresh salt soothed me as Luna curled up on my chest, keeping me warm. Like a cat basking on a sunny ledge. We were nestled together on the lounger we'd converted into a bed. Nova was not so gracefully snoring, fast asleep on the other lounger she had claimed.

I ran my fingertips over the plush robe that we used as a makeshift blanket, and wrapped my arms around Luna Streaks of sunlight beamed in and reflected off the glass table, making little rainbows. Casting a glow on the half-eaten chocolate cake. A stack of vintage cards peered back at me.

Last night felt like another dream. One I couldn't imagine waking from. But I had been reckless. I should have used it to tell her the things I'm sure Azul would soon enough. I could imagine him lying in wait for the perfect moment, like the proverbial snake. But I had wanted last night to be perfect. And I'd been greedy and taken it. I wanted as much time together before . . . *I'm sure there will be a right time today.*

"Now I can get used to this." Luna's light breath warmed me as her eyelids fluttered.

"You're welcome to have chocolate cake and sleep on my balcony every night." I teased.

"Ok, but remember you offered." She joked back.

I would love nothing more. I'd do anything to make that happen. That was the thing. I kept feeling like I was against a clock with her. So, I was capturing every moment I could, especially perfect ones under the stars. Soothing my heart and risking it a little more with every moment she gave me.

"So, are you still up for some sightseeing before you

perform tonight? I can call Louis and let him know we'll be ready soon."

"Well, maybe not too soon," she teased. "I think some more balcony room service would be nice. I had my eye on some banana French toast." And I smiled at her, guilt consuming me. I *would* tell her today. After she performed tonight. It was the only way.

ONCE WE DEVOURED MORE of the delicious room service, we departed from a distraught Nova who was most upset to be left behind. We made our way down to the lobby. And before I knew it, we had mapped out the sights for the day and Luna was sitting on my lap in the car. Somehow, we'd convinced the driver to let us be together in the front seat again. He was kind enough to take mercy on us, even though it was illegal. Louis' horrific story of my vomiting extravaganza may have swayed him. He made it sound like I was the girl from *The Exorcist*. I didn't know if we would keep getting so lucky. But Louis was pretty persuasive and people on the island were always kind.

Luna hopped out of the car and extended her hand to me when we reached Chinatown. The hotel had told us there was a great market on Sundays and it seemed like something Tutu and Louis would particularly enjoy. And while I wasn't much of a shopper, I was learning it was who you surround yourself with in life that truly mattered. It made every experience different.

We wove around the walkways featuring storefronts filled with everything from handmade wares, herbal remedies, Asian eateries, to trinket filled tourist merchandise. The curious writer in me was always up for exploring. I especially enjoyed learning about new cultures. So, I was immediately drawn to the ancient herbal remedies. Luna appeared equally intrigued.

As we stepped inside the herbal remedy shop, it was like entering an old world Chinese medicine store. As we browsed the shelves, I was pulled to some herbal mixtures that were good for anxiety. And when the shop owner saw us browsing the selections, he came over to offer his expertise.

A voice rang out from behind us, "Reishi mushrooms are very popular. They're great at calming the body and countering the effect stress has on the nervous system. It can help train our body to respond in a healthier way to triggers in the future, too."

The older gentleman's gravelly voice caught me off guard. Luna eyed the capsules that my fingers had been hovering over and smiled. "There's even a cocoa mixture–"

"Anything chocolate would be perfect." I chuckled.

With my remark, the long gray whiskered man disappeared into the back, returning to ask Luna a few more questions. After a deep discussion, he led her through some mantra techniques. Very similar to what I had done the other night. At least some good instinct had kicked in.

"There's also an ancient technique of moving your eyes from side to side so your brain can move from one hemisphere to the next. A little mind trickery." He began moving his eyes to the left and right in demonstration as he placed his fingers on his temple. Storelight glinted off the gold pattern of his old world robe. I looked over at Luna, quite impressed.

We were just about to set our goods on the checkout

counter when his methodical voice rang out, "What about you, young man? I have tea to open up your chakra that will help with blocked emotions. We offer acupuncture therapy as well. It can help you open up your feelings in a safe environment, even old wounds you may have kept buried."

"How did you . . . ?" I began, but I'm sure his sixth sense picked up my scarred aura. "The tea would be great." I wasn't exactly fond of needles. It was pretty remarkable what he'd been able to sense with us. Maybe at some point I'd be ready to try something more.

I suddenly had a powerful urge to come clean right here and now in this shop. *But I'll tell her tonight, like I planned. I don't want to make her concert any harder.*

So, we caught up with Tutu and Louis and finished looking through the rest of the market. Tutu found some beautiful silks, which Louis happily bought, telling her how gorgeous she would look in them. Her face lit up at his words. And I hoped I could make Luna feel that special, especially when we were their age. Tutu's radiant smile in response to Louis's words made her look like the most beautiful woman in the world. It was amazing what words could do. Words to build someone up instead of tearing them down could make such a difference in someone's life. If there was a choice, why wouldn't you choose compassion?

"So?" Louis asked, looking up at me, catching my expression. "Is there still time for lunch and Pearl Harbor?" He put the silks back in the bag and offered Tutu his arm.

Luna looked down at her watch. "Yes, plenty of time if everyone is still up for it. I can't believe none of us have never been there before. It's one of the most visited sights on Oahu."

Louis looked at Tutu. "Yes, I'd love to see it. My friends

say it's quite a beautiful, but emotional, sight to see." We all nodded in agreement.

We made our way to a lunch spot and then out to the harbor, where a small boat took us out to the monument. As we journeyed on the vibrant aqua water, there was a quiet that fell upon us. The ocean boosted its brightest colors as we looked out from the monument. But among all the perfect colors, you could still see oil floating up from the sunken ship. A reminder of the tragedy that was just below the surface. The oil was said to be the tears of the soldiers who had given their lives that day. A profound sense of weight and sadness washed over us as we contemplated the monument and the tragedy that unfolded in this most beautiful of places. It didn't seem real that something like this could happen here.

We forget how many sacrifices people made for us to live as we did, and how many people helped us get where we were today. In a world filled with so much hate and malevolence, it's easy to forget about the goodness of humanity. Most of all, we forget peace and freedom aren't free. It was fought for. It took sacrifice.

I stared fixedly at that oil bubble, rising to the surface. A rainbow of color depicted in its inky texture. Something so beautiful created out of something so ugly. It popped to the surface and the rainbow spread.

Luna tightened her hold on my arm. To survive, we need to find the rainbow. *Our rainbow*. And happiness was spreading it. I gazed at Luna who had nestled into me, knowing very well that she was a rainbow in the dark storm of my life. And my eyes wandered over to Louis, who was clutching Tutu just as tightly.

Luna

CHAPTER 42

As the sun lowers
And the waves inch higher
A burst of warm colors fly by
Basking us in a Kaleidoscope of Maui
And there's nothing but safety net

-LUNA MANU MELE, *365 DAYS AROUND THE SUN*

With the wind whipping around us as we returned by boat across the sparkling sea, my gaze fell upon a distracted Reef. This was not the first time today that concern clouded those handsome features I adored.

I worried things had been moving too fast for him. He said he'd wanted to take things slow, but going from a childhood friend to a fake boyfriend overnight was a lot. Especially when you found out your childhood girlfriend had never wanted to break up with you; that she broke up with you to 'protect you'; and oh yeah, she continued to write songs about you. Because she still loved you and no one else would ever be you. I think I may have freaked him out just a bit.

I looked back over at him. He stared out at the horizon, his face frozen in a mask-like expression. *Yup, you definitely freaked him out, Luna.* We're going to have a runner. It's all sinking in now.

As we waited for a car, Reef reached for my hand and smiled. Tutu's soft voice drifted over to me. "I love seeing the two of you like this again." Her eyes looked at us and trailed down to our intertwined fingers. "I always thought you were ʻuhane hoa."

"You thought we were 'soulmates' when we were that young?" I was astonished. "How could you tell?"

An impish grin spread over her face, and she leaned into Louis. "I have my ways," she teased. "You always understood and took such good care of each other. The way you would care for a part of yourself–for your other *hapa*. And you were so reserved when you were without the other one. Not like you needed each other to know who you were, but you were so much stronger with the other one around. You brought out all the *best parts* of each other. It was a truly beautiful sight. Still is."

Using the word *hapa* for 'half'–in such a positive way– gave it new meaning for me. I'd always associated the word with unkindness and isolation. Making me feel wrong for being me. But that was the power of Reef. He could turn the difficulties in my life into something positive. Reef could change the narrative. I couldn't believe after twenty years he still could.

I searched Reef's face, his soft expression in total agree- ment. *Hapa*, my lips uttered in silence. Just testing the word out. How it would feel with no essence of hate–being replaced with love. I could feel it tingle on my lips.

I nestled into him further and explained to Tutu and Louis. "Reef helped with my anxiety so much when we were growing up together. I always felt free to be myself, like I didn't have to apologize—no, I didn't *want* to apolo- gize. I just wanted to be me," I said, not taking my eyes from him.

"Same here. I never had to apologize for my choices or hide from my dreams." Reef added as nostalgia overtook us.

Tutu smiled broadly. "Soulmates don't want to change their partner or wish they were different." She looked at us. "They see the beauty in every piece, even the ones we think are flawed or ugly."

I reached up, straining on my tiptoes as I found Reef's lips and locked my arms around him. "Now that is new." Tutu giggled, "but I like it." I blushed, but agreed. I loved it, too.

As we made our way back to the hotel, I turned to Reef. "Why don't you hang out by the pool? Or you could take Nova and let her explore the beach?"

But he just looked at me with a steady gaze. One that felt so practiced with me. I already knew what his answer would be. "I'm sure Nova would love to do that after your concert. There's no way I'm missing your festival as long as you want me to go."

As I returned his supportive gaze, Tutu's words rang in my ears. *Hapa.* My lips formed the letters again and Reef's lips twitched upward. After everything, he was still right here beside me. Still supporting me and loving me just for being me. She was right. Reef was my *ʻuhane hoa.* My soulmate.

Reef

CHAPTER 43

Just give me one more hour
And I'd give anything to show you
How I've kept loving you

-REEF AKUA, ONE
MORE HOUR

Something changed after our conversation with Tutu. For too long, I carried a negative self-image, a broken reflection haunting me everywhere I went. And Luna had been doing the same thing with the broken image of herself she'd presented to me the other night. The one that men like Azul appeared to use to their advantage. The moment after our conversation with Tutu, I'd seen relief in her eyes, as if she was letting go because someone wanted her *exactly* the way she was. No pretending or changes needed. And she finally realized they weren't going anywhere.

I was glad that her relaxation carried over into tonight's performance. As I reveled in her beautiful music, I eased too, melting into my seat. I smiled at Luna as she finished her last song, feeling at peace.

Azul came onto the stage to switch places with Luna. Musicians were alternating at the festival to allow for breaks. As Azul came over to the mic, he put a hand on Luna's shoulder.

"Stay, for a minute, Luna. We haven't gotten to chat with you in a while." My body tensed at his words. I knew musicians were supposed to work the crowd, and switching sets was an opportune time, but this just didn't feel right. With Luna's social anxiety, she sometimes introduced her music, but she rarely addressed the crowd.

The hairs on my neck stood up as Azul continued. "Catch us up on what's been going on in your life." He looked back at the projector screen behind them, which had been a video loop of butterflies to go along with Luna's music. Suddenly, a picture of us halted the flap of their wings.

I turned sharply to Venice, who returned my look with

unease. "I don't know, Reef. This isn't planned. That's not part of the slides—"

I turned my attention back to the stage as my hands tightened. The crowd had broken out with calls of "oohs" and "awws." There was no way Azul was doing this out of the goodness of his heart or for the sake of good publicity for Luna. He had some sort of plan. Probably a nefarious one. I started toward the stage, but Venice pulled me back, shaking her head. And a protective ache tore through me.

"You two are the cutest couple. Makes me have hope that I might find someone, too." He smiled slyly and handed her something. "I'm thrilled for you. Maybe we could do a duet for old time's sake?" He managed a look of pitiful nostalgia somehow. I rolled my eyes. He was clearly going to get his way. If he couldn't have her, then he at least wanted to share in her musical talent. Maybe he'd decided to play nice. You caught more flies with—

No, oh no. My eyes landed on Luna, whose head was shaking a little too adamantly to be looking at lyrics on paper. No, he wasn't playing nice at all. This vulnerable ache washed away all her peace. He'd gotten to her. My eyes squeezed shut, knowing exactly what was on those pages. He came off looking like the bigger man to the crowd, when in actuality he was single-handedly destroying a relationship. What did he think would happen? She'd be so furious with me that she'd sing with him? That she'd take him back? Or maybe he was just doing it because he could.

"What is this, Azul?" But she didn't give him time to answer. She just shook it off and handed the papers back to him. "It's time for your set. Everyone is waiting for your beautiful music."

She started to get up, but he just kept his hand on her

shoulder, pushing her back down. My fists tightened even more. "Just one duet, Luna. I'm sure he wouldn't mind since you're clearly each other's muses. We'll make it a tribute to him. Funny, you were always mine. Seems you're still inspiring people."

He tried to keep the hurt out of his tone, but I could hear it. He'd figured out that none of her songs were about him. Not even the one he'd stolen from her. His big hit. This was more than just revenge for being dumped. Something that probably didn't happen to him. This was heartbreak and he wanted her to feel it, too. Just as publicly as he had. He was punishing her for all the things she'd done wrong: being more talented than him, taking away his means of success, and most of all, taking back her control when she left him.

He forced the papers back into her shaky hands as her eyes looked over them more thoroughly this time. "Can we get a spotlight?" he asked. "They really are so cute together. What song should we sing for him?"

He pointed over to me and suddenly a glaring spotlight was highlighting all my insecurities. I could barely see Luna through the blinding light, but my imagination could certainly fill in the blanks. I cringed.

No. This is not happening. No, no, no. My mind was whirling as my eyes adjusted to the insane spotlight. Desperately, I tried to make Luna out. Finally, she came into focus as my hand shielded my eyes. Right when she did, I saw her face drop.

"Reef, is it true?" Her voice barely made its way over to me.

But I just stood frozen in place on the outskirts of the Waikiki shell. Stuck in the literal spotlight that shone on me, thanks to Azul. I swallowed and her face fell even more.

Her ukulele dropped from her grasp, clattering to the ground as she left the stage. Racing past me, I watched her leave as she headed toward the park.

"Luna, wait!" At last, I managed to call, my body unfrozen. I took one last look at Azul; his satisfied smirk landed a gut punch. I was propelled forward by "the impact" and chased after her. She soon appeared to be losing momentum, her shoulders falling as she stopped at an empty grassy patch near the park. Secluded under palm trees, the spot offered privacy against the backdrop of a twinkling night sky.

I tried to think of what to say, but she spun back on her heels and faced me, shocking me completely. I thought I'd have more time. I never expected to tell her this way. My mind pictured a serene beach scene with Nova tonight.

"Reef, what is going on?" My face went slack. "Explain this to me." She held out the papers.

I could see all the heat in her face. I saw her determination illuminated by the night sky. Usually I would love her guard dropping, but right now I felt like I might need it back. She had to hate hearing this from Azul, of all people. He'd put her in an awful position. Just the way he liked it, I presumed.

"Reef," she prodded again, her brows furrowing in the waning moonlight. My eyes pinched momentarily, and I heard a pained sigh escape her. That brought me back. It didn't do any good to wish I'd had the courage to do things differently. Those deep-rooted fears had been wrapped around me for far too long.

I glanced at the moonlight bathing the space between us, wishing this moment was something else. Wishing the beauty wasn't lost on my shortcomings. "Luna," I tried. She waited, giving me a chance to explain.

Crisp starlight mingled with my heavy breathing. "I write under the pen name Cece LaRue." She looked at me, stunned. "I began writing romance novels for therapy, and it wasn't supposed to be for anything else. My writing wasn't supposed to be seen by *anyone*. I was just messing around with Locke one day and I let him read some of my writing and. . . He said it was great that it needed to be published. He knew I'd never have the courage to submit it myself, so he did it for me. And I guess he thought if I got rejected, I would never have to know. But I didn't. Or at least he only told me about the ones who accepted me." I laughed tersely.

I looked at her frozen expression and forced myself to continue. "Locke helped me have the courage to believe I was good enough to be published. He helped me feel like my dreams were possible, just like you had when no one else did. That *I* was good enough and had something to offer. But I told him I would only do it if I had a pen name. There was no way I wanted people to know I wrote romance, especially–"

"Your family," she breathed.

I nodded, exhaling when she finally spoke. "I felt like I'd let them down and would be an embarrassment to them as a romance writer. Not that I particularly wanted anyone to know about my work. So, one night, we were just joking around, and suddenly my porn star name was on the contract and mailed off. I had no recollection of doing it when I woke up. It felt like a bad dream. Not exactly the professional way to go. I doubt it would have happened without the liquid courage. Definitely not without Locke. And I'm so grateful that I've gotten to do what I love."

Luna just stared at me. "But no one knows. That doesn't bother you?"

"No, not really. That's not why I write. Sure, it would be nice to discuss that part of my life, especially with readers, but the trade-offs are too steep." A melancholy overtook me, which was echoed in her features.

"But I'm not just *anyone.*" Her deep ache haunted me. "I told you *everything*, Reef. I didn't hold back. I told you about the most painful parts of me . . . Did you think I'd react like other people? That I'd—"

"No, Luna. It's just . . . There's more." She gave me a look of deep longing. I didn't want to hold anything back. I wanted to do what she'd done—trust her with everything. "Luna, you said you really related to Cece's characters. That you've never seen—"

An understanding dawned across her face. Emotions written on it that tugged on my being. "Reef, are you saying?"

"Luna, you're not the only one who's pulling inspiration from what we had. You're my muse." It hung there. This new understanding formed, an invisible tether anchoring us. Unlike anything I'd ever felt before.

"They're all you, Luna. You're the inspiration. I didn't do it on purpose—I didn't even know I was doing it. But it was nice to live on those pages with you again. And I wanted other women to feel seen in ways you hadn't. To know they should be loved for *all* of themselves because they're beautiful *exactly* as they are. And well, that might be a problem with the sample you have." I looked down at the paper clenched tightly in her hands.

A silent realization came over her as she parted her lips. As if she now knew why she loved my books so much.

"Me?" she breathed deeply, overwhelmed.

I nodded. "Yes, they're you." The words felt so good

leaving my lips finally. To have this moment with her. To be completely open and honest.

"But I told you I did the same thing. Why would you hide this from me? You had so many opportunities–" Her voice hitched as her brows sewed together. "I even told you about the letters I wrote to *her.*" Realization hit her.

I squeezed my eyes shut. This was the worst part.

"You knew? You knew all along? All those things I told Cece, I was really telling *you?*" Her voice fractured and something inside me did, too.

I reached out to her, but she backed away as if she'd never known me. A stony facade was resurrected on those lovely features. Stronger than I'd ever seen before.

I could barely whisper, "That's why I didn't know how to tell you–"

"You *replied,* Reef. You *knew* it was me. And you *kept* reading them. You kept replying." Luna's voice rose to new heights. "They were personal. *Private. Extremely* private." Her voice cracked.

"Luna, I'm so sorry–"

"You knew from my letters I couldn't have kids? That was *you* giving me advice?" Her pitch grew higher, spiraling out of control.

I doubted anything I said was going to register now. I tried reaching out again, but this time she yanked away. "Luna, there were so many things I didn't know. I never knew what happened to us or the reason you couldn't have kids. And I know that doesn't help, but there's a reason I answered your letters."

Her stained eyes stared at me wildly. "There can't be a reason, Reef."

I inhaled deeply. "I know I shouldn't have read *any* of your letters in the first place, but I didn't want your letter to go unanswered if it was something . . ." Then, I tried again. "I just needed to know what you wrote in the first letter. And I thought I'd read it and if a response wasn't dire, then I wouldn't respond or read any more. As long as I knew the nature of the letters, then I would be done. But I read that first letter, and I *had* to respond. I couldn't let it go unanswered. And I didn't think we would ever be in each other's lives again, at least not significantly. So I thought I could at least be in your life in this way and be there for you in *some* capacity. I thought it was innocent, I never thought—"

"You never thought that I was still in love with you and that maybe it was a huge invasion of privacy? That there were some things I should tell you myself? There were some pretty big clues to show you how deep my feelings still were for you . . . Or did you think I wouldn't tell you and that you should just find out everything while you had the chance? After how I ended things, that was only fair, right?"

I tried to utter something, but she continued on without blinking. "I *knew* something's been off with you. I had this nagging feeling all day. But I feel *so stupid*. How could I not have *known?*"

She paused briefly to catch her breath as the puzzle pieces fell into place. "You used her closing in the song, but I couldn't place it. And I always thought there was something about her characters, but I just thought all her readers felt that way. That's why they were best sellers. And when I told you about my infertility, your response felt so familiar. The way you reacted, it was like déjà vu in a way."

"Luna—" I tried.

"And you kept bringing up her books. What were you hoping for? More information? Because I'm pretty sure you already got plenty." Her voice broke.

"No, that's not it *at all*. That's not why I wrote you back and you know it. You know me better than that, or at least I hope you do. And I was hoping by bringing up Cece's books you might tell me what was in the letters. I felt terrible about it. It's been tearing me up inside."

Disbelief clouded her features. I steadied my voice. "Luna, would you have told me *all* of this? If Venice hadn't hinted at the songs and Azul hadn't said what he did? Would you have trusted me with all of this already? I think it just would have taken us *both* time to open up."

She stepped back at my words, as if wounded. "But that's not what happened, Reef. I told you *everything*. You had the perfect opening and you let me be vulnerable all by myself. Because you still don't trust me, do you? Not really. You haven't truly forgiven me for the past. I'm one of those *other* people to you. The ones you're too afraid to tell. Too afraid they will hurt you. *Again*."

Her words landed like a knockout punch. Finishing me off. Stunned, I could only stand there. Too paralyzed by my worst fears to speak, even as she made her way back to the stage. Dejection trailing behind her. It seemed the last thing she wanted me to do was go after her. So, I didn't. I didn't deserve to.

Maybe it was better this way. Perhaps we were two stars that were supposed to cross and help each other along their paths. And that was all. We inspired each other's success and happiness, without being together. We couldn't have it both ways. Just like Emma Stone and Ryan Gosling in *Lala Land*. It would never work. That was the thing about star-crossed lovers. Stars were fickle. They didn't align when you wanted them to. Perhaps they were never supposed to align at all.

As I took one last look toward the stage, I accepted my

fate, taking any leftover dignity with me while it was still intact. I slipped back into the hotel room and packed my bags, collecting Nova to return home. Going back to the life we should be living. Only taking one last look around the room, at the world that could have been. The only one I wanted to live in.

Reef

CHAPTER 44

And for a few fleeting moments
It's like she's there with me
My soul feels completed
No longer just a muse
What can I do to make it all come true?
How do I keep you?

-REEF AKUA, THE MUSE

N ova and I had stood by the ferry railing, looking
helplessly out to sea the whole way back. Her tail
hadn't even wagged once. It was actually heart-
breaking. And the journey back home wasn't much better.
But Nova and I were slowly settling back into our normal
routine. If normal was classified as a plethora of takeout
containers strewn about the apartment and endless
romance movie marathons—classics preferred—then yeah,
life was normal. We'd eaten all the vanilla ice cream stock
on this side of Maui. Then, we were getting back to a
routine that now seemed so lonely with just the two of us.
Too empty when it had almost been filled with three.

My bag still lay abandoned by the front door. A ghost
of the past week taunting me. I wanted to get it out of
sight, but I also couldn't bear to move it. Like it was a time
capsule or something. Or maybe the last vestige of hope. I
don't know why I thought this would end any differently.
Somewhere deep down, I think I'd always expected to get
my heart broken again.

Nova was curled up on the worn leather of my writing

chair. Its creases molding around her like a familiar cocoon. Her amber-colored eyes tracked me with her own over-whelming sadness. I wasn't the only one I'd let down. Upon our return, Nova and I had been moping around in a similar fashion. She had gladly licked her matching conso-lation prize of ice cream.

"Well, what do you want me to do?" I looked at her as she laid her head down with the grandest of sighs. Those eyes kept getting bigger as they tracked me. "Nothing is going to help. I had a lot of opportunities to make it right and I didn't take any of them. I messed up badly."

I was met with more stares from the golden eyes of her pure liquid heart. "Yeah, I know there's no excuse. What do?–"

But there was a knock on the door. I stared at it as if it was a portal into another world. My shoulders dropped with an imaginary weight, anchoring me in place. The weight felt too heavy for me to make it there. If it was Locke, I didn't want to explain all the ways I'd messed up. And if it was someone else, I didn't feel like putting on any kind of mask. Worst of all, an absurd, petty part of me hoped it was her.

With an impressive sigh, my feet trudged over that way and cracked open the door. Before I knew what was happening, Mrs. Ailana and her bird had burst into my apartment.

"You cannot just come in here, Mrs. Ailana. Especially not your bird. Nova is in here."

She waved me off as the bird flew off her shoulder and into my living room with total disregard. "I haven't seen you exit this apartment in a week since you came back . . . alone."

"It's none of your business, Mrs. Ailana. "You have to stop spying—" I tried to say, closing the door, only to find her already settled in my writing chair.

"What you should do is go to her and stop talking about it with your dog. Make some big romantic gesture like in those Nora Ephron movies. Find the Hawaiian equivalent of the Empire State Building."

I kept shaking my head like a cartoon, waiting for this hallucination to fade. But she just kept getting brighter and louder. The Wizard of Oz bursting into full color.

"Reef, you sulking around and talking to yourself in your apartment is not helping anyone. You're making me so depressed that all my work looks like Picasso's blue period."

"Were you a spy or something?" I asked incredulously. "Do you have some type of sound amplification? The walls are *not* that thin." Especially not to hear my muttering and moping around. She'd been sending that bird over here again. Probably as soon as she'd realized I'd come back without Luna. I had to keep my balcony doors shut more often.

She rolled her eyes and shooed me away again. Her hair was styled in her pink foam rollers and tied with that hot pink silk scarf she liked so much. Clad in another vibrant, fuzzy bathrobe. Daisies gracing it this time. I'd originally thought she was in ill health and didn't have the energy to get dressed. But as I looked at her sunken face, I realized she was just exhausted and lonely. She probably only got halfway dressed every day. And I suddenly didn't care so much that she was so invested in my life.

"Reef, it needs to be dead silent to paint, and your living room is right next to my art room. You continuously break my concentration, rustling around over here or playing your music. Now when I don't hear it, I think something's wrong. Plus . . . It's comforting to know I'm not alone in my work when I do hear it. Plus, if you haven't figured it out by now, the bird helps. He's the true spy. Although, I didn't need a bird to hear about your sad movie marathon. That was plenty clear through the walls."

"It wasn't sad—" It was seriously creepy how much she knew about me. Good thing I hadn't brought Luna back here very often. If I ever got another shot, I wasn't planning on it. I'd probably try to kiss her, and Mrs. Ailana would bang on the wall, and tell me all the ways I was doing it wrong. I swear she had a peephole somewhere.

"Oh, but it was. *Sit.*"

I stammered. "This is my house."

"Sit!" She pointed to Nova, who was standing upright on the sofa, staring at the bird that had landed on my bookcase. Great, she'd probably poop all over my proof copies. That would be a new form of critique for me.

I rolled my eyes, but obeyed. Mrs. Aliana responded, "Wonderful. Ok, let's figure this out so we can get you out of the doldrums," she began emphatically.

But there was another knock at the door. I sighed heavily. Mrs. Ailana waved it off. But the knocking just continued.

"Reef," Locke's voice boomed. "Reef, open up. I heard from Louis, ok? Just open the door. We can talk about it. I promise I'll just listen or we can sit in silence."

By this time, Mrs. Ailana had gone to the door, most likely to get rid of him. She'd completely taken over. My head was now in my hands. The entire world would have to know.

"Oh." Locke's eyebrows raised at the sight of her.

"Come in, if you must. But I'm the lead on this plan. If you come in, then you're agreeing to those terms. You obviously haven't gotten him very far." Locke's eyebrows arched even higher at her bluntness.

"Fair," he said as he made his way to my sofa. "I've had a long time to help. A *very* long time."

I rolled my eyes. "Can we not? I'm fine, everyone. Thanks for dropping by, but the show's over."

"Yeah, man, I'd say you're not." Locke looked around my apartment. Cartons were all over the place from the past week and I didn't exactly look wonderful myself. Probably didn't smell great either. Now that they're back, have you considered talking to her? Since things have calmed down. You know that's *not* the craziest thing in the world. She's probably over it by now. This is Luna."

"Yeah, definitely over it," I remarked sarcastically. "She just told 'me' her deepest, darkest secrets and didn't even know it was me. Then told *me* all her most intimate secrets when she knew it was me and I still never told her any of mine. Or that I already knew hers. Yup, totally over it. Completely. Why don't I just go over and ask her out to dinner?"

Locke was about to say something, but Mrs. Ailana beat him to it. "You writers make everything so much harder than it needs to be. You overthink everything. Why don't you just go over there, give her some romantic note, tell her you screwed up, say you're sorry and that you love her?"

"Is that what you did with your muse?" I shot back. I closed my eyes, immediately feeling bad about my remark.

"No, I did nothing, Reef. And look where I am. He started seeing the other woman I used to paint. Probably to make me jealous or wake me up. But he's gone now. You want to be like me? Still painting the same person? Still pining for them?"

"I bet you know exactly where he is. You could contact him."

"He didn't want me. Your situation is different."

"You keep telling yourself that." Our eyes met in a deadlock, seeing the same fear in each other, and something shifted inside of us.

"Reef," Locke's oddly soothing tone interrupted us. Somehow we'd forgotten about his hulking presence. "Do you really want to keep living life this way?" He looked around my apartment, but I knew he didn't mean the superficial clutter.

Locke had stood by me all these years and watched me struggle with my identity. But he could only help me so much. Self-acceptance was something only I could accomplish. I had to learn how to be proud of myself. It was one thing not to claim my work. It was another not to claim myself. And I'd seen what that was like with Luna, how different it felt. The love I felt for her wasn't complete without knowing all of her. Without her being willing to accept herself so she could share all those pieces with me. I'd watched her open up, and I had loved her even more for it. *So why hadn't I done the same with her? Why can't I live that way with everyone in my life?*

Locke's gaze held mine. A silent, brotherly conversation brewing. "I think you know what you need to do." He handed my cell phone over to me. "You've got to decide. Before you lose her."

My fingers hesitated over the keypad.

"Yes, he does," Mrs. Ailana said, and I nodded in reply. "Call her!"

"That's not who he's dialing," Locke said as he looked at Mrs. Aliana's puzzled face.

As the phone rang, my flight response kicked into high gear, but Locke just kept gently nodding, like the ebb and flow of the tide. A brotherly strength transferred to me as he placed a comforting hand on my shoulder.

"Hi, Dad," I began, speaking into my cell phone.

Reef

CHAPTER 45

She's the girl from childhood
The one who's always known me
The one I've always loved
The one I could never forget
The one who has made me come undone

-REEF AKUA, THE MUSE

"Dad?" I asked when the phone clicked on. A tremble had already started inside me. *It's time, Reef. Find your voice.*

But my mom's comforting tone rang out instead. "Oh honey, it's me. Your dad is out back working in the yard. Do you want me to get him?" I gulped as the line went eerily silent. "Reef. Are you ok?"

"Yeah, fine. I just . . . I have—" Locke's hand squeezed my shoulder as I looked at it for support. "I just need to tell dad something."

"Oh, well, today isn't the best day, dear. He's been out in the yard, working hard. And you know how the heat can affect him. Why don't you call back later? You can tell me how you've been instead." There seemed to be a lot of 'heat' on this island. There was always some excuse.

I swallowed back the urge to do as she suggested and end our call. To let her continue to 'protect' me. But there was only so much she could do. There always had been. And I couldn't run from this any longer. And I finally realized I didn't want to. It was time to live my life.

"I need to talk with him, please."

"Reef, I *really* think you should wait." Her voice was smaller as she attempted another warning. She wouldn't be able to shield me after this.

"I'm sure. And I'd like to tell you as well. Can you put me on speakerphone?"

"Well, alright. I'll go get him. Just wait a minute, ok?"

I heard rustling and then an unnerving silence. A numb feeling took over me. While I didn't especially want my mom to hear the news with my dad, I also didn't want her to find out from him.

"Ok, we're here," my mom said, as I heard her click

some buttons on the phone. I looked at Locke, who nodded.

"Um, I need to tell you something," I began, hearing the tremble now.

"I'm halfway through the yardwork, son. Can't this wait until another time?" My dad's sharp voice cut through the line.

"Oh–" I began, but Locke squeezed my shoulder. "No, no, it can't." And as I looked at Locke for encouragement, I told them about *everything*. My pen name. How I had started. What I wrote. For how long. And how popular the books had become.

"Son, I can make some calls. There are plenty of jobs, if you know the right people. I'm sure some of the men who have worked for me can call in a favor."

Respectable jobs. Manly jobs. Not something as trivial as romance writing. "No dad. I have a job. One I love and I'm proud of." This heaviness lifted off of my chest, feeling like I could breathe for the first time in twenty years.

He grunted out a sound.

But I just continued while I had the courage and couldn't feel the impact. "I'm able to provide an escape for people. Connect with readers. Travel through writing. Teach them about a topic, one I get to research and explore, too . . . Maybe even show them a new perspective, if I do my job right. I wouldn't trade it for *any* other job."

"Romance author," my dad scoffed. "I've got to finish cutting the trees. This really could have waited. We can discuss your future later, after you've had time to think a little more clearly."

The line went dead and I could imagine him walking away in a brood. "He'll come around, Reef. Don't worry about it. He just wants you to be happy and stable. I think we're just in shock. It's so incredible, honey–"

"Kala, stop indulging him and come help." My father's voice boomed in the distance.

The line went silent again, but this time there was a painful silence. "It's ok mom. I'll talk to you later," I finished, dejected.

"No. No, it's not." She spoke up, surprising me. "I'm really proud of you, honey. He'll come around and if not. . . well it's his loss, isn't it?"

I swallowed hard at the implications. Shock registering on my features. "Thanks, mom. You don't know what that means to me . . ."

"Kala!" my father yelled louder. "Where are you? This tree limb is about to crush me."

"I'm telling your son how proud we are of him, like you should have done. I'll help when you do the same." Complete silence swept the background. Then her voice flowed softer through the line. "I don't know where that came from." She breathed. "I better go, sweetheart. I love you."

"Love you too, mom. Thank you," I managed, with tears misting in my eyes. Love was showing up for someone. Never letting them feel small.

Maybe he would come around one day, like she'd said. Maybe he was just worried about my future and would explain his side of things. But it didn't really matter anymore. The worst that could happen already had. I knew how that conversation ended. And it no longer had any power over me. I was free.

"Reef, I'm really proud of you," Locke as he gripped me tightly.

"You know what? I am, too," I replied softly, feeling a weight soar off of me.

LOCKE AND MRS. AILANA continued to pace the room while I had a long conversation with my literary agent. The one I'd always dreaded and been too afraid to have.

I sat down on the sofa with a thud and both of them just looked at me from their positions on either end.

"Reef—" Mrs. Aliana began hopefully.

But Locke stopped her. "That was thirty years of emotions, Mrs. Aliana. I think that's enough for today."

She peered around me at my best friend. "Not when someone who wants to love and accept you just as you are is waiting. There's a window on these things."

I buried my head in my hands, feeling like a shell of a person. Still not able to process what I'd done. I'd just shattered any illusion I'd been able to build with my father—with the world.

"Reef," her voice came out softer than I'd ever heard it. "Do you really want to live in a world where she doesn't know you love her? Where she doesn't know you want her? At least let that be the last thing she hears from you. Because there's no way she's just a muse to you. And she deserves to know that. You deserve to tell her that."

I nodded, but Locke intervened again. "I'm pretty sure that's why he just did what he did. He's wiping the slate clean for her. No more lies."

And I just kept nodding, not capable of anything else.

Mrs. Aliana actually nodded at me. "When you're ready, Reef, you've got to show her you're *all in*. No more pretending."

As I stared at Mrs. Ailana, a plan formed in both of our eyes. I knew exactly what I had to do. I had my romantic gesture in mind, my *Sleepless in Seattle*, and I would lay my heart out on the line. I'd show her once and for all. I was *all in*. I was ready to stop pretending. No more lies. Like Mrs. Aliana said, no matter the outcome, at least that would be the last thing Luna heard.

Locke chimed in, "Yeah, they have always been way more than just muses for each other. And that will always be true. But, uh guys, I don't speak 'artist'." Locke looked at both of us expectantly. "Could ya help me out here? I feel you have something elaborate in mind. And it's making me a little concerned. So what's the plan?"

Luna

CHAPTER 46

*In a room full of people, no one is equal
I realize everyone else has just been the prequel*

-LUNA MANU MELE, THE ONLY
MAN I COULD LOVE

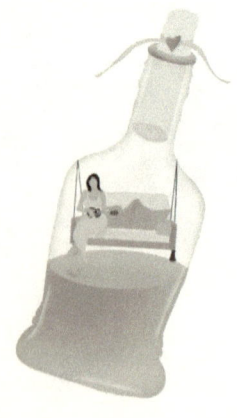

I swayed gently on my porch swing. Letting the familiar creaking sound and the comfy cushions soothe me. The pitter-patter of rain was hitting the roof, lulling me further into my daydreams. This was my favorite time to write, but not even nature's rhythm could inspire me.

"Luna?" Louis called from the kitchen, where he was making breakfast at four o'clock in the afternoon. Louis had dropped by to cheer me up. Apparently, I'd been moping around since we'd returned home. I'm not sure how I finished the rest of the festival and made it back home. Everything was a chaotic mess, as if a corrosive substance had damaged parts of my memory.

Things must be dire, because Louis didn't even bother handing me a uke when he came to visit. Something he'd been doing ever since I'd gotten sick. Nor did he try to hand me a romance book. Besides his comforting presence, none of his usual tricks were working.

From my little hideaway, I could hear the static of the radio and the scent of pancakes. I think he'd purposely left the windows open to my porch, hoping to entice me inside. I'd been in this swing so long, it was going to be ruined with a permanent Luna butt imprint. All I could muster today was looking out at the raindrops as they journeyed off the porch roof. I couldn't squeeze out any more bandwidth today. I was enjoying nature, echoing my solitude, commiserating with me. These conditions took a lot of energy, and sometimes there was hardly any left. Especially on days like today. It was like waking up with a cell phone you'd forgotten to charge. Trying to regain that energy all throughout the day, making it even more exhausting.

Suddenly Louis appeared in front of me with a skillet in hand, sporting my frilly lavender apron. "Honey, you're going to want to hear this."

"No thanks, 'Anakala. I've been avoiding music and social media. Or just social period." He raised an eyebrow with an all-knowing look as I continued. "I just want to stay out here if that's alright. Can we eat out here, too?"

He glanced at me sharply, but went back inside without another word. When he returned, it wasn't pancakes he brought with him. Rather, he was carrying my little vintage radio that I'd had since I was a kid. The one I used to listen to as I dreamed about playing my lyrics on the radio one day. The radio Reef had helped me find and buy, because I'd wanted one exactly like his.

Louis came over and set the small radio down on the cushion beside me. Then he just stood in front of me as it played. With the speaker crackling from today's storms, my foggy brain tried to make sense of the sound. I immediately recognized my favorite Maui radio channel. I still dreamed about being aired live on it. This performance type, with its small, intimate audience, was the only one I believed I could genuinely enjoy and be fully present at. And I could still reach a huge audience.

My eyebrows scrunched together because my brain couldn't make sense of what I was hearing. I recognized the voice. It sounded like—*no.* My eyes shot up to Louis, whose arms crossed. With a pointed expression, he started nodding.

The on-air announcer asked, "So, Reef—or do you prefer to go by your pen name? . . . Can you tell us a little about this song?"

My mouth dropped. *Pen name?* I bolted upright in my seat, my hands clutching at the edge of the porch swing. The cool bamboo material under my palms was the only thing grounding me to this world right now. Because I was pretty sure I'd entered an alternate one and this was all a dream.

Reef let out his friendly laugh that warmed everybody's soul. And I blinked my eyes rapidly, trying to wake up. But Louis just kept nodding at me.

"I definitely prefer my real name. Thanks, Noa. Actually, this song was written for the woman who finally helped me claim my writing and reveal my pen name to the world. And of course, like the title of the song suggests, she's the one I very much have to thank for these novels. They wouldn't have happened without her."

My eyes widened as my uncle tipped his head. *What was happening? Was he finally doing it? For everyone to hear?*

"Wow, that's romantic, Reef. Your romance writer is showing." The announcer teased, and they both laughed. "Well, we're all very glad she came into your life. So, how did you start writing?" He asked in his booming radio tone.

"I've always wanted to write, but I never thought I was good enough to actually be a professional writer. But my real impetus was to write about people like myself, and the woman I just mentioned, so we could feel seen and less alone. And not a day goes by that I'm not incredibly grateful that I get to do what I love. But the novels happened because I wanted to see her again. To be with her, if only through my writing. I wanted to belong to a world where we existed together again and there was a happy ending. Even if it was for just three hundred pages."

Reef's tone ended on a jovial note to keep things light, but the host got more serious. "Sounds like a romance as epic as one of your novels. Are you going to share any of it with us?"

"I think I'd prefer to just sing the song," Reef replied.

But the host must have given him some sort of look because a silence fell.

"You've got to give us something after that. At least set the scene for the song. Don't leave us on a cliffhanger. You writers are good at that." He teased, setting the bait.

"She's the only woman I've ever loved. Since the first day we met making flower crowns as children. And I'm hoping she's listening right now because I'm afraid I may have lost her forever." A dire ache echoed through my crummy little speakers.

There was painful silence in the air again. The host obviously didn't know what to say. I looked up at Louis, feeling equally lost myself. I'd never had a man do something like this for me. No man had ever cared like Reef. Had ever taken the time to do the things he did. To show they cared in their actions, from the smallest to the biggest things. It was one thing to have roses delivered to you. But it was something completely different to have someone pick flowers and build a princess crown with you, while talking about your dreams and helping you believe they'd come true. That was the difference between the type of man Reef was and the relationship we had. *Still have.*

I stared at the radio. He proved that as he took his biggest swing of all on this radio station. The one he'd helped me build my dreams on. He was showing me he was ready as he claimed himself, and his art, in front of the world. It was all I ever wanted. To be happy, he had to love himself. And at that moment, I wanted nothing more than to go to him. I didn't need to hear anymore.

I could feel my eyes swell as I looked at Louis. "You should go," he breathed. "Bring him back for breakfast."

I laughed lightly as I wiped away the tears. I looked down at my yoga pants and oversized lavender sweatshirt.

This *would* be the day I didn't wear a dress. But I'd continued to feel chilled to the bone. Like I was hollowed out. Missing pieces.

"Go as you are *now*, Luna," Louis advised strongly. And the words resonated deeply within me, giving me courage in ways I didn't know I even needed. "He's always known you better than anyone. And he has loved you even more for it. That's obvious."

Louis stared down at the little radio and more mist overtook me. I thought of all those beautiful letters he'd written to me. His replies had gotten me through so many dark times. I'd fallen in love with the letters. And I knew now that he'd *always* been there for me. The letters took on a whole new meaning as I thought about Reef being the one to write them. He'd known from the very beginning and he'd wanted me. He'd wanted *every* part of me.

Those letters proved something to me: his soul would always call to me. Regardless of the circumstances, we would always find each other. I was destined to be in love with him.

My feet began before my mind could catch up as I bounded down the front porch steps. Letting the cool, rejuvenating rain hit my skin. I halted abruptly, feeling like I'd forgotten quite a few things. I turned to find Louis right behind me with my purse and keys in his hand, still hanging on to the skillet in the other. Hissing sounds igniting the air as rain hit the cast iron.

"You might need this," he sang out.

I kissed his cheek and looked at him. Overcome with emotion, I whispered, "I love you, 'Anakala."

"He's a lucky man. Never forget that. Now, go to him." I smiled, but his words only made my eyes brim over with joy and gratitude.

Luna

CHAPTER 47

And I'll never be able to hide it
As much as I've been told to fight it,
You are the only man I could love
Forever and always

-LUNA MANU MELE, THE ONLY
MAN I COULD LOVE

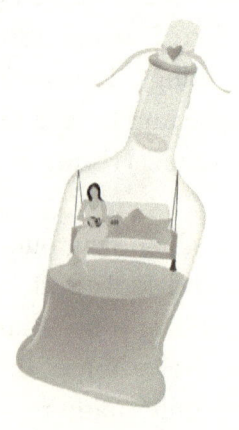

I raced to the radio station, my wipers battling the downpour as I listened to the broadcast. The host continued to prod Reef, but he wouldn't budge. He appeared to have gone on the show to reach me, and he had no intention of sharing any more of our story than was absolutely necessary. However, the host pried a little more information loose about his journey as an author and what it was like to be Cece LaRue, which I found very interesting. *Is Reef doing all this to fill airtime? Is he waiting for me?*

"I'm going to need more time, Reef." I muttered toward my baby blue island cruiser's speaker. And time to think. *I don't think they're going to let me just waltz in there. What's the plan here, Reef?*

At least he'd picked the radio station in Kaanapali, so it was only about five minutes away. Frantically, I pulled into the parking lot and stared at the radio knob on my car dash. My freshly damp fingers hovered over the knob, not wanting to be disconnected. But I cut the ignition and headed inside, getting soaked, yet again, as the rain came down even harder. As I ran through the downpour, it felt as if the water was giving me a fresh start. Wiping my slate clean.

Soaking wet, I began making my way to him. I read the signs in a frenzied blur, redirecting myself like a lost kid at a carnival. I could hear the blood whooshing in my ears as adrenaline became the enemy. Disorientation kicked in as my anxiety flared.

Finally, I found a studio with an 'on the air sign' lit up outside the glass windows. As I peeked through the control area, I could see the broadcast room . . . and Reef.

I lifted my water-logged sleeve, but knew it was no use since his back was to me as he sat across from the host. My fingers slipped on the metallic door handle as I fumbled to open it.

As I opened the door to the control room, I heard Reef's voice cut in. "Ok, I think it's time for that song I promised you." Nervousness laced his tone, mixing with a bit of defeat. So, he had hoped I would come. I guess by now he didn't think I was going to show. It had taken Louis some time to get me to listen to the radio.

I waved my arms to get his attention, droplets of rainwater flying off of me. But I stopped short when I recognized Guin sitting beside Reef. The staff was adjusting their mics and bringing over a ukulele for her. It was the first time I'd seen Guin out since her transplant surgery. And then I realized it wasn't the crew bringing Guin, her ukulele. I recognized Locke, bending down and gently handing it to her, checking on her. The gesture was simple, yet so very sweet. The type of gentle love and affection Reef had described when he talked about them. What I missed so much. Had taken for granted.

Reef had done all of this for me? Even Guin was here. I knew she had to be extremely careful about exposure to illnesses with her immunosuppressant medications, since she was recovering from her surgery.

I stood there, unable to move my arms even if I had wanted to get Reef's attention. The last thing I wanted to do was disturb this beautiful moment he had created. Unfortunately, a man in the control room had taken notice of me. Probably upset I'd left a gigantic puddle.

"Hey, you're not supposed to be in here. How did you?–"

The other man spoke up. "I've been telling management they've got to get better security. Anyone can get in here. It's not cool when we do all this work and just anybody . . ."

Their eyes scanned over me at the same time. "Hey that's not just *anybody*, that's Luna Manu Mele!" One of them exclaimed. They both stared at me. I couldn't believe they'd recognized me like *this*. Their eyes traveled over to Reef. *Slowly*. "No way. No freakin' way. That would be like—"

"Yeah, that would be like the island version of Sonny and Cher. . ." The first man finished in excitement.

But my eyes were too transfixed on Reef to work on diffusing the situation. We'd already put our fake relationship on social media. So what did it matter? Only this time, it would be true. I wondered if it was too late to—No, *I'm done hiding.* That was the point of all this, wasn't it?

So, I continued to moor myself to him. And the men just let me. Until one finally said, "Luna, if you want to go into the recording room to see him—"

"No," I interjected. "No, I don't want to interrupt him. I'll just stay here . . . if that's alright. Unless you think he doesn't want to do this. I mean, I've heard everything I need to hear."

They both looked at each other, their brows crinkling.

Then one of them finally ventured, "The song is wonderful and I think he really wants to sing it for you. He wanted to do the show in a certain way. He had to go through *a lot* to set this up."

I nodded and let my feet sink deeper into the ground. I hoped I was doing the right thing, and he truly wanted to do this. But his eyes stayed downcast with uncertainty.

With his eyes fixed on his mic, Reef's gentle voice came through the speakers. "This is called *The Muse*. I'm going to be accompanied by the talented Guinevere Summers on the ukulele. Soon to be Guinevere Kaleo." He smiled, trying to ease the tension, but his shoulders stayed rigid.

He cleared his throat, and then abruptly leaned into the mic. "And um, this one's for *her*. She knows who she is. Hopefully, she's listening . . ."

His eyes wandered up, and nervous energy rushed through me. Pumping deep in my veins and flooding my body. I swallowed as his eyes caught sight of me. A long pause suspended in mid-air. I could only hear my heavy breathing and the whooshing of my heart pounding in my ears. Reef's gaze fixed intensely on me and then a soft smile began pulling at the corners of his mouth as his features filled with what I can only call love. As he took in my soaked glory, his smile became even brighter. This felt like a scene from one of my romance books. Only better, because the leading man was him.

Guin put her hand on his shoulder and smiled. The mic picked up her quiet whisper as she did. "I guess she's listening."

There was a loud chair creak as the show's host whipped his body around, followed by Locke's iconic laughter. I guess I'd successfully messed up this segment. The host's face scrunched with annoyance, but then he did a double take and his eyes grew wide.

But Reef just nodded to Guin and leaned into the mic, continuing to make eye contact with me. Guin began playing before the host did anything. And as soon as Reef's voice hit the mic, something broke free in me. I felt *everything* when he sang. All the spectrum of colors from our story. The first time I met him. The moment I fell for him. Hearing my diagnosis. The devastating feelings that overpowered me when I made a clean break. Over a decade without him. Being reunited. The moment I realized I'd never fallen out of love with him, even as hard as I'd tried. Realizing that he would always be the *only one* for me. And the moment I fell for him all over again.

I felt warm, wet tears easing their way down my cheeks, finally feeling all of my buried emotions. I didn't know it was possible to feel *this* much with music and I had felt a lot. I had spent a long time repressing a significant part of who I was. All the things I wasn't supposed to feel or show as a woman, an artist, or any of the other plethora of labels I wore. My anxiety and depression hid all the things I had refused to confront. Beneath all my masks was just the young girl with so many dreams and insecurities. Wanting to be loved and make her mark on the world. And not knowing how to do it.

And suddenly, it all felt so perfectly clear. All we had to do was remove our masks. Watching Reef speak set my nerves on fire; making me feel bold and alive. Showing me love and giving me a chance to begin again if I choose. All I had to do was let go of the past. If only I could let go of the burden I've carried for so long, I would be free. No more conforming to others' expectations, no more fear of disappointing, being insufficient, or failing to please . . .

The time had come to do what we always did so naturally when it was only the two of us: be ourselves. His readiness was clear from his grand gesture. The question was, am I?

When the music stopped, the room quieted, all eyes turning to me. Even the host seemed to forget himself. Finally, the man who had placed his hand on my arm in solidarity came back to his senses. He began gesturing wildly to remind everyone in the booth that they were *still on the air*. But they looked like a 3D rendering in a museum case.

My eyes were locked on Reef's, and I was unable to look away. I felt an irresistible pull toward him, my heart deciding for me. With Reef's tender gaze upon me, "I love you," escaped my lips in a slow whisper. A smile burst forth on Reef's face, taking over all of his features. And I brushed away the tears that were becoming more prominent.

He mouthed, "I love you, too . . . *Obviously*." Which made me laugh under my breath.

The talk show host stared, completely stupefied. The men in the control room were now standing up with their headsets on, loudly barking commands in his ear.

"Sorry about the singing," Reef began. "I'm a writer, obviously not a singer. So, I appreciate the station's generosity at my request. Maybe one day someone special will sing it for me." He stared at me.

"Uh, oh." The host bumbled. "Yeah, I'd say so," he said, completely dumbfounded.

"About that—" Reef began innocently. "I left out *a good bit* of the story. Writers do that. We hook you *just* enough. A bad habit, I guess." The host laughed politely, yet glared nervously at Reef. "I didn't tell you about the two little kids who grew up listening to this station, planning their dreams together. Believing in each other *so much* that their dreams came true. See, the little boy wanted to be a writer and, well, the little girl wanted to write songs to be sung on this very station."

The host was flabbergasted. "Reef, you didn't tell me—"

"But see, the girl could sing. *Man, could she sing.* And play, too. Just one of the many pieces of her I fell in love with. And I made a promise to her. Actually, I made a lot of them . . . I promised to always be her friend. To always believe in her. To never let her give up on her dreams. But I think there's only *one* promise I haven't kept. I promised she would be on this show. That I would find a way. No matter what."

The man's jaw dropped. "Yeah, way to bury the lead. I'm gonna make it a rule never to let a romance writer be on this show again." His eyebrows raised as he straightened and arranged some items on the desk, trying to take back some control.

"Well, I was thinking you might let her sing on the show, actually you might *want* her to sing today. Maybe a song from the Oahu Ukulele Festival. The one that she— well, I'll let her decide what *she* wants to tell you."

Apparently, the network producer had been summoned because there was a boisterous man frantically talking behind me. He'd quickly taken over a headset mic. "Noa, if you don't let Luna Manu Mele in that room, I will kill you. Your career is dead. Time of death, now." Noa pursed his lips, obviously none too happy his boss had been called to handle the situation.

Without further ado, the network exec kindly waved me forward. An invitation I'd never expected to get. I looked at Reef, who nodded in encouragement. I took my first step, feeling like I was wading through blackstrap molasses. A strange paradox: time felt both slow and rapid simultaneously. But I just kept looking at my true north, breathing steadily.

A man pulled up a chair for me so I could sit beside Reef, provided me with a headset, and placed the mic between us so we could share it. Shirley Chisholm's quote, "If they don't give you a seat at the table, bring a folding chair," echoed in my thoughts. My eyes were so deep underwater, I was unsure of how I would play.

Guin handed me her ukulele. "Here, I think you might

need this." A warm flush rose on her face as her smile widened. And Locke beamed from behind her.

I slipped into the chair, my shoes squishing awkwardly. I breathed in deeply and then spoke into the mic as I looked at Reef. "Actually, I was hoping you'd sing the duet version from our Oahu performance with me. After all, I wrote it to *you*. Remember, you're not the only one with a muse here."

The host's jaw dropped in total disbelief at this turn of events. He sat silent, not knowing what to do with us. I guess *we* were going to close out the show.

"I thought you'd never ask. I'd be honored to sing a duet with my favorite musician and the woman I love." Reef leaned over and reached for my hand. Love shone fiercely from his eyes.

I leaned into the space between us, filled with safety and possibilities. Endless lifetimes of chances just waiting for us. I let myself be surrounded by the unconditional love he provided. I brought my hand up to his neck as I bridged the space between us and found his lips. The ones I had craved for a lifetime. Our headphones knocked into each other along the way.

"This is an audio show, not a visual one," Noa reminded us, irritated we'd hijacked his show and left him with too much dead air. "No one can see you kissing."

"I'm pretty sure the mic's picking something up," Locke started laughing.

I pulled away from Reef slowly, not ready to break contact as my forehead rested against his and my hands on his shoulders.

My lips silently formed the word *"hapa"*, letting it out in a whisper. This time, the word made its way out on its own. Morphing and shifting in the air. Making me realize we have the power to change the narrative and framework in our lives. Especially given the kindness of people we surround ourselves with.

"*Hapa*," he whispered back, as he nestled against my forehead. That word warmed me to my core, something I'd never felt before. No one saw me like Reef. Changing the framework was easy when he was around.

The host cleared his throat vehemently, and Locke laughed louder. Which warranted a fierce finger pointing from Noa. I guess that was his strong warning.

I turned to the mic, still partly intertwined with Reef. "I'm Luna Manu Mele," I smiled brightly and nodded to Reef.

"And I'm Reef Akua."

"And together we're going to be singing a special version of my song, *One More Hour,* that was written to the love of my life. But I don't want just one more hour with you, Reef. I want all of them. Because I'm so in love with you." I could see Reef's eyes go hazy with emotion. And in the background, the exec clutched his hands together in sheer happiness.

But for me, the background blurred as I melted into Reef and this moment with him. I was singing in a new way, owning my art again for all the reasons I had started it. Feeling like I was in that tree house with him again. I was now ready. At that moment, my world turned technicolor, and I truly began living. I was free.

Epilogue

LUNA | 6 MONTHS LATER

T he radio show had set fire to our world and kick-
started a chain of events. It became the biggest
moment of my career. People loved our version of
the song. Done *our* way.

And that moment with Reef gave me the wings to fly
and break free from my contract with Steve and the music
label. It wasn't without penalty, but Reef and Louis stood
by me as I did it. I wanted to get back to the joy of music
and remember why I made art: to heal myself and hopefully to give something to others. And I wanted to enjoy the
creative process again, and remind myself *why* I made
music.

Louis helped me to fight for my song rights that the
record label had control over. Or at least win back enough
control so we could work within the contract terms and
release new versions. And his efforts allowed me to produce
a record with our version of *One More Night* and Reef's song,
The Muse. Both of which were duets.

Reef insisted I get a professional singer or at the very

least someone who could sing better than he could. But I loved his voice and what I wanted–along with everyone else–was his authenticity and pure heart. Something special happened when he sang those lyrics. Plus, it meant he had an excuse to travel with me and even perform at concerts to help ease my anxiety. Which he did without hesitation.

Performing took on a new enjoyment for me after the radio session, and I had a new, special connection with the audience. Everything felt different once I finally took creative control. Finally, asking for what I needed as Reef encouraged me along the way.

And with a little encouragement from Louis and a lot from me, Reef started writing more lyrics. He needed little persuading since he'd wanted to help me and to become a part of my creative process again, just like when we had worked together in our younger days. Any time we could spend together, we savored. I don't think I'd ever been so happy to do the dishes with somebody.

But working together creatively and supporting each other's dreams was my favorite way to spend our time together. I read each new chapter he wrote, and I became his brainstorming partner for all things romance. Which was kind of dangerous because it rarely ended up with us writing, but with our lips getting lost on each other. I figured it was more material for the novel, so I was helping either way. His agent didn't seem to feel quite the same way. But Reef coming out of the romance closet had been fantastic for sales. It was the exact opposite of what he'd expected.

Readers were loving the sexy, nerdy guy who wrote romances and swooned over the story behind it. They loved when Reef brought me to his book signings. But mostly, they just loved that they actually got to talk to the author now. I know how much I loved talking to 'her'.

I even encouraged Reef to think about that drink line I'd suggested. I'd love to open up a shop with him one day. Incorporate our music and books together somehow. Have a mental health book and gift shop with a coffee and non-alcoholic drink bar. Name it something like the 'Moonlight Reef'. His agent thought it was a fantastic idea, suggesting he could include recipes in his books. So far, Reef hadn't taken me up on the idea. But his confidence was growing every day.

Reef had continued to work with his agent on his previous line of books. And they were currently undergoing rebranding and new edits. Adding in bonus scenes for parts of the book he felt he'd compromised on. Once he'd opened up to his agent, she'd started working with the publisher to help Reef with his vision, fighting hard for him. They'd been through a lot together over the course of his career, and she was proud he was standing up for his work and finally telling her how he felt. They'd become close friends through the process. And since there was a new face to Cece LaRue, it was time for a new branding, anyway. At least that's what she had convinced the publisher needed to happen.

A new face to Cece, meant a new face to the male leads, too. He was re-writing some of the characters, so he could see himself more in fiction, as well. And we could have *our* happy ending.

And just like that, the stars aligned. Our art allowed us to live out our dreams in the way we chose. There is something so powerful about living and speaking your truth. Believing in yourself enough to go after your dream. And if you're lucky, having someone who believes in you along the way.

I gazed over at Reef as I took his hand, and we walked down the steps from Locke's bungalow. Now that Guin's recovery has progressed, we could visit them more frequently. And tonight, Locke had been kind enough to have us over for his incredible fish and plantain dish. We came over several nights a week for game night, dinner on the lanai, or to watch a movie. It was like old times again. As if we'd come full circle. Maybe someday our kids would do this together, too. The thought made me warm as I envisioned our kids growing up together on the island, just like we had. It also made me blush at how quickly I envisioned those kids being with Reef.

I had missed this Ohana so much. When Guin was having a good day, I even played the ukulele with her. She had been shy about it at first, but it only took a little encouragement. Now, we played together any chance we got. I'm sure there was going to be a spot for her on my next album. There was always a special spot for Ohana. Guin was steadily getting stronger, but it was a slow road. One I knew too well. And I knew we were fortunate to be a part of Guin's journey because I hadn't been able to let anyone be a part of mine.

I enjoyed watching Locke alongside her. He showed so much patience and kindness; staying by her side this whole time. Never once disappointed they couldn't do more activities or go to more places. Actually, the exact opposite. I think he loved having this time with her. I looked over at Reef, knowing he would have been the same way with me. It was all about how you looked at things. How you framed your perspective, and I'd had the narrative all wrong. I'd written it for Reef. The biggest mistake you could make for a person was taking their voice away.

My body gravitated over to Reef as we made our way down to the beach access, with Nova trailing beside us. She'd been enjoying these visits just as much as us since Guin and Locke had service dogs for her to visit. That's essentially what Nova had become for me.

Nova stopped to sniff all her surroundings as we enjoyed the short walk, loving that she always got to be included. Our little Ohana unit didn't go anywhere without her if we could help it. Reef chose two palm trees and started making good use of our pocket-size foldable hammock. In no time at all, the Eno's bright colors were waving proudly in the breeze. The soft, salty sea air teasing my skin at this most perfect time of day. The first change of colors in the sunset were providing a cotton candy pattern in the sky.

I looked over my shoulder toward the beach access. Guin had encouraged us to go ahead without them, so we might get lucky enough to see the green flash, insisting she'd be too slow. But I was pretty sure I'd used up all my luck the day I'd met Reef, and I was perfectly okay with that.

Reef slid into the hammock before helping me into it so I could rest against him. I snuggled closer, feeling the warmth of his chest as he cradled me. His familiar scent caressed me, making me completely content. In all of Hawaii, this was my favorite spot. *He* was my favorite place.

I'd say it was the simple things in life that made it the most worth living, but there wasn't anything simple about this. I had everything. A wonderful Ohana, and someone who cared and loved every piece of me. I would never take it for granted again.

Reef had tied Nova's leash around the tree. But it didn't stop her from trying to get in the hammock with us, per usual. She was extra energetic from seeing her doggie friends. I wanted to console her with ear rubs, but I always felt like I was going to tip us over when I did.

"Do you mind checking her pocket?" Reef asked. "I think Locke might have put something in there, trying to be cute. Maybe that's why she's more insistent today?"

"Sure. I bet you it's a bogus treasure map of the beach. Something we definitely would have fallen for as kids." I laughed, but Reef didn't. His face was oddly serious.

I slowly felt around and, sure enough, my fingers rubbed up against some paper that was stuffed inside. My hand brought out a paper scroll, and my eyebrow raised.

"Yup, I'm sure he's got some cheesy pirate map. Probably 'Goonies' inspired."

Reef laughed lightly as I slowly unrolled the paper. My lips scrunched up to one side as my eyes looked over at Reef, confused by the image that appeared at the top of the page. But the pieces quickly fell into place as the paper unfurled. In my hands was a certificate, stating Nova was now a certified emotional support dog. I stared at Reef. A stinging sensation taking over my eyes.

He had generously shared Nova with me ever since I had come back into his life, allowing her to become like my own. And she had helped more than any technique I'd ever tried for my anxiety.

"Reef–" I started, but his face just filled with unconditional warmth. The kind he gave to me so easily, without hesitation or question. And all I could say was, "Mahalo."

"I think there's something else in there," he whispered.

I grinned, reaching back in the pocket and pulling out another scroll. Slowly I unrolled it, trying to buy more time for my emotions to settle. I assumed there would be more paperwork, but what I found was a handwritten note.

> Dear Luna,
>
> I think we may have gotten something wrong. You were looking for a star shining in the dark, but we never thought about how badly the star needs the moon. I forgot to mention that. Actually, I'm pretty sure in a lunar eclipse you can't see the stars. They can't shine. They can't fulfill their purpose— they can't be themselves. Please never forget that.
>
> This 'star' will always be incredibly thankful for you,
>
> Cece (your Reef)
>
> P.S. I hope you like the latest novel.

I LOOKED BACK AT REEF, my eyebrows raised inquisitively. But he just swallowed as he tipped his head toward Nova again. I guess Locke had been very busy packing her vest while I wasn't looking. I thought it strange how they insisted she wear her neon life vest with the attached pockets to visit the beach.

My fingers hurried, waiting to be met with the same paper texture, but they hit something slick. Like photo paper. And ever so slowly, I pulled out a small paperback novel. Printed just to fit the vest. *Only Reef.*

I glanced up at him and saw his complexion pale. My fingers brushed over the glossy cover, idling over its features. A beautiful woman swinging from a palm tree with her ukulele peered back at me. She was nestled under the stars and a glowing moon. And the title, *The Woman and the Moon*, felt thick beneath my fingers with its 3D font. Underneath it was Reef's name. His *given* name. My lips parted, but no sound escaped.

"Do you like it? There's a dedication–" But my fingers were already flipping to that page. He chuckled lightly.

> To my moon. You light up every part of my world and help me find my way in the dark. I will always love you. Just as you are.

I didn't know what to say. "Reef, it's so beautiful." I was at a loss for words as tears stung my eyes. I continued to turn the pages and there beneath the copyright was his name and the publisher. His *own* imprint. A mist formed in my eyes.

"I'm glad you like it." He drew me close.

"I love it. Reef the name–" I pointed down at the imprint logo . . . Little Moon Publications. I'd been trying to help as he decided what to do about publishing his next book. The one with the infertility representation. But he'd kept the imprint name a secret. I knew he'd been working with his agent to make it happen.

"I thought it was only fitting. This imprint never would have happened without you. Nor would this book." He gazed at me and then whispered. "I hope it helps someone who reads it feel seen and to know how worthy they are of love. And maybe someday, a little boy out there who's too afraid to write will see things differently."

I couldn't keep the stinging in my eyes at bay any longer. I stared down at the book that he'd poured his heart and soul into. The one he had found the courage to publish exactly the way he wanted it to be. He'd decided if he was going to release a book like this, then he wanted complete control over it, especially over the representation. He wanted ownership of his voice. Hopefully, his imprint could do the same for others. And I couldn't be prouder of him.

It was kismet that we'd come back into each other's lives when we did, our paths paralleling one another's. Funny how you find people like that in life. I'd felt helpless in so many aspects of my life, especially with my art. And Reef had as well, feeling like he was selling himself short because he didn't have the courage to publish his art the way he wanted. Self-doubt appeared like it had won.

My fingers traced the logo on the book tenderly. What a change life had taken. I could feel our hearts changing as we grew together. We reconnected at a time when we both desperately needed each other, *again*.

A tear fell on the beautiful gift, and I tried to blot it away, wishing I had something to give him in return. He'd always given so much of himself to me and I didn't know how I could ever begin to convey how much he meant to me. For a lyricist, you would think words were my forté, but I never felt they were adequate.

I was trying to think of how best to express myself when the words rushed out of me, "I'd like to give you a key?" Butterflies took over my entire being.

"Well, if I'd known a book was all it took, I would have sent you those instead of letters."

I put a hand up to my face, covering my blush. I

couldn't believe what I'd just asked, blurting it out there. *What was I thinking?*

He dragged my hand down from my face. "Luna, I'm pretty old-fashioned." I laughed nervously at his response.

"Uh, huh? Where was that bundling in the honeymoon suite?" I teased.

"Excuse me, I slept on the floor. I can't help it if someone took over my bed." I pushed at him playfully and he nodded at Nova's pack.

"What? You can't be serious. She's not a camel, Reef. How much did you put in there? Are you having her do all your dirty work?"

He grinned, laughing harder. "I'll have you know. She was *keen* to be part of the plan. I thought you'd be more likely to say yes to her than to me. After my letter experience, I've learned to play a little dirty."

I leaned over and rummaged deeper in her pocket. I raised up slower this time. A plastic bottle filled with sand in my hand. One similar to the sand art projects we used to make as kids. I just looked at Reef, waiting for him to explain.

"Well, I think you should ask me properly. At least I came prepared," he teased, nodding toward the bottle.

I shook my head in total confusion. *Did we have the same idea?* Well, at least that made me feel better. I peered inside the bottle to see a string attached to the cork. The key must be inside. I couldn't wipe the grin off my face.

"Well, I guess since I asked first." I teased back.

"Yes," he said with an even bigger smile, loving this.

"Reef," I got out of the hammock and made my way down on one knee. "Since Nova is now my emotional support dog and you're going to need access to me 24/7 to write the rest of your bestselling series—"

"Well, yes, of course . . . that only makes sense. This is just such a romantic—"

But I shushed him jokingly. "Will you make me the happiest woman ever and accept this key? Help me burn dinner in the evenings and inspire me to write every afternoon?"

"Gee, when you put it like that—" he began, and I uncorked the bottle and began pulling the string out with it. But the sunbeams started reflecting off of the end of the string. Keys don't sparkle in the sunlight like that.

"Reef!"

"Yes?" he replied cheekily.

"That's not a house key!"

"Yes, I told you I was old-fashioned."

No wonder Guin had been so insistent we see this "green light." I looked back over to their building to see if they were out on the balcony. Instead, I saw Locke's Jeep in the parking area. No doubt they were waiting for news. Typical Locke.

Suddenly, everything blurred, and when I looked back over, Reef was kneeling by my side. "Could you stand up for me? It kind of ruins the whole look I'm going for. I didn't expect you to steal my move."

I swallowed hard as he helped me stand. He gently took the ring from my shaking hands with the string and cork attached. The wind bobbing the cork around in the breeze like a fishing bobber on a strong sea.

"I know it's kind of fast, but I don't want to wait any longer. And neither does Nova. She doesn't enjoy being parted from you. And I have to say the feeling is *very* mutual."

I made a little snuffling sound as my emotions started taking over me, and he squeezed my hand. Then he continued, "I want to make music with you every day and create together until we're old and gray. And then I want to create stuff that makes little sense to anyone except us. But more importantly, I want to love you every day and create a life with you. I've loved you my whole life, Luna. So, Mahina Liilii, will you marry us?" Reef asked as Nova came over by his side and he wrapped his arm around her, taking the cork with him. Nova looked up at me, too. *Had he rehearsed this?*

I was speechless as Reef and Nova sat patiently, waiting for a response from me. Finally, I started nodding vigorously, unable to do anything else.

"Yes?" Reef asked.

"Yes, of course, yes. A thousand times, yes." I responded with an uncontrollable smile.

He beamed as he slid the ring attached to the cork on my finger. Laughing at my continuously bobbing head as he got up from kneeling.

"Reef, I hope you know how much you mean to me . . . How much I love you. How much you've always meant—" Tears got stuck in my throat.

His hands went around my waist, pulling me in close, leaving goosebumps in their wake. Electrifying me with his touch. He nodded gently. "I know because it's the same for me. That's why I've been here waiting. There will never be anyone else for me."

Just as he leaned in to kiss me, Reef's eyes sparkled with mischief as if he spotted something over my shoulder. "Just so you know, Locke wants a double wedding. I told him no, but I think he's going to have to hear that from you. Three dogs as ring bearers would just be a nightmare. Even if they are service and emotional support dogs." Reef chuckled.

I knew Locke and Guin must be close by, ready to

congratulate us. "I don't know . . . that doesn't sound so bad."

"I doubt everyone will agree on the lavender farm for the wedding venue." I smiled at his words.

"Well, I was thinking a helicopter elopement sounds pretty incredible." I grinned mischievously.

"You need the groom to be conscious in order to say 'I do', Luna." I laughed at his joke. "But you know I would do whatever you wanted." He relented as he looked into my eyes, getting even more lost than ever before.

"Ok, maybe not there. But I really don't care as long as I'm with you. I never dreamed about my wedding, only about the groom . . . Maybe being stuck on a tree limb would do."

"With flower crowns," he added. "Oh, the press would love that."

"I love it, too. I'm pretty sure Louis can officiate. And we know Tutu and Guin can provide the music."

His eyes sparkled. "How about the aquarium instead? It can be our 'something blue'. Our radios the 'something old' and Nova stands for the 'something new.'" He grinned. "Your album just released and my book is ready to print . . ."

I chuckled. "It couldn't be more perfect."

Reef looked back over my shoulder again, and I glanced to see both Guin and Locke waiting impatiently on the beach access walkway, edging their way closer. Reef called out to them, "We're getting married. Can we go now in your car? We'll need Guin's uke."

Locke's face went blank. "You literally *just* asked her? It doesn't work like that. Have you learned nothing from me? . . . So, she said yes?"

"Thanks for being *so* surprised," Reef joked.

"Well, I figured you didn't use any of my suggestions," he teased. "So, I wasn't sure how it would go."

"Yeah, good thing I didn't. And yes, Locke, she said *yes*." Reef held up my hand triumphantly, the cork wildly bobbing around in the breeze. I beamed at Reef, tucking myself into his chest. Reef continued, "And it works like that if you elope. Maybe the aquarium will let us rent it out for the evening. We'll be right behind you. Or do you not want to be the best man?"

I could see Locke rolling his eyes from here, but he was already headed toward the car, not going to miss out on his best man privileges. "This is not an educational overnight school trip, Reef. But I'll start making some calls. I'll begin alerting people. I bet Tutu can find you a cake. Maybe I can even find you *another* honeymoon suite."

He shook his head like we were crazy, but proceeded to the car, anyway. Guin followed, calling out her congratulations.

Reef looked back at me with the most loving gaze. One that helped me see an entire lifetime of possibilities and happiness in our future. A little Ohana of our own dancing in my mind, a flip book of the stages of our life going by. There was no doubt in my mind. I would always choose him.

"But first, I want to kiss the bride." Reef's lips turned upward as he said it. The ones I'd grown to know so well, yet sent butterflies through me every time. Lips I continued to appreciate even more, especially through the loving things he said to me.

"I'll allow it," I replied cheekily, even as desire grew inside me. Reef's grin only stoking my need further.

"Now, where were we? Oh yeah, 'perfect,'" he finished. Allowing his eyes to wander over every part of me, he let his lips show me just how much they agreed with his words. Our lips molded together as if destined to be; reminding me of all those times I longed for his kiss when we were young, our fateful reunion, his soothing presence during my anxiety, and our future together. I was finally home.

ENJOYED Reef and Luna's story? Check out the other soulmate books at brookegilbertauthor.com/books and sign-up for newsletter to join the book family! If you'd like others to be able to find this novel, please consider leaving a review or spread the word! THANK YOU!

Join the Newsletter

I'd love for you to become part of our book family! :) You can sign up to become a newsletter subscriber and gain access to the growing bonus content library at brookegilbertauthor.com! Deleted scenes and extras, such as the original music in this novel, are available at www.brookegilbertauthor.com/bonuscontent.

By becoming a subscriber, you will receive the secret password to unlock these bonuses, a book boyfriend quiz, plus the monthly newsletter (there's a giveaway in each one), release alerts, and blog post notifications :) If you're already a subscriber, then you can access it now! Each newsletter has the secret password in it and you can always message me! As a subscriber, you will be the first to know about the progress on my latest work and get a behind the scenes look. We really are a book family and I can't thank you enough for being a part of mine!

All the love and spoons!

Brooke

The Aloha Soulmate Series

The Aloha Butterfly Kiss: Under the Hawaiian Skies

If you want to learn more about Guin and Locke's story, check out my novel, The Aloha Butterfly Kiss! This book also features Tutu and Louis and how they were reunited :) Available in eBook and print from major retailers and directly from the author's website and Etsy store! Special Edition hardback cover drawn by the author available on Amazon! Add to your Goodreads reading list. Learn more about the book and read an excerpt on the launch page.

Also by Brooke Gilbert

The Paris Soulmate: A Sweet Romance Novel

A woman with a "no dating policy." A mysterious, cocky British stranger. A dream trip to Paris. What could go wrong?

Reeling from the reality of turning thirty soon, Christine decides to take her bucket list trip. She has dreamed of going back to Paris, but since being diagnosed with several rare autoimmune disorders, she never imagined she would get the chance. Now, she finds herself on her way to the City of Love with a surprise . . . An extremely handsome British stranger seems to have mysteriously fallen onto her path. Is it just a coincidence that they are both traveling to the city of love? It all seems too good to be true.

"Own Voices" Crohn's, Lupus, Mast Cell Disorder, & Mental Health Representation.

Also by Brooke Gilbert

The Irish Fall: A Sweet Romantic Comedy Novel

A woman goes to find her heart in Ireland, what she doesn't realize is she will leave it there.

Eyre decides on a desperate whim to take the first appealing flight out of town. This lands her right at the gorgeous cliffs of Moher where she meets the attractive, but infuriating, tour guide Darby– not to be confused with Jane Austen's Mr. Darcy. Darby shows Eyre the heart of Ireland and in doing so, shows her how much heart she still has left to give. But Darby has demons of his own. Can Ireland's healing powers mend a wounded heart?

"Own Voices" Crohn's, Ovarian Cysts, & Mental Health Representation. PTSD and endometriosis are also represented.

Movie List

In need of ideas for a movie night? Grab some popcorn and relax with the movies/TV shows mentioned in this novel. Haven't heard of some of these references? That's okay! I'm hoping you will find some new ones to enjoy along the way as you read this novel!

The Wizard of Oz
Batman (1989)
The Dark Night Rises
The Wedding Planner

Thelma and Louise
Scandal
Runaway Bride
Cast Away
Jurassic Park
The Breakfast Club
Short Circuit
Austenland
Moana
Alice in Wonderland
Baywatch
The Little Mermaid
Dr. NO (1962)
Octopussy (1983)
Rocky
10 Things I Hate About You
The Notebook
Looney Tunes: Back in Action
The Pink Panther (1964 and 2006)
Twilight
From Here to Eternity
Castaway
A Cinderella Story
Some Like it Hot
Vertigo
Fight Club
Coco
Butch Cassidy and the Sundance Kid
Nightmare on Elm Street
Home Alone
LaLa Land
Sleepless in Seattle
Goonies

Original Songs

The lyrics in this book have been turned into original songs :) Find the songs on the Spotify playlist and YouTube as music videos.

Coming soon!

Panic Attack & Anxiety Tips & Tricks

• Lavender is a great natural remedy for anxiety. I use it in all different forms! I enjoy lavender tea, lavender syrup in drinks, lavender capsules to sleep or for an anxiety flare, and lavender oil for diffusing, shower steamers, or baths.

• Lazer Tapping as mentioned in The Irish Fall is a great technique. I love the blog, Listen to Your Gut, and I learned the technique there. I recently used it during some medical testing when I was riding the edge like Luna.

• The mantra and brown paper bag technique came from Katie Atchison, who kindly responded to one of my Instagram posts about panic attacks. Taking a mantra with you into stressful situations like medical testing can make all the difference. This was the inspiration for Reef repeating one to Luna.

• I had Luna keep a brown paper bag with her. We see her pull it out in her car. Just knowing you have it can be comforting. But if necessary, actually seeing your breath can be incredibly soothing. This is a step beyond the breathing techniques Luna was doing. And I am so grateful for Katie's suggestion. There are also breathing necklaces, which are great for those with anxiety.

• Likewise, carrying an object you can pull out and rub or squeeze in your palm might help. A best friend gave me a key with strength written on it. I took it to all of my infusions. I squeezed it in my hand while I did breathing techniques. I still have it and keep it as a cherished possession.

• I love Tara Brach's meditations on YouTube. They're free and amazing. It's the first meditation I've been able to do. Apps like Curable, Insight Timer, and Calm have also been recommended to me. I have trouble focusing, I'm finding out that I'm probably on several neurodivergent spectrums, so adding some movement can help. I find doing gentle Pilates for 10-15 minutes each morning (I do one for EDS/hypermobility–Jessica Valant is amazing) in the morning followed by Brach's meditation helps how I handle stress throughout the day.

• Finding what stability looks like for you is key. Or at least it was for me. And my "stable" means making time for this short exercise every morning (or let's be real, sometimes just stretching) and some meditation. Or even some simple Savasana where I'm being mindful and focusing on gratitude. Or five minutes of gratitude journaling in the evening if I don't have time in the morning. And stable also looks like getting a certain amount of sleep, eating a certain way, being able to say 'no' so I don't put too much on my plate (I know, it's a foreign concept for us people pleasers), pacing myself and knowing my limits, surrounding myself with healthy relationships, and making time for the important things in life.

• My health doesn't allow me to get to everything I want in a day. Sometimes I just get a few good hours. And recently in an EDS class I learned something very important. If you have a good day or a few good hours, and have the opportunity to spend it with the people who are important to you or are able to do something special in life, you should take it. Just take the other penalty. Which has been a hard concept for a perfectionist like myself, but an important lesson. Getting a B on a paper instead of an A+ for example isn't as important as getting to spend those couple of quality health hours with family. Or at least for me, it isn't now.

• There are studies now that massage can also help with depression and I'm sure it could help with anxiety as well. Fascia and lymphatic massage can help so much. On a low budget, one of those handheld devices can be great on your lymph nodes every morning or evening! It definitely boosts serotonin!

• Moving your eyes from side to side is an actual technique I researched, and one I plan to try!

• Reframing your thoughts. I've been working with a pain psychologist on this concept and cognitive behavioral therapy. It has been an amazing experience. As someone who had a terrible experience as a child, I can say this was completely different and wonderful. There's some great CBT apps out there, too!

• Another coping mechanism mentioned in this book was

emotional support animals. I've seen people's lives change with emotional support dogs. But there are other ways to seek this type of therapy. I used to volunteer at a local animal shelter and it always helped.

• And of course, I'm sure you knew it had to make the list . . . art therapy. I've been substitute teaching and I always try to take art or special ed positions. I love seeing how much art can help students because I know how much it has saved me. Writing, drawing, painting, coloring, crafting, reading, making music etc. It's not about being good, it's about enjoying yourself and expressing your emotions. As I now say to myself, it's time to give myself grace and space.

So even though I poured my heart into this book, there are likely errors. Lol. Brain fog, neuralgia, chronic pain, c0vid, and severe migraines were just some of the things I was battling over the year I worked on this book. If you find some errors, please message and let me know! I always appreciate it and will update it so others have the best reading experience possible :)

Wishing you the best mental health,

Brooke

The Luna

~

DRINK RECIPE

I created this recipe as I was writing the book. I love anything lavender—it's true the flower is great for anxiety! There's a great homemade lavender syrup at a local coffee shop that inspired this drink. I bought lavender syrup on amazon to make this one, and it's been addictive.

FILL a glass with ice and add:

- 1/2 cup condensed milk (I love Let's Do Organic. Replace with coconut milk for a less sweet and lighter version. I love forager the best! Others have so many additives.)
- ½ cup lemonade (If you want something more refreshing instead of creamy, replace the condensed milk with sparkling water!)
- 1 tablespoon lavender syrup poured over top
- Sprinkle lavender buds on top
- Make it alcoholic: add 1-3 tablespoons of vodka.

SIT BACK, enjoy, and read!

The Reef

DRINK RECIPE

This is my version of Tommy Bahama's pain chiller, which I think is perfect for Reef! Before the pandemic, I could only bake and make mocktails. Lol. My grandmother is a bartender and I like to think I got some creative genes from her :) This is one of my favorites!

FILL a cup with ice and add:

- ¼ cup pineapple juice (Lakewood is my favorite brand. It's preservative free)
- ¼ cup orange juice (Natalie's is my favorite brand. It's preservative free)
- 1 / 2 cup oat milk (I love forager the best! Or Oat Malk. Others have so many additives. Also, buy one that is labeled gluten-free! I've made this mistake before)
- A squirt of agave or honey will also work!
- Mix it up and top with a sprinkle of organic nutmeg (I love the Whole Foods brand).
- Make it alcoholic: add 1-3 tablespoons of clear or coconut Bacardi rum.

SIT BACK, enjoy, and read!

Discussion Questions

A few questions to start the discussion at your next book club meeting. If you are choosing *The Heartbeats of Aloha* for your Book Club meeting, I would love to join your discussion! Send me a message at brookegilbertauthor.com, @brookegilbertauthor on IG, or email me at brookegilbertauthor@gmail.com.

Question 1

• How do you feel about the mental health representation in the novel? Can you relate? Did it make you feel more connected to the main characters?

• Was it portrayed differently than in other novels you've read? If so, how?

• What did you think about the portrayal of childhood cancer and its lasting effects? What about the infertility rep?

Question 2

• What is your favorite quality about Reef?

• Did you think he was a good fit for Luna?

• What did you think about Reef's career as a romance novelist? What did you think about him channeling his feelings into his books?

Question 3

• One of the things the author often hears is how relatable her main characters are with their health concerns. Can you relate to Luna?

• What is your favorite quality about Luna?

• Luna feels like she had to protect Reef by leaving without explanation. How do you feel about that choice? Can you relate?

• How did you feel about Luna's struggle with anxiety and depression following her childhood cancer experience and later feeling trapped in her career?

Question 4

• Luna's uncle plays a pivotal role in bringing them back together. How do you feel about his matchmaking scheme?

• What did you think about the uncle's relationship with both Luna and Reef?

• Do you think the uncle was right to interfere, or should he have stayed out of it?

Question 5

• What did you think about the fake dating arrangement?

• Do you think Luna and Reef handled the fake relationship well, or would you have done things differently?

• How did you feel about the record label's original PR plan with Luna's ex?

Question 6

• Luna left Maui abruptly as a child due to her cancer diagnosis. Have you ever had to leave a place or person suddenly due to circumstances beyond your control?

• Have you ever had to make a difficult choice to protect someone you love, even if it meant hurting them in the process?

• Reef spent years not knowing why Luna disappeared. How do you think you would have handled that uncertainty?

• Do you think Luna was right to keep her cancer diagnosis secret for so long? Would you have pursued answers like Reef, or accepted the mystery?

Question 7

• How do you feel about the mental health representation in the novel? Which character do you feel grew the most in their struggle throughout the novel?

• Luna experiences panic attacks and feels trapped by her music label, losing joy in her passion. How did you feel about Reef helping her rediscover her love for music? Have you ever lost passion for something you once loved?

• The theme of childhood trauma and its lasting effects is present throughout. Do you think discussing it in literature helps normalize these conversations in society?

Question 8 (or you could insert it earlier as Question 4 and renumber):

• Infertility is a major theme in the novel. How did you feel about Luna's struggle with feeling "broken" and unworthy of love due to her inability to have biological children?

• What did you think about Reef writing letters to her as Cece, telling her she's worthy of love despite her infertility? Did his words resonate with you?

• How did you feel about their discussions around adoption and building a family in non-traditional ways?

• Luna believes no one will want her because she can't have children. Can you relate to feeling like a health condition or personal struggle makes you unlovable?

Question 9

• What do you think about how Reef and Luna reconnected? Was their reunion different from typical romance reunions you've read?

• How do you think Luna changes throughout the book? What growth and changes did you see in her?

• What about Reef?

Question 10

• Both Luna and Reef have been hiding aspects of themselves—her health struggles, his writing career. How do you feel about these secrets? Would you have been able to maintain a relationship with someone who couldn't initially be fully open?

• How did you feel when Luna's cancer history was finally revealed?

• Do you think they handled their revelations well?

Question 11

• What do you envision for Luna and Reef's future?

• Do you think they'll stay in Maui or split time between there and Luna's music career?

• How do you see their creative careers supporting each other going forward?

Question 12

• What is your favorite scene in the novel?

• If you had to pick one place to visit mentioned in their story, where would it be? (The tide pools, Mount Haleakala's lavender fields, the mermaid coves, etc.)

• If you were going to travel with one character from the novel, who would it be and why?

Question 13

• Reef navigates the challenges of being an indie-published author versus traditional publishing. What did you think about the author's portrayal of the publishing industry?

• Did learning about the pros and cons of different publishing paths surprise you or change your perspective on how books reach readers?

• How do you think Reef's experience as a writer affected his understanding of storytelling in his own life?

Author's Note

Thank you for taking this journey with me! I hope you enjoyed Luna and Reef's love story. Over the past year, my anxiety increased as I sought more answers on my chronic illness journey, and I started battling panic attacks and depression. Before last year, I had only experienced medically induced panic attacks. And journeying with these characters was like a salve to my soul. I hope it helped you too. And maybe you could feel seen or relate. That's the entire goal of my writing. To provide an escape, but also help people like myself feel seen, because that's why I read. I also hope to spread awareness through these novels and to de-stigmatize conversations in our society.

I often hear that my novels are not a 'normal romance' or romantic comedy, and I cherish those comments!! That is the whole point of my work. So, if you felt seen or heard, please don't be shy, I'd love to hear from you. And if you would be kind enough to leave a review, that would be greatly appreciated, as well. Being different is sometimes very difficult, and without your kind feedback I've received from readers like you, it would be impossible to keep publishing. Reef is very fortunate to have been backed by a big traditional publishing house before he begins his self-publishing journey. I do not have any such backing. It's just me producing these books. Using all the spoons I can find. So, your kind words, messages, reviews, and recommendations make ALL the difference. Truly, you don't know how much of a difference you make in my life. Thank you for all your love and support :)

There were a lot of reasons for writing this book. Several readers were curious about Reef and I had to admit that as I wrote *The Aloha Butterfly Kiss*, I couldn't help but imagine this romance between him and Luna. But it was the many discussions I've had with readers about being "broken" that made this book come to fruition. Recently, I even heard the term thrown around in the elevator of a medical center. And that's when I knew I had to keep pushing on this novel even when I was borrowing spoons.

It was heavy on my heart to put this topic in my book. I've often discussed with readers that I love the song lyrics, "there is a crack in everything, that's how the light gets in." And I hope this book embodies that quote. I hope that Luna's journey and the way Reef saw Luna helped you to see yourself differently, too. You are ***not*** broken. You are so wholly beautiful, just as you are. What we deem as weaknesses can become our unique strengths. It's just all in how we shift the narrative—how we position our framework.

Reef never saw her infertility as a defect, but as an opportunity to provide a child with a home if she wanted that one day. Likewise, her anxiety was something that shaped her into the person she became and led her to share music that affected others. Music that made people feel not as alone and comforted them. Nothing about that was broken to him. And I hope we can shift our narratives. As 1 John says, "there is no fear in love." That's how we know the difference. Please never undervalue your worth. I am here to tell you that you are NOT broken and you are a beautiful human being.

If you enjoyed this novel, please consider leaving a review on Amazon, Goodreads, BookBub, The StoryGraph, LibraryThing, Barnes & Nobles, or recommend my book to family or friends who you think might enjoy it! Reviews are invaluable for authors and help us be able to continue to do what we love and hopefully what you enjoy us doing too. I also love seeing readers post photos with the book on social media! Meeting readers is one of the most exciting parts of this journey :)

Sending all the love & spoons,

Brooke

Sign up for the newsletter at www.brookegilbertauthor.com and receive a free romance quiz to see what type of man is your perfect match! You'll also be matched with a leading man from one of my current or upcoming novels! There's also a giveaway in every newsletter!

I am constantly writing and hope to release more novels soon. I am currently working on publishing my next one. It's my healthy addiction. I'd love to connect with you whether to discuss writing, literature, pets, hobbies, travel dreams, spoon theory, or everyday life!

Donation Suggestions and Resources:

A donation will be made based on book sales. Please consider making one, too 😊

To make a donation to the Maui Strong Fund: https://www.hawaiicommunityfoundation.org/maui-stron
To make a donation to St. Jude's Hospital: https://www.stjude.org/donate/donate-to-st-jude.html?sc_icid=header-btn-donate-now
Panic Attack Resources:
https://www.anxietycanada.com/anxiety-disorder/panic-disorder/
Anxiety Resources:
https://adaa.org/understanding-anxiety/panic-disorder/resources
Depression Resources:
https://www.everydayhealth.com/depression/guide/resources/
Need Help Now?
Dial or Text 988 (USA) for the Suicide and Crisis Lifeline

Connect with Me:

Official Website: brookegilbertauthor.com
Email: brookgilbertauthor@gmail.com
Instagram: @brookegilbertauthor
TikTok: https://www.tiktok.com/@brookegilbertauthor
Youtube: https://youtube.com/@brookegilbertauthor
Facebook: www.facebook.com/brookegilbertauthor
Pinterest: www.pinterest.com/brookegilbertauthor
Twitter: https://twitter.com/brookegauthor
Story rocket: https://www.storyrocket.com/the-paris-soulmate

Follow Me On:
Amazon Author Central: https://www.ama-zon.com/author/brookegilbert
Goodreads:https://www.goodreads.com/author/show/23026582.Brooke_Gilbert
BookBub: https://www.bookbub.com/authors/brooke-gilbert
The StoryGraph: https://app.thestorygraph.com/authors/5826ed0e-5120-433f-90b7-bceb6d8ed7f0

LibraryThing: https://www.librarything.com/author/
gilbertbrooke#https://allauthor.com/author/
brookegilbertauthor/
Storyrocket: https://www.storyrocket.com/the-paris-
soulmate
Allauthor: https://allauthor.com/author/
brookegilbertauthor/
https://linktr.ee/brookegilbertauthor
Audible

Acknowledgments

I would like to thank every person who takes the time to read this novel. I know there are so many options, and that you read my book truly means the world to me. You truly make this experience so fulfilling and meaningful. I am humbled and honored that you have taken this journey with me. And if, by chance, it resonates with you or provides some escape, you will have made this writing journey worthwhile.

Thank you to all the ARC readers, Bookstagrammers, and Book Tokers who have encouraged me daily. Becoming a part of this community has been one of the best experiences of my life. I have never met such a welcoming community. I think I lost ten pounds the month my first book was released because of fear and anxiety, but you accepted me as your own, and through your kindness and encouragement, you strengthened me. I will never forget your compassion, kind words, sweet postings, beautiful reviews, and fun book discussions. And I also want to thank the spoonie community, who makes up part of the book community as well. I have found such a wonderful support group with you, and I no longer feel alone with my conditions. Your beauty and strength encourage me every day. And I hope you know my door is always open if you need to talk.

To my wonderful editor, Isabel, and alpha readers,

Annie and Brie. Thank you for seeing the possibilities in such a rough draft and for encouraging me when I was ready to chuck my manuscript out the window. Lol. And thank you to everyone who has ever been a beta reader for me! You have always shown me nothing but kindness from day one. On days when critical book reviews came in, when I doubted my abilities, or when I didn't think I could continue, you all were there. Thank you so much for always being there! You are such a very special and beautiful group of women :)

I'd be very remiss if I didn't include the authors and voice-over artists I have had the pleasure of meeting along the way. I am always amazed at the encouragement you give one another, and I am so thankful you have accepted me as one of your own. From the first moment, you made me feel like I belonged. Coming from the competitive world of medical sciences, I can say it was an extremely pleasant shock to my system! I have loved learning from you and hope to pay it forward one day! I have been blessed with meeting my "rainy day" author/partner in crime, Tomi Tabb, who is always there to discuss book ideas, book covers, and even boring book logistics. Lol. I have loved getting to know you and truly feel I've found my kindred spirit, especially in loving all things Jane Austen :)

To my parents, who have supported every creative dream I have ever imagined, I want to say thank you sincerely. I know having a creative daughter who marches to the beat of her own drum has been a handful, but I appreciate all the love you've always shown me. I'm sure you never envisioned having "Mrs. Maisel" as a daughter, but just as her parents did, you have always supported me and fought for me. Thank you to my mother, who always wanted me to be a writer and encouraged me. I never imagined I'd ever become one. It's still surreal to have written a novel. Your love has been a light and a guide, especially in times of trouble. Thank you to my father for shaping my sense of humor and always providing laughter in my life. It is laughter that has made the difficult times bearable. You have helped mold me into the person I am today, and I will be forever grateful. Your continued support has meant the world to me. I love you both very much.

To all my friends and family who have helped me through my rare autoimmune conditions and reminded me of my self-worth, I cannot express my gratitude. You have been such a blessing in my life. Your love and support have made a wonderful difference in my life. I am so fortunate to know you.

To all the caring doctors, nurses, and healthcare workers who have helped me in my journey, I want to say thank you. Your compassion in the most difficult times of my life has been appreciated more than you could ever know. To all the people that made this experience bearable, I want to say thank you, and I hope to pay it forward.

Most of all, thank you to God for showing me that "all things work together for good for those who believe in the Lord" (Romans 8:28). And for proving that faith can overcome all odds. I am humbled and unbelievably grateful for this Job moment.

About the Author

Brooke Gilbert is a Tennessee native, a microbiology grad-
uate of the University of Tennessee, and a border collie
mom. She is, as you may have already guessed, a hopeless
romantic and a lover of Jane Austen. When she isn't writing, she works as a jewelry designer, an audiobook narrator,
and a graphic designer. Her writing features characters with
autoimmune disorders, something she deals with herself.
She believes it is important for these types of characters to
be seen in modern literature and started writing so she
could see someone like herself in literature. She is considered a medical mystery and has several rare autoimmune
disorders. These disorders caused her to withdraw from
Physician Assistant School, but she is happy to be pursuing

her dreams of designing, creating, and writing. She thanks God for leading her heart on this new path and recites "perhaps this is the moment for which you were created" in times of doubt (Esther 4:14).

She loves watching classic films (thrillers and romantic comedies, too), reading, playing the ukulele, painting, dancing, Pilates, and spending time with her dog, family, and friends. One of her favorite quotes is from Flashdance: "When you give up on your dreams, you die." She believes that if you're waiting to pursue your dreams, stop waiting and start doing. Your time is now. And may you never stop being a hopeless romantic. Contrary to popular belief, it's a very good quality. She's still looking for her Mr. Darcy. Visit brookegilbertauthor.com to connect and stay updated on her latest projects.

Song Index

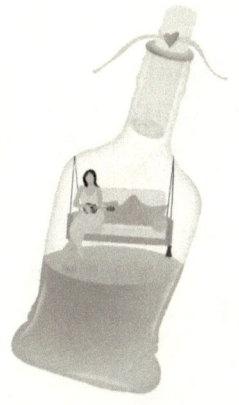

Always been told what I needed in life
Always been told how I should be loved right
But love isn't so simple
At least not to a heart like mine

Never been treated right
Not by those type of guys

491

Never been much of a woman to stand by a
  man's side
Just for the status, just for the privilege, just for the
  right

Because behind closed doors is different
And there I'd blissfully evaporate into the ether
I stay because I'm loyal, because I'm a 'healer'
 because I'm a pleaser, because I'm stuck in a fever

But with you, everything is new
With you, I feel I've come unglued
In a room full of people, no one is equal
I see everyone else has just been the prequel

Because here I realize
You'd never push my dreams aside
Or expect me to compromise

And I'll never be able to hide it
As much as I've been told to fight it,
You are the only man I could love
Forever and always

-LUNA MANU MALE, THE ONLY
MAN I COULD LOVE

So long ago, you and I
were lost in a dream
So long ago, you were the only
Place I could run to and be free.

Just give me one more hour with you

And you'll see
Just give me one more hour with you
Anytime or place will do
And I swear I'll make it back to you
Just give me one more hour
And this time, I'll be the one you need

Anxiety was my only company
A cycle of belittling
Until you intervened
And took the time to care for me.

Just give me one more hour
And you'll see, you're the only man for me.

Not so long ago, you did what no one else would
What no one else could
Just give me one more hour
I'll do anything to show you
How much you mean to me

-LUNA MANU MELE, ONE
MORE HOUR

Arms intertwined, smiles combined,
Why can't I call you mine?
Lost in a lavender daze
I never wanted to part this way.

Lost in a lavender daze
I never wanted to part this way
Salty, sweet air mixed up with you
All wrapped up in a haze

On that perfect summer day
Arms intertwined, smiles combined
Why can't I call you mine?

-LUNA MANU MELE, LAVENDER
WAYS

[Reef]
So long ago, you were the only one
Who could truly see me
The only one who believed
So long ago, it seemed we had forever waiting
And were always meant to be
Just give me one more hour with you
But I'd gladly spend forever with you, too
Just give me one more hour
And I'd give anything to show you
How I've kept loving you
Just give me one more hour
And you'll see, you've always been the only one
    for me
Please let the stars guide you
Because I've always been here waiting

[Luna]
Anxiety was my only company
A cycle of belittling
Until you intervened
And took the time to care for me
Not so long ago, you did what no one else would
What no one else could
Just give me one more hour with you
Anything will do

Just give me one more hour
I'll do anything to show you
How much you mean to me
Just give me one more hour
And you'll see, you've always been the only one
    for me

- *One More Hour Duet*

    I can still see her so clearly
    a vestige of the past floating through
    the clouds of lavender hills
    Soaking every ounce of my memory

    The way her body moves
    Her smile from ear to ear
    A soft hum of her melodic tune
    The faint smell that's purely her
    It's the way of my muse

    And people ask me
    After all these years
    How it could still be her
    How she could still be imprinted on me,
    And I tell them it's easy

    She's the girl from childhood
    The one who's always known me
    The one I've always loved
    The one I could never forget
    The one who has made me come undone

    She slips in and out of my memory

like a distant reverie
A word, a sound, a smell
All brings her back to me
she's my everything

I'd do anything to keep her
Grasp out into the ether to reach her
But words lie there like vapor
Surrounding me until I put them to paper
Setting my muse alive again

And for a few fleeting moments
It's like she's there with me
My soul feels completed
No longer just a muse
What can I do to make it all come true?
How do I keep you?

-Reef Akua, The Muse

Beach waves storm the castle
As your fingers intertwine in mine
Clouds float by upon the sea breeze
with the sun high in the sky
And I think how safe I am in this spot
sliding into textures in the sand
our warmth
Our hands
Endless smiles
Nothing but miles

As the sun lowers
And the waves inch higher

A burst of warm colors fly by us
Basking us in a Kaleidoscope of Maui
As our laughter tumbles I see
Your eyes
Our bodies
That Endless summer
And there's nothing but safety net

It's not until the waves start roaring
The darkness takes over
And a castle lay demolished
That I see Summer can't last forever
Even if it is you & me

Some forces are stronger
Some tides pull harder
Some darkness falls faster
Time was never our friend

Why did summer have to end?
Why did the darkness creep in?
What do I have to do to make it back to you?
I'd gladly travel 365 days around the sun
Just to steal one more day with you
So until the summer sun rises,
Just know I'll be missing you
And you'll always be my one

        -LUNA MANU MELE, 365 DAYS
            AROUND THE SUN

Book Quote Index

> Some say childhood is when we can be our truest selves. Maybe that's why this flame burns so brightly. And feels like nothing can ever extinguish a childhood love.

-CECE LARUE, WHEN YOU WERE MINE

" With love, he wanted to trust his gut. But his intuition felt broken. That's why he needed lightning in a bottle to wake him up. And from that very first moment, she was it.

-CECE LARUE, PACIFIC PULSE

" When he kissed her, it was like a part of her became imprinted on his soul. And every time he did so, he gave a little more of himself. Or at least he imagined that's what it would be like if he ever got the nerve to actually do it.

-CECE LARUE, LOVE ON ISLAND TIME

" I can't help but see you when I look at the stars. And I wonder, are you looking at them, too?

-REEF AKUA, ECHOES OF THE ISLANDS

" A Greek myth says we were ripped in two, sentenced to search for our other half—our soul-mate—as a reprimand for our pride. But my punishment must be different because searching was never my problem.

-REEF AKUA, -TIDES OF LOVE

" How can someone smell like home when you just met them?

-REEF AKUA, PASSION IN PARADISE

66 The ghost of her always caught up with me. From simple everyday objects to dinner dates. Everything always came back to her.

-REEF AKUA, WHISPERS OF WAIKIKI

66 Give a man a gift and he'll be happy for a day. Give a man a dog and his life will be forever changed.

-REEF AKUA, -STRINGS OF SERENDIPITY

66 If you knew it was the last time you would see someone, what would you do differently?

-REEF AKUA, WHEN YOU WERE MINE

66 "One day she'll realize I was always right here waiting."

-REEF AKUA, BEATS OF PARADISE

66 'Just breathe with me,' he repeated as the world seemed to melt away. And he continued to repeat it until there was nothing but her and their breaths, which sounded like calm waves. And he wouldn't have had it any other way.

-REEF AKUA, PASSION IN PARADISE

That omnipresent thought reverberated in his head again. 'No one would ever be her.'

-REEF AKUA, ECHOES OF THE ISLANDS

She showed up in my dreams so often; I was sure her presence was a fantasy.

 -REEF AKUA, WHEN YOU WERE MINE

She always made him feel like a 'man'. No matter what current trends dictated that definition to be. She let him choose his own descriptors of masculinity.

 -REEF AKUA, TIDES OF LOVE

When did we stop seeing people and only start seeing their labels? I certainly wanted to be seen as more than that. Not to love her wholly would be such a mistake.

 -REEF AKUA, WHISPERS OF WAIKIKI

In our cookie cutter world, nothing appealed to him more than someone who broke the mold.

 -REEF AKUA, STRINGS OF SERENDIPITY

When you fit with someone, it was easy. You felt it in every fiber of your heart and soul.

 -REEF AKUA, SPARKS IN THE TROPICS

If only she could only see herself as I did, then she'd never doubt herself again.

 -REEF AKUA, HAWAIIAN HEATWAVE